Family Resemblance

ADVANCE PRAISE FOR
FAMILY RESEMBLANCE

"*Family Resemblance* is one of those all-too-rare literary anthologies that's as informative for contemporary writers and their readers as it is for students learning about contemporary writers. Surprise, risk, the energy of the new; the work collected here engages literary history while doing things that have never been done, and readers will take away a broader sense of creative possibilities in writing."

—Mark Wallace, author of *The Quarry and The Lot*

"If there is one way to contain all that hybrid texts can be, this book does it. With open arms, *Family Resemblance* brings together video, napkins, electrons the size of gnats, Hot Wheels, Yvor Winters, Laura Petrie, chess, homebirth, the color blue, a guy named Jason, a woman named Mary, Santa Claus, Malcolm X, card catalogues, perfect heavens, graphics, and maps. The plentitude of subjects embodies the plentitude of form. This book creates its own hybrid, binding discourses, making them snap with electricity."

—Nicole Walker, author of *Quench Your Thirst with Salt*

Family Resemblance

AN ANTHOLOGY AND EXPLORATION
OF 8 HYBRID LITERARY GENRES

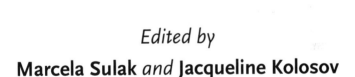

Edited by

Marcela Sulak *and* **Jacqueline Kolosov**

Rose Metal Press

2015

Acknowledgments for previously published works appear on page 417, which constitutes an extension of the copyright page.

Rose Metal Press, Inc.
P.O. Box 1956
Brookline, MA 02446
rosemetalpress@gmail.com
www.rosemetalpress.com

Library of Congress Cataloging-in-Publication Data
Family resemblance : an anthology and exploration of 8 hybrid literary genres / edited
by Marcela Sulak and Jacqueline Kolosov.
    pages cm
  Includes bibliographical references.
  ISBN 978-1-941628-02-7
1. Literary form. 2. Cultural fusion in literature. 3. Literature--History and criticism-
-Theory, etc. I. Sulak, Marcela Malek, editor. II. Kolosov, Jacqueline A., editor.
  PN45.5.F37 2015
  808--dc23
  2015034695

Cover and interior design by Heather Butterfield
See "A Note about the Type" for information about the typefaces used.
Cover art: *Pass It On* by Debi Pendell
More information and artwork can be viewed on the artist's website: www.debipendell.com

The epigraph on the following page is from Carl Jung's *Psychological Types*, the 6th volume of the 1971 Princeton University Press edition of *The Collected Works of C.G. Jung*.

This book is manufactured in the United States of America and printed on acid-free
paper.

FOR OUR STUDENTS, WITH GRATITUDE

• • • •

"The creation of something new is not accomplished by the intellect
but by the play instinct acting from inner necessity.
The creative mind plays with the object it loves."

—*Carl Jung*

TABLE OF CONTENTS

. . . .

LOCAL, ORGANIC, AND LIVING
A Preface
Marcela Sulak

What is a literary genre but a family of works that resemble one another—in style, form, technique, goal, or philosophy? A family resemblance defines a particular genre, and for this reason, genre can be viewed as an affiliation, rather than a fixed point of identification. Within each affiliation, a critical mass of reproducible structural patterns overlap, so that it becomes helpful or efficient to refer to individual representations as an affiliate of a single kind or type—which is what the word *genre* means—of literature.

Genres have, at least since the age of print, been characterized according to whether the lines of words on a page consistently continue to the right margin (prose), or whether they consistently stop somewhere before the right margin (poetry). Before print, Plato characterized poetry by the overwhelming emotional effect of its rhythms. Aristotle characterized literary genres by the presence of multiple speakers (drama), or a single speaker but multiple perspectives (narrative), or a single perspective and/or speaker (lyric). We can even catalogue genre affiliations according to the kind of narratively significant time-space operative in them, as Mikhail Bakhtin does. Or according to the relative strength of the main character compared to the world around him or her, or according to whether or not the character was portrayed as better (tragedy) or worse (comedy) than the average person. Genre also refers to the medium in which we create art: literary, plastic arts, dramatic arts, cinema, and so forth.

When we speak of hybrid literature, we are speaking of individual works that do not replicate any previously existing pattern of literary affiliation.

Rather, they take features from multiple parents—multiple genres—and mix them to create a new entity. Writers experiment and innovate, combining elements of traditional genres until they find a form that fits their subject or story.

Interestingly, these innovative works actually take us deeper into our literary heritage because many incorporate forms that precede the main four genre distinctions we recognize in literature today—poetry, fiction, nonfiction, and drama. Novels, novellas, scientific catalogues, literary criticism, philosophy, history, news, myths, magic spells, and religious incantations were historically carried from place to place in verse form, at least until the invention of the printing press and the spread of literacy.

Susanne Paola Antonetta introduces this anthology by referencing the Sphinx, the creature that is half lion and half woman (in the Greek version) or half woman and half man (in the Egyptian version), which guarded the seam between the sacred and the secular—the entrance to the temple. The temple, of course, guarded the seam between the present and the eternal, the life now and the afterlife. The Sphinx was nothing less than the keeper of magic and power. What I would add is that the word "sphinx" is itself a Greek corruption of the Egyptian term *shesep-ankh* for "living rock," rock that was there, on the scene, from the beginning and not harvested and brought in from elsewhere. We can think of hybridity as local, organic, original, and living, and therefore, mutable. And we can think of generic literary forms into which the hybrid has broken as simply genetic mutations, though today we tend to think of hybrids in literature as the mutations and innovations, rather than as original sources.

When Jacqueline Kolosov and I met online by chance in a writer's group in 2012, I'd recently converted a multi-genre writing workshop into a workshop on hybrid forms. I was astonished at the Sphinx-ish energy, power, magic, and excitement that hybridity generated in class, and the exceptional quality of literature the workshop produced. At the same time, at the Shaindy Rudoff Graduate Program in Creative Writing, which I direct, we were planning how to accommodate the needs of students in our pilot creative nonfiction track, since we could not afford to offer an entire schedule of nonfiction workshops yet. One of the options on the table was changing our entire program into two tracks: "poetry" and "prose." This felt incredibly wrong to me for reasons I could not completely articulate, except that I write both nonfiction and poetry, but I cannot write fiction, unless it is flash fiction. My own writing and teaching practices tended to blend documentary poetry and personal essay, research and lyric.

I was finding myself increasingly incapable of championing genre distinctions based on external structures such as the absence or presence of line breaks, even though I teach poetic prosody and am a practitioner of syllabic verse, and I understand the power of meaning-making music that line breaks facilitate. Jacqueline had been experiencing a similar crisis in genre faith, and so one day when discussing the issue, we turned to the Bible, as they say. But there was no Bible. The closest thing I found to the single-volume anthology, field guide, or craft manual that I was looking for was something like Janet Burroway's *Imaginative Writing: The Elements of Craft*, because each of Burroway's chapters focused on an "element of craft" that transcended generic distinctions. Her writing examples were multi-genre ones, though few of them were hybrid, in the sense that few were such a thorough combination of genres that assigning a single label to any of them would have radically changed how one read the work.

We discovered the ambitious *American Hybrid: A Norton Anthology of New Poetry*, and, of course, the Rose Metal Press *Field Guide* trio, which focuses on the individual hybrid forms of prose poetry, flash fiction, and flash nonfiction, along with Rose Metal Press' exploration of novellas-in-flash, *My Very End of the Universe*, which appeared in late 2014. These were immensely helpful in describing individual genres and genre combinations, and I did use them for teaching.

Such literary journals as *Tarpaulin Sky* and *Diagram* have been embracing the cross-/post-/trans- approach to genre since the beginning of the twenty-first century. Certain exciting critical studies, such as Jahan Ramazani's 2013 *Poetry and Its Others: News, Prayer, Song, and the Dialogue of*

Genres (University of Chicago Press) reveals poetry's dialogue with other genres, forms, and discourses, albeit, in a way that highlights the difference between poetry and "not poetry." Yet sometimes, the proliferation of scholarship and hybrid collections seemed to reify genre distinctions by creating even more micro demarcations within each genre.

We, on the other hand, dreamed of a single anthology that would map combinations of all the major literary genres, as well as extra-literary genres like graphics and performance, onto a single terrain. That said, *Family Resemblance* is not meant to be exhaustive. We simply wanted a single tome on hybridity that we could use in our classrooms—one that carried exemplars of exciting work, with artist's statements preceding each piece. Jacqueline and I sensed that, at least to a certain degree, we would need to approach an anthology and exploration of hybridity from the point of view of hybridity as the original source of literature. And here I really did turn to the Bible: to the Biblical account of the beginning of people, and to Greek stories of origin. The Adam of Genesis 5:2 was a human who preceded gender: "Male and female created he them; and blessed them, and called their name Adam, in the day when they were created." In the beginning, gender (and genre) distinction is unimportant, as both male and female are Adam. Distinction only becomes relevant later, when it becomes politically, socially, and culturally useful.

We see the same concept in Aristophanes' tale at Plato's *Symposium*, which features spherical people who have two sets of female sexual organs and others with two sets of male genitalia, and others with one set of each. Since their severing by a jealous god, humans have been wandering in search of their missing half. And in various other cultures, hermaphrodites/androgynous/intersex people were considered sacred and charged with special tasks, such as storytelling and prophecy. Gender and genre have the same root, after all. They just mean "type" or "kind."

After the earliest creation stories, classifications of gender appear with hierarchy. Later in the biblical Genesis the hierarchy appears so that we'll know who's in charge, and so we'll know who to blame for the apple incident in the garden. In literature, it seems there is also a hierarchy that enters with genre—the poets get kicked out of Plato's ideal republic in his *Republic,* and literary genres have been in competition ever since. As Kevin Young pointed out in his *The Grey Album,* and others elsewhere have highlighted, distinctions between "history" and "myth," or "memoir" and "folk-story" are also used to bolster particular versions of "truth" that disenfranchise, incarcerate, or otherwise subjugate people of color and their personal and cultural narratives.

In envisioning an anthology of hybrid forms, we gravitated immediately to the topic of family precisely because hybrid literary forms have historically been associated with statements about identity as it navigates hierarchies of various kinds. Indeed, the malleable, up-and-coming genres of improvisation, self-invention, and the disjunction of texts that are "neither this nor that," or rather, "both this and that," have long been used by writers whose identity is hyphenate. N. Scott Momaday, a Native American of Kiowa descent, uses a blend of myth, history, and memoir (as well as illustrations by his father) in his 1969 *The Way to Rainy Mountain* because a single genre cannot serve as an appropriate vessel to contain the different types of content his mixed heritage requires. Maxine Hong Kingston, likewise, requires a memoir/myth blend in her 1976 *The Woman Warrior* to make narrative sense of elements of two different heritages, one of which contains a gender-specific secret. Earlier in the twentieth century, writers employed strategies of multiple genres to portray mulatto culture in the South, as in Jean Toomer's 1923 *Cane,* or the blend of frames (northern/southern, lyrical/socio-economic/visual/audio) to capture life caught between this and that, such as James Agee and Walker Evans' Depression-Era *Let Us Now Praise Famous Men.* More recently, we see this tradition continued in C.D. Wright's documentaries of social injustice and the people who fight against it: *Cooling Time* (2005), *One Big Self: An Investigation* (2007), and *One with Others: [a little book of her days]* (2010).

At times, hybrid literary forms have been used to express the desire for families and lands that do not exist, as in the Japanese writer Takashi Hiraide's prose poem essay on the work of Donald Evans, a miniaturist who invented countries and then painted their postage stamps. Sometimes hybrid forms have been used to metaphorically erase what does exist, what came before, as in William Carlos Williams' blend of essay/manifesto and poetry in his 1923 volume *Spring and All*. Think of the Futurists, Dadaists, and other early-twentieth-century "ists" and "isms."

Hybridity is increasingly used to depict the dislocation of the subjective "I" in the experience of familial bonds and particularly motherhood, as in Alicia Ostriker's 1980 *The Mother/Child Papers*. She began writing the book after her son's birth, in the wake of the shooting of four students at Kent State. In a dialogue between poetry and prose, Ostriker juxtaposes meditations on war against musings of motherhood and the experience of birth. Other contemporary writers not included in this anthology who use hybrid forms to articulate family are as diverse as Aimee Nezhukumatathil, Lance Larsen, Claudia Rankine, Bich Minh Nguyen, Joy Castro, and Junot Díaz.

Hybrid literature is powerful. It is also fun. There are those who innovate for innovation's sake, with the verve of Galileo, Leonardo da Vinci, and Thomas Edison. Charles Simic won the 1990 Pulitzer Prize for a collection of prose poems, *The World Doesn't End*, and has since created other hybrid explorations. Randall Jarrell, Judith Kitchen, Dinty W. Moore, Michael Martone, Jayne Anne Phillips, Mary Ruefle, and many others have joyfully performed their alchemy of genre malleability.

Hybrid literature has existed for hundreds of years, all over the globe. As Eileen Myles points out about the label "hybrid" in a personal email: "It seems old fashioned to coin a term and worse to stick to it to describe a new diasporic state in which all genres are inadequate and fail." She adds, "Everything indicates a free flow of ideas and perceptions and communication that makes multi-disciplinary, hybrid, multi-genre last-chance-to name approaches and even the formation of 'schools' seem archaic. Time to get our collective dress dirty and admit it's writing and beyond that we don't know." Creek-Cherokee writer Joy Harjo, whose 2012 memoir *Crazy Brave* uses all the creative elements and paths at her disposal, puts it like this:

This world is [...] an active state of creativity [...] We are in a continual state of creation. We make choices by our thoughts, by each act, and as well are influenced by the thoughts and choices of others. Each thought or road of action makes an impression. They are layered. Massacres gouge and continue to erode the psyche. The smallest kind acts make the brightest lights. The kind of story I want to inhabit is one in which everyone has a right to their own way of life, are not forced by an oppressive state or religion to conform. In this story the arts are as important as football, and everyone has worth and value, no matter race, sex, or culture.

[Joy Harjo, Facebook update, January 23, 2015]

The term "hybrid genre": we, too, dislike its limitations. But we decided to create this anthology and use "hybrid" to describe the literary work in it because we felt that, despite everything, the idea of hybridity retains its ancient magic, its calling into existence imagined ways of being and seeing that have not been articulated, and that, therefore, do not exist in the cultural map of the master social narrative, though they exist in the physical world.

For our anthology, we chose eight different concentrations of hybrid affiliation, which derive from oral, written, and graphic sources: diaries, novels, correspondence, various poetic genres, various genres of documentation and personal essay, forms of story-telling, map-making, etymological dictionaries, photography, drama, film, art. We grouped these eight amalgamations/affiliations under the headings "lyric essay," "epistolary," "poetic memoir," "prose poetry," "performative," "short-form essay," "flash fiction," and "pictures made of words." Given our disposition to view genre as an affiliation of techniques and goals, our own eight categories are not meant to be the final word, but rather, a place to start when we gather to examine the energies that are released when various genre fields are used and combined, and the new terrain that is created in our doing so.

The individual introductions to each section will explain our philosophy behind breaking the hybrid genres as we do. Because authorial intent is such a large factor in determining hybrid affiliation, we felt it was absolutely essential that this volume be not just an anthology, but also an exploration. Thus, our representative authors are given nearly as much space for their artistic statements as they are for their art.

Identifying the section headings—the hybrid form categories—was the most difficult and time-consuming portion of the anthology. Originally we wanted to focus on formal strategies to avoid distinctions based on truth telling or market concerns, such as those that underlie such categories as fiction and nonfiction. Especially since notions of truth and fact are increasingly problematized, and since greater critical attention has been given to the faultiness of memory. Keepers of public records are notoriously subjective in their vigilance, we decided. We'd considered naming one section "flash," and including all short forms there, for instance. Although in the end we conceded to the existing hybrid categories of "prose poetry," "flash fiction," and "short-form essay," we did acknowledge truth and fact and memory are often performances, rather than absolute states, hence the "epistolary," "performative," "poetic memoir," and "lyric essay" sections. "Pictures made of words" encompasses a range of art-text works whose dust jackets contain the labels "poetry," "memoir," and "journalism." The graphic also bleeds over into the performative and into prose poetry.

In fact, just about any of the hybrid pieces we chose to include could easily have fit into more than one section, which is what makes this anthology *hybrid.* Placing them depended on the particular conversations we felt were most interesting and important to initiate, deepen, or explore. However, we encourage readers of this anthology to move writers around and to see what aspects of their work are highlighted when you do so. We hope that *Family Resemblance* will generate new possibility, new alchemy, and new fields of play, and provide a guidebook for those writers and teachers like us, who were searching for a way to study, teach, and celebrate literary innovation.

RIDDLING THE SPHINX

An Introduction to Hybridity

Susanne Paola Antonetta

Outside the city of Thebes, once upon a time (as the formula goes for events that never happened and yet somehow never cease to happen), a young man who had just killed his father and not yet met his mother stopped to answer a question. The Sphinx—sister of the three-headed Cerberus of Hell, daughter of the Chimera (himself a lion, a snake, and a goat merged into one form)—flapped her eagle wings, arched her lion body, thrust her human breasts, and spoke these words from her woman's mouth:

What has one voice, but walks on four feet in the morning, two in the afternoon, and three in the evening?

The answer, from the human Oedipus, was us, humanity: we who crawl in infancy, walk upright in the vigor of adulthood, and lean on canes in old age.

The hybrid asks her fellow hybrid to recognize his hybridity. When he answers correctly she kills herself.

. . . .

Susanne Paola Antonetta's most recent book is *Make Me a Mother* (2014). She is also the author of *Body Toxic* (2001), *A Mind Apart* (2007), the novella *Stolen Moments* (2014), and four books of poetry. Awards for her poetry and prose include a *New York Times* Notable Book Award, an American Book Award, a *Library Journal* Best Science Book of the Year, and a Pushcart Prize. She has also been a Lenore Marshall Award finalist. Her essays and poems have appeared in *The New York Times*, *The Washington Post*, *Orion*, *The New Republic*, and many anthologies.

Where else to begin a discussion of hybridity? The Greek myths soar, snort, and crawl with creatures made from bits of more than one species. While the word *hybrid* comes to us directly from Latin, it is almost certainly a Greek import to that language—most likely a relative of the Greek word *hubris*. From hubris—a pride that ruffles the gods with its overreaching—to hybrid—a work built out of multiplicity—the family resemblance is worth noting: our concept of hybrid art continues to resonate with its Greek root. In his essay "Short Lessons in Hybridity" in *Essay Daily*, Ander Monson, editor of the text-art journal *Diagram*, writes that "Interspecies dalliances generate a lot of heat and sometimes shame. So says the lonely Minotaur deep inside his labyrinth."

True, we cringe before the Minotaur and the Medusa, and we feel the Sphinx's despair: figure me out and I cease to live. But to understand the hybrid creature, we must also remember the teacher the Greeks celebrated above all others: Chiron the centaur, half-man, half-horse. Chiron was lauded in myth as the greatest of teachers, pedagogue to gods and heroes, including Apollo, Hercules, and Achilles. Centuries later Niccolò Machiavelli in *The Prince* praised Chiron, noting the peculiar genius of elevating a centaur as teacher, uniting the cool intellect of the human with the brute strength of the beast. In the dual body of the hybrid is the force the weak unitary self needs.

· · · ·

How to pin down the hybrid, to get our Sphinx to tell us who she is? We have the physical hybrid, like the liger, bred of a tiger and a lion; the hybrid plant, such as the apple tree waving a branch of pale pears. Theorist Mikhail Bakhtin in *The Dialogic Imagination* defines hybridity as a "mixture of two social languages within the limits of a single utterance, an encounter, within the arena of an utterance, between two different linguistic consciousnesses." This anthology is filled with such encounters: Khadijah Queen, writing of *Black Peculiar*, notes that "compartmentalization doesn't seem honest; blending and cross-poliination does." Among other moves,

Queen hybridizes traditional narrative with the structure of a play, nudging the reader to recognize the "performative aspects of identity-making," particularly for writers of color. As Queen puts it within these pages, "Cultural assumptions and social expectations [...] create situations that require intellectual, physical and psychological acrobatics."

A contemporary theorist, Australian Catherine Beavis, extends Bakhtin's definition, writing in her article "The Literary and Artistic Merit of the Graphic Text as New Textual Genre and Hybrid Literary/Artistic Form" that the hybrid is a work in which "more than one meaning making mode—writing, image, movement, sound, etc.—is used to create the narrative world."

This definition resonates with today's hybrid, which may encompass any number of forms, many of them digital: film, hypertext, photography, graphics, and so on. We don't need computers to achieve a stunning hybridity, but we in the computer age have fallen back in love, more than in any recent literary period, with hybrid work. We have presses like Melville House, Jaded Ibis, this book's Rose Metal, and many more that specialize in hybrid texts; and anthologies with names like *Bending Genre* and *The Far Edges of the Fourth Genre*. We have literary journals like the Spring 2014 "Beyond Category" issue of *Seneca Review*, which arrives in a box containing a bound journal, the pages of which carry art, sketches, and words skewed across the page, accompanied by rolled-up tubes of paper unfolding their text, a magnifying glass, temporary tattoos reading "don't *wax poetic*" in heavily serifed script, and a digital accompaniment on the web.

We see, as the "Beyond" issue of *Seneca* illustrates, a new regard for materiality: book arts flourish. At my local bookstore I can buy Anne Carson's *Nox*, a poem unfolded from a box (boxes again!), on tea-stained paper, juxtaposed with photography, sketches, collages and letters, and an exploration, on each page facing the poem, of one of the words—just one word per page turn—of the great elegy for his brother written by the Roman poet Catullus. In his excerpt in *Family Resemblance*, Craig Santos Perez uses all the spatial possibilities of the page as well as fragments of many discourses—official documents, oral histories—to create an elegiac poetics invoking his written-over homeland of Guåhan (Guam).

Hybridity can also be less rather than more. Flash fiction, that hybrid of fiction's made worlds and the diamond-concision of the prose poem, has been growing in popularity in the U.S. since the 1980s, when the *Sudden Fiction* anthologies brought the short short back to the American literary scene. The genre had previously peaked during the first part of the twentieth century. Its counterpart, the short essay, has also become more and more popular in our era, though it too has been around in one form or another since classical times—and was charmingly dubbed the "essaykin" by William Makepeace Thackeray (see the Rose Metal Press *Field Guide* series for more discussion of the historical arcs of these forms). Flash forms—known as the "smoke-long story" in Chinese, the idea being that you can read such a story in the time it takes to savor a cigarette—have become equally important internationally. Etgar Keret, an Israeli, and Julio Ortega, a native of Peru, demonstrate flash's reach, contributing short-form works to the flash section of this anthology. And every country has its own particular linguistic and cultural perspective to bring to flash. Keret, for instance, discusses the translation issues between traditional written Hebrew and the slang of the oral, in the same way his piece explores the slippage between life lived and the realities created by the camera.

Shorter and shorter: in a brilliant exploration of permanence and transience, "Ineradicable Stain: The Skin Project," author and artist Shelley Jackson had a story tattooed—one word per person—on over 2,000 volunteers. Jackson referred to these participants, after they had been tattooed for the project, simply as *words*. Jackson's call for subjects has these notes at the end: "As words die the story will change; when the last word dies the story will also have died. The author will make every effort to attend the funerals of her words."

And thus the hybrid plays pin-the-word-on-the-hybrid.

． ． ． ．

If we look to the roots of the word "hybrid," and to the Sphinx's story, we shouldn't wonder that most hybrid writers regard this process of uniting languages, of combining meaning-making modes, as uneasy: a fertile tension rather than a smooth mix.

Ander Monson—in correspondence I initiated for this project—elucidates this creative tension:

> A hybrid is a thing that's not entirely comfortable with the container it's placed in. At least from my perspective what I talk about when I talk about hybridity is this feeling of otherness that produces some pressure against the walls of the container. Containers need walls, but the hybrid in the container pushes back and tries to find where it might become more electrically porous. If there's not electricity there then there's no real advantage and the hybrid becomes pointless, but usually I find that the physics change up against the boundaries—or past them—in interesting ways.

Without the pressure—without the sense that each container has morphed into something it was not when singular—the hybrid work cannot be said to have achieved the fullness of hybridity. Chiron uses his human mouth to teach the wisdom his equine body intuits; the humanizing of that knowledge changes it. It is important for hybrid authors to distinguish between the work of a hybrid text and mere illustration and decoration.

Kristen Radtke, who creates video essay and graphic memoir, as well as word-only works, writes in her contributor's note to her video piece entitled "That Kind of Daughter" that "perhaps the biggest obstacle we face as artists and writers is how we can craft visuals that do more than just offer a narrative that mirrors the text." Graphic novels and memoirs—what Mira Bartók in her essay here calls "sequential art"—have today become popular forms, yoking together the literary and the cinematic, creating a blended visual, spatial, and linguistic way of making meaning. For many authors, the visual aspects of their writing have become essential in any text. Bartók, for instance, in her process essay in this book, describes how sketching helped her create the highly visual structure of her memoir *The Memory Palace*.

The late Judith Kitchen, writing to me of her photography/nonfiction hybrid *Half in Shade*, echoes this feeling:

> But I'd say that illustrations don't do it [create hybridity], because they are serving the text. There has to be some equality, or balance, or interaction between two media, I would think, for it to become hybrid—like a grafted tree with two colors of blossoms, or something like that. Or a mix, a twining, something that makes it neither one nor the other but a combination of both.

· · · ·

As artists, the ancient Greeks were more than willing to do their own mash-ups, with choruses in their plays that commented on the drama, performed in the action, and also danced, probably to engage the audience while props and costumes were changed. Lyric poems, laments, and other shorter forms were embedded throughout the Greek long narrative poetic form, the epic.

Nor were the Greeks alone in hybridizing or in their fascination with hybrid forms. Classical China, like most civilizations, produced many word-image texts. Many of these, like the Ch'u Silk Manuscript and *The Classic of the Mountains and the Lakes*, had calligraphy inked around sketches of hybrid beasts and spirits. A text that dates back in its earliest form to 400 BCE, *The Classic of the Mountains and the Lakes* blends geography with bestiary, descriptions of locales with their cross-bred inhabitants. Creatures included the Lu-Shu, which had tiger stripes, a horse's body, a red tail, and, according to the author, a lovely cry like a human singer's. For those travelers willing to risk an encounter with his hooved and potent body, wearing a piece of Lu-Shu's skin would result in plentiful children and grandchildren.

. . . .

Where we find literature, we find hybridity—from the Bible, with its story, aphorism, prophecy, erotica, and song; through the Mahabharata of India; all the way to the Popol Vuh, the great creation story of the Mayans, which offers legal code wrapped in creation story wrapped in family history. The Arabic *The Book of the Thousand Nights and a Night* samples story forms whose origins range from Persia to France.

Nor does it take a history of accretion to produce hybridity. Look no further than Boccaccio's *The Decameron* in Italian or Chaucer's *The Canterbury Tales* in English. The *Tales* incorporate prose and verse and cover everything from a lecture on the Seven Deadly Sins to an extended fart joke. The first written text we have, the king Hammurabi's legal code, is itself a hybrid of stately content and intimidating form: what spoke to his Sumerians more, the code itself or the great stone steles containing it, looming over their city?

During the Renaissance in England, in a crowded theater that jutted out into the audience, Shakespeare's Romeo and Juliet met at a masked ball, placed their palms together, and jointly uttered a sonnet within the play. Then they kissed. The poem irrupted into the dialogue with its 14-line message: *love*. Or perhaps it bore a darker subtext—that, because the poet who introduced the sonnet to England, Petrarch, never touched his love Laura, the touch is the thing to notice here, and not in a good way. The hybrid, as we've seen, speaks in riddles.

So too does the hybrid cause us, as riddles do, to question what we think we know. In her essay "How I Became a Detective," Carol Guess describes the process of writing poems based on the ground-breaking crime scene dioramas of Frances Glessner Lee, poems (also included in this book) that wrestle with the withheld narratives of the dioramas, the deliberate seeding of clues, forcing the reader. like the student of crime, to "stand very still until the truth reveal[s] itself."

. . . .

If a hybrid work were a snack food it would be chocolate-covered pretzels rolled in chipotle dust.
If a hybrid work were a song, it would hum the words.

These quotes are not mine. I created a set of sentences to complete ("If a hybrid were _____ it would be _____, " for instance), sending them to writer friends whose work entails hybridity to finish. Thus I made of the question of hybridity a Mad Lib, drawing on one of the first, most loved hybrid forms of childhood.

. . . .

Part of our new artistic drive toward hybridity has to do with changing cultural attitudes, as well as our recent surge of technological growth. It might well have been the case that the late twentieth and early twenty-first centuries would have seen an outpouring of hybrid work with or without the computer. Throughout the Renaissance and well into the nineteenth century, the concept of hybridity tended to be a negative one, a notion associated with boundary violations, and one that challenged ideas of aesthetic purity which drew on and paralleled racial thought. The twentieth century emphasized what Sabine Mabardi, in "Encounters of a Heterogeneous Kind," calls "the concept of heterogeneity which has replaced the modernist credo of universalism, essentialism, binary opposition and purity." This shift led, slowly and not without pain, to a revaluing of the rich potential of the margins, cultural cross-overs, and blending.

The hybrid has been both an entry point and a weapon. Remember, the Sphinx guarded the gates of the city only to let Oedipus the subverter pass.

Amy Moorman Robbins, author of *American Hybrid Poetics: Gender, Mass Culture, and Form*, writes that "hybridity can be understood as an implicitly political strategy, one that forces encounters between hitherto incompatible literary traditions and that thereby brings to the surface competing ideologies." Kazim Ali puts it more simply in this anthology, describing the composition of *Bright Felon* (also excerpted in these pages), "I did not mean to innovate but knew I could not speak." *Bright Felon*, a hybrid work ("Is it a book or is it a filmscript or is it (I suspect it is) sculpture?" Ali asks), grows partly from, he writes, the thought that "a belief in genre manifests as a belief in gender—they are rooted in the same impulse: that a body (or text) must 'behave' according to the social rules that govern it."

· · · ·

To explore all that is going on now in the larger world of the hybrid, the parable of the humanzee and the cyborg may be instructive. In 1997, a professor from New York Medical College applied for a patent to create a hybrid creature made of human and chimpanzee DNA. His creation was to be called the "humanzee," both *homo sapien* and chimp. The professor, Stuart Newman, had no intention of actually doing such an experiment, though it was technically possible; he wanted to force bioethicists to consider the fact that no system existed to stop him, and that such a creature could not only be forged, but also legally experimented on, and even enslaved. His gesture, much talked about both in and out of the scientific community, has not prevented other scientists from brewing up, among other things, rice enriched with genes from the human liver, and mice with brains made of human neurons—mice whose brains could conceivably be 100% human. Entirely human, yet rethinking the family cat, I'd imagine, as its glowing eyes narrowed above the homo-rodent's cage.

On the other hand, N. Katherine Hayles, in her influential book *How We Became Posthuman*, brings up the category of the "cyborg," the image of the "human being [...] seamlessly articulated with intelligent machines," a category to which she has no resistance, and which she evaluates no further than to say hybridity is a fact of life in our age, one to which we must accept surrendering our bodies.

We live in a time of hybridity, and we're not sure how we feel about it and all of its stitched-together singularities. It has become a passion in artificial intelligence to create a robot that will make its own choices—to wean our creation from ourselves—even as we create the literary text, like Julio Cortázar's choose-your-own-ending novel *Hopscotch,* that proves its dependence on the existence of the reader.

. . . .

A hybrid work must seduce but it cannot consummate. Hybrid work must go forth and multiply but it cannot simply combine.

We are ourselves hybrids: we carry the genetic codes of many of the viruses our ancestors suffered, as viruses can insert themselves into our DNA, and if that process should happen within an egg or sperm cell, the viral genetic code gets passed along as surely as anyone's eye color. We may have far more virus DNA than active human genetic code.

Advances in DNA testing have also taught us that there are human chimeras—the name for the condition in which a single human contains more than one kind of DNA, caused by absorbing DNA in utero from a twin, or by a fusing of parents' reproductive cells. This chimericality can cause humans to develop mosaic qualities—more than one color in the skin, or even the hair. Our evolutionary vestiges hang on in the body: we wear a flesh suit that stows rather than loses its anachronisms: a bone that would wag a tail if it could; wisdom teeth, forcing their way into a jaw that's grown too small for them, needing, with our refined diets, only to be removed. Perhaps understanding the mixed messages of the body may be the start of a kind of hybrid wisdom.

The hybrid is a chimera; its head is a revolving door; its body is a silo; its tail is what's left in the field.

The hybrid is a chimera; its head is protective; its body is edible; its tail is poisonous.

I am amused that two of my sources chose the word "chimera" to fill in this sentence.

· · · ·

For the purposes of this anthology we need a further act of definition. Any literary or artistic work will bear evidence of hybridity. We have languages and authors and forms that are all in some sense hybrid; and all texts are hybrids, not just in themselves, but of who we are when we're reading them: the quality of the air in the room, the view from the window, that whine of mosquito that causes us to lose our place and miss the moment that tells us the killer is actually *all* the passengers on the Orient Express.

I will borrow another concept from Bakhtin, who distinguished between conscious or "intentional" hybridity and hybridity that came about through organic or unconscious means. Organic hybridity happens because cultures, as well as art forms, cross over, meld, unthinkingly appropriate from one another.

Conscious hybridity involves an element of choice. Conscious or intentional hybridity happens, says Bakhtin, when symbols from different symbolic realms are brought together on purpose; they fuse, and each exerts its shaping magic on the other, reforming, redefining. Conscious hybrid writers are greedy, I would say, for all the meaning-making vessels they can find, for all they can grasp of the readers' senses and their thoughts.

· · · ·

What might this uneasy blend of modes, this warped-container quality of the hybrid look like? We encounter, within the manuscripts of Romantic poet William Blake, these stanzas from "The Tyger," written in the nineteenth century:

Tyger! Tyger! burning bright
In the forests of the night,
What immortal hand or eye
Could frame thy fearful symmetry?

In what distant deeps or skies
Burnt the fire of thine eyes?
On what wings dare he aspire?
What the hand dare seize the fire?

And what shoulder, & what art.
Could twist the sinews of thy heart?
And when thy heart began to beat,
What dread hand? & what dread feet?

What the hammer? what the chain?
In what furnace was thy brain?
What the anvil? what dread grasp
Dare its deadly terrors clasp?

And then we look down Blake's beautifully crafted page and see his drawing of this beast, a being neither symmetrical nor fearful, nor likely to have much truck with dread. In fact, the creature appears to have wandered out of the Hundred Acre Woods, with Winnie-the-Pooh and Tigger lost somewhere in the high grass; the big cat is less frightful than Blake's image of his Innocent counterpart, the Lamb.

Here, we think, we see Bakhtin's "conscious" hybridity. At some point Blake wrote a poem, and he illustrated that poem with a tiger who seems to drain the lines' chanting fearfulness off into his cuddly stripes. Two discordant elements continuously remake each other, to refer back to Bahktin, in an act of apprehension creating too many questions to ever be complete. The meaning-making modes do not echo one another, but tug on one another, remolding. This narrative world, as Catherine Beavis would put it, is large.

Hybrid works have their resonances within our country and our English language, but they have been important—and burgeoning in the last century—around the world. The Russian poet Vasilisk Gnedov declared art dead in 1913, yet wrote a book of death-to-art poems, minimalist works that grow shorter and shorter until the last poem is just a title ("Poem of the End") and a hand movement, performed to his audiences. It is the poem brought up against the silence of its own mortality; the move as opening and closing at once.

In contemporary Russia, Ry Nikonova publishes "gesture poems" that, among other things, incorporate mathematical formulae and drawings. She calls for far more morphing of the body of the poem, a wing here, a haunch there—imagining a literal pillow book, or the book-pinwheel or the *book-mill*, a poem that should be read while the pinwheel's wings are flying. The more wings on the pinwheel, the greater the reader's options creating her own coming-and-fleeing text.

An American contemporary of Nikonova, David Shields, appeared on the mock talk show *The Colbert Report* (itself a hybrid of humor and pundit-news) calling for writers to steal words from other writers, to forget attribution, to recombine. ("The book is a call to arms to writers to ignore the laws regarding appropriation," said Shields, citing sampling in music and the like.) Shields was on the program to discuss his *Reality Hunger: A Manifesto* (excerpted in this book). Shields claimed he wanted no one to know the origins of the quoted material in his book; his publisher insisted on a list of sources in the back, he noted, but he showed Stephen Colbert the dotted lines where he asked readers to take a box cutter and remove that record.

Colbert indeed ripped out those pages but he kept only them, tossing away the rest of the book. In this way, Colbert made of *Reality Hunger* yet another, different work.

. . . .

If a hybrid work were a window it would be fogged on one side with nose-prints on the other.

. . . .

So we have calls to arms and gestures back at them; being the hybrids that we are, unwilling to forgo any form of meaning-making, we will probably ignore these calls and paint or mime or whistle others of our own. We are all human. We have all faced the Sphinx and answered her question. We have all wronged our forerunner-parents somehow, taking more from them than they meant to give us, going away and returning unasked, but in this wronging we become most fully, like Oedipus the king, who we were meant to be. We hope the container can contain, but not too much.

. . . .

And so we turn to this anthology. Forty-three authors of hybrid works contributed to *Family Resemblance* both their creative pieces and an accompanying essay, describing—to the extent the authors can articulate it—how the works came to be as they are, how these grafted forms achieved themselves. Some authors, like Kazim Ali, reveal to us the new plant that arose, like Jack's beanstalk, out of the small seed left to them from a larger cultural famine. Others, like Arielle Greenberg and Rachel Zucker, joint authors of *Home/Birth: A Poemic*, limn for us a process that grew out of pregnancy, friendship, and bodily necessity and bodily claiming: the hybrid as human connection. Poet Gregory Orr revisits the violence and loss that led to his coming to poetry in his lyric memoir, *The Blessing*, which channels the etymological origin of the word: "to wound, to spatter with blood." Each hybrid creation story is different, as of course it must be.

We see wounds in these hybrid processes, like the cuts on a tree branch where a graft can grow. We see authors who borrow one form, like theater (Queen) or journalism (Miriam Libicki), keeping it in something like its original shape—one set of aesthetic demands exerting its dialectic pull on the other(s).

The eight hybrid forms presented here—Lyric Essay, Epistolary, Poetic Memoir, Prose Poetry, Performative, Short-Form Nonfiction, Flash Fiction, and the Pictures Made of Words—indeed bear a family resemblance to one another. Each work in the book has its own gestation story, yet we hear again and again in the author's comments the push to find what nineteenth-century memoirist Daniel Paul Schreber called a "fleeting improvised body" to contain the uncontainable, the suppressed, and the impossibly complex. Sarah Vap in "Assault Hybridity" calls these the "multiplying strands and multiplying strands" of our lives. Many authors, like Greenberg, Zucker, Vap, and Ali, push to write the reality of their bodies, seeking a structure that captures, like Chiron's teaching, what the body knows.

We come to these pages with questions, and we hear the authors tell us what they cannot tell us. With that humility, we can proceed beyond the gates.

1
. . . .
Lyric Essay

LYRIC ESSAY
An Introduction

The lyric essay is an act of perception that is aware of itself as an act of perception. It can be a personal essay suspicious of the myth of objectivity, or a critical essay practicing the wisdom of compassion as it sings in verse. It can be an attempt to make sense of an issue too large to be grasped in its entirety by a single mind or from a single perspective. It can be an attempt at comprehension performed by an "I" that is dislocated, fragmented, or cursed with stuttering—that stop-start-repeat that prevents one's forward movement. It can be an attempt at understanding that understands that linear progression does not necessarily arrive at understanding, and that the action of turning back—which is the etymological root that gives poetry the name "verse," the ploughman's turning at the end of a field row—may be the most fruitful tactic.

The five lyric essays presented here have precursors that reach back half a millennium. Alexander Pope's 1711 "Essay on Criticism" and his 1734 "Essay on Man" are written in heroic couplets. Michel de Montaigne, who lived from 1533 to 1592, was often called the father of the modern essay, and was a significant philosopher in the French Renaissance. He has recently enjoyed a popular revival for his essays and essaylets, but perhaps his "commonplacing," his practice of keeping a book of notes on which he drew for his essays, is really the forerunner of today's lyric essay. A commonplace resembles a journal, but it contains far more: quotes, recipes, vocabulary words, gossip, facts that the owner had learned, as well as observations, weather, and records of flora and fauna. The European Early

Moderns were fond of this practice, aware that knowledge of a particular topic requires a multitude of approaches and genres.

The term "commonplace," or *locus communis* in Latin, comes from the Greek *tópos koinós*, meaning literary topos, "topic or theme." So a commonplace for the Early Modern writers was simply writing on a common theme approached through various genres. Later, when William Carlos Williams sought the symbolic destruction of all former thought patterns and ways of seeing that prevented direct apprehension of the thing itself, he did it through a lyric essay, a blend of essay/manifesto and Imagist poetry in his *Spring and All* (1923).

Perhaps a good way of defining the lyric essay is to suggest that it is an *essai*, or an assay, an attempt at understanding a particular subject, in which the form of the essay performs the content. David Shields' process essay in this anthology, for example, discusses the form as a means of overcoming a dehumanizing stutter, so as to enter the human world of language. Nearly all the lyric essayists included in this anthology approach the lyric essay as a means of integrating a lived experience by combining multiple generic perspectives where one genre or mode of inquiry alone has proven insufficient. Sarah Vap says about her piece "Oskar's Cars"—which documents motherhood's physical, emotional, and spiritual assault on her very being—that "no existing form (not lyric poem alone, not academic or critical or nonfiction essay alone, not narrative alone) would come close to containing this thing that I was experiencing/enduring/being. So hybridity is what happened." Susanne Paola Antonetta's contribution results from a recognition that scientific objectivity is a myth like any other. For Antonetta the lyric essay is a way of eliminating the unnecessary binary between "truth," or science, and metaphor. Her "Dark Matter" explores the "antitheses that make up the world."

When it comes to form, as opposed to the content discussed above, the lyric essay has been characterized by fragmentation and interruption; it often blends, braids, or synthesizes narrative elements from various genres: myth, history, science, personal essay, lyric poetry. Sometimes merely rendering the critical or personal essay in lines, as Kathleen Ossip does, or as a poem in prose collage, like Julie Carr, is enough to introduce a physical sensation of temporality, of which the lyric essay is constantly aware. In their process essays, Ossip and Carr helpfully explain that distinct literary forms are really just distinct tempos and temporalities. Ossip calls her poetic lines "shreds," which are "thinner and quicker than paragraphs, and without the neat transitions that tend to tie one paragraph to the next." Her piece is a passionate critique of the "objective" stance of literary critic Yvor Winters, and she notes, "my feelings don't allow for neat transitions." Julie Carr, writing about gun violence in Colorado, says: "form is about time [...] Form is the visual presentation of the bodily experience of temporalities."

And this is the strength of the lyric essay—it allows an embodied exploration, richly textured and fully human. If, as Leonard Cohen says, "there is a crack, a crack in everything. That's how the light gets in," then the lyric essay embodies both the crack and the light.

—*Marcela Sulak*

WRITING VIOLENCE, WRITING TIME

Julie Carr

I wanted the human element to live inside a tin can, to peer out from within that tin can.

Or, I wanted the human element, the shards of a face, the scrap of a face, visible under layers of dust and rot.

I found these lines in my notebook—I wrote them at the Whitney Biennial in 2012 where I saw, for the first time, the work of Luther Price. Price is a filmmaker who works with found materials: home movies discovered at yard sales and in the trash, industrial films, medical films, old pornography—junk footage. The work at the Biennial, "Meat," was actually a series of slides—photographs of filmstrips that Price had, in one way or another, destroyed. He buried the film and dug it up, or spilled stuff onto it, or ruined it with chemicals and bugs. Then he photographed whatever was left. Occasionally the film was so damaged that it became illegible as narrative, just pure abstraction, color and shape, bubbles of oil. Or, the narrative was only the narrative of its transforma-

Julie Carr is the author of six books of poetry, including *100 Notes on Violence* (2010), *Sarah—Of Fragments and Lines* (2010), *RAG* (2014), and *Think Tank* (2015). She is also the author of *Surface Tension: Ruptural Time and the Poetics of Desire in Late Victorian Poetry* (2013), and the co-editor of *Active Romanticism: The Radical Impulse in Nineteenth Century and Contemporary Poetic Practice* (2015). She lives in Denver where she helps run Counterpath Press and Counterpath Gallery. She teaches poetry and poetics at the University of Colorado, Boulder.

tion. More often, a face, a hand, a body, could be just discerned through the bleeding, morphing, damaged film.

If there is such a thing as retroactive influence, my encounter with Price's work would be it. Writing *100 Notes on Violence* also involved finding materials, doctoring or injuring them, sometimes abstracting them while retaining, or hoping to retain, the human face or body, broken as it might be.

100 Notes is an effort to see into something I cannot see, to look at something I cannot understand, to recognize the way writing always moves between abstraction and mimesis in its reach toward truer fictions. Because the book took up a topic I knew I would never exhaust, never come to terms with, it had to be a chronicle of failure. The form had to be partial, broken, fractured, and interrupted.

My daughter was writing a wish list. "I want a horse," she wrote. And then, thinking about that a bit, she added, "but I am a horse." I *am* the big frightening foreign thing that I desire. Maybe the person shopping for weapons online, this person looking to buy a heavy dangerous foreign thing, is that thing he thinks he wants.

I read and I read, all the experts on violence (Hannah Arendt, Slavoj Žižek, Georges Bataille, Elie Wiesel, Walt Whitman, and Emily Dickinson). None had an answer for me. Or all did, and their answer was, "You cannot fold a flood / and put it in a drawer." And then when I wasn't reading or writing I was doing all the things I'd done before—driving, cooking, walking around—but now these things had a slightly sickly aura on them.

The lens gets wide and the lens gets narrow. For moments we focus on patterns, on statistics, on laws that support such statistics, on a cultural adherence to the erotics of murder. Then, because life is real, it's really *not* a movie, we look close by, at our own kid making a wish list, at our student going hunting drunk, at the dad at the bus stop whose other son was shot, at our own jeans and boots. It's not like we're outside of it. To see something that is happening means you've got to look at how you're making it, allowing it, even needing it to happen. How you are that dangerous thing you're thinking about buying.

Something far away was suddenly right here. Something right here was suddenly foreign.

Writing into violence, writing into anything, there is no formula—no pre-ordered pattern to follow. Perhaps one could say that prose introduced itself when my lens got larger, and the poetry happened when I looked closely or down or in. But I suspect this attempt to make form or genre conform to some logic, some law, won't hold. I can say with more confidence that whether prose or poetry, whether list or dialogue, whether propulsion or whisper, form is about time—about manipulating the time in and of language—making it move in particular velocities: pick it up, slow it down, breathe here, pause, now run. Forms of all kinds are strategies for listening to, and making audible, the way language works time. If I break a line, it's because I want to hear it alive on its own for just a second longer than I would if I didn't break. Form is the visual presentation of the bodily experience of temporalities.

Cole Swensen defines prose as the willful refusal to see the line as a physical thing. "Prose," she says, "exists somewhere other than the page"; it is always pointing outside of itself to that "somewhere other." A science fiction writer I met once said pretty much the same thing, that the best writing in her genre made sure that no one would pay attention to it. Instead they would pay attention only to the "somewhere other" that the writing pointed to, would "forget" that what was before them was only, to quote the Italian poet Franco Loi, "insects running on snow."

If we accept this definition of prose, then I can say, with Swensen, that I don't write it. For whatever shape the writing takes on the page it carries a series of rhythms that matter. Every shape—block or fragment, line or paragraph—is an attempt to make visible some music.

Like the premonitions of Philip Glass heard through a pillow, language keeps arriving, and keeps failing to resolve.

· · · ·

We're writing not in order to control what's in front of us, but in order to continue beginning, as one by one the victims recede to make space for new ones.

"The field is lethal but pretty in Autumn," wrote Apollinaire.

Something hurt, so we opened a book.

HYBRID WORK
Excerpt from 100 Notes on Violence

58.

MORE SHOPPING

Gunaccessories.com is pleased to offer one of the world's largest selections of firearm accessories, gun parts, tactical gear, police equipment, Gerber knives, Buck knives and an assortment of upgrades for handguns, rifles, shotguns, AR-15 and AK-47 military style guns. Our vast selection of gun parts includes barrels, grips, magazines, clips, bolts, hammers, barrel bushings, springs, recoil pads, recoil buffers, mag wells, mainspring housings, sights, scope mounts, slide components, extractors, ejectors, triggers, sears, pins, pistol grips and frontstraps. I want a horse and I am a horse.

Our selection of Gun Parts will fit handgun and rifles manufactured by Armalite, Auto-Ordnance, Beretta, Browning, Bond Arms Inc., Bushmaster, Chricket, Charter Arms, Colt, Comanche, European American Armory, Firestorm, Glock, Hastings, Hi-Point, Legacy Sports, Magnum Research, Mossberg, Navy Arms, New England, North American Arms, Phoenix, Ruger, Savage Arms, Snake Charmer, Spartan

Gun Works, Taurus, Tikka, Verona, Walther Handguns and Weatherby. I want a horse and I am a horse.

Military style rifle owners will be pleased with the massive selection of components and accessories for AK-47 and AR-15 style rifles. Items include barrels, bolt carriers and assemblies, buttstocks, folding stocks, free float tubes, handguards, flashiders, muzzle brakes, flash hiders, gas tubes, gas blocks, bayonets, receiver covers, and match sights. AK-47 builds are very popular and we carry U.S. compliance parts for building AK-47 rifles and AK-47 pistols as well as dress up parts for your favorite AK-47. AR-15 rifles are again readily available as well as AR-15 pistols.
     I want one and I am one.

In addition to the firearm items and gun parts, we carry a large selection of Knives from leading manufacturers such as Almar Knives, Anza Knives, Benchmade Knives, Browning Knives, Chef's Choice, Cold Steel, Columbia River Knife & Tool, Hen & Rooster, Ka-Bar Knives, MOD, Spyderco, Tomahawk Brand, Wyoming Knife Corp., United Cutlery, EZE Lap.

Want, am.

59.

The book about violence must be a book of quotations.
For everyone speaks about violence.
Is a book of memories, for everyone's life is riddled.

Whereas the floating hand of sexual love stirs the baby's within, the floating arms of Godly love lift the earth to the sun. Whereas trees by the river greening. Girls in the coffee line, ravened and foamed.

Precise in their aging, the bodies roam. Not every day's a
happy day; my plays are peppered with crime.

Agree,

agree to take me with you.

60.

Man goes constantly in fear of himself. (Bataille)

Let us accept the dead in their irrevocable 'situation.' By
what right can we suspect them of actions that, under other
circumstances and in face of other pressures, they might
have committed? No, we cannot look for the murderer
among *them*. (Wiesel)

Tenderly—be not impatient, / (Strong is your hold, O
mortal flesh, / Strong is your hold O love.) (Whitman)

The sight or thought of murder can give rise to the desire
for sexual enjoyment for the neurotic anyway. (Bataille)

Others wonder if our lack of success at contacting other
forms of higher life, despite an array of satellites and
detection equipment, could possibly mean that higher life
forms destroy themselves and that extreme violence, a by-
product of intelligence, has obliterated them. (Dutton)

Cathy: convicted of the murder of the 3-month-old Brandon
B. had been babysitting the boy and his 2-year-old brother.

Cruelty is only the negation of the self, carried so far that it is transformed into a destructive explosion: insensitivity makes the entire being tremble. (Blanchot)

Violence akin to vim: strength; and to vaya: meal.

I'm on a mission. I can't stop. (Shaw)

But ah, but O thou terrible, why wouldst thou rude on me / Thy wring-world right foot rock? (Hopkins)

Now I will do nothing but listen. (Whitman)

61.

COLORADO

Colorado has the highest rate of teen depression in the nation. Believe it. In a class of 13 19-20 year-olds, two are bipolar, two are alcoholic, one can't wake up, one's best friend has just been shot. Sores around their mouths. Skin burned red. One misses class, bailing her friend out of jail. Another's being stalked and must get a court order. Kid you not. Most are on meds. Sunny skies. Lots of skiing. Who can account? Littleton, Colorado, whereof the Columbine Massacre, is an unimpressive suburb. But pretty. Mountains in the distance. Lots of skiing. Lots of churches. Sad, sad mothers and fathers.

I'm done. Done doing this and doing that and saying this and saying that I'm done. Done for and done in, done

doing for and being done to. Under delicate bits of dust,
I swim backwards. Now that's a trick. If you must make
a racket, do it somewhere else, someone said. Someone
said, Everything I do is a text. I filter my life through the
text of my face. That's big, someone answered, that's
really big. Wanna share a foot-long? No, I can't do that.
Someone said, This should be put on hold, but later,
somewhere, we'll come upon its true sense. Someone
said, I cannot enter normal places, but instead stand
outside, tapping on store windows. It has something to
do with the heat. Something to do with the wayward. She
ran down the street in her heels, sobbing as he pursued
her. As soon as I'm done here, I'm going to fall asleep.
Do I have no stamina? None whatsoever. Did you own a
gun? Never did. And why didn't you? It was redundant,
he says. *Quiet, quiet, still.* Said, Want that well done or
rare? But what could be more rare than you?

Than you, sad mother, sad father?

BLURRING THE MAGISTERIA
Science as Fact, Science as Metaphor
Susanne Paola Antonetta

Stephen Jay Gould, a scientist, proposed the doctrine of "non-overlapping magisteria," a chalk line he scrawled on the playground asphalt to divide science and spirituality. The magisterium of science houses the "empirical constitution of the universe," Gould writes, while religion contains "the spiritual meaning of our lives." Gould did not refer to a domain between science and art, though I think his stress on factuality has tended to keep nonscientists away from his magisterium. To be empirical is to be evidence-based, to approach the world from a place far removed, seemingly, from the leaps of art and the lyric essay. Yet what constitutes our world—from a physical and existential standpoint—frets at all of us who dance on the skin of this planet, twirling its lopsided way through our galaxy.

Many years ago, I went to a conference on fractals meant to draw creative writers and scientists together. After a few writers spoke about fractals, a mathematician got up—I remember his arching auburn beard and look of dismay equally well—and said, "You writers don't understand this theory at all. You're reducing it to poetry."

Susanne Paola Antonetta's most recent book is *Make Me a Mother* (2014). She is also the author of *Body Toxic* (2001), *A Mind Apart* (2007), the novella *Stolen Moments* (2014), and four books of poetry. Awards for her poetry and prose include a *New York Times* Notable Book Award, an American Book Award, a *Library Journal* Best Science Book of the Year, and a Pushcart Prize. She has also been a Lenore Marshall Award finalist. Her essays and poems have appeared in *The New York Times*, *The Washington Post*, *Orion*, *The New Republic*, and many anthologies.

Poets might feel, of course, that imagery is not a reduction, but what struck me was the needless binary: a fractal, which is a repeating geometric or mathematical pattern (think of the little stalks of broccoli leaning out from a large stalk of broccoli), can be a metaphor in a literary work, but it can also be itself in a literary work. We do not need to pledge ourselves to use scientific material only factually or only metaphorically; rather, we writers can do either or both—though if we use scientific fact only as metaphor, we ignore the fundamental forces that shape our lives.

To put it another way: we need to put the metaphor-making into the hands of those who understand that metaphor—what my bearded mathematician meant by "poetry"—is not some kind of metaphysical decoration, but a means to grasp how the physical world we encounter is most fully real. Metaphor is a way to capture the reverberations of reality. To use a physics image to describe the phenomenon, metaphor is the multiverse model of the universe—it gives infinite versions of the world that out-fold from one another as parallel universes would. Imagery, like multiverse theory, gives us a version of the world that can answer far more of our questions and satisfy more of our longings than a unitary model ever could. And science is not something apart from us; it *is* us. As the lyric essay moves us to recognize the poetry in prose, the reality of the image, so too can it help us encounter the rich levels of being of the physical world.

This universe holds us captive in the rigor of its laws. If you have ever snapped a towel at someone, the bone-break sound came from you breaking the sound barrier. If you have ever cursed at static on your television set, you have the echoes of the Big Bang to thank for the Cosmic Microwave Background snowing up your screen. Here is Niels Bohr's explanation of the atom: if the atom were the size of a football field, the nucleus would be a football on the ground and the electrons would be gnats circling crazily above the stadium. This reality is void and emptiness. This is you, still cramped enough to develop blisters from the pinch of those new shoes.

Every day, you muddle around in a cosmos that is both an answer to human reason and an affront to it—like the infinite universe that we find, nevertheless and irrationally, has a shape.

I'm fascinated by the strange scale of the things physics claims to know—a Big Bang at the starting gate, and Higgs boson particles that allow for mass, including your Higgs-bosoned hand wrapped now around this book, instead of being a soup of particles that can't latch onto one another to make atoms.

I'm equally fascinated by what physics fails to know. So much of the universe consists of forces that can't be found, like dark matter and dark energy. We know these forces exist because of what they do—we see their curves in space, observe their gravitational pull.

In my lyric essay "Dark Matter," these dark forces create a template for the sweeping antitheses that make up our world—matter and antimatter, dark matter and known, and so on—and the more personal antitheses of my life, as a manic-depressive woman and an embodied creature with more than her share of dualities. The fact of my manic-depression partakes of science and medicine: there are genetic oddities you could chart on my genome; there are chemicals I put into myself that alter other chemicals and systems found there. And those genes and those chemicals provide a scaffold in which my spirit and my imagination do what they do. I cannot tell one story without telling the other. Dark matter, in this essay, gives me a way of understanding my body, its sudden and unexplainable darknesses. It presents another container for the story, another mode of making meaning: my small self as part of a cosmic *modus operandi*.

Metaphor and the lyric are often the writer's way of grappling with the many dark matters of our world, I think; they give us a way to approach the unsayable things we cannot apprehend directly, but the pull of which works us mercilessly. A hybrid genre is one concerned with blurring, with crossing lines. I want to see what dark matters the dark matters of our universe can hold.

HYBRID WORK
Dark Matter

> *What does Athens have to do with Jerusalem?*
> —Tertullian

So many opposites in this our universe: matter and antimatter, the Big Bang and the Big Crunch, dark matter and known. Athens and Jerusalem, cold intellection and leaps of faith. I've wondered why this bipole world of mine feels so normal. It has breathed through me lo these many years, and though people ask me the question, I can't even say if it's strange. I have two different names. My mail carrier, my bank, accept them, at times with a bit of mild interrogation: whom are you hiding, and where?

I lived under dual names even as a child. One girl with a short form of my given name, one with a name unrelated, signed not just my school papers but my diary, in different inks. Both of them, for completely different reasons, loved risk. They walked away from things—crumpled cars melded into trees, boyfriends who hung knives above their beds, a toxic milk kindling in the blood—no one would seem likely to walk away from.

And later: there's an S------- who supernovas; physicists would call her a *standard candle*. And one scarcely knows where the rain stops.

· · · ·

Perhaps it took a Carthaginian—which Tertullian was—to understand the terms of the world so wholly in terms of place, Athens at odds with Jerusalem. The Romans fetishized the destruction of Carthage, a destruction they pursued, several centuries before Tertullian, through the Punic Wars. The general Scipio finally defeated Carthage and sold every living inhabitant of the city into slavery, then sowed the ground with salt. The defeat of Carthage was an astonishing destruction, a creation of nothing out of something comparable in ways to what our modern bombs do, but slow and steady and requiring piecework, the loading of individual human beings onto ships bound for slave markets, the plowing of acre after acre of land.

Carthage rose again, as a Roman African city, home of saints: Tertullian, and Augustine, who studied in Carthage and fathered an illicit child, a sin he would spend the rest of his life famously confessing.

An Augustinian prayer: *Light of my heart, do not let my darkness speak to me.*

. . . .

Nothing, true nothing, as the Romans learned, is hard.

Even the universe has errors of plenitude. There's far more matter in our cosmos than astrophysicists predicted, until they invented ways to measure the gravitation within galaxies and found off-the-charts quantities of matter, far more matter even than there is antimatter, though if two things existed that called out for symmetry, it would be these.

When I was a young woman and doctors went exploring in my body they found two uteruses, one dark, closed off, prone to illness. It seemed like a just physical architecture for a manic-depressive, and one that should have parallels all over: two hearts, one hard and dry, two spleens.

. . . .

Space has its own attendant force, dark energy. Space comes into being all the time, and as it does, it brings with it more and more dark energy and causes the cosmos to fly apart faster and faster. Space is probably flat, and it's very plastic, bending, flexing, rippling like water under a skipping stone. The universe and the space that makes up most of it have an end point, a place into which it expands, a ludicrous fact that bothers nonscientists to death.

Popular shapes for the universe come and go—the sideways cone or technically, Picard horn; the dodecahedron; the doughnut; an infinite flatness. If space didn't end, darkness would not exist, but every millimeter of night sky would reflect back some sort of light from somewhere. We would have the light of the sun during the day and the light of true infinity at night, and they would look much the same.

Here where I live, in the northernmost part of the Pacific Northwest, we have short days in winter, with dim skies all day and sunset at three, and long days in summer, the sun finally exhausting itself after 10:00 p.m. It is, doctors warned me, a hard climate for a person with bipolar disorder, and for that matter, everyone. Seasonal Affective Disorder touches much of the population; someone invented a baseball cap here with a lightbox built into the brim. Summer makes you giddy, like swallowing a lit bulb, while winter is live burial. These facts tell me if the universe were infinite I would be somebody else.

Two unknown pieces of the universe exist, dark matter and dark energy. Dark energy's a quantum force and constitutes about two-thirds of the cosmos: dark matter, which we cannot see or uncover, about 25 percent. We have not the dimmest idea of 90 percent of our world.

It may be shameful that we know only 10 percent of our universe, even well enough to label it star or galaxy or comet or supernova, little as we understand these. 10 percent seems to be a threshold fraction of ignorance; I remember an aunt of mine saying we only use 10 percent of our brains, as she sat at her country-style kitchen table in her boxy suburban house, licking color over her fingernails with a brush. *If only we knew what the rest does, if only we could get at that part of our brain,* she would say. *Probably as Einstein did.*

The notion of this dark matter in the brain—though the only-10-percent theory turned out not to be true—seized my imagination as a child. I don't think I ever dreamed of being an Einstein. This same aunt told riddles to pass the time: in one, a boy's father rushes him to the emergency room after an accident, where the surgeon says, I cannot operate on him, he's my son.

Who is the surgeon? riddled my aunt. She gave us a day to come up with the answer but, stumped, my girl cousin and I never did: the surgeon was the boy's mother, my aunt finally told us, and we stared at her when she gave us the solution: absurd.

. . . .

Whether the dark matter in the brain struck me as something that could help me, or something that had accidentally been unleashed, I don't recall. I was aware of being bipolar decades before receiving the diagnosis or understanding there could be a term for such a thing. In place of medicine I divided myself up: A moods and B moods, this girl and that one, Athens and Jerusalem. I separated compulsively, as if I knew I could annihilate myself and I needed to hold myself apart. Only a small fraction of people have the condition I do, and a doctor warned my parents they would have to institutionalize me. No one would be likely to give this advice now, not because we've learned more, but because we choose to spend less on care.

Too, I was born into the age of the medical journal *Eugenics Quarterly*, when the thinking of the eugenics movement begun early in the century still knocked around. Ten percent became a eugenics target, the "submerged 10th" of the population who should not be allowed to continue their bloodlines, stopped from doing so by segregation—institutionalization—along with sterilization, and among the more hardcore eugenicists, discreetly putting people to death. Back then, in the 1960s, shutting someone away for life smacked of sparing the general population from their freaks and their genes. Eugenics doctors did perform tens of thousands of sterilizations, some in institutions, some simply by telling patients they needed an operation without saying what kind, carting them to the hospital for the purpose, then releasing them.

Dark energy works mysteriously, free from gravity, and dark matter likely has a different atomic structure than ours, with our clingy electrons and stuck nuclei. If we could endow these dark forces with sentience I'm sure they would find us weak, swinging along with the nearest weighty thing, voids orbiting voids. We have failed to uncover their secrets. Unlike Augustine, we pray for our darkness to speak to us.

ASSAULT HYBRIDITY

The Disintegrating Lyric/Mother I

Sarah Vap

The hybridity of "Oskar's Cars" evolved directly out of an assault of emotion, of physicality, of time—launched directly at my body, my personhood—in the form of a baby. The person I was before the birth of my first son was a person who had boundaries of body, more or less. Or rather, she had a fairly consistent degree of boundary to which, after 33 years, she had become accustomed. Ditto boundaries of time. Ditto boundaries of noise. That person, she had a chair to sit in and no one else sat in it simultaneously. She generally could walk across a room, or from one room into another, and no one screamed their fucking head off. The person who existed before the birth of my son had some degree of control over the level of noise around her, the amount of time she spent around other people, the hour more or less when she would fall asleep and wake up, and who she would do that with. She was a person who didn't have to strategize or call in help in order to brush her teeth (comb her hair, sit down to shit, eat an apple), and when she did, didn't feel for three minutes like she was *failing another human being utterly.* Nor, for three minutes, did she have to hear

Sarah Vap is the author of five collections of poetry, including *Dummy Fire* (2007), winner of the 2006 Saturnalia Poetry Prize; *American Spikenard* (2007), winner of the 2007 Iowa Poetry Prize; *Faulkner's Rosary* (2010); and *Arco Iris* (2012), named a Library Journal Best Book of 2012. Her book *End of the Sentimental Journey* (2013) initiated Noemi Press' Infidel Poetics Series. She is the recipient of an NEA Literature Fellowship for Poetry. Her book *Viability* (2015) was selected for the 2014 National Poetry Series.

the cries of an innocent's heart being ripped out. She was a person who when she had a thought could generally think it without interruption for at least a few seconds. These things were not only her life conditions, but also her working conditions as a writer.

When my son was born, the boundaries of body, heart, mind, even spirit—they dissolved, were battered, foundered, split apart, in ways that I wanted. And also in ways that stressed me deeply. That gave me unprecedented joy, and unprecedented frustration—as a person and as a writer. The dissolving, the battering, the foundering, the splitting—when I sat down to write "Oskar's Cars" (feeling almost barely there anymore)— these actions manifested themselves in a hybridity that occurred without, it seemed, any decision on my part. Different strands of old and new self(ves), different strands of Oskar's emerging personhood and his absolutely present physicality, and strands of myth (This assault had to mean something, didn't it? Be part of something larger, ancient, even holy? It helped me to believe that it did.) slammed at each other and warmed with each other and fought against each other to exist, even if in remnants.

I thought for a time, while I was writing "Oskar's Cars," that one strand of the essay—the lyric or the narrative strand—might win out over the other. But one never did win. I tried pulling the strands into different documents and developing them apart from one another, but that wasn't it. That wasn't the thing I was trying to say. I was trying something like this: how do you scream out that you love something more than you've ever loved something and also it is destroying "you" and you hate that destruction and perhaps also you don't mind/you crazily desire that destruction—but no, you don't, and it's happening anyway and for that you are profoundly grateful and this is somewhat, somewhat how that whole deal is going. I was trying to document the "content" as well as the process, and no existing form (not lyric poem alone, not academic or critical or nonfiction essay alone, not narrative alone) would come close to containing this thing that I was experiencing/enduring/being. So hybridity is what happened. Like my son, it seemed as if "Oskar's Cars" made itself.

I do think that as more voices produce and publish/disseminate their writing—more voices of women, more voices of people of color, more voices of people who are not of the socioeconomic elite, more queer of all kinds voices—the more the old genres will break apart and new ones will form. (Our existing contemporary genres, didn't they evolve toward this moment expressing a fairly particular experience of the world? White, white-ish, male, male-ish, wealthy, wealthy-ish, straight, straight-ish?) I do think that as more human experiences are put into writing—and disseminated increasingly apart from traditional publishing houses—that writing will continue to change. Morph. Blend. Break.

And six years after writing "Oskar's Cars," all the strands that I worked with, plus many, many more strands—the multiplying strands of Oskar, and the multiplying strands of our next two sons, Mateo and Archie, and the multiplying strands of our partnership as parents, and the multiplying strands of our "own" "selves" as we grow and change and experience the world, oh and also the increasingly complex strands of technologies, of capitalism, of racism, of misogyny, of systematic and systemic violence, as well as all of the enduringly nourishing things that are mythology and story and language—all these strands still swirl around the soup of my body, the soup of my mind, and the soup of my writing. My work continues to move in the direction of what one might call hybridity. I think it's the wave of the future. I think our world demands it. I think it's only getting worse/better.

HYBRID WORK

Oskar's Cars:
A Mothering Mind and the Creative Process

Anyone who knows my son Oskar knows how he feels about cars. And trucks. And heavy machinery.

Oskar falls asleep at night, between his father and me, tightly holding two small cars in each hand. We wake in the night rolling over the metal race cars and backhoes that he has tucked into bed with us. Every morning, he sits up half asleep and slightly frantic to search for the vehicles that he's dropped in the night. His movements are still shaky and confused with sleep, adding to the urgency of finding the cars.

Every few days the cars in our bed change, but each morning Oskar remembers exactly which ones he must find between the blankets and under the pillows—he remembers exactly who he held in the night.

He can't stand it until they are each accounted for, and back in his arms.

> The sources of Love? The sources of Poetry?—The attention,
> the connections, and the details of one's world loved and pieced
> together. Mother-splitting. Mother-echoing. Echolalia not only of
> the child, but also of his mother.

Sometimes we have had trouble understanding a new car's name, or how he refers to it: Broken Truck, Old Blue Car, All-Terrain Vehicle, Red Race Car, Snow Tractor, and inexplicably, on a delivery van painted over with phoenixes, Agba Truck. But after a couple tries we, too, know his cars and trucks by the names he gives to them. Between our house, his grandparents' houses, and his great-grandma's house, Oskar must name and care for 200 cars.

> The source of him. The source of the decision to love. Or how
> we came to love him.

Oskar has just turned two years old, and his love of cars has been enduring. His love of cars has covered more than half of his life.

But the first obsession he held was for cats.

He found and declared cats everywhere. He loved every cat—inspired, I know, by our own dear cat, Iris, who cuddled with him when he was an infant, in the months before she died. Oskar meowed in his sleep once. He wore the little cat outfit that he chose for Halloween when he was a year old—tight orange pants with black cats on them, a black vest with a pink cat nose and tongue, and cat ears on his head—with glorious pride for weeks. I had to hide the orange pants from him around Valentine's Day—they were just too tight.

> If my source of love, my source of poetry, used to be dream, memory, landscape, and feelings so intense as to alter, momentarily, the world that I shared with other people—now, Source is simply what my life has become.

> If before, I pushed my head through and through some hole back into a childworld, a wombworld, a dreamworld, to gather a poem together, now I have fallen complete into that world. Now I attempt to push my head back out. Back into the world of time and chronology. Back into the world of words.

> If before, my poems were lyric, outside of time or fixed place, then now my whole self is lyric. The world in which I live is outside of Time. Outside of fixed Place. Not outside of word, exactly, but parallel with word.

Vacuums did not replace cats, but he loved them equally and alongside one another for several more months. Even in the most unlikely of places, if Oskar hooted his word—"Vaaaa-coooooom!"—we looked until we found the vacuum. Once Oskar began to love vacuums, they were everywhere around us. We vacuumed four or five times a day. He knew which closet held the vacuum in each house or restaurant or place of business we frequented.

Everywhere we went, for those months of his life, our friends, neighbors, relatives, and barely acquaintances would pull out the vacuum and the cat for Oskar.

Then he had brief affairs with spatulas and clocks.

> Since Oskar's birth, I have both unhitched completely from time, and am shot through with bullets of pure small time. Daily time, moment-to-moment time. The paradoxes of time, the paradoxes of place, of identity, of separation and cohesion—they are more complete.

> Paradox now moves in more than two directions—is more completely paradoxical than duality, than the pair of opposites both true at once.

> Now, in this world where the ordinary is a miracle to Oskar, in this world where anything is possible and nothing yet constrained by language—and in this world where he and I are not yet separate human beings—everything is true for us at once. And everything is only partially true.

> And nothing holds true at all.

But sometime before his first birthday, Oskar gave his heart to cars. And he hasn't looked back. Cats and vacuums were completely forgotten. Spatulas and clocks were dropped cold and ignored. And by the time Oskar was a year and a half old, his vast vocabulary of animal sounds (he had dozens and dozens!), and his vigorous vacuum-motor growl, and his bird-like hooting of "vaaa-coooom," and his sweet "tick-tock" to point out the clocks, and his surprisingly clear rendering of "spatula" at one year old, were replaced almost entirely by his Car-and-Truck vocabulary.

If every opposite had to be the perfect opposite of 12 other things simultaneously, and if each of those 12 things lived in 12 different dimensions, and if truth and reality melted into dream and possibility like butterscotches melting—this is how I now experience paradox.

The only descriptions I have for this mothering feeling are physical.

The only descriptions I can muster have to squeeze themselves back down into the four mere dimensions of which we speak.

He can now communicate almost anything in the world by speaking Car-and-Truck with us. And we are learning to communicate back with him, I believe, in Car-and-Truck.

I mean this: there is something I can't yet explain about poetry and about mothering. I don't want to make parallels; they aren't parallel. A baby is not a poem, and a child has nothing in common with a book.

But it is true that women are saying *something* about mothering and poetry. And saying it more and more. There are anthologies. There are entire courses and writing programs. This isn't new, what I'm struggling to explain. But it still feels... unexplained. Or perhaps truer, it feels inexplicable.

Oskar doesn't just enjoy cars and trucks. He isn't just interested in cars and trucks. He attachment-parents his cars and trucks, says my husband. Last night, he bathed each of a dozen or so cars he took into the bathtub with him. We washed Oskar. He washed his cars. We poured water over his hair while he covered his eyes, and then as quickly as possible we wiped off his face with a towel while he sputtered trustingly. Then he poured water over his cars to rinse them off and wiped their front bumper as quickly as he could with his wet washcloth. Before he left the tub, he asked me to dry off each of his cars in his waiting towel. Only after they were dried off, and set in a straight line on the counter, could I dry and put pajamas onto *my* son.

What is happening? What is happening?

I want to whisper this question over and over to anyone watching my life, hearing me, seeing me, these two years after Oskar's birth.

Oskar wants to understand his cars, and he wants to be understood by them.

Neuroscientists and mythologists describe the brain like the tree of knowledge. Dendrites and neurons and pathways that connect and reconnect and push endlessly out through the body and into the ether.

Push out from the tops of our heads like roots and trunks and leaves made of the material and made of the invisible.

Right now he is sitting on my lap, watching a cartoon that features talking cars and trucks, and he is holding four cars that look like the characters in the movie: Old Blue Car, Police Car, Broken Tow Truck, and Red Race Car.

When Oskar's hands were even tinier than they are now, he held just one car in each. Now that he is two, he can just barely manage to hold two cars in each hand. For over a year, for more than half of his entire life, I haven't seen him for more than a few moments without at least two cars in his hands.

I'm saying something like this: motherhood has wiped that tree in my mind clean away, and left me pure soil. Motherhood has wiped the tree away, and left pure space.

Motherhood took the tree, and left me air, soil, space.

When I dressed Oskar this morning, he set down Yellow Stripe Car, Pump-er Truck, Mama's Car, and Yellow Bug Car, and stuck his arms straight up in the air. I pulled his pajama top off. He bent down again and touched each of the cars where he'd set them on the floor, while I unfolded today's shirt. He stood back up, stuck his arms straight up in the air again, and I pulled the shirt onto him as quickly as I could. Then, almost frantically, as if he'd set his own baby down in the middle of the road, he picked up his cars again, and arranged all four of them, with difficulty, in his tiny hands.

This shirting process probably sounds reasonable, but it is a compromise a long time in the making. For months, we stretched his sleeves and tugged them, one at a time, over his fist and its two cars—neither of us able to endure the agony of taking his beloveds right out of his hands.

And where this soil, and air, and space are, I tell my husband, a new tree of knowledge is growing to replace my lost mind.

And exactly where my new tree of knowledge is growing, I tell him, within it and around it—this is where Oskar's tree of knowledge is growing.

And exactly where my tree and Oskar's tree are growing, simultaneously and in that exact spot, are the trees of every other mother that ever there was. And of every other child that ever there was.

And exactly where my new tree grows, I tell him, there grows also my own childhood's tree.

And these billions of trees are made of materiality and invisibility.

And the joint of the material mind and the invisible mind, is it language?

Oskar wakes in the morning exceedingly tender from his dreams. He wakes from his nap in the afternoon exceedingly tender from his dreams. During these times, he won't put his cars down, not even to eat. *Mama feed*, he will say, with two cars tight in each hand. Several cars arranged around his plate. I feed him because I, too, wished someone would feed me while I held him, newly from my dreams.

> What I could try to tell you is that in mothering, I've lost the mind that I had before. I've lost my solitude, my body, my privacy, my time, my concentration. Mothering, I have lost my seriousness, my access, my connection to, my inclusion. Mothering, I have lost my sleep, my dreams, my mornings, my nights, my money, my job, and my time with other adults and other poets. As a pregnant woman, as a nursing woman, as a mothering woman, I have lost nearly all of the ways and props and yearnings and communities that defined who I previously understood myself to be. What I mean is, I no longer remember or recognize myself, mothering as I am.

Oskar began to love cars during the months he was sick. At one year old, around the time we moved from Phoenix to the Olympic Peninsula, Oskar began to get fevers. For the next several months we spent much time with doctors, in emergency rooms, at Children's Hospital. On and off medications. I associate his love of cars with his decision to remain in his body—imperfect, painful, material.

> However, who I am now is becoming deeply known to me. Or, I might say, I am simply becoming this new woman—this strangely concentrated and scattered, more selfless, bodied woman.

> I remember a different woman as Sarah, as poet, as lover, and as friend.

She has been cast through with a clear and splitting shadow, shearing a hard and enveloping clear space. Split. Clarity. Bright shadow.

Wide sheets of glass slice through that body. That spirit and that mind.

I associate his love of cars with his body. Tiny and vulnerable and perfect. I associate his love of cars with his acquiring of language. Vulnerable and perfect.

It is not just a loss or confusion of my own body and my own personality and my own spirit of which I am trying to speak. It is a loss and confusion of time itself. A loss and confusion of material itself. Of invisibility and quiet themselves.

A loss and confusion of way.

The thousands of hours of breastfeeding, day and night. The thousands of hours of helping him fall asleep. Two years of not being separated from him for more than four or five hours at a time. Being more than doubled, and less than whole. An imposed, and self-imposed, form of meditation. Of sitting. Of bondage, claustrophobia, need, responsiveness, selflessness, koan.

Oskar is still so tiny. He weighs just 22 pounds. He is only 25 months old, and it's sometimes difficult to understand his words if you don't know him well.

I sat down with my mom and my son. He pulled five or six cars into a line, and said: "combibibil." He was right: he had just pulled out every convertible from the pile on the floor.

But I am still all those things: daughter, friend, lover, and poet. Sister, teacher. Though now I have four to six legs, three or four hearts, the perspective of a two-year-old, of a baby in utero, of a 35-year-old American woman. And now, of women ancient and of all time. A woman of anyplace in any world.

A female of any kind of animal.

STUTTERING INTO RELATIONSHIP

Excerpts from *How Literature Saved My Life*

David Shields

Writing was, and in a way still is, very bound up for me with stuttering. Writing represented/represents the possibility of turning "bad language" into "good language." I now have much more control over my stutter; it's nothing like the issue it was in my teens and twenties and into my thirties. Still, Edmund Wilson's notion of the wound and the bow persists in my mind. (Samuel Johnson had scars all over his face, he twitched, every time he walked past a tree he had to touch it, he was sexually masochistic, and out of his mouth came wondrously strange and funny things.) Language is what differentiates us from other species, so when I stutter, I find it genuinely dehumanizing. I still feel a psychic need to write myself into, um, existence. So, too, due to stuttering, I value writing and reading as essential communication between writer and reader. It's why I want writing to be so intimate: I want to feel as if, to the degree anyone can know anyone else, I know someone—I've gotten to this other person.

And vice versa: because I stutter, I became a writer (in order to return to the scene of the crime and convert the bloody fingerprints into Abstract

David Shields' 16 books include *Reality Hunger*, named one of the best books of 2010 by more than 30 publications; *The Thing About Life Is That One Day You'll Be Dead* (2009), a *New York Times* bestseller; and *Black Planet* (1999), a finalist for the National Book Critics Circle Award. His most recent book, *I Think You're Totally Wrong* (2015), is appearing as a film in 2015. The recipient of a Guggenheim and two NEA fellowships, he has published in the *New York Times Magazine, Harper's, Esquire, Village Voice, Salon, Slate, McSweeney's,* and *The Believer*.

Expressionism). As a writer, I love language as much as any element in the universe, but I also have trouble living anywhere other than in language. If I'm not writing it down, experience doesn't really register. Language has gone from prison to refuge back to prison.

Picasso: "A great painting comes together, just barely" (I love that comma). And this fine edge of excellence gets more and more difficult to maintain.

Yeats said that we can't articulate the truth, but we can embody it. I think that's wrong or at least beside the point. What's of interest to me is precisely how we try to articulate the truth, and what that says about us, and about "truth."

What separates us is not what happens to us. Pretty much the same things happen to most of us: birth, love, bad driver's license photos, death. What separates us is how each of us thinks about what happens to us. That's what I want to hear.

Texting: proof that we're solitary animals who like being left alone as we go through life, commenting on it. We're aliens.

The moment I try not to stutter, I stutter. I never stutter when singing to myself in the shower.

The perceiver, by his very presence, alters what's perceived: Plato, *Dialogues of Socrates*. Eckermann, *Conversations of Goethe*. Boswell, *Life of Johnson*. Malcolm, *The Journalist and the Murderer*. Schopenhauer: "The world is my idea." We don't see the world. We make it up.

Ancient Sanskrit texts emphasize the ephemeral nature of truth. Sanskrit writers use fiction, nonfiction, stories within stories, stories about stories, reiteration, oral history, exegesis, remembered accounts, rules, history, mythological tales, and aphorisms to try to get to the "truth," often dressing it up in narrative as a way to make it appear comprehensible, palatable. Sanskrit works revolve around the question: "Who is the narrator?" Subjectivity is always present in the recitation: the nature of reality is ever elusive. We spend our lives chasing it.

Maggie Nelson claims that it makes her feel less alone to compose almost everything she writes as a letter. She even goes so far as to say that she doesn't know how to compose otherwise. When I'm having trouble writing something I often close the document and compose the passage as an email to, say, my friend Michael. I imagine I can feel the tug of the recipient at the other end of the wire, and this creates in me a needed urgency. The letter always arrives at its destination.

HYBRID WORK
Excerpt from Reality Hunger: A Manifesto

The Reality-based Community

248
We're living in a newsy time.

249
We live in difficult times; art should be difficult (my goal is to make every paragraph as discomfiting as possible.)

250
Tying my shoes in the lobby of the recreation center, I saw someone reading what looked like *Checkpoint*, Nicholson Baker's novel about a man who fantasizes about assassinating then-president George W. Bush. I'd just finished reading the book, so I asked, "Are you reading *Checkpoint*? How do you like it?" The reader seemed wary and was strikingly reluctant to respond with any specificity to my question. He asked if I was the writer David Shields. I am, the one, the only (actually, there's at least one other writer David Shields, a scholar who's the author of a book called *Oracles of Empire*). Still, we talked about *Checkpoint* and Baker only circumlocutiously. When I was ready to go, I well-meaningly but ill-advisedly said, "I'm David Shields; I guess you know that. What's your name?"—which,

of course, reanimated the entire spy-vs.-spy subtext, so he said, very slowly, "I'm Wes." No last name. End of conversation. A new moment in the re- public, so far as I could tell.

251
Shortly after 9/11, the Defense Department hired Renny Harlin, the writ- er-director of *Die Hard 2*, to game-plan potential doomsday scenarios; in other words, fiction got called to the official aid, reinforcement, and rescue of real life, as if real life weren't always fiction in the first place.

252
I have invited my fellow documentary nominees on the stage with us, and they're here in solidarity with me because we like nonfiction. We like nonfiction because we live in fictitious times.

253
People like you are in what we call the reality-based community. You be- lieve that solutions emerge from judicious study of the discernible reality. That's not the way the world really works anymore. We're an empire now, and when we act, we create our own reality. And while you're studying that reality (judiciously, as you will), we'll act again, creating other realities, which you can study, too, and that's how things will sort out. We're history actors, and you—all of you—will be left to just study what we do.

254
The person who loses the presidential election is the person who seems most fictional. In 2000, Gore simply was Mr. Knightley from *Emma*. So, too, in 2004, Kerry—Lord Bertram from *Mansfield Park*. During the 2008 presidential election, reality hunger in the face of nonstop propaganda resulted in regime change. Obama won because of his seeming commit- ment to reality, the common sense of his positions. Obama came off as completely real, playing basketball and texting people on his BlackBerry

and tearing up over his grandmother's death. Both Hillary and McCain campaigned with all the logic of a Successories poster: they appeared to believe that could will their presidency into being simply by desiring it; no matter how behind they were by every real-world metric, they could still win by wishing it so.

255
Facts now seem important.

256
Facts have gravitas.

257
The illusion of facts will suffice.

258
In our hunger for all things true, we make the facts irrelevant.

THE NEW CRITIC ON THE COUCH

Kathleen Ossip

When I was a graduate student, I heard Anne Carson read from *Eros the Bittersweet*. She explained that she'd been asked to write an academic essay, but she felt incapable of that. Instead, she said, the piece she was going to read gestured toward the form of an academic essay but was only pretending.

I feel the same way about "The Nervousness of Yvor Winters," except that my piece doesn't even have the form of an academic essay and no one had asked me to write one but myself.

For years I had kept on my bookshelf a paperback copy of *Approaches to the Poem: Modern Essays in the Analysis and Interpretation of Poetry*, edited by John Oliver Perry, taped along its spine to keep it from falling apart and filched from my parents' house, the house where I had grown up. I have no clue why my parents, neither of them literary scholars, had this book from 1965, but I used to dip into it when I was a teenager, not a literary scholar but at least a bookworm. The lofty tone and heady content were frankly beyond me, but something about the mid-century-bookish-white-male tone of authority provoked me to keep trying. For

Kathleen Ossip is the author of *The Do-Over* (2015); *The Cold War* (2011), one of *Publishers Weekly*'s best books of 2011; *Cinephrastics* (2006), a chapbook of movie poems; and *The Search Engine* (2002), which won the *American Poetry Review*/Honickman First Book Prize. Her poems have appeared in *Best American Poetry*, *Best American Magazine Writing*, *The Washington Post*, *Paris Review*, *Poetry*, *The Believer*, *A Public Space*, and *Poetry Review* (London). She teaches at The New School and teaches online for The Poetry School of London.

that reason, I guess, I had "borrowed" it permanently and kept it on my grownup shelves.

Of all the mid-century bookish white males (New Critics, I eventually learned) included in this anthology of lit crit, Yvor Winters pissed me off the most. I found his judgments supercilious, besides being proven by history to be plain wrong, as I say in greater detail in my own "essay."

The ironic quotation marks above mean that I still don't know what to call this piece. Like Anne Carson, I wanted very much to write a true academic essay, complete with closely reasoned arguments and sub-arguments, incontrovertible and serious. I wanted to beat Winters at his own game. This fantasy kept me from writing the piece for several years. I would make attempts, get a few paragraphs in, and the tone would make me want to puke, or at least delete—it was so far from anything I could recognize as my own voice. Nor could I recognize my intention (although I wasn't even sure what my intention was) in the dry prose.

Finally I thought: What is the real reason I want to write about Yvor Winters? At bottom, what was the essential point? I realized that it was because I felt he was an asshole. I'm sure my rage, focused so specifically on Winters, was also rage against the literary branch of the patriarchy. Then I asked myself: What do you do when you meet someone who strikes you as an asshole in real life? The answer was: I try to find some compassion for them. And then my thinking/feeling began to come quite easily.

In my vain attempts at the essay, I suppose I'd been trying to pull a Winters myself: to keep the feelings out of my writing. Once I realized (so belatedly) that my (anyone's?) best writing is always driven by emotion, I saw my path: I put Yvor on the couch. What made him write so wrongheadedly, yet in a manner that was so absolutely sure of himself? The simple answer: his anxiety in the face of chaos and uncertainty. The complicated answer is in my essay/poem/piece.

I still don't know what to call it. I think of the form as "shreds," thinner and quicker than paragraphs, and without the neat transitions that tend to tie one paragraph to the next. My feelings don't allow for neat transitions. Personally, I think it's more essay-like than poem-like—it is, after all, argument-driven—but most people who talk to me about it call it a poem. One review called it an "essay/poetic sequence/tribute"! Whatever it is, I'm grateful to have written it at last: in what might be the writing equivalent of a therapeutic breakthrough, I'm no longer obsessed with those mid-century bookish white males.

HYBRID WORK
The Nervousness of Yvor Winters

> *We must never lie, or we shall lose our souls.*
> —Yvor Winters

> *The tears held back—barely held back—his voice would frequently almost break when he was reading the poems that he loved.*
> —Thom Gunn, recalling Yvor Winters in the classroom

> *Well, intensity with ignorance—what do you want worse?*
> —Henry James, *The Ambassadors*

In 1947, Yvor Winters published a volume of criticism called *In Defense of Reason*, from which is excerpted his essay "The Experimental School in American Poetry: An Analytical Survey of Its Structural Methods, Exclusive of Meter."[1]

In the essay, Winters harshly assesses poets he termed Experimental (Moore, Crane, Eliot, H.D., Pound, Stevens) whom we recognize as the geniuses of Modernism.

It takes time for literary criticism to turn literary text, but turn it does. Winters's essay now reads as a tragicomic monologue spoken by an exceptionally nervous and absolutely defended man.

The essay takes the form of a taxonomy. It could easily be outlined by a fourth-grader.

What are the structural methods possible in poetry? Winters attempts to list and rank them.

Repetition is OK in small doses but lax and diffuse in longer forms (e.g., Whitman).

Narrative is acceptable; *logic* ("coherence of form and content that gives the poem a clearly evident expository structure") is preferred.

Pseudo-reference is despicable. Moore, Crane, and Eliot are guilty of it. Poems organized by pseudo-reference retain the form of logic or narrative but without rational coherence or content.

Qualitative progression makes no attempt or show at a rational progression. Pound's *Cantos* are the perfect example, since their progression is that "of random conversation or of revery."

Non-rational progression is "a vice wherever it occurs."

So is irony, a doubleness of mood that should have been resolved by the poet before he/she committed the poem to paper, an "admission of careless feeling, which is to say careless writing." Wallace Stevens a culprit here.

•

Yvor Winters was born in 1900 and diagnosed with tuberculosis while he was studying at the University of Chicago. He wrote his first two books, experiments in free verse published in 1921 and 1922, in a sanitarium:

From *The Magpie's Shadow* (1922)

From Part 1. "In Winter"

No Being
I, bent. Thin nights receding.

From Part II. "In Spring"

Spring
I walk out the world's door.

Song
Why should I stop for spring?

From Part III. "In Summer and Autumn"

The Aspen's Song
The Summer holds me here.

Alone
I saw day's shadow strike.

What happens in tuberculosis is this: A specific bacterium is transmitted from one person to another through the air. As the bacteria multiply, they attack and destroy tissue primarily in the lungs, but they also can spread to the brain, kidneys, or bones. During the first stage, the immune system fights the disease by walling off most of the bacteria in fibrous capsules. Some of the encapsulated bacteria remain alive and may reactivate if the person becomes stressed or depleted. If the disease proceeds to the second stage, lung damage reduces ability to breathe.

The body fights off multiplicity and chaos, that which doesn't belong. In Winters's time, a retreat to an orderly, white, dry environment was part of the cure.

Which is easier to attain, sickness or health? Which is easier to accept? "Early in 1928 I abandoned free verse and returned to traditional meters...."[2]

After which:

Sonnet to the Moon

Now every leaf, though colorless, burns bright
With disembodied and celestial light,   .
And drops without a movement or a sound
A pillar of darkness to the shifting ground.

The lucent, thin, and alcoholic flame
Runs in the stubble with a nervous aim,
But, when the eye pursues, will point with fire
Each single stubble-tip and strain no higher.

O triple goddess! Contemplate my plight!
Opacity, my fate! Change, my delight!
The yellow tom-cat, sunk in shifting fur,
Changes and dreams, a phosphorescent blur.

Sullen I wait, but still the vision shun.
Bodiless thoughts and thoughtless bodies run.

•

"The problems of unity and form became the obsession of the New Critics."[3]

Incredibly, Winters's logic led him to the conclusion that he could "find few implicit themes of any great clarity, and fewer still that are explicit" in Pound's *Cantos*.

Pound replied (this a footnote in Winters's essay): "The nadir of solemn and elaborate imbecility is reached by Mr. Winters [...] [who] deplores my 'abandonment of logic in the *Cantos*' [...] [He] thinks logic is limited to a few 'forms of logic' which better minds were already finding inadequate to the mental needs of the XIIIth century."

Winters shot back: "[...] the abandonment of the denotative, or rational, [power of language] [...] results in one's losing the only means available for checking up on the qualitative or 'ideographic' sequences to see if they really are coherent in more than vague feeling. Mr. Pound, in other words, has no way of knowing whether he can think or not."

For Winters, a poem that yielded to a good paraphrase was very desirable; it allowed him to *check up on*. This need to check is a sort of critical OCD, which stems, we know, from fear and rage.

The critics became obsessed with meaning because meaning was perceived to be under attack. It is difficult to believe that one good hard look out the window wouldn't have convinced them that their ideas of logic were inadequate to the mental needs of the XXth century.

It is a frightening thing to take a good hard look out the window.

What is the relationship between this type of denial and chaos?

It is thought defended against feeling (i.e., everything else).

What pleasure is being denied? The pleasures that are not filtered through intellect/reason.

What is reason? Thinking that follows certain familiar rules or forms. It is usually contrasted with feeling/emotion.

Well, what produced this split in Yvor Winters? Fear. Of chaos.

While his body was shutting off and encapsulating the tuberculin, his mind was rejecting the chaos of emotion.

But emotion is not the right word. There is no word I know of for the miniverse of feeling, sensation, causation that falls outside the capsule of reason and logic.

"Winters came to realize that accumulated and juxtaposed intensities of image do not amount to thought."[4]

(He wasn't alone: "Feelings do not belong in a thought-work. [...] In the serial progress of a piece of thinking we may be treating a great many objects about which we have stored-up feeling-responses, but we do not release the feelings. [...] Thinking is a game of suspense, like holding one's breath when we dive, in which we postpone feelings and attend to our undertaking, at least until we have achieved the specific goal and can relax." Said John Crowe Ransom in a piece from the same critical anthology.)[5]

Winters wanted poets to analyze feelings rationally before they wrote, which he believed would result in thought.

Actually, though, the thoughts tell you what the feelings are.

Winters's rational, thought-based argument against Experimental poetry revealed his feelings about change (fear, rage).

Also: Where there is hostility that has not been provoked by hostility, there is usually envy.

•

"In the 1930s for literary scholars to attempt to criticize the work of their con-temporaries was looked upon as bizarre and strange, and possibly even ir-responsible and subversive. English departments were dominated by philolo-gists and grammarians who saw their goal as instructing students in ways to write properly and by scholars whose life work often resulted in the produc-tion of an annotated edition. [...] Winters's career did not proceed smoothly as a result of his interest in contemporary experimental poetry. The chair of the English Department at Stanford, in a notorious confrontation, denounced Winters for having written works that were a 'disgrace to the department.'"[6]

He had his controversy and ate it too. He had his conservatism and ate it too.

•

When the modernists exploded the notion of "argument" in a poem (Yvor Winters's real objection) it would seem to have been a change not in aesthetics but in technology. Aesthetic fashions swing pendulum-wise; but technology goes only forward. Thus: technophobia, the effects of a loss akin to mourning, but defended against intellectually.

Winters demanded not logic, not reason: but reassurance. He required not coherence but explication. Comfort, really.

Winters thought he was attacking bad (scary) writers but really he was showing himself to be a technologically obsolete reader. He did not want to admit what he already knew.

•

Proposed: A poem without a present vulgarity has no legs. If a poem does not put off its reader to some degree, it is probably no more than a conglomeration of received ideas about beauty (or literary expression). Ideas withering even as we read them on the page.

•

Update on pseudo-reference (retaining the form of logic or narrative but without rational coherence or content): it is rampant, in life and in poetry. It has been acknowledged (but not officially). It won.

Winters said: "This kind of writing is not a 'new kind of poetry,' as it has been called perennially since Verlaine discovered it in Rimbaud. It is the old kind of poetry with half the meaning removed. Its strangeness comes from its thinness."

Now this hits home. Or at least it makes me nervous.

It is amazing how much current prose poetry sounds exactly like passages out of *Ulysses*.

Winters spent so much time wondering how a poem works. Is our how so transparent?

How could we describe the present period style, various as it is? Varnish of Modernism applied to the wall of Romanticism?

Also tragic, and also inevitable and necessary, is the wash of irony on every word, image, sentiment. A split self. I grieve it. But I don't trust my nostalgia.

•

If we can know what we want from a poem before the fact, and we can know it definitely and in a very clear way, we may feel comforted or vindicated when we get it, but we won't feel ecstatic.

When we read a poem, are we looking for ecstasy or an opportunity to check up on?

There is something titillating about a theory of poetry. Read a polemic and you start to think "Poetry can do *that!*" But then go and read the poetry of the person writing.

Because a poem costs and earns nothing, it seems to invite judgment. Judgment, serious judgment, the more judgmental the better—the thinking maybe goes—will justify the importance of this money-free product.

Do we want to understand poems, or do we want poems that understand us?

What strangenesses, scarinesses, are we closing ourselves to?

Notes

[1] The essay discussed here may be found in *Approaches to the Poem: Modern Essays in the Analysis and Interpretation of Poetry*, edited by John Oliver Perry (Chandler Publishing Company, 1965). My title owes a debt to the title of David Yezzi's essay "The Seriousness of Yvor Winters" (*The New Criterion*: www.newcriterion.com/archive/15/jun97/winters.htm).

[2] From Yvor Winters's introduction to *The Early Poems of Yvor Winters, 1920–1928* (Swallow Press, 1966).

[3] Arnold L. Goldsmith, *American Literary Criticism: 1905–1965* (Twayne Publishers, 1979).

[4] From Thom Gunn's introduction to *Yvor Winters: Selected Poems* (The Library of America, 2003).

[5] John Crowe Ransom, "Poetry: The Formal Analysis," in Perry.

[6] Modern American Poetry website of University of Illinois at Urbana-Champaign (www.english.uiuc.edu/maps/poets/s_z/winters/bio.htm).

2
. . . .
Epistolary

EPISTOLARY
An Introduction

The word "epistle" comes from the Greek *epistole* meaning "letter" or "message." The Greek-language New Testament Epistles, dating from the first century CE, contain specific components that were considered standard to the form, and that historically would have always been included in this genre of writing: an epistolary prescript, a thanksgiving formula, the letter body, and a closing formula that included news and a farewell. The New Testament's Epistles make up 21 of its 27 books, reflecting the form's prominence in the ancient world—and for centuries afterward—as the primary source of communication for people who did not live in the same place. Many of the elements of early letters endure today in such forms as email and various official memoranda.

The epistolary novel—unfolding in a series of hybrid-form documents that may include letters, diary entries, newspaper clippings, and other miscellany—became an established literary genre in the eighteenth century. Aphra Behn's three-volume *Love-Letters Between a Nobleman and His Sister*, published in the 1680s, was the first work to demonstrate the complexity of the genre, presenting multiple points of view and including counterfeit letters, intrigue, and other duplicitous interaction. Other examples include Samuel Richardson's *Clarissa* (1740), Johann Wolfgang von Goethe's *The Sorrows of Young Werther* (1774), Jane Austen's early novel *Lady Susan* (written in 1794, but not published until 1871), Mary Shelley's *Frankenstein* (1818), Bram Stoker's *Dracula* (1897), C.S. Lewis' *The Screwtape Letters* (1942), Alice Walker's *The Color Purple* (1982), Stephen Chbosky's *The Perks of Being a Wallflower* (1999), and Marilynne Robinson's *Gilead* (2004). One reason for the epistolary novel's endurance is its ability to create the illusion of re-alism via a multiplicity of documents while avoiding the intrusions of an omniscient narrator. Another is its feeling of naturalness. The reader seems to have walked into another person's life via privileged access to personal documents. In a novel that integrates texts from several individuals, reading becomes about assembling a puzzle, literally putting the texts into conversa-tion and/or sequence. Equally important, epistolary novels embody the ways in which human beings communicate at certain moments in time.

The six writers included in this section are all working with book-length epistolary sequences that attest to the continued flexibility and expansive-ness of the genre. They variously explore the interiority of the writer as character, play with the form's traditions and uses, and engage in cultural critique. Take Joe Wenderoth's *Letters to Wendy's*. Ostensibly written over the course of a year on comment cards from the fast-food chain restaurant, the letters follow an unnamed narrator obsessed with Biggies and Frosties, but also with consumerism, pornography, and mortality.

The epistle, by definition, invokes an individual who is both listener and reader. Amy Newman cites Emily Dickinson's letter to Thomas Wen-tworth Higginson in April 1862 as one of the motivating sources of her own *Dear Editor*. "Mr. Higginson," Dickinson begins, "are you too deeply occupied to say if my verse is alive?" In Newman's words, Dickinson's first letter to her editor "distills down all the complications of writing and sending out one's work to this one intense, accurate query." Each of New-man's own prose poem "epistles" begins "Dear Editor: Please consider the enclosed poems for publication."

Julie Marie Wade's *Postage Due: Poems & Prose Poems* explores the liter-ary possibilities of the fan letter and brings these into dialogue with mem-oir. Wade crafts her triptych of letters to Mary Tyler Moore/Mrs. Laura Petrie after discovering her teenage self's fan letters to various celebrities. By dating the letters of "Triptych" to Moore/Petrie at various stages of the epistolary "Julie Marie Wade's" development, Wade stages a growing self-awareness through this "range of narrative distances," dramatizing the evolution of interiority and encapsulating the desire for intimacy that is a hallmark of the epistolary tradition.

The desire for intimacy is also a driving force behind Diane Wakoski's *Medea the Sorceress*, a sustained meditation on personal past and the secret nature of reality. Wakoski began writing the poems within the epistolary body, discovering in the process that "this new poem-embedded-in-a-letter format echoed the poetry reading experience." She actually sent her letters with poems out as correspondence, further blurring the lines between the art and utility of the epistolary form.

Takashi Hiraide's *Postcards to Donald Evans* is addressed to the very real artist who had created postage stamps for a series of fictional countries: "Goodbye, Donald. I just left the world, and I'm bound for another. Everything is so different, dear Donald, and everything is new to me, too." Hiraide's collection alters the reader's way of seeing by staging a dual encounter of two artists via the mediums of postage stamps and letters.

In *The Book of Anna*, a fractured, lyric exploration of the life of memory following trauma, Joy Ladin brings into being Anna Asher, a fictional Czech-German Jew who spent her adolescence in a concentration camp and is writing journal entries and poems about her life in mid-1950s Prague. The creation of *The Book of Anna* became for Ladin "a five-year process of discovering the hybrid of poetic forms, prose diary entries, and narrative modes that Anna's story required." Ladin's myriad engagement with forms, and with the bending and blending of those forms, speaks to all of the work included in this chapter.

Epistolary writing can be intensely pleasurable for the reader because of the challenge as well as the sense of play that accompanies piecing together the various forms of writing. The epistolary genre, in particular, places front and center the relationship between writer and reader, both by distinguishing between the two roles, and by placing the reader in close or allied proximity with the writer via the active and dynamic process of reading.

—*Jacqueline Kolosov*

THE EPISTOLARY ENTERPRISE

Fusing Artifact and Art

Julie Marie Wade

I was born in 1979, the only child of conservative Christian parents obsessed with the ideals of 1950s television sitcoms like *Leave It to Beaver,*
Father Knows Best, and *The Donna Reed Show.* With the advent of Nick
at Nite in 1985, I came of age watching many of the same programs my
parents watched while they were growing up. Since I was restricted from
engaging with much of the popular culture of my own time, I arrived at
junior high school unable to recognize iconic images of such present-day
celebrities as Madonna and Michael Jackson. I had never heard of MTV,
The A-Team, or *Dirty Dancing.* I found myself mystified by the candlelight
vigils held in my Seattle hometown for a long-haired stranger named
Kurt Cobain.

My deep engagement with the popular culture of my parents' era also
left me largely isolated from my peers. I can remember saying to a girl
who sat beside me in seventh grade, "Hey, did you catch that episode of
The Dick Van Dyke Show last night? How surreal were those walnuts in the
closet?" She looked at me like I had just sprouted horns.

Years later, as a graduate student in creative writing, I was encouraged
to use the stuff of my life as fodder for developing a distinctive, idiosyncratic voice. I was encouraged to ask myself, "What made your coming of

Julie Marie Wade teaches in the creative writing program at Florida International
University in Miami. She is the author of four collections of poetry, most recently
SIX (2016), and three collections of lyric nonfiction, the latest of which is *Tremolo: An
Essay* (2013). Her fourth collection, *Catechism: A Love Story,* is forthcoming in 2016.

age unique?" As I mulled, I realized that I had grown up, not "ahead of my time" as many creative types claimed, but quite literally behind.

One of my favorite pastimes as a teenager was writing fan letters to the stars of classic television shows. Often, I'd forget that the actors and actresses to whom I wrote were 20, 30, even 40 years older than their televisual alter egos. The eternal present that syndicated television creates caused me to wince with confused dismay when a signed photograph arrived from Barbara Hale (Della Street on the *Perry Mason* series), and the woman in the picture was—well—*old*!

Rooting through diaries from that time, I found that I had written long, besotted letters to several television characters themselves. My diary didn't have a name, but it might as well have been Laura or Mary, since the characters of Laura Petrie from *The Dick Van Dyke Show* and Mary Richards from *The Mary Tyler Moore Show* (both played by Mary Tyler Moore) were the women I most often sought to confide in, the women to whom I believed I could safely raise the most vexing questions of my youth. These preoccupations from my early years, when revisited in a creative context, offered a unique perspective from which to personalize the universal experience of coming of age. But until those first graduate classes, it had never occurred to me that a letter could hold aesthetic possibilities beyond the practical purpose of correspondence or the private therapeutics of a journal entry.

In "Triptych," my series of three recreated letters to Laura Petrie, Mary Richards, and Mary Tyler Moore, I use the epistolary form to trace my evolving self-concept—first, as a 12-year-old junior high school student in 1991, then as a 15-year-old high school student in 1994, and finally as a 19-year-old college student in 1999. The younger self idolizes Laura Petrie and seems to long for her as a surrogate mother figure. Three years later, the speaker's tone is more self-aware and realistic. The most telling moment in the second letter, and perhaps the most poignant also, comes near the end where the speaker ventures cautiously into the subject of sexual orientation. She says, "I guess I wondered if you had ever kissed a girl, or thought about kissing a girl—maybe even a friend—maybe even Rhoda.

And if you ever thought (or worried even) that it might make you into a lesbian." Not coincidentally, I had begun my own process of coming out in graduate school, and I was repeatedly struck by how absent all representations of same-sex attraction, let alone lesbian relationships, had been from the popular culture I consumed in my youth. The third letter, addressed to Mary Tyler Moore, comes from the perspective of a college student who is able to discern important differences between the fantasy of television and the exigencies of real life. The writing evolves into a thank-you letter to a hero from the speaker's past while also suggesting that a certain chapter of hero worship has come to a necessary close.

It wasn't until I entered my Master of Arts in English program that I learned the word *epistolary*, and suddenly, just as the Baader-Meinhof Phenomenon predicts, I noticed epistolary poems and essays and stories everywhere. They seemed to fall around me like confetti. I recalled my Bible as Literature class in college and considered how the New Testament Epistles (from which the word *epistolary* clearly derived!) had been presented to us as exemplars of literary prose, the same way Psalms and Song of Solomon had been presented to us as exemplars of spiritual and erotic poetry. Awakened to these possibilities, I began work on a hybrid collection called *Postage Due: Poems & Prose Poems*, subsequently published by White Pine Press as the 2010 winner of the Marie Alexander Poetry Series.

While I was exploring the literary possibilities of the fan letter in my own writing, I was also reading a transformative memoir by Toi Derricotte, my soon-to-be thesis director at the University of Pittsburgh. *The Black Notebooks: An Interior Journey* is a work of literary prose written by a poet who incorporates both original and recreated letters and journal entries as illuminating extensions of her larger personal narrative. Even the word "notebooks," with its connotations of something piecemeal and ever-in-progress, suggests Derricotte was working consciously close to the line between what I had begun to discuss with my own students as *artifact*—the thing itself, the original document—and *art*—the crafted, nuanced, and necessarily distanced entity that is often derived from an unmediated document like a letter or journal entry. What Derricotte achieves by mixing documents of lived experience with literary translations of lived experience is an intriguing range of narrative distances I hadn't encountered before. Her hybrid literary journey allowed for a deeper kind of interiority than most confessional work I had read to date, and the intimacy she forged with her readers was something I sought to emulate.

Derricotte writes in *The Black Notebooks*, "We talk about the pain of revealing ourselves, of getting out what is inside. Later I may ask students to write a letter of unfinished business to someone from their past." While I was never given this specific assignment by Derricotte, reading about it in the context of her memoir helped to expose the false binary between artifact and art for me—or at the very least, to complicate that binary in favor of integration. When I went back to drafts of old fan letters I had written, I found myself selecting lines from the original documents and embedding those within literary recreations of what I wished I had said—what I had been longing to say. For instance, in my letter to Laura Petrie: "I'm also writing with a practical question even though I tend to get philosophical from time to time & am currently not using commas." This detail from an old journal entry made me smile at the self I had been, and it also informed the stylistic decision I made not to include any commas in the first letter of this sequence.

With Derricotte's memoir as exemplary model, I learned how artifacts, written without aesthetic concerns at the forefront, could strengthen the authenticity of a work later shaped into literary art. Ultimately, I found this hybrid mode of writing enabled me to convey a more complex self to my readers, a truly hybrid and evolving self (as all selves are) than either the artifact or the art alone would allow.

HYBRID WORK
From Postage Due: Poems & Prose Poems

Triptych

I.

46 Bonnie Meadow Road
New Rochelle New York

November 3 1991

Dear Mrs. Laura Petrie

You can't imagine what it means to me that we are meeting now in syndication. I am a seventh-grade honor student at Calvary Lutheran School in West Seattle. When I grow up I want to be a writer an oral surgeon & a private investigator like Paul Drake on the <u>Perry Mason</u> series (also in syndication). Do you know him by the way or Della or Perry? They're black-and-white like you but from L.A.

I would also like to be a wife and mother.

You do it so well—always with Capri pants & a smile. And when you get mad it isn't like my mother's mad. It's like a tunnel with a light & the anger's just a train that's passing through.

I think I'd like to <u>be</u> you. I have big white teeth from my father's side of the family but my skin is a bit of a problem. Not perfect for pictures. In fact nowhere near close.

But did I tell you I'm on the cheer team? We're such a small school they don't even hold auditions. Every girl is automatically enrolled. I'm no great cheerleader & no great dancer either nothing like you in the USO show before you found & fell in love with Rob Petrie. And I wonder what that's like because I haven't been in love yet though I did see <u>Barefoot in the Park</u> performed last Christmas.

The fact is though despite skipping sixth grade & not even (yet) shaving my legs I've already had one boyfriend. My mother says I'm too young to have had my heart broken but she's not enlightened like you Laura Petrie. Nowhere near close.

Lee Bennett & I were "hot & heavy" for about a year but then he met Marissa Sheldon. She's no Millie Helper I'll tell you that but I did wish that she had been my friend. She was the prettiest most popular girl in the whole school & I couldn't keep Lee from losing interest in me.

So how do you make it work—love I mean—& how do you keep thin after having kids & do you ever wish you had a job outside the home?

I'm also writing with a practical question even though I tend to get philosophical from time to time & am currently not using commas.

See an anonymous person entered a picture of me (pre-acne) & a statement about my so-far accomplishments (tap jazz ballet piano choir track swimming spelling bee champ six years running & now cheer) in the Miss Pre-Teen America Pageant preliminaries. I have a chance to compete: make a speech wear a prom dress in front of an audience answer questions from judges & perform a talent. My mother thinks a piano solo of Beethoven's <u>Für Elise</u> would please the crowd.

But please Laura Petrie what do <u>you</u> think? I'm afraid of losing & afraid of winning. Does that make sense? On the one hand I just want to meet a nice man & be 10 years older so I can skip adolescence altogether & go directly to a home of my own. Be something to somebody who will see me in my pajamas & not laugh. We probably won't even sleep in separate beds. But if I become a hit on the pageant circuit then what? A lot of dating & parties & I won't know what to wear...

I just want it all to be over & done with: a husband who trips over the ottoman & a little boy I don't have to see too much.

Please write when you can.

Sincerely
Julie Marie Wade
from Fauntlee Hills

2.

119 North Weatherly
Minneapolis, Minnesota

October 19, 1994

Dear Ms. Mary Richards,

I am choosing the prefix "Ms." instead of the more traditional "Miss" because I know you are a classy & progressive kind of woman. Allow me first to introduce myself. My name is Julie Wade, & I am a first-term sophomore at Holy Names Academy—a Catholic school, even though my parents are Protestant.

(I know you're Presbyterian; they're Lutheran.)

To tell the truth, I am quite unsatisfied with my life thus far, & at 15 now, I'm not sure what to expect from the future. I don't have a lot of friends at school. I'm not the kind of high school girl you were. Once, a long time ago, I was in a beauty pageant, & I didn't even make the semi-finals. I used to be better at math, but I'm only pulling a B in Honors Geometry, & my mom is really fit to be tied. If I do all the extra credit, though, I should be able to eke out an A for my final grade.

I don't know what kind of student you were. My guess is probably average. Not that you aren't really smart, but Roseberg High didn't sound all that demanding. In the old days, average was ok. It was <u>average</u>. Today the "average" GPA at my high school is 3.6. Excellence used to be oatmeal, & now it's eggs benedict.

But—I'm really not writing to complain. I'm writing to find out a little more about "making it on your own" & how it's done. Do you ever get scared at night, all alone in your own apartment? My friend April & I—she's kind of like my Rhoda—are planning to move in together after college when we go to live in the city. (Our addresses say Seattle, but we don't really live there. It's just a trick the postal service likes to play.)

So here's the thing: you always say that you want to get married, but you've turned down at least three proposals that I can recall. If I had even one guy offer to marry me—as long as he wasn't in prison (or likely to be)—I'd accept that proposal in a hurry. I have a hard time picturing married life, & you seem to be having a fine time without one. And look at Rhoda—she got divorced. Who's to say that couldn't happen to you, too?

So are you playing the field or what? Are you still looking for Mr. Right? Do you ever feel like there might be something wrong with you (not that there is) for being single so long?

I have an aunt—we call her "Lindabird"—& she's at least your age & probably older. She's not as pretty, but I like her clothes, & so far she's basically kept her figure. She wanted to get married & have kids, but my mom says she's close to menopause & it's a shame. Aunt Lindabird hasn't even had sex yet because she thinks it should be saved, but I'm not sure you can even have it after 50.

Which brings me to another question, Mary Richards, which I think I can trust you to answer. I'm a bright girl. I can read between the lines of your dialogue—what the censors will (& will not) allow. But you've had sex, haven't you? You're not waiting. You even lived with a man who was training to be a doctor.

I'd like to know how you knew when you were ready to—& if you were even a little bit afraid God might strike you down. I'm around celibacy all day long, & it's starting to be kind of a drag. I still want to be a writer & maybe a counselor. I was thinking maybe I could work with teenagers who need to get laid & get out of religion.

Because frankly, I feel my religion is holding me back, & I notice you don't even go to church at all. Is that because you don't believe in God, or just because you don't believe in the kind of people who believe in God?

There are some nuns here who've got it in for me pretty bad. I'm a good student, but I think annulment's crap, & I've essentially stopped taking communion on the grounds that if transubstantiation is actually real, then we're all a bunch of cannibals & that can't be good for your soul.

Pretty much I'm conflicted because I think I could like being single & having sex with different people—men—& the rest of the time just hanging out with my friends. My parents are Republicans, but once I get to college, I'm joining the Young Democrats. I know you & Phyllis & Rhoda all belong.

I guess I should be wrapping things up because you've had a long day in the newsroom & I have homework to do. More proofs. I hate them. I'm not that certain of anything, & I don't see why we should accept these theorems at face value. (Probably why I'm not on the fast-track to earning an A, & Miss Benedict is a stickler for accuracy.)

Mary Richards, did you ever do anything in your whole good & pretty life that you felt ashamed of?

See, I sit next to this girl in Psychology class—Sara—& she's kind of worldly & agnostic & all that, & she's also dating another girl—Heather—at school. And once, I don't know why, but I told Sara Timmons how I kissed Mandie

Salazar in fifth grade, even though I already had a boyfriend. She said that probably meant I was a lesbian & the next step was coming out of the closet. But I once had a babysitter named Deanna who had a friend named Heidi, & they got caught making out in a closet with both their shirts off by Deanna's dad. (Sorry if this is too much information.) But by rights then, by Sara's theorem, Deanna had to become a lesbian. Instead, just last year, she married a doctor, & my mother said, "She's set for the rest of her life."

So I guess I wondered if you had ever kissed a girl, or thought about kissing a girl—maybe even a friend—maybe even Rhoda. And if you ever thought (or worried even) that it might make you into a lesbian.

I have another friend, Laura Wissing, who says just going to a Catholic girls school can turn you gay. She also says if you're not married by a certain age, you become a "spinster," which is one of several euphemisms (vocab word!) for lesbian.

What do you think, Mary Richards? I'm desperate to know.

Gratefully yours,
Julie Marie Wade,
Class of 1997,
Agnostic & Democrat

3.

Mary Tyler Moore, Inc.
Culver City, California

January 14, 1999

Dear Mary Tyler Moore:

I'm sending this letter to Mary Tyler Moore, Inc., hoping it will actually reach you and not just someone sorting through your mail. My mom's friend found the address when writing to celebrities to request items for a church auction, and she said you were very kind and sent an autographed copy of the "Chuckles Bites the Dust" script, which I hear garnered quite a bit of money for Calvary Lutheran and its related ministries.

This letter isn't a request so much as an expression of gratitude. As it is, I'm probably too old to be writing fan letters (sophomore in college), but there's some part of me that just can't seem to resist. You've been my favorite actress for such a long time, and I feel like I've grown up with you. I started watching The Dick Van Dyke Show when it debuted on Nick at Nite in 1991, and then The Mary Tyler Moore Show followed the next year, and I was immediately addicted. I started reading books about you (The Woman Behind the Smile, etc.) and watching films you'd been in—your performance in Ordinary People is especially good—and I think in a lot of ways, just being able to focus on something (someone) outside the tiny bubble of my upbringing has enabled me to grow up and become the questioning and open-minded 19-year-old woman I am today.

I recently ended a relationship with a guy I've had an on-again, off-again romance with since the beginning of freshman year. We fought terribly toward the end, and Ben (that's his name) said something to me that I wanted to dismiss as just sour grapes but that I'm thinking now might have been more true than not. He said my problem is that I don't tailor the relationship to the person I'm with; I already have a pre-set notion of what a relationship should be—I guess kind of a Platonic ideal—and I'm always trying to make the person I like fit into an already-drawn picture. Ben said he felt like I wanted him to play Rob Petrie (play or be, I'm not sure which, or if it would have mattered) so I could play Laura, and we could imitate some version of some TV show that never even existed anyway.

I have to admit I really like the idea of the simple, easy life those characters shared with each other. I mean, it's a far cry from the family in Ordinary People. I like the idea of being someone's beautiful wife and a dancer and giving big, well-attended parties where people entertain each other with songs and comedy routines. It seemed so safe there, but not boring. There were problems of course, but nothing life-threatening or damaging long-term.

Sometimes I think you gave me two portraits of how life could be for a woman: the married life and the single life, and both of them seem like so much fun it's hard not to *want* to emulate them. When I'm not dating anybody, I tell myself it's better that way because of being with your girlfriends and having that freedom to be open to whoever may come along. I think about the theme song and "love is all around," and everything feels charged with potential. You never know who you might meet or where you might live, and your character is so brave to pack up her car and drive to a big, unfamiliar city, find her own apartment and a job and make friends and hobbies, and I want to do that, too. It scares me a little because I've never lived farther than an hour away from home (in a dormitory, no less), so I haven't really been on my own for real yet, and I'm not 100% sure I can "make it on my own." But I want to try, and Mary Richards motivates me to keep trying to be braver and more independent. Next year I am even planning to study abroad.

But then there's Laura Petrie, who I keep coming back to, and that possibility for sharing a life with someone. How would that work? I mean, you've been married three times and gone through two divorces. You've had a miscarriage and had your own grown child die. Clearly, your personal experiences are far less ideal than those you've portrayed.

I remember that interview you did with TV Guide (back in 1993, I think), and you said—I underlined it and still keep the quote on my bulletin board—"I'm not so fearful anymore. I've already seen the darkness." But how does that work for you? Are you ever jealous of the women you've played? Do you ever wish your own life had been more like theirs?

[...]

I remember this song from church (it's hard to get all the old religious clutter out from the brain...) about knocking and the door would be opened unto you, but then I heard somewhere else, in a story or a myth of some kind, about knocking and a door shall appear. I like that second idea better. I think in a lot of ways you've been the door other people have knocked on to have it opened for them. You've showed us options for our lives, particularly as women. Laura Petrie wore pants, and it caused a scandal. Mary Richards slept with men she didn't marry. For your time and in your way, you were being radical. I can only hope for my time and in my own way, I will be too.

Maybe I will even make a door appear that no one else has ever walked through.

No guarantees of course, but here's to trying.

Yours truly,
Julie M. Wade
Ordal Hall #106
Pacific Lutheran University
Tacoma, WA 98447

POEMS EMBEDDED IN LETTERS

On *The Archaeology of Movies & Books*

Diane Wakoski

I was an avid writer of long letters in 1988, and my primary correspondents were the American novelist Jonathan Carroll, who lived in Vienna, and an American poet who lived in Southern California, Craig Cotter. Having recently visited Jonathan in Austria, I kept flashing on glimpses of his lifestyle, which included sitting with his dog and writing in cafés for chunks of each day, an aspect of European culture that hadn't yet invaded the U.S. One morning in the Midwest, sitting in my dining room, at our big butcher-block table, northern light streaming in the casement windows, I got it! Rushing upstairs to my desk, I grabbed my tiny Olivetti portable typewriter (this was also before personal computers) and ran down to the table, where I sat down and pretended I was in a café, talking to Jonathan. It is important to say that I couldn't have invented these cafés or the mood I put myself in to write the letters and the poems embedded in them at my own desk. I needed that shining wood table and the morning light, the sense of having to move my typewriter down to it.

Typing my first "Café" letter, giving myself instructions to imagine my own café, I typed the name that occurred, "Café Eau de Vie." Everyone knows that the *"eau de vies"* are clear white brandy liqueurs, fiery and

Diane Wakoski began her poetry career in New York City (1960–1973). Her selected poems, *Emerald Ice* (1989), won the William Carlos Williams Award. Her newest collection is *Bay of Angels* (2014). She has retired as University Distinguished Professor from Michigan State University after 37 years. She lives with her husband, the photographer Robert Turney, in East Lansing, Michigan.

fruit-flavored, and I particularly loved these scented, heady, and often hard-to-find after-dinner drinks, like *framboise* and *poire*. They seemed as cosmopolitan and elegant as I longed to be. The Café Eau de Vie represented myself, as I wished to be.

When I composed this first café letter, I improvised a first draft of a new poem while typing. It became my custom to compose the first draft of a new poem in each of the letters I sent. I suppose this was an act of trust, indicating that I was willing to show my intimate self, the unrevised self, to the recipients of these letters. I devised different café names, often to indicate my mood, or where I was, or to whom I was writing. This evolved later into a map of locations for the cafés, indicating important people or events in my life.

Writing poems, which often came out of some discussion I might have been having about books, movies, beauty, gambling, or my ideas about love, sex, and romance, into the context of an epistolary body mimicked not only my process of composing, but also the style of poetry readings I gave, wherein I almost always prefaced each poem with some talk, an anecdote, or a personal observation. This natural process also led me to realize that I could create a bigger structure for my poems in printed form, using quoted material, the way we use epigraphs sometimes to open a poem. Like many intelligent readers of the 1980s and 1990s, I found it exciting to work my sense of quantum physics into this larger structure and used a book called *Quantum Reality: Beyond the New Physics,* by Nick Herbert. There is a kind of *frisson* one feels in recognizing an idea, e.g. parallel universes, which can give the poem a different arc. It's a bit like seeing your lover, whose body you know intimately with clothes off, out on the softball field in uniform throwing a pitch or hitting a ball. You recognize where the action is coming from.

Soon after I began writing these letters embedded with poems, I began to shape the first book of what was to become a quartet, *The Archaeology of Movies & Books.* At first it was just one volume, *Medea the Sorceress,* a persona I'd chosen in earlier poems, beginning with myself as a teenager in Orange County. I turned the orange into the fruit of the Garden myth and gave Jason the designation of "Sailor," because my father was in the Navy. Jason and Medea's doomed romance is probably a metaphor for my doomed *family romance,* the Freudian father-daughter drama. In my map, the River of Life (a play on *eau de vie,* which means "water of life") separates the origin story from the other stories that swirl around the other cafés from which the letters come.

Throughout my poetry writing life, I have often identified myself as Moon/Diane in poems, and in these café poems I began also to call myself The Lady of Light (sun and moon). Invoking the title "Lady" is a gesture toward my belief that I come out of the literary, courtly tradition of *The Romance of the Rose.* Being a "Lady," I must have knights, men whom I love, idealize, long for, or feel some connection to. *Rosenkavalier,* Knight of the Roses, both alludes to the opera and to my desire to be served by these Knights of Romance. Thus, in Los Angeles I write from The Rose Diner, and Craig, who is one of my correspondents, lives in a town near L.A. that is famous for its annual Rose Parade. One of my great friends and mentors was David Smith, who built a house in Point Dume, where I locate The Seaman's Bar & Grill.

Though my cafés are all in my imagination, created at my sunlit table, usually in the morning, the letters are real. I sent the letters I wrote, along with the embedded poems, and later in the 90s, this led to my writing what I called "my big letters," which distilled material from various letters but which also contained an original first draft of a poem, composed during the compiling of other letters. Some years into the project I was mailing out as many as 40 copies of these big letters. It stopped when I stopped writing physical letters to my friends, the computer having usurped this activity.

Though the project of *The Archaeology of Movies & Books* was the beginning of my creating poems embedded in epistolary text, it was actually a simple progression of my usual writing style, letting my poems follow my feelings and ideas spontaneously. It called attention to the fact that I do write poems as if to speak to a specific person. Incorporating my poetry into these real-life letters put me one step closer to a lifetime goal, to make poetry a seamless part of my physical universe.

HYBRID WORK

From Medea the Sorceress

Dear Craig,

You were once my student and now you've grown
into my friend. Though I call you my Rosenkavalier
and we meet here at the Rose Diner on Melrose
Avenue in L.A., our love is the shared love of The
Word, of poetry, not of physical lovers. I see you as
my Knight, and myself as The Lady you serve,
though such medieval images don't actually fit in with
my Southern California heritage and your real life
there in the City of Angels.

When I was young, I fell in love with the story of
Medea. I identified completely with the betrayed
sorceress, with her jealousy of the fake (beautiful)
princess whom Jason dumped her for. How prophetic
this tale was to be in living my own life, though at
the time I first felt any passionate identification with
Medea, no man had betrayed me for another woman.
Unless we count my father, who left me for his ship,
for the ocean, the Navy, the sea.

. . . .

*Quantum Reality #4: The many-worlds interpretation
(Reality consists of a steadily increasing number of parallel
universes.) Of all claims of the New Physics none is more
outrageous than the contention that myriads of universe
are created upon the occasion of each measurement act. For
any situation in which several different outcomes are possible (flipping a coin for instance), some physicists believe
that all outcomes actually occur. In order to accommodate
different outcomes without contradiction, entire new
universes spring into being, identical in every detail except
for the single outcome that gave them birth. In the case of
a flipped coin, one universe contains a coin that comes up
head; another, a coin showing tails.*

· ſ · ·

I love thinking about these poetic theories of the
universe. The idea that many worlds exist
simultaneously explains to me how I can be living my
middle-aged, middle-class life in Michigan while
simultaneously meeting you, my Rosenkavalier, at the
Rose Diner in Los Angeles and my friend Jonathan at
the Ritter Café in Vienna, and also be at the Mailbag
Café that I, the Postmistress, own in Las Vegas, or
be meeting all the rest of you at the Café Eau de Vie in
Michigan. I can still be the young girl, the teenager
who identified with Medea, and simultaneously, the
sorceress who escaped and who is beyond all that.

Jonathan told me that he goes to Munich sometimes
to visit a beautiful woman friend who lives there, and
that the train he takes is called The Rosenkavalier. I
was meditating on this for a while this morning
while waiting for you here at the Rose Diner.

ROSENKAVALIER (KNIGHT OF THE ROSE)

You rode the
train from Vienna to Munich,
        —Wien-München—
A woman who wears only a black
lacy garter belt is waiting at the
end of the line/ no,
she has also a dog, a white spade-faced
bull terrier: "Greetings from your father
who passed this way recently," she says
and this reveals she is a fraud.

But she is beautiful.
"Wait, before you dismiss me,"
she says in German.
It is too painful. You don't
want to wait; you know she isn't
really a fraud. It's just that she comes
from another world, a world of Booth cartoons,
framed, a world of marble green fountain pens
filled with Pelikan ink, a swirl of
fingerprints like ghost faces
of unborn characters.

Famous for 15 minutes,
postmodern fate.
Steel Man offers The Silver Surfer
some of his popcorn, but movie theaters defraud you, then draw you into
    a world
which is only light play. No matter how many
times you watch a flick, it is never more
than a woman wearing a black lacy

garter belt over her creamy linen-finish
bond paper thighs, never more than
the beautiful woman meeting you at the
train station in Vienna
with her, also white as paper, sweet
dog on a leash, his paws like splayed
garlic bulbs, nails clicking on
the stone floors of the train station,
never more than images which seem
less interesting each time you use them.
You leave the theater fat from popcorn and thin
from the film which has no angels,
no devils, but is a fraud. "Wait, before you dismiss
it," I hear Maverick calling over
my shoulder.

"Tom Cruise," I reply, "you will never top
Top Gun." Even if I ride this train every day,
you will not come more alive than this first
time I saw you. In fact, Woody Allen is wrong.
Mia Farrow can't bring Jeff Daniels down
off the screen. What she does is
go crazy. She enters the screen, showing
The Purple Rose of Cairo, only half there
of course and only half at home.
But sometimes when you enter this train,
you think for a minute
that München and Wien are only
metaphors, not names of towns;
sometimes, you think that the Rosenkavalier
stops in Beverly Hills, then goes on
to Orange County and stops in La Habra,

sometimes you think it winds back up
to Altadena, then heads out to
the desert, making for Las Vegas.
What you think
matters.

What you think
is like a movie.

        "I'm at the flicks,"
makes everyone laugh. "No, not Diane!"
They don't know that I am redesigning
my life; instead of the boy who loved
and betrayed me when I was 18, there is Maverick
shooting down all the enemies and returning to
Orange County with "that lovin' feeling."
He passes me on to John Cusack, who learns
that is "no sure thing," and writes me into his
life where I can *Say Anything*, and like Debra Winger
marry *An Officer and a Gentleman*.

Americans invented these movies; we invented
        adolescence.
Teen-age films are
our genius.

The truth takes me to the American Desert;
John Cryer in *Dudes* reinvents
the Western; take me to meet Clint Eastwood
for dinner. Clint Eastwood has a new role:
he's playing Steel Man, a mythic character based on
the life of Robert Turney in East Lansing,
a man who married a poet, who, until she met him,

only rode trains from one continent to
another. But there can only be
Strangers on a Train, and perhaps
poetry. In movies and books
we shape our own destinies,
and call ourselves
whatever we want to.

· · · ·

And I will call myself Diane the Moon, Diane
the Lady of Light. In one of the many simultaneous
worlds I'll occupy, I'll tell the real story of my life,
the deep reality. This archeological dig to show the
layers of ascent and descent, and one of our guides
will be that one-eyed poet, Creeley. "O love,"
he says, "where are you leading me now?" And
the echo of the good doctor, "no ideas [no reality]
but in things."

You do know Creeley's poem "Kore," don't you?
And of course Williams' obsession with the
Persephone figure, evolving from his early images and
ideas in *Kora in Hell?* Both poets are obsessed with
the beautiful image of the young girl enthralled by
love. So am I, I guess.

Yrs,

Diane, Moonlight

TAKE A LILY, FOR INSTANCE
Trying to Capture the "Real" of Writing Poetry

Amy Newman

> *Chess problems demand from the composer the same virtues that*
> *characterize all worthwhile art: originality, invention, conciseness,*
> *harmony, complexity, and splendid insincerity.*
> —Vladimir Nabokov, *Poems and Problems*

Dear Editor is a book of poems in the form of cover letters to an imaginary, all-powerful editor. This form came about because I was interested in what makes a poem a poem, in what makes a poem *poetry*. The line break seems to be a visual clue that says, *here is a poem,* but while a news article broken into stanzas may look like a poem, it would not have that "animating presence" noted in R. P. Blackmur's definition that "adds to the stock of available reality." Yes, *that*: What is poetry?

When we write poems we use the mind in a different way than when we are doing our taxes or backing the car out of the garage, activities during which we must purposely avoid the kind of wandering, wondering mind that is open in poetic composition, and focus instead squarely on the

Amy Newman is a Presidential Research Professor at Northern Illinois University. Her books include *On This Day in Poetry History* (2015), *Dear Editor* (2011), *fall* (2004), *Camera Lyrica* (1999), and *Order, or Disorder* (1995), and her work appears in *The Iowa Anthology of New American Poetries*, Sentence's *An Introduction to the Prose Poem*, *The Rose Metal Press Field Guide to Prose Poetry*, *Lit from Inside: 40 Years of Poetry from Alice James Books*, *The Mind of Monticello: Fifty Contemporary Poets on Jefferson*, and *Heart of the Order: Baseball Poems*.

subject at hand. Similarly, I don't use the poetry mind when I compose the submission letter that accompanies a selection of poems that I'm sending to an editor; that's a standard template that always begins the same way: *Dear Editor: Please consider these poems.*

But one day I thought, as a drafting exercise: what if the girl who is composing the submission letter to the editor can't or won't turn off the poetry mind, and the poetry enters into the writing of the letter? In this example, Amy Newman moves seamlessly from the salutation to a beseeching gesture akin to prayer:

> Dear Editor:
>
> Please consider the enclosed poems for publication. They are from my manuscript *X=Pawn Capture*. If you are familiar with chess openings such as the Caro-Kann Defense or the Benoni Defense, you are ahead of me, for although my grandfather suggested I try the attempt at early checkmate, he never explained them. His silence may be compared unfavorably to that silence which is the proper response to my submissions.

As the days went by and the exercise continued, the Amy Newman who wrote the letters became more real—she became complex and dimensional. Who was this person and why was she so interested in writing? I began to perceive a similarity between her relationship with the absent, unknowable editor, and my own drafting; the very act of submitting poems, of sending work into the world, I now understood as not only pro forma, but also an act of obeisance and discipline and devotion to something that felt indefinable, some state for which there is no exact word. How do we describe this mix of anxiety and belief in which writers exist, of doubt and faith at the same time? In any case, I'm not the first writer to experience it. Emily Dickinson's missive to Thomas Wentworth Higginson in April 1862 begins: "Mr. Higginson: Are you too deeply occupied to say if my verse is alive?" Dickinson's first letter to her editor distills all the complications of writing and sending out one's work to this one intense, accurate query. Synonyms for *submit* include both *deliver* and *surrender*.

In what is obvious to me now, my drafting—the daily, silent, unobserved, and nearly obsessive activity—mirrors the behavior of the Amy Newman of the letters. But she is an imaginary creature. Yet what is inside my head is certainly as real in any number of ways as the material world. Which is the real world, anyway?

Dear Editor was also inspired by Vladimir Nabokov's insights into the nature of the creative imagination and his problematic narrators. Take, for example, Charles Kinbote's explication of John Shade's poem in *Pale Fire* (and readers of that novel will understand immediately how troubling the "facts" of that sentence are). It's Nabokov who, in his afterword to *Lolita*, tells us that reality is one of the few words which mean nothing unless it is contained in quotation marks. Nabokov understands reality as "a very subjective affair" based on who is doing the observing. "If we take a lily, for instance," he writes:

> or any other kind of natural object, a lily is more real to a naturalist than it is to an ordinary person. But it is still more real to a botanist. And yet another stage of reality is reached with that botanist who is a specialist in lilies. You can get nearer and nearer, so to speak, to reality; but you never get near enough because reality is an infinite succession of steps, levels of perception, false bottoms, and hence unquenchable, unattainable.

The Amy Newman of *Dear Editor* is similarly Nabokovian, recognizing the inability to represent all the complexities of experience. In a letter dated 20 December, she writes: "I am having so much trouble [...] because such details as flesh and belief are tough to arrange as metaphor." Like her, I want to hold the flux of reality in language, to express something inexpressible ("a verbal means to a non-verbal source," as A. R. Ammons says), and so the experience of the shadowbox of the real—an ever-deepening, disappointing, and delighting journey—is a part of a poetic experience.

Amy Newman's fascination with chess, or at least her desire to write a manuscript of poems using chess as a metaphor, may be puzzling because she writes that she doesn't know much about the game. But the letters—in which she can be her utilitarian self and her poetic self at once—tell the editor differently; once in a while she sees the world in precisely chess-like structures, not only its hierarchies but also its harmonies of form, originality, escape, capture, and relation, in all its Nabokovian "complexity, and splendid insincerity." Fyodor in Nabokov's *The Gift* sees in the formulation of chess problems "an inner impulse [...] indistinguishable from poetic inspiration." For the Amy Newman of *Dear Editor*, chess and poetry are similarly intertwined, sharing beauty, complexity, and mystery, and the architectures of both are her immense, imaginative kingdoms.

HYBRID WORK
From Dear Editor

17 March

Dear Editor:

Please consider the enclosed poems for publication. They are from my manuscript, *X = Pawn Capture*. If you are familiar with chess openings such as the Caro-Kann Defense or the Benoni Defense, you are ahead of me, for although my grandfather suggested I try these attempts at early checkmate, he never explained them. His silence may be compared unfavorably to that silence which is the proper response to my submissions. For I only have to exercise my faith to know grace in our intercourse, whereas with my grandfather it's a little harder to observe the strength of the faithful and to believe in familial love. Still, I cared for him amongst his tobaccos and his soft clothing, tick-tocking his starry and willful avoidance of me all over the dining room.

It was my grandmother I could speak to, even if our conversations might hover around the idea of sainthood and its challenges. For each opening gambit in chess there is an equally ornate story I may imagine, such as those martyrs of Saragossa—Lupercus or Quintilian or the four Saturnii—of which nothing is known except that they were appallingly slain for their faith. Sometimes my grandmother filled in the blanks in the kitchen, sweet pies accompanying her narratives about the martyrs' plush red hearts still beating fresh waves of blood after death, and the horrified faces of the tormentors who see Proof of The Way and The Light in the flesh of the flayed skins. *Real blood of real faith, not mere wooden pieces on black and white squares, old man.* Where my grandfather saw the rank and file of order and conflict my grandmother perceived *slashes of nonsense that cross the afternoon with diversion,* and a *game of secrets* compared to the truth and bloodshed of our march toward *perfection,* which is also our *burden.* The cherry pastry crackled and softened its plump sacrifices into my unclean mouth and my imperfect body within this reverie of paradise we must trudge through, the pie tin littered with wan fruit skin parings and the leftover crumbs of flesh. Your move.

Thank you for your consideration, and for reading. I have enclosed an SASE, and look forward to hearing from you.

Sincerely,
Amy Newman

21 March

Dear Editor:

Please consider the enclosed poems for publication. They are from my manuscript, *X = Pawn Capture,* a lyrical study of chess as my grandfather invented it: the first move has to be made when my grandmother lifted her knife to begin chopping vegetables for the evening meal.

The sound of her chopping is hard to put down in words, but I have tried: *restless, resigned, determined.* The workshop says those are all clichés, and I needn't revisit with you why we should not use clichés. But where is the word that says the knife understood her weariness and expressed her will in its repetitive rush to the wood beneath the carrots? How to say it rang my grandmother's acuity in a pattern of messages while my grandfather either didn't notice or made no response to her alarms and cries, her information telegraphed through the carrot's core in an obsolescence of her heart's *dot dot dashes?* And you know he noticed, and he made no response. There is more going on in the room than details, such as the anger of the pin-dot curtains and a rude cigar judging the air in increments. I assure you the afternoon appeared quiet and useful but underneath, as the scribes say, the landscape was rising up to meet it, and when the chessboard was put away in the sideboard, and the bowl of softened carrots consumed, the evening became something more than what letters arranged to make sound blocks can achieve. The shaped dark that gathers beneath my window has a way of making me dream the oddest pictures in my head when my eyes are closed, in forms and manipulations and sounds. Where is the Morse code for something like that?

Thank you for your consideration, and for reading. I have enclosed an SASE, and look forward to hearing from you.

Sincerely,
Amy Newman

23 March

Dear Editor:

Please consider the enclosed poems for publication. They are from my manuscript, *X = Pawn Capture,* a lyrical study of chess as it was played in my family: only my grandfather could move the pieces, his hand halfway through an arc to land on a dark square while in the kitchen my grandmother smoothed the pages of her calendar of saints near the square for Saint Fedelemia, who as you know met Saint Patrick by the fountain of Clebach before rising waiflike to her clean destiny in a beautiful sheer cloth outfit.

My grandmother would say of me: *she is a young body but any unclean girl has an open door for sin down there, is burgeoning with sin as is a pigeon with maggots.* I know that the boys who walk me home after practice should not inspire my heart, even if it feels like the definition of ecstasy, all my senses suspended to that one sense, the outer world diminished to a creak or a hiss or stripe of noise through a door. Fedelemia died in that language of rapture, suffering her name onto the list of saints in a sacred branding, like the permanent mark on the livestock, only tender and ever charged. I am not elated but confused when a boy pins my body to the brick of the corner posts and his hands move like playing cards all over my blouse. And sayeth the grandmother: like maggots I have it.

I wish I had a sister as Fedelemia had Eithne, as they had each other, so that when they died in their excitements for all good reasons beneath the fountain where they met their Patrick, to be herded, gathering in the weight of all that innocence as though it were a damask hem, all their hair uncoiled and they left behind the earthly nothings, and they could chatter and giggle and gossip as they rose. I am a lone body with an open door that needs to be guarded, so sayeth the grandmother.

Thank you for your consideration, and for reading. I have enclosed an SASE, and look forward to hearing from you.

Sincerely,
Amy Newman

17 April

Dear Editor:

Please consider the enclosed poems for publication. They are from my manuscript, $X =$ *Pawn Capture*, a lyrical exploration that tries to be about everything and to contain everything, but fails like the periodic table of the elements or the categories of physics. I can find you in neither, but both are lovely to study when the footsteps of a grandfather so tired of it all insinuate themselves into any given room. Let my words be acceptable to you, to magnify and be magnified, in order that we may one day be fully aware of whatever gift has been sent our way, even though it's obvious to me there isn't anything there to see, to actually see. The dimension is private. My longing is the deer's longing, which I can place not under Velocity or Torque but maybe Pressure, Reflection, or Relativity.

You can see I'm thinking of Saint Philomena, the saint of having been forgotten, who was discovered as bones only, and later catalogued without the blood-soaked and blossoming-from-torment virginity and martyrdom histories that are my grandmother's bedtime stories. On the calendar it says Philomena was effectively forgotten since there is nothing to know. She should have been the saint of Momentum and Light, against desperate causes, against lost causes, against everything that seems forgotten, as she moved through the ether and made soft impressions and threw grass stems at her brother or, if she had no brother, she at least looked at water in a stream and noticed how it rushed or, if there was not a stream, she maybe had a horse. She existed, she had dimension, and you'll forgive me, it doesn't seem fair she should be forgotten, having come all that way to be and put so much of herself into a little slip of wandering. Of what consequence are the elements of which she is made as they passed by the elements of which the tree is made if she only left little marks of nothing on nothing, all that rotation of Field and Force and Image and Mass? And not turned into a shower of roses or golden twisted cables of burning holy love or a field of almond blossoms. Did she look forward to hearing from you? She sent out her breath into the air and I think that is enough to write a history, albeit unseen. It is not enough to come to nothing. So I see her.

On her holy card Philomena is always breathtaking, impossible to forget, represented by a combination of anchors and arrows, the anchor I guess because she was weighed down by the sobering fact of being a human girl, and I'll say for her, since she has no history, that arrows are a metaphor for praying, for the rising volley of expectation and belief propelled through currents, and thank goodness when the arrows fell, if they fell, it was out of her view. All proposals, whatever the crest, should seem to remain ever buoyant. Here is mine, as the earth shifts its properties to fit inside my head, and the heavens flutter and everything should be trumpeting glorious, and we'll all have a good cry: please consider these poems for publication.

This petition is a good example of what I mean. Belief requires my sending my postage stamp crest and white vanes, those agitations of my heart's velocity, forcefully into the unseen, and there it all levitates, and nothing coming back.

Sincerely,
Amy Newman

BUFFOONERY AND THE POETIC
Writing Short Letters

Joe Wenderoth

Allen Grossman, in his helpful work *Summa Lyrica*, writes:

> The limits of the autonomy of the will discovered in poetry are death and the barriers against access to other consciousness.

> The abandonment of the autonomy of the will of the speaking person as a speaker constitutes a form of knowledge—poetic knowledge.

I like this description of poetic knowledge, and I've often used it to describe the difference between the "poems" I've written and the "letters" that comprise my book *Letters to Wendy's*. The poet's access to poetic speech begins with an unusual action: "*the abandonment* of the autonomy of the will" (emphasis is mine). The poetic act is unusual because, in truth, it is not an act at all. It is a *ceasing* of action; it is where consciousness becomes estranged from willful action, i.e. from "the speaker." And if consciousness becomes estranged from the autonomy of the will, said autonomy is implicitly vacant, a puppet with its strings cut. The poetic act is unusual because it is an action performed *upon* the puppet rather than *by* the puppet. The writer of a letter, in contrast, evidences the puppet calmly at work,

Joe Wenderoth teaches in the Graduate Creative Writing Program at the University of California, Davis. He is a writer, performer, and filmmaker with six books to his credit, including four books of poetry, an epistolary novel, and a book of essays. His most recent collection is a book of poems, *If I Don't Breath How Do I Sleep* (2014).

quite unaware he *has* strings that might be cut. He is a character—a someone—in a social space, which is to say, *addressed to some other someone.*

The letters from *Letters to Wendy's* are comical because they suggest and
explore the abandonment of the autonomy of the will even as the ground
they traverse[1] obviously locates them in a world that is wholly dependent
upon (and only ever sensible in) ongoing *devotion* to the autonomy of the
will. This is something of a variation on a particular comedic skit, probably best or most *succinctly* put by Beckett: "I can't go on. I'll go on." To
describe how my *Letters* vary the joke, picture Beckett's two sentences as
two separate paintings. Each painting is on a transparency, say. Lay one
transparency on top of the other. Each *Letter* is that way: "I can't go on" and
"I'll go on" spoken simultaneously. The key, I think, to this particular gag,
or to my use of it, is the devotion implicit in my main character's *regularly*
returning to the Wendy's environs. The writer of the *Letters,* that is, *goes
on... and on... and on*—every day for more than a year, even as the *Letters* he
writes obsessively approach or outright decry *I can't go on.*

The joke can be thought of as a kind of stumbling. I stumble, but I go
on. The autonomy of the will is threatened on all sides by such stumbling.
The specific orientation and alleged destination implicit in the one who
stumbles are not typically dislodged by his stumbling, at least not in any
significant or lasting way. To *abandon* the autonomy of the will, however, is
different from *stumbling* within it. People stumble all the time within their
established intentions, and their stumbling, of course, can be funny. Co-
medians master the art of stumbling, recounting familiar, non-threatening
examples in order to demonstrate their (and our) mastery of them.

"I can't go on," however, as an act of abandon, is a *response* to, rather
than a recounting of, a stumble (or more likely, *many* stumbles). It is,
moreover, a radically serious response, bespeaking the potential to abandon movement (destination/identity) altogether. It is, indeed, the last sin-

---

[1] The ground between the consumer and the corporate entity to which he is
addressed is *literally* traversed by mail carriers, whose deliveries disappear every
day behind the closed doors of large, secure office buildings.

cere utterance the autonomy of the will can lay claim to; it is the surrender-and-relinquishing wherefrom the poetic might accrue. Where, then, is the humor in following up such a dire utterance with "I'll go on"? What is funny here is the abject failure of seriousness, i.e. of the dramatic, i.e. of the poetic. "I'll go on," in Beckett's formulation, disproves the space of the poetic almost before it can even finish resonating in our ears. Where poetic speech might be, there is only the slightest of silences—the silence between two non-poetic utterances. Thus, for Beckett, every sign of seriousness is, *a priori,* a ridiculous misunderstanding.

Two kinds of humor, then. The humor of stumbling is by far the most common sort—indeed, there are many who know of no other sort. It's the humor of stumbling that precedes (and prevents) "I can't go on." This is the realm of the comedian. The comedian stumbles not toward "I can't go on," but toward "I'll go on." That is to say, the comedian has always implicitly weathered his stumblings, and recounts them from a place of "understanding." If he is funny, it is because he is able to articulate the peculiarity of the little stumbles that are most common to us.

The second kind of humor concerns a different realm, the realm of the *buffoon.* The buffoon does not stumble, and does not recount stumblings. One does not laugh *with* the buffoon—one laughs *at* the buffoon. This is because the buffoon is not *in on* the joke. The buffoon is a would-be poet; he believes *it is possible* to be serious. He believes, moreover, that seriousness has the capacity to transform the crude and absurd *modus operandi*—eating, banking, teeth-scrubbing, oil changes, ejaculating, taking out the trash, etc.—in which he is mired. It is this belief—this faith in the poetic—that makes him ridiculous. Each of the *Letters* in my book opens up the slight silence between "I can't go on" and "I'll go on." The writer of the *Letters* is a would-be poet, trapped in anti-poetic space. He screws himself up into the towering silence-tantrum of "I can't go on," only to find himself going on, making an order, and returning to the absurdly satisfying teats of the mire.

HYBRID WORK
From Letters to Wendy's

July 27, 1996

So many drive-through people. Of course, there is really no such thing as driving *through*—one drives *by*. And who would drive *by* a Wendy's? Who would be so ridiculous as to assume that he could simply *extract* what he needs from a visit without actually making the visit, without standing awhile inside the blessed delusion of a manned source? How fast the dead have learned to bury the dead.

August 18, 1996

We've become a *throw-away* society! they gasp. Well, could this be because we've discovered, *finally*, that we're a throw-away organism... living in a throw-away land? I think it's just this discovery that's prompted so much righteous organization against "waste." I'm happy to every day get a brand new ornate yellow cup, drink half my Coke, then abandon the thing altogether and forever.

August 22, 1996

There used to be a little Ma-and-Pa restaurant across the road, but it couldn't keep up. Everyone over there acted all familiar and cozy, like they knew exactly where they were. Like they were *natives*. Natives!! *Execute the natives*, insofar as they claim to be! Build Wendy's everywhere and all alike—and do not fear: you cannot, you CAN NOT ever step into the same Wendy's twice.

September 20, 1996

Today I had a Biggie. Usually I just have a small, and refill. Why pay more? But today I needed a Biggie inside me. Some days, I guess, are like that. Only a Biggie will do. You wake up and you know: today I will get a Biggie and I will put it inside me and I will feel better. One time I saw a guy with three Biggies at once. One wonders not about him but about what it is that holds us back.

September 30, 1996

I don't like the idea of "old fashioned" hamburgers. The desire to dwell in *the ways of old* reduces being to tourism. It puts a "Ye Olde" in front of every location. Ye Olde Drugstore, Ye Olde Restroom, Ye Olde Prison, Ye Olde Strip Club, Ye Olde Convenience Store. The only place that still is a place—and Wendy's is, despite this silly slogan—exists primarily *before*, not after, history.

POETRY THAT ISN'T POETRY

The Fragment as Center in
Postcards to Donald Evans

Takashi Hiraide

Donald Evans was an American painter who created imaginary countries and then drew stamps supposedly issued by these imaginary places. I first saw Donald Evans' artwork in early summer of 1984 at a gallery in Tokyo. More than seven years had passed since the artist had died at the young age of 31. I was moved by his approach to making art, one that did not bother to keep up with the latest trends, and by the subtle order of this other world that he had carefully built up. A friend who was the publisher of a small press had also seen the exhibit and suggested I write something about Evans. It just so happened that at the same time I had been asked by a quarterly publication to do a serialized piece for them, which would appear in a number of installments in their magazine. We were already discussing what the theme would be, what form the piece would be written in, and what publisher to use for any future publication in book form. Finally, there was the question of how to write it.

Simultaneously, I was looking for an alternative approach to writing. I wanted to write criticism that wasn't like criticism; essays that were more than just essays. These thoughts were connected with my earlier desire to write poetry that wasn't like poetry.

Takashi Hiraide is a Japanese poet, writer, and critic whose work includes *The Guest Cat* (2014), an internationally bestselling novella, and several genre-bending essay collections. Seven of his books have been translated, and *For the Fighting Spirit of the Walnut* (2008) won the 2009 Best Translated Book Award for poetry. His work is in dialogue with that of contemporary artists On Kawara, Mitsuo Kano, Gerhard Richter, and Donald Evans. He currently teaches at Tama Art University and lives in Tokyo.

Writing in installments for a quarterly magazine would mean that I could write at a leisurely pace. And it also meant that I would be able to travel at the same time I was working on the assignment. But even more so, I would be able to give myself to the current of reality, no changing of dates or proper nouns. In other words, I would not fictionalize things in my writing. I decided that this would be the rule for this serialized piece. At the same time, there was one important point in the project that was fictitious—I would be writing postcards to a person who was dead, and this would of course be done as if it were completely natural.

I just happened to be spending three months in Iowa City while preparations were going on for the serialized piece, and this became the backdrop for its opening section. The piece starts with the description of an actual event—the rejection of my attempt to send a letter to the parents of the painter, Donald Evans, at the Iowa City Post Office. My two months touring the United States that followed then gave form to the first section of the book. Finally, the third section of the book, completed three years later, comprises my journey to Amsterdam where I would fulfill the original impetus of the work. There I followed in the footsteps of the dead painter, and at the end of the story crossed over to a remote island where he himself had attempted to travel, but was thwarted by a storm. The island is actually in British territory, but it is officially allowed to issue its own local stamps. Hence fiction and reality got mixed up here as well.

My leisurely magazine assignment made it possible for me to write in the form of a series of postcards, or as one might write diary entries on slips of paper. I was always enamored of the ability to write letters and diaries with great facility, and yet I was somehow unable to do so, and over time had come to consider it an impossibility. When I was in college my attraction to the letters and diaries of Kafka exceeded even my love of his other writings, so much so as to become an obsession—I became totally immersed in my readings of them. But this literary obsession simply made writing in that form even more impossible. No writer has ever

POETRY THAT ISN'T POETRY

focused on the impossibility of the writing of letters and diaries as Kafka did, or continued to produce works out of that very impossibility.

I continued gradually producing this series of letters to the dead. In doing so, I wrote about my own daily life, as well as the things around me and of course the dying of people who were close to me. This type of content is what formed the second section of the book, produced during my time back in Tokyo where I had returned to the day-to-day drudgery of an office job.

I finished writing the serialized piece in 1989. My readers and friends assumed that it would be published in book form soon after completion, but I continued to betray their expectations. In fact, it would be 12 years before the book was finally published. There are two reasons that publication took so long. One is simply that I could not come up with a good title. But the other reason was that most of the second section is comprised of a diary of the dying of people who I was close to, a kind of homage, and there's rawness to the language that was unavoidable.

In the end, the Japanese title was quite simply as it appeared in English—*Postcards to Donald Evans*. But translating the same title word for word into Japanese produced something that was somehow uninteresting, more like an explanation of the contents rather than a title. The title of the original serial piece in the magazine was "Imaginary Correspondence with Donald Evans," but this didn't seem right either. Calling my own fiction fictional in the title just seemed odd. My journey to Donald's imaginary country was actually quite real.

In the end I went with *By Postcard—to Donald Evans*. It finally came to me that a title like this would be workable in 1998. I had a kind of epiphany while reading the end notes of Kafka's collected works in Japanese. One of Kafka's letters is referred to as "by postcard—to Odstrcil."

Yet something still remained that prevented me from publishing the book. This was the simple fact that the memories of those years remained so vivid, so real. I would have to completely separate myself from the past before I could let go of this work and send it off into the world on its own. The way I was finally able to do this came down to a simple matter of editing. It took me nearly 10 years before I figured out how I should approach editing. Originally, there were a total of 186 postcards. Like dropping frames when editing a film, I threw out about 30. This is what I wrote in the afterword of the book—"Of the 186 postcards which were sent, some turned up over a period of over 10 years damaged or arrived from various places in a disorderly state."[1] Yet this is actually another fiction that I created to explain the loss of some of the postcards, using the 12 years that had passed since then both as an excuse for some being missing and as something that also felt strongly as being real.

The fragment takes up the center of my writing methodology. This is because I believe that the essence of poetry is in its fragmented nature. I instinctually feel that any attempt to bring closure to poetry or to explain it is what kills the poetic nature. And this is how I have approached all of my works—by playing with these fragments that I have produced in various ways. Letters and diaries have a certain universal power, and this also comes from their essentially fragmented nature. The term postcard used in this work could easily be substituted with the word fragment.[2]

HYBRID WORK
From Postcards to Donald Evans

OCTOBER 19, 1988
LUNDY

Donald Evans,
Here a house is just like a house; a road a road. Everything is exposed to the sea wind, and there is no transportation whatsoever. That is why,

---

[1] I have used my own translation rather than the one appearing in the publication (ES).
[2] The words for "postcard" and "fragment" in Japanese are not complete homonyms, but very close.

in fact, the salt-parched house is like nothing but a house and the road merging with the field is like nothing but a road.

I landed, climbed up the cliff, and went into the only shop, a restaurant that also sells souvenirs. I was, however, shut out immediately. The shop was going to be closed between two and six. This is the one and only building here that you can enter. To walk around was the only option I had.

I noticed, then, that the birdwatchers who came with me in the ship had vanished into thin air; not a single figure could be seen on the meadow where you command a 180-degree view.

I took a road to the Marisco Castle. There was nothing but grass, rocks, and sheep. In the void you lose a sense of distance. Until I got to the castle, my five senses were torn to pieces by the strong sea wind; my mind was empty.

OCTOBER 19, 1988
LUNDY

Dear Donald Evans,
Don't make fun of this foolish trip. This Marisco Castle, allegedly built by Henry III in the thirteenth century, is very small. One of the island's residents seems to live here. In the courtyard, some laundry is even hung out to dry. There is a bench, on which I'm sitting and writing this postcard. From my date book I took out a leaf, the Japanese maple leaf I tore off in Morristown. I've had it with me all the time for two years. I think I'll leave it in the middle of this ruined castle. On the leaf I'll also put the Dutch stamp of the old woman in black.

I'll leave it in the middle of the king's castle where briny winds roll; in the smallest, weirdest kingdom of the world. Don't make fun of my foolish trip on your behalf: this is meant to make one of your dreams in this world come true.

OCTOBER 19, 1988
LUNDY

Donald,

I'm wandering in a field full of sheep. The island is flat, but its end is not visible, so I don't think I can walk all the way from the southern tip to the northern one in time for the returning ship. A low fence charged weakly with electricity surrounds the sheep. I cross it just as I walk through the Berlin wall at one of the designated points. Having crossed the "wall," I wander.

As I near the cliff, a hare pops up from a hole in the rock by my feet. Every time I look up, the sun is setting in a magnificent way upon the Atlantic. I run down the cliff to a decaying warship battery, where I can catch the sun from the turret. There are no puffins. According to the birdwatcher I passed a few minutes ago, it's from April through August that you can see puffins. At this time of year they have migrated to a different sea. Judging from the low angle of the sun, I decide not to walk along the western cliff toward north any more. The shadows are getting longer.

OCTOBER 19, 1988
LUNDY

Donald,

My own shadow has started to get longer and longer. I guess it's grown to be as long as 30 meters. With nothing to interrupt it, it seems to be stretching endlessly. I saw some freshly killed rabbits. Behind the old lighthouse there is a small graveyard. As soon as a small dog made a fearsome jump out of the shadow of a low tomb, a hare ran away past my feet. The Jack Russell terrier ran after it, its teeth exposed.

The sun was about to set in the Atlantic. Once again, I saw my shadow, which was now extremely long. Turning around, I waited for the sundown beyond the cliff where sheep grazed. I waited, because I had a hunch. Then I saw a miracle.

A green flash of light, a rare phenomenon in the air seen only in coastal areas, and only in perfectly clear weather. The moment the sun set on the horizon, the green light radiated from there.

OCTOBER 19, 1988
LUNDY

Dear Donald Evans,

While waiting for the returning ship that departs late at night, I'm writing this important postcard. I've also just written brief notes to Yteke, Benno, Ad and Thea, Bill, Mr. Yokota, and Belta. To my great surprise, this restaurant is also a post office. I asked Ian the waiter for Lundy stamps and made some detailed queries about Lundy's postal system. Which took me by surprise—it differed from my London friend's account on a crucial point.

A stamp with a puffin picture, its value denoted in "puffin" currency, is the only one that is valid when you send mail from here. One puffin equals one penny. Wherever in the world you send your mail, even to the nearby port of Bideford on the mainland, you have to buy a 10 puffin stamp of Lundy at this restaurant and stick it on. Though it's a fictitious stamp from the world's point of view, it's the only real stamp here.

Ian kept explaining, accepted a bunch of postcards from me, switched quickly from waiter to post office clerk, and rushed to the upstairs office to imprint Lundy Kingdom's original post-marks on them.

OCTOBER 19, 1988
ABOARD THE OLDENBURG

Dear Donald Evans,

Stars seem to fall without ever spoiling the entire constellation. I climbed down the steep cliff road in pitch black to the bay where the Oldenburg was moored. On my way, a cat presented itself, getting tangled up with my feet. Whenever I nearly stepped on it, the cat quickly went down a few feet ahead and then got tangled up with my feet again. You couldn't tell if the cat was hindering me or leading me. Something like a walk on the border of a dream was going on.

When I finally reached the bay, the passengers taking the ferry were already waiting, whispering, like shadows. The cat was gone.

I took the ferry along with these strangers and then went aboard the ship that must be carrying my mail. As it now started to push its way through waves, more and more stars seemed to be falling.

Goodbye, Donald. I just left the world, and I'm bound for another. Everything is so different, dear Donald, and everything is new to me, too.

AUTOBIOGRAPHY OF A HYBRID NARRATIVE

Finding a Form for Trauma

Joy Ladin

The self is a hybrid, a churning hodge-podge of feeling, experience, shared narratives, memory, fantasy, and clichés, to name a few of the self's concatenated genres that our ongoing process of self-narration stuffs into the pronoun "I." As Daniel Dennett and others have argued, this process of self-narration—the process of telling ourselves the story of what we are doing, have done, will do—generates our sense of self, implying a coherent, continuous perspective, an "I" who both lives and tells this story. The process of self-narration conceals the hybrid nature of our selves, enabling us to stuff the disparate materials that compose "us," and the disparate modes through which we make sense of them, into a single baggy form, a sort of picaresque autobiography.

It's often said that trauma shatters the sense of self. More precisely, trauma interferes with the ongoing process of self-narration, collapsing the distance between suffering and the story we try to tell about it, undermining the narrating perspective, the "I" that stands beyond experience reflecting upon it, interpreting it, relating one experience to another and incorporating all of them into an omnivorous narrative that subsumes and digests them all. Trauma is experience that cannot be subsumed or di-

Joy Ladin is the David and Ruth Gottesman Professor of English at Yeshiva University. She is the author of seven books of poetry, including *Impersonation* (2015), *The Definition of Joy* (2012), and *Transmigration* (2009). Her memoir, *Through the Door of Life: A Jewish Journey between Genders* (2012), was a 2012 National Jewish Book Award finalist.

gested, cannot be narrated as past because it is always present. Trauma interrupts our self-generating story, exposing the multifarious materials that self-narration enables us to think of as coherent, continuous selves.

For writers, representing characters wrestling with trauma presents an opportunity to explore the hybridity of self, to see what's at stake, on the most intimate level, when we confront the incompatibility of our various modes of making sense of ourselves, and to see if we can develop more capacious modes of self-narration that embrace rather than conceal the hybridity of the self.

Those questions are at the heart of *The Book of Anna*, which consists of diary entries and autobiographical poems written in the voice of Anna Asher, a fictional Czech-German Jew who spent her adolescence in a concentration camp and now lives in mid-1950s Prague. When that brief biography came to me, I had no idea that Anna and I would spend the next five years struggling to find ways to tell the story of her life.

At first, I thought that I would have it easy. A handful of short, brutal first-person lyrics alluding to Anna's concentration camp experience tumbled out in a matter of days. My drafts seemed successful by lyric standards—the voice was urgent, the language dense with suggestive image and metaphor. But when I tried to revise them, I realized that the lyric form was excluding rather than expressing Anna's character and life. It took me months to break down and break open my lyric conception of form. I was afraid of what might lie beyond lyric's safely circumscribed allusions, afraid that if I let myself discover the details of Anna's life, her traumas would expose the inadequacy of my familiar modes of representing the self. For months, I tried to avoid admitting what seems obvious in retrospect: Anna's character and life couldn't be expressed in a single form; her voice, her story, her self, demanded hybridity.

Anna's voice, emotionally charged and wildly associative, was a natural fit for first-person lyric, but that voice was trying to tell a story, a story composed of many stories of narration—confounding trauma. Indeed, part of Anna's story was her inability to tell these stories; her concentration camp experiences had destroyed her faith in narrative, along with all the other means she had to give meaning to her life. As Anna attempted to tell her stories, her narratives kept erupting into lyric outbursts that implied further narrative. Anna's life would only allow itself to be told through a hybrid of first-person lyric and narrative forms.

Once I committed to discovering Anna's stories, I saw that Anna's skepticism about self-narration was well-founded: there was no single narrative form that could fit abandonment by her mother, repeated rape, forced concentration camp bedspring abortion, to list only a few of her traumas. Each trauma posed different psychological, moral, and narrative problems; each required different forms and combinations of narrative and lyric.

As these poems grew into a sequence, Anna's life and self were emerging. But each poem-story was too long, too fragmented, too complex, a fiction-writer friend told me, for readers to understand them as parts of a larger story. He suggested adding another layer of hybridization: interspersing the poems with prose in which Anna reflects on how each poem relates to her life in the present. Those prose entries became a diary (two entries of which are reproduced in this volume) that revealed aspects of Anna—her writing process, her relationships with neighbors, her obsessive sexual behavior, her chain-smoking, her idiosyncratic exploration of Jewish tradition—that offered context for the poems.

The juxtaposition of Anna's blunt prose about the present with her poetic narration of the past generated dialogic relationships between these forms and their content. The prose self-narration foreshadowed and commented upon the poetry, embedding traumatic past in writerly present; the poems challenged the bitter assurance of the prose, exposing the pretense, the fragility, of Anna's present-tense "I." As this dialogic relationship continues, prose and poetry transform one another, and begin to interpenetrate. The diary entries grow more allusive, more lyric; the voice in the poems less high-flown, their narratives more coherent. As the book progresses, this dialogic relationship brings past and present closer and closer, until, in the final lines, they meet.

When trauma exposes the hybridity of the self, it exposes the multiple, often incompatible, discourses—familial, cultural, aesthetic, psychological, religious, and academic—through which we give meaning to what we live through. Anna's traumas destroyed her faith in these discourses as thoroughly as they destroyed her faith in self-narration. But just as she can't stop telling the story of her life, even when she doesn't believe there can be any such story, she cannot stop invoking discourses whose meaning-making pretenses seem to her pathetic and obscene.

Of all the discourses Anna transmogrifies through hybridization, the discourses she invokes most obsessively are those that represent Jewish tradition, particularly those that participate in the Biblically rooted, rabbinically elaborated conviction that Jewish history reflects and reveals the presence of God. Using bits of Biblical narrative and poetry, Talmudic and post-rabbinic traditions, to tell her stories of meaning-mooting trauma, Anna mocks Jewish tradition's inability to escape or explain the Holocaust.

At the same time, though, by forcing them into the service of her self-narration, Anna revitalizes these discourses, freeing them from piety and predictability, imbuing them with her own urgency, her skepticism, her obscenity, her despair. For example, in "Song of Songs: 8 Sessions with Dr. Solomon," excerpted in this volume, Anna combines language drawn from the Biblical Song of Songs, rabbinic interpretations of the poem as an allegory of the love between God and the Jewish people, and the "Jewish science" of psychoanalysis to portray her concentration camp experiences as a series of violent sexual encounters between God and the women who designated the teenage Anna their survivor. This God is Lord of both life and death, a hybrid God who presides over incomprehensible murder and equally incomprehensible deliverance.

This hybrid space catches God in the act, exposing God as unforgivably implicated in the horrors Anna witnessed and endured in the camps. But at this point in the book—midway—Anna is also trapped in the "harem of the dead," experiencing its horrors from each of her hybridized perspectives. By the final poem in the book, Anna has found in hybridization a means not just of expressing the past but of surviving it. Hybridization becomes, for her, a mode of self-narration, one that is capacious enough, skeptical enough, and generous enough to combine the traumas she has suffered, the love she has known, the discourses she has scorned, and the Jewish traditions she has pastiched into a sense of self, a self that, despite it all, because of it all, remains alive and writing.

HYBRID WORK
Excerpt from The Book of Anna

The following is an edited version of the first section of The Book of Anna, *which consists of prose diary entries and long narrative poems written in the voice of Anna Asher, a fictional concentration camp survivor living in Prague in the 1950s.*

7 April 195_

Wischnauer's fever has broken. I managed to get some penicillin, even without a doctor. The pharmacist, like the grocer, finds my small talk very persuasive.

Wischnauer would hate to admit it, but even for her, my job has its advantages.

Soon Wischnauer will be well enough to throw me out of her apartment. I'll be back on the street at night, at my usual post above the river. *Many waters cannot quench love...*

I plan to keep reading that song made of songs. It's become a favorite. Not just because of the sex. Because God is so utterly absent that the rabbis decided—what else could they do?—to see Him everywhere, as shepherd and King and leaping gazelle, wooing from every side at once His lonely rose of Sharon, His maiden Israel, who lies awake at night radiating per-

fume from between her breasts, ripening like a cluster of dates just beyond His grasp.

Black but comely, most beautiful of women, she somehow—that's
the nerve of this girl, this allegory of devotion and abandonment—
thinks she is entitled not only to her Beloved's love, but to the love of
the rest of the harem. She wheedles their apples and bits of bread, cries
on their shoulders, faints in their arms, screams for their protection.
In the final chapters, when she's made her escape, she has the gall to
survive them.

11 April 195_

A day altogether bad, beginning to end.

That dream again—the harem, the scarab—then Wischnauer pounding
the door with her shoe, taking my screams for the screams I scream with
men. Then I overslept, missed the bus, arrived at work half an hour late after
a long walk through the pouring rain, looking, according to one of my fellow
girls, like a rat fished out of a bottle of milk, and was threatened with termina-
tion by our local war hero—a man I've slept with three times—who accused
me of no longer taking seriously my "social obligations." As if I ever have.

When I arrive home, Wischnauer immediately knocks on my door. It's
been days since I've seen her.

"Anna," she says, without greeting or explanation, "call this man." She
holds out a cardboard rectangle, white, with gold lettering.

Dr. A.M. Solomon. Psychoanalysis.

That, again. "A doctor, eh? And Jewish, no less." Her face remains expressionless. Not a crack. "You want to fix me up, Wischnauer? Worried
I'm running short of men?"

It's dim in the hallway. I won't step out; she won't step in. The rectangle
floats between her fingers, extending across the sill like a fragment of a
bridge. Her face too floats against the shadows—they will never replace

the bulb in the hall—fine and lined and the color of old linen, like the heirloom tablecloth my mother inherited from her great-great aunt.

In this light, this close, it's one of the most beautiful faces I have ever seen.

Footsteps at the end of the hall. Keys in a lock. A hinge squeaking open.

Wischnauer pushes the card into my hand. Pulls my door shut behind her.

From the first section of "Song of Songs: 8 Sessions with Dr. Solomon"

Yes Dr., the same dream the harem,
Bags of myrrh between their breasts.
Henna tattoos on their wrists.

The terminally noble
Daughters of Barracks 10
Who made the suicide pact

To husband me as their—

Their vineyard, Dr.
Their designated fruit; the shoot
They'd plant beyond the camps.

He must be here they murmur. *His scent is growing stronger.*

The Rebbetzin trembles like a veil;
The Physicist giggles;
The Whore straightens her hem.

It's a tense moment, Dr.
God returning to the harem
To kiss us with the kisses of His mouth

Stud us with gold shower us with silver
Lay us on couches of leaves
Between panels of cypresses.

The Rebbetzin was right: the Whore

Was a dangerous influence.
The others shunned her;
With me, she could reminisce—

Soft Jewish boys; firemen; lawyers; grandfathers
With whiskey on their breath.
It was a living, Dr.

No guns, no boots.
Just small dark rooms,
Need and nakedness.

After every *tête-à-tête*
The Rebbetzin would mutter supplications
To shield me—she was serious Dr.—
From growing up like *that*.

．　．　．　．

Is this too much for a first session?

You're looking a little pale.
Your predecessor accused me of using his office
To violate the dead.

He was no Solomon, Dr.
It isn't that easy to violate
Daughters of Barracks 10.

In your professional opinion, Dr.,
What do I owe them?
For the Physicist, a skeptical smile?

Kinder for the Rebbetzin?
For the Whore, a steady job
And steadier diet of men?

And for the King whose Name is like perfume, unspeakably intimate,

Who has brought me to your couch
To recount what the Rebbetzin called
His merciful deliverance?

Where was I oh yes
The dream the harem myrrh
The footfalls of His Nibs.

I take my place
Between Whore and Rebbetzin
Blink and have no lids.

My jaws keep moving,
The chant goes on,
But my mouth is full of flesh;

I'm eating my way
Across a face
Familiar, immense—I have

No hands no skin hidden wings
A sweet-tooth
For the dead.

A scarab-beetle; yes.
Uncanny Dr.
A truly inspired guess.

Black but comely,
Part Rebbetzin, part Whore,
Consummate Physicist,

Living tribute, Dr.,
To the daughters of Barracks 10.
Return—isn't that what you call it?—

Return on their investment.

3
. . . .
Poetic Memoir

POETIC MEMOIR
An Introduction

A memoir, as distinguished from an autobiography, tells *a* story *from* a life, rather than *the* story *of* a life. The word "memoir" comes from the Old French *memoire*, and earlier, from the Latin *memorandum;* hence the genre's fragmented nature. A memorandum is a memory device: a group of ambient details or a set of notes that gestures toward a whole to be constructed in the future. The earliest memoirs took two divergent forms: formal, public oration by military or political leaders, or unpublished, incomplete "memos," which an author might use to jog the memory at a later date for a more complete written piece. These two forms emphasize the play between the individual or private life, and the culture, society, or public in which an individual's life stories receive their context and significance.

Perhaps the best way of defining the poetic memoir is by suggesting that the genre straddles its two separate and yet related roots, drawing formal attention to the fact that it is a fragment of a whole or larger narrative, and that the whole is the society or culture of which the individual is a member. This tension is evident in some of the earliest and best-loved memoirs, from Augustine of Hippo's *Confessions,* written in fourth-century Hippo (in modern-day Algeria), to Jean-Jacques Rousseau's *Confessions*, written in eighteenth-century Paris, and the spiritual memoirs by Catholic saints and mystics in between. The influence of the memorandum is also evident in such works as *The Autobiography of Benjamin Franklin*, which Franklin himself called a memoir, and which is full of anecdotes, letters, sayings, and various narrative threads.

Each of the selections included here negotiates between poem and prose, and personal and public (or social or cultural). They begin before birth, exploring the medicalization of birth and death, questioning the extent to which a person can be said to have any autonomy over his or her body in the face of state control. They address the autonomy of family units, drawing attention to the family as a microcosm of the state, and exploring social resistance to alternative familial models. They focus on the tension between the individual and the family, testing the family's elasticity, its ability to forgo its primal goal of biological reproduction and to adapt to homosexuality, or its ability to endure loss. Each of these pieces demonstrates that fragmentation is an apt response to the crisis that is each individual life, and an honest response to the attempted integration of two or more complete human beings—the integration that is necessary to create family, society, and culture.

These poetic memoir pieces are generative: they are writing into being a life—a way of being in life—that has not, to the writers' minds, been available to them before. Several of the memoirists included here view the fragmented form of their work as a way of reconciling the individual and the social, the binary that has historically animated poetic memoir. As Jennifer Bartlett, writing about physical disability and alternative familial arrangements in "My Body Is (the) Marginalia; The Sun Drawn a Saw Across the Strings," notes, "Genre, grammar, and form safely mirror society's restrictions, and this is not a wholly bad thing." But for her, hybridity is born when a writer resists prescribed forms.

The most prominent formal feature of the poetic memoir is the use of poetic lines or blocks of poetic prose or dialogue, rather than the traditional first-person narrative prose account. However, many of the writers here warn us against reading their work as just poetry. Perhaps they have in common most what they are not. Kazim Ali finds it "depressing" that people call *Bright Felon* poetry for the simple fact that it is written in sentences instead of paragraphs; to him, lines are not "verse." They are merely individual sentences, the basic components of a paragraph.

Maggie Nelson also notes that she does not consider her book *Bluets* poetry, though when readers do so, it "happily expands the notion of poetry."

Arielle Greenberg and Rachel Zucker view their *Home/Birth: A Poemic* as formally emphasizing and mimicking "the cyclical, gynocentric, and uniquely liminal space that is the birthing process." The work is a dialogue that does not indicate which interlocutor is speaking, and sometimes it is a chorus.

On another side of the spectrum of formal possibility is Gregory Orr's *The Blessing*, which, while it may look like prose, is "not straightforward narrative prose." Orr, a lyric poet, explains, "Lyric wants to go vertical, whereas prose seems to me strongest when it flows confidently with the horizontal, the time-bound particulars of observed action and interaction." Thus, Orr alternates narrative prose with associative imagery, "or prose poem-like chapters."

Whatever else a poetic memoir is or is not, the selections here work as ancient memos for the ever-evolving relationship between the individual and society, the private and the public, the inner and the exterior, individual agency and institutional exigency, gender, genre, and the generation of humans and literature, chaos and order. It's an exciting time to write poetic memoir, for the genre is perhaps the "it" genre of our present moment. Consider the popularity of reality shows; consider that nearly every notable figure in the political, economic, or entertainment world will, at one point, produce a memoir. Consider writing your own memoir, embracing each little chaos and contradiction that makes up your life, without trying to reconcile them.

—*Marcela Sulak*

FRIENDSHIP AND PROCESS
This Project's Birth Story
Arielle Greenberg and Rachel Zucker

For more than 13 years, we have been close friends and dedicated readers of one another's poetry and essays. Our friendship has included many literary projects, including starting a peer poetry workshop, attending and then giving poetry readings together, helping one another navigate the pleasures and frustrations of publishing, co-teaching a poetry master class, and co-editing the anthologies *Women Poets on Mentorship: Efforts and Affections* and *Starting Today: 100 Poems for Obama's First 100 Days*. Somehow, despite all of this shared creative work, we had never found a way to write poetry together, though we often tried.

In the fall of 2007, Arielle was teaching a graduate poetry semi-

Arielle Greenberg's most recent books are the poetry collection *Slice* (2015) and the creative nonfiction book *Locally Made Panties* (2016). She's co-editor of three anthologies: most recently, with Lara Glenum, *Gurlesque* (2010). Her poems and essays have been featured in *Best American Poetry*, *Labor Day: True Birth Stories for the 21st Century*, and *The Arcadia Project: North American Postmodern Pastoral*, and she writes a regular column on contemporary poetics for the *American Poetry Review*. A former tenured professor in poetry at Columbia College Chicago, she now lives in Maine and teaches in Oregon State University-Cascades' MFA.

Rachel Zucker is the author of nine books, most recently a memoir, *MOTHERs* (2014), and a double collection of prose and poetry, *The Pedestrians* (2014). Along with poet Arielle Greenberg, Zucker co-wrote *Home/Birth: A Poemic* and co-edited *Women Poets on Mentorship: Efforts and Affections* (2010). Zucker lives in New York City with her husband and three sons. She teaches at New York University.

nar at Columbia College Chicago on the work of C.D. Wright, whose hybrid forms and book-length investigative projects she has long admired. Arielle asked the students to write poems or essays in Wright's style: students were to employ lyric fragments, lists, overheard snippets of conversation, text from billboards and diner placemats, etc., with the goal of capturing the vernacular, the artifacts, and the other details of an American culture or subculture in which they were invested, but that are relatively unexplored in literature.

Arielle gave herself the same task, and began working on a lyric essay about the homebirth subculture of which she herself was a part. As she began to write her essay, she realized that she had happened upon a project that might lend itself to direct collaboration with Rachel. Homebirth was, after all, one of the most intimate connections between the two of us and a topic about which we both cared passionately.

In 2004, when Arielle got pregnant for the first time, she asked Rachel to attend the birth. Rachel already had two children (born in the hospital) and was worried about Arielle's decision to plan a homebirth. Rachel was also deeply moved by Arielle's invitation and wanted to be at the birth. Knowing instinctively that she should not attend the birth if she wasn't fully supportive of Arielle's choice, Rachel began to research homebirth. Rachel quickly became convinced that homebirth was an excellent choice for Arielle, and she decided to become a certified doula so as to better prepare. The certification process required a six-week workshop, reading several books, writing an essay, taking a short exam, and attending at least three births.

Newly certified and tremendously excited, Rachel flew from New York City to Chicago when Arielle called to say her water had broken. It turned out that Rachel arrived in plenty of time, as Arielle had a five-day labor! Two years later, when Rachel became pregnant, she decided to plan a homebirth herself. That pregnancy ended in miscarriage, but a year later (and one day after Arielle realized she was pregnant with her second child), Rachel gave birth to her third child at home, just as she had hoped to do.

So, when Arielle (newly pregnant) approached Rachel (newly postpartum) with the idea for a collaborative lyric essay on homebirth, Rachel was thrilled. Arielle sent Rachel what she'd written—a handful of pages of material, mostly lists and little notes—and Rachel wrote in between those lines, adding and questioning, augmenting where needed. The book was passed back and forth over email for four months, timed to be finished by the birth of Arielle's second child. The book grew organically, from the center outward, in a non-linear fashion, with new sections, arguments, ideas, and threads inserted here and there, rather than from front to back, and moved freely between essay, poem, and memoir. The book's evolution also mimicked the call-and-response, argument-and-negotiation patterns of our long friendship. We decided early on not to identify who's speaking, in part because so much of the book is collaged from other voices (medical articles, other women's birth stories we retell, maternal care experts, etc.) and in part because we felt it was a feminist strategy to unravel notions of Authorship and Authority, especially for a book about the collaborative, feminine work of childbirth, midwifery, and female friendship. Sometimes even we can't remember who wrote what, or who found a particular quote or bit of research.

Shortly after we finished a complete first draft of the book, the baby Arielle was pregnant with died. In the weeks that followed, as Arielle waited to birth her stillborn son, we spoke or emailed daily and continued to work on the book, which took on new significance and felt more urgent than ever. To Rachel's great sadness, she was not able to attend Arielle's second homebirth, but Arielle was fully supported by her husband, midwives, and doula. In the period of grief after the death and birth of Arielle's son, Arielle wrote the Afterword, and together we continued to revise the text. We decided to split the book into sections loosely organized around specific threads of the story—waterbirth, for example, or the misogyny of the medicalized birth industry—and to create lyric pieces in between those sections with language culled from the longer prose sections in order to further emphasize and mimic the cyclical, gynocentric, and uniquely liminal space that is the birthing process.

Working on this book was more exhilarating, gratifying, profound, and sustaining than either of us could have anticipated. And because the process of writing *Home/Birth: A Poemic* required us to not only rely on someone else's language, but also to work in a more direct manner than either of us had before—utilizing more outside research and less opacity than usual, writing in short bursts of plain-spoken prose, occupying an overtly political, even polemical stance—the project continued to influence our individual writing and relationships. In the years that followed the book's completion, we both wrestled to locate and redefine our own individual writing voices, our relationship to the act of writing itself, as well as the nature of the next phase of our friendship.

This essay is a revised version of the appendix that appears in Home/Birth: A Poemic. *It was revised especially for this anthology.*

HYBRID WORK
Excerpt from Home/Birth: A Poemic

I want to be clear about this: I believe that for most people the *safest* place to birth a baby is at *home*.

One (male) OB, Dr. De Angelis, says to Jennifer Block in *Pushed*, *Why do women put up with [hospital birthing practices]... Back in the 80s, when I was in residency, there was a feminist movement. The women back then would never have tolerated this.*

Do you know how they keep the internal fetal monitor inside the mother? They screw it into the baby's skull.

I wonder if they tell vegetarian and vegan moms that Pitocin is derived from the pituitary glands of cattle.

Let's just think about this stuff. Let's not think about this stuff. We need to.

People say about homebirth, "Wow, I don't know if I could be that brave," but they don't get it: when I think about being in a weird-smelling room in weird-smelling clothing strapped down with monitors and denied food and water, and with strangers pushing me to make choices I don't want to make, I think that's terrifying. I can't imagine how brave you have to be to birth in a hospital.

We must stand together. The women who need interventions should get them and not be made to feel badly. The women who don't need interventions should be left to their glory.

But all women need to know how infrequently we actually need interventions, and how interventions can make everything harder and more dangerous, instead of easier and safer. There is nothing easy about having Pitocin, or a C-section.

Now so many women have had interventions and births like the terrifying ones on television. And some are angry when I talk about homebirth, because they feel judged.

But you can't just say that birthing choices like inductions, epidurals, and planned C-sections are the right of modern women. A feminist issue of choice. Because the birthing industry is a conspiracy to keep women from trusting themselves. I believe this rabidly.

So we are pitted against each other, against other women, rather than the institutions that fail us and fail to treat us humanely.

We've hardly even begun to talk about homebirth, really.

I think my sister-in-law is angry with me. My brother-in-law too. They feel judged by my homebirth activism.

Tell their story.

Who is the villain here?

Hospital birth is a volume business.

Lola planned a homebirth. But on her third day of prodromal labor, the baby turned breech and they transported. "I can't come to your screening," she wrote. "I still have too much to process."

Lay blame where blame is due.

Every time I go to the regular OBGYN-Certified Nurse-Midwife practice, I feel like I'm an undercover investigative reporter finding out how bad it really is.

Powerful strangers.

The baby just kicked when I typed that.

Sometimes, by talking about this, you hurt a woman's feelings. She feels judged. "I was induced with Pitocin and had no trouble at all bonding with my baby," said M. after the film.

The way we welcome babies, the way women feel (physically and mentally) after and about their births has profound and lasting consequences for our society.

Transport is what they call it when a homebirthing mother and/or baby has to be transported to the hospital. There's a special Meetup about it tomorrow at Bloom Yoga Studio in Lincoln Square in Chicago.

Bag of waters. AROM. Sacred knowledge.

What does prodromal mean?

She was having contractions for days but wasn't yet in active labor.

Oh, like me.

Sometimes I feel I have a responsibility to be very normal so that people will not think that only freaks can have homebirths. Do you ever feel this?

I feel both the desire to appear normal and the desire to seem like a total hippie freak radical at all times. I think this is one of my mother's many complicated legacies.

I wrote a blog entry about how homebirth made me a radical. Even being a poet didn't do that for me.

When Josh thanked me afterward for being the impetus for your home-birth that seemed like a big deal. Even Josh could see how important it had been for you all.

After the screening Rita came up to me and said, "Daria was born with a C-section and afterwards I had absolutely no interest in her for two days."

We haven't even begun to talk about transport.

Shelby said, "After my C-section it was very, very hard."

All homebirth midwives in an area tend to know each other, and there is a lot of helping and sharing of knowledge and also a lot of gossiping. Maryn tells me about it.

Vital Signs. Doppler. Meconium. Dystocia.

I have hardly even begun to tell Maryn's story, how she had an awful, normal hospital birth with her first and then a homebirth with her second to which Tracey almost didn't make it in time and then Maryn decided to become a homebirth midwife and moved out of state to apprentice with Jerren and then had a homebirth with her third and then moved again to join a new practice in Arizona.

At Abram's birth, in the hospital, what I needed was for someone to say, "You *are* having a baby. I know you don't feel ready. I know you feel you can't. Give that to me. I'll hold it for you. You can have it back, after the birth. Now you need to let this baby out."

Did I tell you about how Maryn's birthing tub had a heating pad in it but Egan was coming so fast they turned it on full blast and then it was too hot? You don't want to cook the baby. So they had to dump in a bag of ice cubes.

I was holding that baby in and needed to let go.

Maryn has started a new natural birthing website and zine, *Indie Birth*. Maryn, who will soon be a licensed CPM for homebirth in Flagstaff.

We are trained this way in doula training. Hold the space. Hold anything the mother has that's getting in the way.

Maryn became a birth junkie. A "birthie." It happens. It's happening to us too.

Orgasmic. How the baby got in. How the baby comes out.

Arizona is one of the good states.

My homebirth was so normal it was borning.

If Maryn was still in Illinois, I could have had this homebirth here.

There's so little to say about a good, normal birth. And it wasn't easy. Of course not. And we tell the story over and over because we need to. Because we brought these babies by hard, beautiful labor into the world.

Do you mean boring? Or do you mean borning?

At Judah's birth, at home, all I wanted was a cold washcloth to lean my head against as I made sounds on hands and knees in the warm, good water. And someone to press down hard on my butt bone when the strong ones came. There was no place else I wanted to go. Nothing else I needed.

Button: *Doulas do it in any position.*

I could listen to birthing stories all day.

Diana's story: First she went to an OB and told him she was considering having her baby at home even though he was breech and he said, "What?! Are you insane?" and she was very turned off by him but she was also scared to have her first baby at home if he was breech, and he was persistently breech. She called a homebirth midwife when she was in labor and the midwife came over and Diana was in the bathtub vomiting and eight centimeters dilated and the midwife could see a foot coming out. The midwife said, "You can have your baby right here. You're having your baby now. You're doing it," but Diana was scared and wanted to go to the hospital and she did and she ended up with the mean OB and of course he sectioned her, even though the baby was almost already out on his own just fine.

In my last pregnancy the thought of the baby crowing was exciting to me. I mean it turned me on. Does that make me a freak? A witch? Oh, well.

Do you mean crowing? Or crowning?

"Crowning." Sometimes I am writing this with Judah on my lap. Sometimes while he is sleeping.

I like the idea of the baby crowing, too. Proud. Greeting the day.

I AM NO HYBRID, NO OTHER THAN MYSELF

On Writing *Bright Felon*

Kazim Ali

I did not mean to innovate but knew I could not speak.

The text wrote itself out of requirement. Had I followed the injunction to say in paragraphs my history I could not have begun.

Because I had to take action in my life (come out to my parents and family) I had to write to know why I lacked courage in the first place.

Begin in the present moment, sitting up late in the night in the apartment in Marble Hill, unable to sleep from both worry and the train arriving one street over and all night long.

There in a nowhere place, Marble Hill, once on Manhattan, then an island, and now attached to mainland.

Go backward in time. Allow the mind to wander. I did not mean to invent.

But my life had to invent itself, queer and Muslim who was I.

Kazim Ali is an associate professor and the director of the creative writing program at Oberlin College. His three volumes of poetry include *Sky Ward* (2013), winner of the Ohioana Book Award in Poetry. His poetic memoir is called *Bright Felon: Autobiography and Cities* (2009). He has also published three novels, most recently, *Quinn's Passage* (2005), and three collections of essays. He has translated Sohrab Sepehri and Marguerite Duras. He is the founding editor of Nightboat Books and editor of the Poets on Poetry Series from the University of Michigan Press.

I did not use the word "gay" in my book because I wanted it to quiver under the pressure of the unsaid.

I used three versions of the word "god"—there was "god" and "God" and "G-D." The copyeditor wanted to standardize but I argued they are three different words and they mean three different things at different points in the text.

Is it a book or is it a film script or is it (I suspect it is) sculpture.

In any case I thought of it as "autobiography" if anything. "Memoir" means you are remembering, or at least interrogating how memory (the way the present constructs the past) acts on or changes the present moment. More than this, I was constructing the past as the present (and the future, too). It was process in motion. That's where I live or where I knew I could find myself.

And "poetry?" I guess you could call it that if you must, but the fact that some consider *Bright Felon* "poetry" is actually depressing to me. So much has music and fervor and fever evaporated from poetry for such a fairly straightforward narrative book to be categorized as poetry simply because it is made of sentences instead of paragraphs, and badly behaved sentences, at that.

Yes it is deeply entrenched heterosexism (a belief in genre manifests as a belief in gender—they are rooted in the same impulse: that a body (or text) must "behave" according to the social rules that govern it) that makes *Bright Felon* into "poetry."

I did not use many question marks and tried to avoid commas. I followed Gertrude Stein who thought these two punctuation marks to be expressions of fascism.

Meena Alexander's book *Fault Lines* taught me that the present and the past implicate each other. And that one could write again the story of one's life.

I found a lifeline in this line of poetry by Gillian Conoley: "I approached as an alias, a trachea without sound, my signature, bright felon."

I did not mean to "experiment"—which in scientific parlance means to repeat actions within a controlled environment in order to learn something new. My life is not experiment after all. Said M. NourbeSe Philip (I heard from Bhanu Kapil who heard from Mg Roberts): "The purpose of avant-garde writing for people of color is to prove you are human."

To place myself: city by city. Was my silence related to the fact I have had no home, that I have moved and moved again and again. Or did I move because I could not be human, could not open my mouth, could not insist on my own life.

My book was a detective novel. I had to know the answer to save the life of the young ingénue. Who was in this case me.

City by city and backward in time though the narrative progressed forward.

Infinity in the heart of me.

And the hero of the book: not me, not the lost lover, not the new one who found me, but a little boy who appears in the epilogue, a little boy in the garden on Montjuïc in Barcelona who is calling out for his mother.

And so I came to understand my life through the writing of it and was able to act and speak. There is conclusion to the book or the life.

Bright Felon continues: to have deleted scenes, alternate endings, notes for the screenplay adaptation. But these are all fictions.

Truth is I could never write the book again. And everything I wrote for it is in it. I wrote it between November 2006 and March 2007. The rest was editing but nothing was added only deleted.

So when one tells a secret one also compromises the resource from which poetry comes. That pressure of silence was released. What is left for me.

I had a secret left to keep. The secret subtitle of the book is written in orange on the cover in Urdu script. It is a couplet of American poetry translated into Urdu and written out.

Only a person who can read Urdu and knows enough about American poetry will be able to read and decipher it.

I'm looking for that person. Is it you.

To tell a life, to know it, you have to include movements of the mind. In my case I refracted the narrative through the classical arts: calligraphy, geometry, architecture.

I imagined a space in which I could breathe, in which I could speak.

It was no experiment. If it is "innovative" for one such as I to live at all, to be brave, then count me in that number. I am mad to recite my own unspelled self.

My every life in language had wandered. Planets stood in a sky loaded with light waiting.

For what. For him or her, the other one out there in the world having read my book to have had already begun.

HYBRID WORK
From Bright Felon: Autobiography and Cities
Washington, DC

Georgetown. The late afternoon sun is dark as honey sliding down
M street in beginning of summer.

There is an Arab restaurant inviting Muslims to break their fasts behind
the high and metal doors.

The fourth of July weekend I should have returned home to visit
Ammi-jaan, sick with cancer for three months, I took Vietnamese
take-out to the small canal now covered with green, sat there reading
a comic book, thick in my loneliness.

Remember, we used to sit on the second floor of the bookstore, in
the café, looking down over the street, each with a stack of books. I kept
thinking I might find myself there, maybe knowing deeply that I would
stay lost.

Still, the sounds of talk and cars, the thick French soup, the warm wood
of the pier, Jason's soothing voice, always putting me together.

Jason loves to put things together.

The night I moved down to Washington, DC, driven by my elder sister
and my brother-in-law my right upper-wisdom tooth broke in my
mouth. The shards stayed there for two more years before I could afford
to have a dentist pull it out.

It would be two more years before I would have enough money to have
the other three extracted.

The late afternoon sun is dark as beginning to break.

Behind the high and metal doors my home.

The small canal now covered with green.

Remember, we used to sit there together, reading.

Ammi-jaan had already died by the time I went home a month later.

Paradise lies beneath the feet of your mother.

My father, as usual, read the services. "If any of you have a grievance against Jaffery Sayeed, forgive her for it now," he said, "and if she has a grievance against any of you beg her forgiveness."

Because I had not come home in time, because I never wanted to come home, keeper of secrets I was, I burst into tears and couldn't stop.

She'd left and turned to tell me.

What.

Nothing.

Afterwards I lay down in the bed praying for something real and for the silence to unfold its hands and show me.

There wasn't any way.

My friend wrote to me from Albany about a new student in her Greek class who reminded her of me in his torment between god and the body.

Having not yet realized there was a mind-self and a body-self inside me along with the third who is with them.

She flirted with him by giving him a poem she originally had written to me.

Which of us would play Apollo and which of us would play Dionysus.
No one who knew us could tell.

Now I know Jason was more Apollo and more Dionysus both
than I ever was. If any opposite pair I am Persephone and Hades
who took her.

The myths do not write me though because I am I. There wasn't one
before me.

When I said what I said in the cold afternoon, when I said finally what
I needed to say in that house, my father asked me, "Are you a Muslim?"

Dumbstruck, I had no answer.

I am I, a driftless star, disowned from his own constellation.

Who will be able to find the polar star now?

How I become a man is an unwritten book.

Because finally, at the end of it, I am not Isaac who cried out in anger
against his father, but the other son, the elder one, the darker one.

The obedient one. The one who said, "You asked me to lie down and
I lay down."

Who said, "Father, if this is God's will, let it be done. You will find me
among the steadfast."

That's how it happened to the son who went into the desert with his
mother and father.

To starve.

Who knows how things fit and what you are supposed to say.

I know how things fit. You are not supposed to paint on your wall, but we did, Jason and I.

He was an echo at first, an earlier version of me. If he was an earlier version of me then he was the one I wished I had been not the one I had been.

The one I had been: ugly, ashamed, frustrated, hedonistic, undesired.

A wretch really who flew from one room to another without any need or understanding.

Staying up late into the night, smoking cigarettes and wondering.

My friend, the classics professor, obsessed with phoenixes and nursing her own desires, saw Jason on the street once near her apartment. She too saw him as a version of me and walked behind him, following him into her own apartment building, a building I myself had once lived in when I was in Albany.

I meet a million and one furies. My first experience being pressed against the earth.

A hot river to drown me or the plates of the earth moving apart and then together to crush me between them.

Have you ever been so thrown down, so twisted to disappear with liquid into the air.

She watched Jason walk down the hall with his keys and then unlocked the apartment that had been mine: 92 Willett Street, Apartment 1D.

After they had become friends, after she had given him the poem, after she confessed it, after he and I started writing to each other, I wondered to myself if the dreams he was having, the conflict between his own spirit and bodily desires were mine somehow, left in the apartment, physical things.

It being a story of politics, he painted two little boys on the apartment in DC—a boy in an arab gelbab and keffiya and another with curly hair, red shirt and black shorts.

When he left I had to paint over this little mural, the failed echo of what I had tried to do—love regardless of my culture, my religion, the social pressure I faced.

When will I break the fast and tell the story of our silence?

Let me not leave it at the failure. I am traveling back in time for a reason.

Let me leave it that first day before I knew him, before I loved him.

He and his friends were traveling down to Washington to see the AIDS quilt. We had arranged to meet.

I was at a breakfast meeting. Leaving the meeting early I made my way down to the National Gallery of Art café.

Had to fight my way through a huge rally and march of striking custodial workers.

I got to the gallery early in spite of my adventures, and sat there watching people walking in, trying to piece together Jason's description of himself, wondering which of them was he. Each time a person roughly matching his description arrived, in the seven seconds between their appearance and realization each was not he, I pieced together a whole imaginary life.

NECESSARY AMBIGUITY

Exploring Hyphenate Identity

Jennifer Bartlett

Genres, like grammar, have an agreed-upon set of rules or conventions. Similarly, societies also impose guidelines that their citizens are expected to follow. In American society, men are expected to refrain from wearing dresses. American marriage, until recently, was "supposed" to be a monogamous arrangement between a man and a woman. And overall, contemporary society remains, architecturally and otherwise, geared toward people who do not have physical, mental, or psychological impairments.

Genre, grammar, and literary form often mirror society's restrictions, and this is not a wholly bad thing. People do need a system of rules in order to communicate and live relatively peacefully. Societal mores such as "Do not murder" or "Please wear clothes while outside" are helpful. However, what happens when the "identity" of any given person resists the narrow societal container: when disability or alternate relationships come into play? How does such a writer, perhaps out of necessity, navigate and resist presubscribed form? Hence, the hybrid is born.

Early in my career, I only desired to be a poet. Working outside of one discipline struck me as awkward, and improbable. I wanted to be deeply involved in the disability poetry movement, and I wanted to resist that desire entirely, too. But as I progressed, I found that I didn't want to do

Jennifer Bartlett is the author of *Derivative of the Moving Image* (2007), *(a) lullaby without any music* (2012), and *Autobiography/Anti-Autobiography* (2014). She also co-edited *Beauty Is a Verb: The New Poetry of Disability* (2011) with Michael Northen and Sheila Black.

just one thing. I wanted to become a researcher and to write a biography of the poet Larry Eigner. I wanted to make visual art as well. I also wanted to write a memoir. I wanted this memoir to be about my 15-year marriage transforming into an "open marriage" and my subsequent exploration of my sexuality; an exploration that had been stunted by societal preconceptions about disability. A hybrid memoir was not a conscious choice. It was an opening, a way to move through the work; I am, at heart, a poet. The piece leaves much unexplained, but I think somehow the affairs of life are necessarily ambiguous. And having an "impaired" body, or one that does not meet society's narrow expectations, necessitates creating a new form.

Something about having a child (or children) can deeply change the way women write and think—it changed me, too. In a letter, Denise Levertov chided Jonathan Williams for slacking off from the busy work of promoting her book—she, a poet and "busy housewife at that." While few women now are jumping to claim the title, the *responsibilities* of the so-called "housewife" remain with us, whether we work outside the home or not. Alice Notley and Alicia Ostriker both write about the separation of the "soul" after childbirth—Notley calls this separation "doubling." How can one's form and considerations in writing *not* change from time to time, especially after the time restrictions placed upon the body and the soul by children? The mere fact that I am a "householder" makes my work all that much more fragmented. My work needs to multi-task. It is written in fits and starts. My considerations not only mirror my life, but my body as well. I have cerebral palsy, and as a consequence, I move more slowly than most and get tired easily. My body is fragmented, my soul is doubled; how could my work not be fragmented as well?

Throughout the memoir, however, the speaker/embodied I assumes central focus. The person referred to as "the husband" is never named and always identified with his title, or the position in the writer's life. The "lover," also not named, is called "you." "You" also addresses the reader. *I want to be part of this unit: not the whole of it* is a fundamental line in the memoir. None of the other characters—the husband, the lover, the parents, and the implied child—are named because they exist merely in relation to the woman. They are not meant to be fully developed characters, but rather symbols of the writer's life.

The memoir is a consequence of my grappling with my own perceived entrapment, in marriage and motherhood. It is a way of coming to terms with the strictures of life in an "impaired" body and with marriage—an institution able-bodied women have been examining for years.

The hybrid form mirrors the hybrid content: the desire for continuity and sense making in my life; the need for rules and containers, and the desire to burst them when they become too small. Thus, most of the memoir is written in very short paragraph form, because paragraphs evoke the narrative. But the paragraphs are short because they are only meant to be representative snapshots and need to cover a lot of territory. The sections in lines are meant to be interludes—moments outside of the lineal space and time of narrative. This memoir is not a case for polyamory; nor is it a case against it. This memoir is a map to myself, the non-standard size and shape to encompass all the non-standard parts of my life.

HYBRID WORK
Excerpt from My Body Is (the) Marginalia; The Sun Drawn a Saw Across the Strings.

how much does one's ability to feel the other depend on one's feeling for oneself
       how much does one's ability to be for the other

depend on one's ability to be for oneself

    we are all windows

hold still in the light

the edginess / every year / o it's so painful / to let go

                                etched on the river's sound
                                the water has to suffer

I was a kind friend
held in the branches of dreamers

and I loved you so

*We went to Grand Central Station. I turned you to the wall so that I could
speak to you through the arch. I had planned to tell you how much I loved you.
But you were so cranky and nervous. Turning your back to all these people. We
sat on someone else's stoop and ate our breakfast. You learned the words solace,
longing. Fall inched closer. Her birthday.*

I'm afraid your fingerprints are far from disabled.

I want to change my pronoun to they
That way there will be one of me
For each of you at all times.

In the bed, I sat next to where you slept and I burned.
In sleep, your body curved toward me
Through dreaming you said *Question.*

I dreamt that my uncle had had all the tattoos scrubbed off his skin
Or was that you, dearest?

Sometimes, the days row me. Sometimes, I row the days.

I like your knees. By this I mean all kinds of things.

Nontraditional relationships remain nontraditional and yet, for all my defensiveness, everyone knows and no one cares, even the people in my life who are religious. There is something about people who have been married who know that marriage is a next to impossible journey. My mother wants to know if I love you. My father simply doesn't understand why I don't lie to my husband, how can he come to terms with my honesty? Society tells us we are all meant for one kind of relationship, but then why do so many people separate?

My husband says he might be bisexual.

The vow to only give my body to only one person for the rest of my life troubled me. Once I chose to give myself only to my husband, I was no longer my own. When I am with you, my body is my own. There is nothing about my body that belongs to you, nothing in you that belongs to me.

I want to be part of this unit: not the whole of it.

As I progress, the four voices become a chorus and it becomes impossible to distinguish one from another. *I wish I had a bed that was you.*

The facts of my life are minimal, and I've named most of them here. I have mild cerebral palsy due to a trauma at birth. I grew up around able-bodied people. My parents divorced. My grandmother died. My mother was found temporarily insane (which is now, perhaps, attributed to post-partum depression) and committed briefly to the mental hospital. During those few days my infant sister and I were in an orphanage. My father moved to France. My mother remarried. I had many responsibilities and few freedoms. I changed parents. I fell in with the gays. Ashley died. I met friends who would stay with me for life. Emma died. Then college, then more college. A love affair. A move East, poetry and so on. Marriage. Elizabeth died. Then John & Louis shot themselves. A baby who grew up to be a brilliant, obstinate boy. Dion died. Sasha died. Feminism. *I met you in a fish restaurant.*

NOT NOTES, NOT APHORISMS, NOT FRAGMENTS, NOT POETRY

Composing *Bluets*

Maggie Nelson

The below is adapted from Maggie Nelson's responses to Ben Segal's interview with her called "The Fragment as a Unit of Prose Composition," in continent. *Volume 3, Issue 1 (2011): 158–170.*

I have always pronounced *Bluets* "bluettes," which is kind of a personal joke about feminization. Like, "majorettes," etc. It's a joke because I think the book has a lot to do with the robustness of being a female human, so I found irony in the diminutive nature of the suffix. I also liked the fact that the word means a kind of flower, as it allowed each proposition, or whatever you might call each numbered section, to be thought of as a single flower in a bouquet. This sounds cheesy here, but I think I talk about this idea in a less cheesy way in the book itself, near the end, when I'm ruminating on its composition, and its surprising (to me) slimness, or "anemia."

Often while writing, I'd re-read the books by Roland Barthes written in fragments—*A Lover's Discourse: Fragments*, for instance—and see what he gained from an alphabetical, somewhat random organization, and what

Maggie Nelson is the author of five books of nonfiction, including *The Argonauts* (2015), *The Art of Cruelty: A Reckoning* (2011, named a *New York Times* Notable Book of the Year), *Women, the New York School, and Other True Abstractions* (2007, winner of the Susanne M. Glasscock Award for Interdisciplinary Scholarship), and *The Red Parts* (2007), as well as four books of poetry, including *Something Bright, Then Holes* (2007), *Jane: A Murder* (2005, finalist for the PEN/Martha Albrand Award for the Art of Memoir), and *Shiner* (2001). She teaches in the School of Critical Studies at California Institute of the Arts.

he couldn't do that way. I mostly read Wittgenstein and watched how he used numbered sections to think sequentially, and to jump, in turn. I read Sei Shōnagon's *The Pillow Book*, and tried to keep a pillow book about blue for some time. (It didn't last long, as an exercise, but some of the entries made it into *Bluets.*) I re-read Peter Handke's *A Sorrow Beyond Dreams*, which finally dissolves into fragments, after a fairly strong chronological narrative has taken him so far.

In a course I taught on the fragment, which was somewhat after the fact of writing *Bluets,* but conceived in relation to it, we studied a kind of taxonomy of fragments: the decayed fragment (Sappho); the contemporary fragment (text messages, Twitter, blog posts, etc.); the Modernist fragment (T.S. Eliot; fragment as mark of psychological disintegration); Freud's fragment (dreams, slips, etc. as thruways to the unconscious); the sampled or plagiarized fragment; fragment as waste, excess, or garbage; the footnote; fragment as frame (Degas, Manet); life narrative as fragment: we can't see the whole until we're dead, and then we can't see it (pathos); fragment as psychological terror (castration, King's head); fragment as fetish, or as "organ-logic," as pornography; fragment as metonym and synecdoche; fragment as that which is preserved, or that which remains; fragment as the unfinished or the abandoned; and so on and so forth.

I think, in the back of my mind, I was aware of all these categories while writing *Bluets,* and put them each into play as needed while writing. The book seems to me hyper-aware of the fragment as fetish, as catastrophe, as leftover, as sample or citation, as memory, and so on. Many of the anecdotes in the book (such as about the decay of blue objects I've collected, or my memory of a particularly acute shade of blue, or the recountings of dreams) perform these concepts quite directly.

I am interested in the notion of collecting, of a collection—and how to know when to stop, when you've amassed enough. While writing *Bluets,* I thought of Joseph Cornell as the ultimate teacher in this respect: he collected enormous amounts of junk, he "hunted" for treasures all over the city, but each box or collage or even film has a certain minimalism, each feels as if it's been distilled to become exactly as specific as it should be. In other words, the composition emanates from the piles of junk left in its wake, but it in itself becomes perfect. It may be unfashionable, but I'm interested in this sense of perfection.

I don't really like it when people called *Bluets* "notes" or "aphorisms" or "fragments," because it's not really any of those things. Aphoristic philosophy—which was one of this book's inspirations—is not made up of just aphorisms, per se. There may be great aphorisms to be found in Nietzsche or Wittgenstein, for example, but neither is writing a series of one-liners. Their projects are bigger than that. They are in dialogue with argumentation as much as with impression. Likewise, I don't really see *Bluets* as poetry. I mean, I don't care if someone wants to call it that—if they do, it happily expands the notion of poetry—but I've written enough poetry to have a lot of respect for its particular tools, which include the line break, and forms of logic unavailable to prose.

Bluets always had a specific set of dramatic personae, and also a sort of narrative arc. It begins by saying, "Suppose I were to begin," which places the whole book, at least for me, in the realm of the novelistic, or at least the speculative. That freedom was important to me while writing. I have a lot of issues, for lack of a better word, with narrative, but I also have no problem with trying to structure a work so that it acts as a page-turner. I wanted there to be a lot of momentum, as well as plenty of opportunities for eddying out into cul-de-sacs. That was the tension—how to make some chains of propositions that pull you forward, and then allow for some to bring you so far afield that you might find yourself wondering, "Why are we talking about this here?" before remembering how you got there, and why it might matter.

While some of the fragments may seem disconnected or distinct, the truth is that they each had to fall into one of the book's major categories, which included love, language, sex, divinity, alcohol, pain, death, and problems of veracity/perception. If I truly couldn't tether an anecdote or factoid to the thread, it eventually had to go. I also spaced out the distinct threads fairly methodically, and had the characters reappear at a fairly regular rate.

I'm sure one could write a book of very disconnected fragments that didn't so overtly weave into a whole—I've read many of them—but it's also true that the mind will always work overtime to put disparate things together; the Surrealists mined that tendency for all it was worth. I think that's a cool approach, to let the reader make the connections, but it's important to me as a writer to make sure that the connections, when made, actually point toward what I want to be pointing at, rather than just reflecting the human brain's capacity to make a bridge.

HYBRID WORK
Excerpt from Bluets

1. Suppose I were to begin by saying that I had fallen in love with a color. Suppose I were to speak this as though it were a confession; suppose I shredded my napkin as we spoke. *It began slowly. An appreciation, an affinity. Then, one day, it became more serious. Then* (looking into an empty teacup, its bottom stained with thin brown excrement coiled into the shape of a seahorse) *it became somehow* personal.

2. And so I fell in love with a color—in this case, the color blue—as if falling under a spell, a spell I fought to stay under and get out from under, in turns.

3. Well, and what of it? A voluntary delusion, you might say. That each blue object could be a kind of burning bush, a secret code meant for a single agent, an X on a map too diffuse ever to be unfolded in entirety but that contains the knowable universe. How could all the shreds of blue garbage bags stuck in brambles, or the bright blue tarps flapping over every shanty and fish stand in the world, be, in essence, the fingerprints of God? *I will try to explain this.*

4. I admit that I may have been lonely. I know that loneliness can produce bolts of hot pain, a pain which, if it stays hot enough for long enough, can begin to simulate, or to provoke—take your pick—an apprehension of the divine. *(This ought to arouse our suspicions.)*

5. But first, let us consider a sort of case in reverse. In 1867, after a long bout of solitude, the French poet Stéphane Mallarmé wrote to his friend Henri Cazalis: "These last few months have been terrifying. My Thought has thought itself through and reached a Pure Idea. What the rest of me has suffered throughout that long agony, is indescribable." Mallarmé described this agony as a battle that took place on God's "boney wing." "I struggled with that creature of ancient and evil plumage—God—whom I fortunately defeated and threw to earth," he told Cazalis with exhausted satisfaction. Eventually Mallarmé began replacing "le ciel" with "l'Azur" in his poems, in an effort to rinse references to the sky of religious connotations. "Fortunately," he wrote Cazalis, "I am quite dead now."

6. The half-circle of blinding turquoise ocean is this love's primal scene. That this blue exists makes my life a remarkable one, just to have seen it. To have seen such beautiful things. To find oneself placed in their midst. Choiceless. I returned there yesterday and stood again upon the mountain.

7. But what kind of love is it, really? Don't fool yourself and call it sublimity. Admit that you have stood in front of a little pile of powdered ultramarine pigment in a glass cup at a museum and felt a stinging desire. But to do what? Liberate it? Purchase it? Ingest it? There is so little blue food in nature—in fact blue in the wild tends to mark food to avoid (mold, poisonous berries)—that culinary advisors generally recommend against blue light, blue paint, and blue plates when and where serving food. But while the color may sap appetite in the most literal sense, it feeds it in others. You might want to reach out and disturb the pile of pigment, for example, first staining your fingers with it, then staining the world. You might want to dilute it and swim in it, you might want to rouge your nipples with it,

you might want to paint a virgin's robe with it. But still you wouldn't be accessing the blue of it. Not exactly.

8. Do not, however, make the mistake of thinking that all desire is yearning. "We love to contemplate blue, not because it advances to us, but because it draws us after it," wrote Goethe, and perhaps he is right. But I am not interested in longing to live in a world in which I already live. I don't want to yearn for blue things, and God forbid for any "blueness." Above all, I want to stop missing you.

9. So please do not write to tell me about any more beautiful blue things. To be fair, this book will not tell you about any, either. It will not say, *Isn't X beautiful?* Such demands are murderous to beauty.

10. The most I want to do is show you the end of my index finger. Its muteness.

11. That is to say: I don't care if it's colorless.

12. And please don't talk to me about "things as they are" being changed upon any "blue guitar." What can be changed upon a blue guitar is not of interest here.

13. At a job interview at a university, three men sitting across from me at a table. On my CV it says that I am currently working on a book about the color blue. I have been saying this for years without writing a word. It is, perhaps, my way of making my life feel "in progress" rather than a sleeve of ash falling off a lit cigarette. One of the men asks, *Why blue?* People ask me this question often. I never know how to respond. We don't get to choose what or whom we love, I want to say. We just don't get to choose.

14. I have enjoyed telling people that I am writing a book about blue without actually doing it. Mostly what happens in such cases is that people give you stories or leads or gifts, and then you can play with these things

instead of with words. Over the past decade I have been given blue inks, paintings, postcards, dyes, bracelets, rocks, precious stones, watercolors, pigments, paperweights, goblets, and candies. I have been introduced to a man who had one of his front teeth replaced with lapis lazuli, solely because he loved the stone, and to another who worships blue so devoutly that he refuses to eat blue food and grows only blue and white flowers in his garden, which surrounds the blue ex-cathedral in which he lives. I have met a man who is the primary grower of organic indigo in the world, and another who sings Joni Mitchell's *Blue* in heartbreaking drag, and another with the face of a derelict whose eyes literally leaked blue, and I called this one the prince of blue, which was, in fact, his name.

15. I think of these people as my blue correspondents, whose job it is to send me blue reports from the field.

16. But you talk of all this jauntily, when really it is more like you have been mortally ill, and these correspondents send pieces of blue news as if they were last-ditch hopes for a cure.

17. But what goes on in you when you talk about color as if it were a cure, when you have not yet stated your disease.

WRITABLE RADIANCE
Notes on the Hybrid of Lyric and Prose

Gregory Orr

I've always relished the fundamental writer's decision: to turn the world into words and then to order those words. It seems to me that the orderings of narrative—chronology, action, description, dialogue and interaction, and character revealed through time—are compelling ways of speaking about human experience. On the other hand, I've spent my life as a lyric poet, and we poets tend to do a lot of our ordering through heightened rhythm, sonic patterns, and metaphor.

The violent and chaotic experiences of my early life were especially daunting when I tried to convey them in straightforward prose. A simple listing of some of the incidents might give an idea of how intimidating I found the material to be: an infant brother's death from swallowing pills; a younger brother's death at eight from a hunting accident in which I, a 12-year-old, held the gun that killed him; my mother's overnight death when I was 14 and we lived in the backwoods of Haiti; my father's long-concealed drug addiction and his own childhood secret, that he'd accidentally killed his best friend with a rifle when he was 13; my adventures in

Gregory Orr is the author of 11 collections of poetry, including *River Inside the River* (2013), *How Beautiful the Beloved* (2009), *Concerning the Book That Is the Body of the Beloved* (2005), and *The Caged Owl: New and Selected Poems* (2002). His memoir *The Blessing* (2002) was chosen by *Publishers Weekly* as one of the 50 best nonfiction books of the year. His four books of essays and criticism include *Poetry As Survival* (2002). He has been the recipient of a Guggenheim Foundation Fellowship and a National Endowment for the Arts Grant.

the Deep South at 18 working in the Civil Rights Movement. The latter included beatings and jail and being kidnapped by armed vigilantes in rural Alabama and held in solitary confinement for a vivid, terrifying week.

I was reluctant to write the story of my childhood and adolescence partly because I doubted the power of prose to stabilize these events and to discover meaning in them. Or, put another way, I doubted my ability to use the resources of prose to successfully communicate my story.

A related issue: I've never had an easy relationship to narrative prose. Its very strengths—the way its language clings to the world and describes it accurately, the way it tends to construct meaning in the light of chronology and cause and effect—can make me uncomfortable as writer and as reader. For some reason, I can feel a sense of entrapment and claustrophobia in prose not unlike what I think Emily Dickinson was lamenting when she wrote: "They shut me up in Prose— / As when a little Girl / They put me in the Closet— / Because they liked me 'still'...." (445).

A part of the lyric temperament seeks to rise up out of the body and out of time—the classical definition of ecstasy. Poets inclined to such "lyric longing" often use metaphor and imagination to rise up—think of Keats in his "Ode to a Nightingale," transported up there where the bird sang, high above all human suffering. Lyric wants to go vertical, whereas prose seems to me strongest when it flows confidently with the horizontal, the time-bound particulars of observed action and interaction.

It's not as if I consciously choose to alternate narrative prose with associative imagery or prose-poem-like chapters in my book *The Blessing*— what I experience in memoir writing is that when the narrative gets too intense, an image appears and this image seems to reveal some aspect of the story or the self or life as I understand it. What I'm calling an image is actually an object or thing: a turtle or a bottle—some item seen in the light of imagination and thus capable of revealing an aspect of being (as the French philosopher Gaston Bachelard insists such items should). Images and symbols carry the weight of the observer's feelings and emotions and yet are real: the bottles I found as a kid in the woods, pastoral trash. They seemed eager, when I wrote about them, to reveal multiple meanings, to hint at how debris can transform into beauty by simply being lifted up—arrayed, luminous and jewel-like, on a windowsill. And those same mundane bottles carry also my childhood longing to reach my mother and gain her attention and love: my wish to be cherished as I imagined the colorful bottles were.

And then there's the issue of beauty, which we lyric poets often feel is integral to meaning in some mysterious way. As a poet, I feel that to seize beauty, the flow of time must be stopped by some imaginative method—perhaps metaphor or symbol. A pause must be imposed so that the object being contemplated can take on that essential, cryptic quality called "radiance"—that place where human mysteries (wonder, love, loss, being a body in time) shine through some object in the world. Without beauty, the story, whatever it is, is too bleak for me.

And doesn't beauty smuggle in the longing for meaning? In writing the "Bottles" section, I had vivid memories of scrabbling in rusty junk piles in the woods, peeling back layers of leaves in search of old bottles I could bring to my mother. But that action, those memories, seemed inert as description, and I knew I needed to find some way inside the boy I was, who spent all those hours like a squirrel scrabbling and scratching the forest floor. An image from a dream of finding the coin with the Roman empress' head gave me access to this subjectivity. The sense I had when I awoke, that that empress was my mother, led me toward the naïve reverence and awe I felt as a child toward my mother, and to the recovery of a vanished world. No one seems to know what beauty is—it has infinite different definitions—but without it meaning isn't possible for me.

We lyric poets can tend to brood over the subjective, emotional dimension of experience. We do our best to try to dramatize it and make it shareable, but when we write prose we're often in danger of being static and boring and self-involved. I love the way action and facts move prose forward. To combine the accuracy and action of embodied narrative with the ecstasy of imagination and metaphor to create poetic memoir—what could be more fun? What could be a more gratifying dance to perform with language: to have both the truth of narrative and embodiment (which is often suffering, and frequently joy) and the periodic need for release.

HYBRID WORK
Excerpt from The Blessing

3 *from* The Accident

...A faint, gray light was just seeping up from the eastern horizon as we arrived at our trench. Our whole group paused there as Bill, Dad, and I removed our gloves and each loaded a single shell into his rifle. My hands trembled with cold and excitement as I slid the hollow-point bullet into the chamber of my .22 and clicked on the safety catch that would prevent any accidental firing until I was ready to shoot. We set the rifles on the ground beside us and began the awkward clambering down into our hillside excavation that had been dug by two somewhat lazy workers [my brother and me] to hold three and was now being asked to accommodate five. It did so somehow and packed us in so tight that what we lost in mobility, we gained in body heat.

Now, all was silence broken only by whispers and the occasional distant caw of crows. As the gray light grew, I watched the frost flowers scattered across the dirt mount a few inches from my face melt like the stars going out overhead. I watched my breath rise up in wisps like the mist off the dew-drenched reeds. I waited as patiently as I could. And then we saw it: a deer slowly working its way along the trail through the power-line swamp and out into the field below us, where it paused to browse the short grass. An antlered buck! Dad whispered that Bill would shoot first. This order, if a whispered statement could be called an order, stunned me. What could he possibly mean? Was this another one of those "you'll have your chance when you're older" routines? Did he mean that if Bill missed, I could shoot? Or did he imagine that our luck would be so extraordinary that if Bill killed this deer, a second one would appear this same morning? Surely he couldn't imagine that I would wait for another day. There was no time to explain to Dad how wrong-headed he was being. No time to tell him I *had* to take part, that it would be impossible for me not to shot at this deer, too. As Bill put his rifle to his shoulder and took aim at the deer, I, too, lifted my .22 with the one bullet in the chamber and sighted along the barrel. And when Bill fired, I fired too, at the exact same instant, so that our two rifles made a single harsh sound that echoed off the woods as the deer collapsed in the green field.

Whooping and yelling, the five of us scrambled down the brush-grown slope and raced to where the deer lay dead in the low grass of the field. We stood around it in a loose circle of awe. By now, my father had calmed down.

"Check your chambers," he said.

At this command, each of us was supposed to point our rifle straight down at the ground and pull the trigger to make sure the gun was empty. If, by some mischance, the bullet had misfired, then the gun would discharge harmlessly into the dirt at our feet. But I was still delirious with glee at what I had accomplished, since it was obvious to me that I, too, not just Bill, had brought down our quarry. I *knew* my pulling the trigger now would only produce the dull mechanical click of a firing pin in an empty chamber.

I was wrong. In my excitement after the deer fell, I must have clicked the safety again and now, instead of pointing my rifle barrel at the ground, I casually directed it back over my right shoulder toward the woods and never even looked as I pulled the trigger. And Peter was there, a little behind me, not more than two feet from where I stood. In that instant in which the sound of my gun firing made me startle and look around, Peter was already lying motionless on the ground at my feet. I never saw his face—only his small figure lying there, the hood up over his head, a dark stain of blood already seeping across the fabric toward the fringe of fur riffling in the breeze. I never saw his face again.

I screamed. We were all screaming. I don't know what the others were screaming, but I was screaming "I didn't mean to, I didn't mean to!" My father was yelling that we must run for help. I started off across the field toward the house as fast as I could. I ran straight across the swampy stream that split the field and scrambled up the bank and through the barbed-wire fence. I felt Bill and Jon running behind me. I was trying to get to the house first, as if somehow that could help, but what I had done and seen was racing behind me and I couldn't outrun it. That's what I wanted to do: run some place where it had never happened, where the world was still innocent of this deed and word of it might never arrive. But I knew that wasn't possible and that even now I was desperately running toward more horror, toward the moment when I would reach the house and when, no matter how exhausted and out of breath I was, I would still have to tell my mother that I had shot Peter....

5 Child Mind

I don't know how adult minds arrive at meanings. I don't know what they need, or how they figure things out. But here are two stories about children and how they think. When my wife, as a child, first heard the opening phrase of the prayer "Our Father who art in Heaven," she imagined a bearded man wearing a smock and a beret, holding a paintbrush in one hand, a palette in the other, and standing before an easel. And why not? Here was a Creator God. Here is the figure who might well have painted the bright primary arc of the rainbow as a symbol of his good intentions toward his people. I'm not surprised my wife became a painter.

The other story about how children think isn't so charming and benign. I heard it from my younger brother, Jonathan, only recently, when he learned I was writing this book. It was a story he had never told anyone except his wife in all the time since the accident. The week of [our brother] Peter's death, Jonathan was scheduled to have a math test, which he knew he couldn't possibly pass. That Sunday evening, just before he climbed into bed, he prayed to God: "God, if you just get me out of this math test, I will never ask you for anything else again. Just help me this once, please." We didn't go to school that week after the accident, and when we finally did, Jon's math test was long forgotten.

As Jon sat in his room, as he watched neighbors enter to dismantle Peter's brass bed and carry it out to be stored in the barn, as the slow days went by and he tried to comprehend what had taken place, an awful realization dawned on him: God *had* answered his prayer. God had heard his selfish request and had granted it by killing Peter.

6 Numb

I was numb at the funeral. I remember almost nothing except a white curtain that was drawn to keep us, the family, separate from the rest of the mourners. We sat in a little alcove. I remember the chairs—the same folding metal ones I'd set up or folded countless times in the school gym or at Cub Scouts or in church basements. I don't remember people, except as kind of whispering around me. And where was I? I was deep in a desert wilderness as desolate as that inhabited by those early, God-tormented, Christian saints who lived their whole lives alone on top of stone columns. Only I wasn't on top of the column, I was embedded inside it, as if it were a shaft of pure shame transparent as Lucite, and I was immobilized inside it, like an insect or some unusual beetle. I heard people whispering around me like the desert breeze around the pillar, but I couldn't move or look up, and so as far as I could tell no one was there.

The gravesite was a two-hour drive from our town—across the Hudson and north into the Heldeberg Hills southwest of Albany, where we had lived when I was first born. As we drove home, in the dark, I felt my faith in the devouring God grow stronger. I saw that Death, his angel, was everywhere, that it had entered our lives and I had opened the door to welcome it. I saw that it could enter in the spectacular, terrible form of Peter's violent death, but that it could also insinuate itself in minor ways, in numberless tiny shapes you might not even notice until they had worked their way toward a beating heart in order to still it. Sitting in the dark in the backseat during that long drive, I saw that death was with us. It was the small white snail of wadded Kleenex my mother kept pressing against her face; it was nibbling holes in her cheek as if it was a leaf. I saw that death was the moonlight's patch of blue mold growing on my father's shoulder as he drove, oblivious, through the deep night.

When I tried to sleep that night and for years after, I could only do so if I began in one position: flat on my back with my arms crossed on my chest and my legs hooked over each other at the ankles. Lying like that in the dark room, in the pose of a mummy in an Egyptian sarcophagus, I calmed myself toward sleep. I imagined I was both the body inside, immobilized in its wrappings of thin linen strips, and the wooden case itself, painted with the expressionless face and figure of its dead occupant. I was afraid of my thoughts and afraid of the dark. I needed a double magic of rigidity to brace me against the violent storms of my dreams.

14 Bottles

In a dream last night I was digging in muddy earth and rubble and found a silver coin with the head of a Roman empress, but somehow I knew it was my mother's face, the features worn smooth yet still discernible. I rubbed it until it was clean, until it grew warm in my hand.

It reminded me that, besides country furniture bought at farm auctions up and down the Hudson Valley, my mother also collected antique bottles. On my various solitary wanderings in the woods around the red house, I'd sometimes come up on a spot where a farmer, years before there was a town dump, had hauled his trash. Usually some large, unidentifiable object rusting among the trees marked the spot. Or I might actually find the cellar hole of a house long gone and vanished from anyone's memory.

When I found such a place, I'd dig down with a stick or my bare hands, rummaging about in the humus for any bit of buried glass that, unearthed, might be a whole bottle. I must have looked odd, on my hands and knees scrabbling through the leaves in the middle of the woods, like a squirrel searching for fallen nuts. My fingers still remember the sensation of peeling back the strata of hickory leaves—the top layers light brown and dry and lifting off in large patches like bandages, then each successive deeper layer darker and more compressed, the leaves now fragmented and finally wet and cold and traced through with white and yellow threads of mold. And every once in a while, the gritty feel of ancient iron where a can has become nothing but a filigreed bracelet of rust.

Often I'd find the remnants of the metal teapots popular on farms at the turn of the century—a white-speckled gray like guinea hen feathers. And many patent medicine bottles, whole earth-hue rainbows of greens and browns and ambers. The cobalt blue of Phillips' Milk of Magnesia seemed especially magical to my child's eyes, though after I'd brought a few home as trophies, I began to grow more sophisticated under my mother's instruction. Soon, I was holding each find up to the sunlight, searching for the varying thickness of walls or bottoms of trapped air bubbles—any irregularities that might show it was hand-blown rather than merely poured in a mold. Once I discovered a dark-green bottle with an ingenious stopper—a glass marble resting inside the neck in such a way that when you tipped to pour, it rolled forward and out of the way of the gushing fluid, and then when the bottle was turned upright again, the marble dropped back to cover the opening.

What I found I took home to her—a way of trying to please her, whose love I was so unsure of. I'd watch her wash them in the sink and place them in rows along windowsills, where they glowed brightly. That was the idea, that was my own vague longing: to be lifted up out of the earth into the light.

4
. . . .
Prose Poetry

PROSE POETRY
An Introduction

Although the prose poem may not utilize the line breaks associated with poetry, forming instead a block of text, it retains poetry's techniques, among them fragmentation, compression, repetition, rhyme, and heightened language. And while the earliest tradition of prose poetry dates back to China's Han Dynasty (206 BCE–220 CE), the prose poem, as we understand it today, began in France with Aloysius Bertrand's *Gaspard de la Nuit* (1842), which in turn influenced Charles Baudelaire's *Le Spleen de Paris* (published posthumously in 1869). Baudelaire's series of "petites poems en prose" invest concrete, often biographical subject matter with abstract, dreamlike energy. The following lines from Louise Varese's translation of "The Double Room" encapsulate this energy: "Here the soul takes a bath of indolence, scented with all the aromatic perfumes of desire and regret."

The prose poem calls into question our sense of what a poem ought to be, one reason it was passionately embraced by France's next generation of writers, most notably by Arthur Rimbaud and Stéphane Mallarmé. The Surrealist poets who followed innovated the prose poem further, and the form soon found itself a part of the French canon. From France the prose poem spread to writers working in English including James Joyce, Oscar Wilde, and Gertrude Stein. Writers in Russia, most notably Ivan Turgenev, and Poland's Boleslaw Prus also worked with the prose poem's flexibility, as did Latin American writers including Mexico's Octavio Paz and Chile's Gabriela Mistral. Japanese poets, too, embraced the form. Yasushi Inoue, who published his first book of prose poems, *Hokkoku* (*The North Country*), in 1958, described the collection not as poetry but as containers he created so that the "poems" he experienced should not escape entirely.

The extensive debate that arose with the Modernists about whether or not prose poetry is actually poetry bears mentioning here. In his 1917 essay "Reflections on Vers Libre," T.S. Eliot argued vehemently against it. Charles Simic, who won the Pulitzer Prize for his prose poetry collection *The World Doesn't End* (1989), famously said: "The prose poem has the unusual distinction of being regarded with suspicion not only by the usual haters of poetry, but also by many poets themselves." Yet the early work of Homer, too, would have looked more like prose poetry than lineated verse given that poetry was initially passed down orally. The audience listened for a change in rhyme scheme instead of a line break.

Echoing Percy Bysshe Shelley's praise of the Bible as poetry, contributor Mark Jarman points out in his essay: "Anyone who grew up reading the Authorized King James Version of the Bible would have believed that its poetry was written as prose because the poetry of the Psalms, of the Prophets, of Solomon's Song of Songs, of Job, of Jesus, in the KJV are all set typographically as blocks of prose." Jarman's words underscore the prose poem's protean appeal for so many contemporary writers, among them Campbell McGrath, whose playful piece "The Prose Poem" enacts part of what he—and others—find so compelling:

> On the map it is precise and rectilinear as a chessboard, though driving past you would hardly notice it, this boundary line or ragged margin, a shallow swale that cups a simple trickle of water, less rill than rivulet, more gully than dell, a tangled ditch grown up throughout with a fearsome assortment of wildflowers and bracken. [...]

Freedom is what the prose poem offers, freedom from line breaks, yes, but also freedom from what William Olsen calls "codification and how-to-aesthetics."

In his introduction to *Great American Prose Poems: From Poe to the Present* (2003), editor David Lehman discusses the origins as well as the specific distinctions of the prose poem in America, ultimately defining the form through its use of the demotic, its willingness to locate the sources of poetry defiantly far from the spring [...] sacred to the muses." The prose poem's colloquial elements, too, can also be central to its liberating feel.

The contributors anthologized here have experienced various kinds of liberation in their own explorations of the form. For Mary Szybist, who worked exclusively in the lyric until late in the writing of her second book, *Incarnadine*, the form allowed for expansiveness: "If a stanza is a lyric 'room,' then perhaps a prose paragraph is the largest room, the one that can hold the most motley and unlikely crowd." In "Invisible Green," which opens *Greenhouses, Lighthouses*, Tung-Hui Hu created a poetic space for nonfiction reportage. "Source documents could be copied wholesale into the text, like any other piece of prose," he notes in his essay.

Subsuming, exploding, and/or interrogating the lyric "I" is fundamental to the works of both Carol Guess and Sabrina Orah Mark. In *Doll Studies: Forensics*, Guess employs prose poems as miniature dollhouse dioramas to depict real-life crime scenes and interrogate them. *Do the patterns form clues?* Guess' poems ask. *Or are the rhymes intended to mislead?* In Mark's *Tsim Tsum,* the reader is tasked with parsing the exchanges of the characters of Beatrice and Walter B. as they undergo a series of disorienting journeys. Dialogue in this collection reads like the characters' attempts to tether themselves to the bizarre world they now inhabit. Baudelaire, a stranger or at least a highly sentient observer in his native Paris, would certainly have admired Mark's opening to her process essay, one that bears on all the work excerpted here: "I write an essay on the prose poem. It begins, 'the prose poem is a home where everything else is in exile, and where exile is where everything belongs.'" Quite simply—yes.

—*Jacqueline Kolosov*

IT'S DARK IN THERE

Confessions of a Prose Poem

Sabrina Orah Mark

Hybrid is from the Latin *hybrida*, which means "offspring of a tame sow and wild boar, child of a freeman and slave."

The opposite of hybrid is pure.

Hi Bird. Hide Bread. Honey bride. Hymn bard. Home blood. Him brown. Her red. High build. Hidden boards. Hem born.

Mongrel. Bastard. Crossbreed. Mule. Half-Blood. Incross. Incross?

My sons, Eli Winter (almost one) and Noah Juniper (almost three), are African-American and White and Jewish and my husband is a fiction writer and we live in Georgia in a big blue house. I grew up in Brooklyn and went to Yeshiva and my husband who is 19 years older than me was a military brat so he grew up nowhere.

So he grew up everywhere.

The opposite of hybrid is pure.

I am asked to submit poems to the Academy of American Poets for their

Sabrina Orah Mark lives in Athens, Georgia with her husband and their two sons. She is the author of the poetry collections *The Babies* (2004) and *Tsim Tsum* (2009). Her poetry and stories have most recently appeared in *Tin House (Open Bar)*, *American Short Fiction*, *jubilat*, *B O D Y*, *The Collagist*, *The Believer*, and in the anthology *My Mother She Killed Me, My Father He Ate Me: Forty New Fairy Tales* (2010).

Poem-A-Day program. I haven't been writing poems. I have been writing something else? What do I call them? Little fictions? Poem stories? Prose poems? No, not really. I send one that stars a bully named Beadlebaum and a husband named Poems and another about milk that has gone wild. I apologize. I say I understand if they're of no use.

They are of no use.

I write an essay on the prose poem. It begins, "The prose poem is a home where everything is in exile, and where exile is where everything belongs."

My son Noah points up and says, "It's dark in there." I say, "Where?" "In there," he says. He waves his hands around as if to signal everywhere.

The Kabbalists call the phase in Genesis when God departs from the world so that the world can come into being a Tsim Tsum.

My husband has been married twice before me. He has two daughters from his first marriage and one daughter, E, from his second. E is, of course, my stepdaughter.

"I loved not being dead when I was a kid." (Maurice Sendak)

The opposite of hybrid is pure.

My husband's daughters from his first marriage are R & M. I go to R's bridal shower. I am introduced by a friend of R's as R's mother-in-law. I try to correct her. I am not my husband's oldest daughter's mother-in-law. I explain my husband has been married twice before so I am and I am not really her stepmother. I am not her stepmother.

I receive a rejection from a literary magazine. The editor writes, "I wish these had more ballast." Ballast. A heavy material (such as rocks or water) that is put on a ship to make it steady or on a balloon to control its height in the air.

There are daughters who are more beautiful than their mothers and then there are mothers who are more beautiful than their daughters.

A well-known young African-American poet tells a friend of mine that no one will ever forgive me for marrying my husband. I understand and I do not understand what he means by this.

Above my writing desk is a print that reads FACTS MUST BE FACED with an image of a rooster standing on top of a sheep standing on top of a pig standing on top of a cow. The cow is wearing the identical hat my grandfather, when he was alive, wore to synagogue.

My husband tells me that in 40 years white people will be a minority in this country.

When I tickle Noah and Eli they are delighted because for a moment I am both their monster and their mother.

"The prose poem is the result of two contradictory impulses, prose and poetry, and therefore cannot exist, but it does." (Charles Simic)

For months I have a blackish floater in my right eye. My better eye. On multiple occasions I shoo it away, mistaking it for a fly. In a story written by my husband called "Uncle Moustapha's Eclipse," a man suffers from the same eye malady I seem to have. But in the story the dark spot that at first flashed on and off just remains there, hanging in the air. And then it begins to grow.

"Writing a prose poem is a bit like trying to catch a fly in a dark room. The fly probably isn't even there, the fly is inside your head, still, you keep tripping over and bumping into things in hot pursuit. The prose poem is a burst of language following a collision with a large piece of furniture." (Charles Simic)

"This is so nice and sweet and yet there comes the change, there comes the time to press more air. This does not mean the same as disappearance." (Gertrude Stein)

Tsim Tsum spelled backwards is Mist Must, which feels apropos to the writing process. First there is the fog (mist), and then there is the necessary thing (must). Or, maybe must here is decay, or fetor, or fustiness. Mist the rot! Spray it!

The opposite of hybrid is pure.

A friend of mine, a teacher, lost her husband to a hideous form of heart cancer, and raised four sons, two of whom have special needs. She is recently remarried to a wonderful man, also a widow, with two daughters. She tells me that being a stepmother is the hardest thing she's ever done. I want to say to her it's because stepmothers have no ballast. The job should come with rocks and water.

Being a stepmother is like being a prose poem. We should not exist, wish the stepchildren, but we do.

"See the moon? It hates us." (Donald Barthelme)

When I gave birth to my sons my mother wasn't there. My midwife was there and my husband was there.

The opposite of hybrid is pure.

HYBRID WORK
From Tsim Tsum

The Saddest Gown in the World

"I do not give anymore," said Walter B., "a fig about you." "Are you sure?" asked Beatrice. "Absolutely," said Walter B. "Not a fig?" asked Beatrice. "Not a fig," said Walter B. "Promise?" asked Beatrice. "Promise," said Walter B. "When do you suppose," asked Beatrice, "you will give about me a fig again?" Walter B. looked up at the sky. "Probably not for many years," said Walter B. "Oh," said Beatrice. "Should I wait?" "Of course," said Walter B., "you should wait." "I'd be very happy," said Beatrice, "if you joined me while I waited." Walter B. squeezed her hand. "One day," said Walter B., "I will make for you a sewing of all the figs I never gave about you." And one day Walter B. would. He would sew all the figs together. It would not be easy, but he would do it. If he could promise Beatrice anything he could promise her this. He would make for Beatrice a perfect sewing of all the figs he never gave about her. She could wear it, thought Walter B., like a gown. And everyone would applaud.

The Name

When Walter B. discovered Beatrice that winter inside his chest, he began to suspect that something for Beatrice had never happened. Something perhaps like a name, he thought to himself, as he carried her. He carried her into the parlor. And he carried her into his bed. All winter he carried her, inside his chest, like a Beatrice without a name. When the spectacle came to town he carried her to the spectacle. And when the spectacle left town, he knew he would go on carrying her without the spectacle for a long time. All winter, he carried her. There were times he did not want to go on with this carrying. There were times he wanted to tie around her neck a thin bundle of sticks and send her out. But something for Beatrice had never happened. Something like a name. And this was a world, thought Walter B., a world inside which a Beatrice could not live without a name. He studied his chest and marveled at its smallness. He could not, like this, go on. If he could find for Beatrice a name, thought Walter B., he could empty her out. If he could find for Beatrice a name, a name that would last, he could go on without her. A name like Poland. Or Abigail, for example. But first he would have to remove Beatrice from Beatrice. But how? How does a Walter B., wondered Walter B., remove a Beatrice from a Beatrice so that he can find for her a name. A name that could empty his chest of a Beatrice. He hadn't meant to go on carrying her for this long. But he went on carrying her. He carried her inside his chest for a long, long time. He carried her until one day she was gone. And the space in his chest where he had once carried her grew large. He marveled at its largeness. And he knew he would go on carrying this largeness, this largeness that was once inside him a Beatrice, for a long, long time.

Long Ago and Far Away

"Doing some housekeeping?" asked Walter B. "What was that?" asked Beatrice. "Housekeeping. Are you doing some housekeeping?" "If by housekeeping you mean time travel, then yes, I am doing some housekeeping." "Can I do some too?" asked Walter B. Beatrice thought for a moment. Lately, it seemed, Walter B. had not a feather to fetch. Not a fish to mangle. Ever since the carousel ride he seemed lost. He should not have gone twice in all that dampness and fog. Beatrice had begun to notice a deep whir coming from Walter B.'s chest. As if somewhere unimaginably long ago and far away Walter B. was still going around and around. "Are you up to speed?" asked Beatrice, hoping for the best. "If by up to speed you mean standing next to you, then yes, I am up to speed."

Walter B. was in fact standing next to Beatrice. "Hello there," said Beatrice. "Hello," said Walter B. "Fine," said Beatrice, "let's help each other into our swimsuits and proceed." "To the ramparts!" shouted Walter B. "Yes, dear," said Beatrice, snapping him in, "to the ramparts." And off they went to look for the Walter B. Walter B. once was before the terrible mistake of the carousel ride.

The Creation

The first time Walter B. died Beatrice announced she would stand in the street until this never happens again. "Until what never happens again?" asked Walter B., embracing her. "Until this," she said. "Until what?" asked Walter B. "This!" said Beatrice, shaking herself loose from his arms. "What are you," asked Beatrice, "new in the neighborhood?" "Yes," said Walter B., "I am new in the neighborhood. That is," he continued, "if it is this neighborhood you are referring to." They looked around. It was, in fact, a new neighborhood.

The second time Walter B. died it was, according to Beatrice, indecorous.

A few moments before Walter B. died for the third time he mourned the fact he would only use the word *crepuscular* once in his life, and incorrectly. "I would have felt this life more complete, sweet Beatrice, had that word referred to a wonderful party rather than to twilight. As in, 'tonight, my love, I am going to the crepuscular without you!'"

The fourth time Walter B. died the man who arrived to break for Beatrice the news of Walter B.'s fourth death resembled Walter B. although his appearance was less ambitious than Walter B.'s appearance would have been had Walter B. arrived to break for Beatrice the news of Walter B.'s fourth death.

The fifth time Walter B. died he seemed distracted. "You seem," said Beatrice, "distracted." "What?" said Walter B. "Distracted," said Beatrice. "Oh," said Walter B. "What do you call this," he asked, holding up one of the children. "A child," said Beatrice. "Oh," said Walter B. "A child."

The sixth time Walter B. died, Beatrice investigated the crime. "Who," asked Beatrice, "has done this to you?" Walter B. shrugged. "For god's sake," cried Beatrice, "tell me. Was it the children again? Was it me? Who has ruined you, my darling?" "If you must know," said Walter B., "it was The Collector with his sack of paper animals." "A suffocation!" gasped Beatrice. "No, my little bird," he said swinging her around by the waist, "it was the most colorful trample I could have ever hoped for. Wish you were there," he sang. "Wish you could've come with."

For three days after Walter B. died for the seventh time, Beatrice moved from room to room calling for him. For three days. And then she stopped. She knew he would die again. "He simply has to," she said to herself, hanging his robes in the trees where he would be sure to find them.

AMPLITUDE

On the Possibilities of Prose

Mary Szybist

A few years ago I decided to read exclusively poetry on my regular bus rides through Portland. Talking about this decision over coffee one afternoon with the poet Endi Bogue Hartigan, who inspired the idea, we reflected that fiction on the bus drew us so completely into its imaginative worlds that we tuned out and missed the experience of each day's ride: its particulars, the people entering and exiting.

Reading poetry is a different kind of experience. When my mind is holding a line, a stanza, a phrase from a poem, I often find myself more alert to my senses, to what is unfolding around me. A poem's language becomes another layer of the present world—and even a lens to magnify or sharpen—rather than an entry point to an alternate one. I've found this true even of narrative poems as their use of lines actively slows the narrative momentum; with each break, I'm thrown back to the page. Through lines, rhythm, rhyme, and so on, poems call attention to their own composition, reminding me that I am experiencing a made thing. Subsequently, perhaps because I have to be cognizant of language and form, and because I have to concentrate harder, they won't let me disappear into their worlds in the way "transparent" prose does.

Of course much of this could be said about some works of fiction, so these distinctions between poetry and prose are crude and problematic,

Mary Szybist teaches literature and creative writing at Lewis & Clark College in Portland, Oregon. She is the author of two books of poetry, *Granted* (2003), a finalist for the National Book Critics Circle Award, and *Incarnadine* (2013), winner of the 2013 National Book Award for Poetry.

and they quickly fall apart. I mention them because, as I try to think about why I turned to prose poetry, the distinctions my own mind has made and carried—the stories I have told myself about their differences—seem relevant. I reached toward prose late in the process of writing my second collection, *Incarnadine,* and the writing seemed, at first, a break from poetry. The pieces didn't initially feel like poems.

As an undergraduate I fell under the spell of Killarney Clary's *Who Whispered Near Me* and Lyn Hejinian's *My Life,* collections of prose poems. They were prose poems that really felt like poems, poems that seemed to me to resist absorption more sharply than most lineated poems. "It is what I'm afraid of that hints at what I desire," begins one of Clary's poems, before skipping forward and opening voluminously—to a "comfortable screened porch on an eastern beach in Indian summer," to "holding a gun," to "good anger" that "won't work toward a finish when there is none"—with an intimate logic of its own. I developed an assumption that lyric "leaps" had to be more radical in prose poetry precisely because there was no leaping between the lines; I developed an assumption that prose poems had to astonish with their strangeness—"we who love to be astonished" (Hejinian). Didn't prose poems have to prove they were poems? Didn't they have to be radically different from ordinary prose? I did not think of them as spaces to relate story, information, or even the vividness of a world—which is what I suddenly felt myself wanting to do.

I think my own early attempts at prose poetry fell flat because I was afraid that my prose would be *prosaic.* I loved the way that Clary and Hejinian included the so-called mundane and swerved between the ordinary and extraordinary, but the mundane made me nervous—so I cut away, far away, from it constantly. I was uneasy that I might be writing prose rather than prose poetry, so I made each sentence move in a different direction, made each juxtaposition willfully bizarre. Whatever energy motivated the poems, I tended to diffuse it into incoherence.

At the same time, prose's ability to engage with the ordinary was also what attracted me to it—"It's what I'm afraid of that hints at what I desire." I reached for prose because it is so ordinary that it is almost invisible as a form; it is steady, predictable, and it can elastically stretch to accommodate what is brought to it. If a stanza is a lyric "room," then perhaps the prose paragraph is the largest, most ample room.

In *Incarnadine* I had been trying to re-write myth. As I worked to complicate that mythic realm, I felt the need for more poems grounded in the everyday historical, human world, its modes of language and thinking. In "Another True Story," I was thinking about journalism and storytelling, the kinds of "proof" both offer (and how quickly one bit of "evidence" often persuades us not only to believe a claim, but to jump to a belief that it is evidence of something larger). In "Entrances and Exits," I began by letting myself simply report the day's news—from the radio, the newspaper, the small happenings in my office. In "Update on Mary," I entertained myself by imagining myself as an anthropologist recording my daily behaviors. In "To Gabriela at the Donkey Sanctuary," I imagined I was simply writing a letter.

At some point I began to consider the possibilities of these pieces as poems, and I liked the challenge of writing prose poems that felt dangerously close to prose. I wanted to invite absorption into a contemporary domestic sphere that inhabited the mundane, to linger there between and even through disjunctions. Not being able to offer "full access" to the imaginative realm of the mythic Virgin-Mother-of-God Mary, I wanted to offer access—more access than was comfortable to me—to my very un-mythic life as *a* Mary.

I have always loved the moments in Shakespeare's plays where the play breaks out (that is how I have thought of it: *breaks out*) of the realm of prose into that of verse. When I was in high school, I played the role of Viola in *Twelfth Night*, and I felt her relief when she was able to untangle herself from the baser prose of the comic characters and enter into more elevated entanglements.

It has taken me longer to appreciate how much real drama—dark and unnerving—unfolds in the prose of that particular play, with its greater skepticism toward "antique tunes." I began to feel the play's prose held more darkness—and more humor. Maybe this was in the back of my mind when I turned to prose: I wanted to hold more of both.

For me, finally, I think what most distinguishes the prose poem from other kinds of poetry is its ampleness, its amplitude, its ability to hold so much at once without breaking. With such room for everyday detail, for the dark and the humorous, I found it easier to create a fuller world within prose, a world that can be entered, not just glimpsed, and that can transport a reader from his or her present reality, whether that is on a bus or somewhere else. Still, even when the prose poem offers such absorption, it also—if by nothing else than its brevity—calls attention back to the made thing on the page. It was my desire to try my hand and ear at making art of everydayness that drew me to this form balanced precariously between poetry and prose.

HYBRID WORK
From Incarnadine

Entrances & Exits

In the late afternoon, my friend's daughter walks into my office looking for snacks. She opens the bottom file drawer to take out a bag of rice cakes and a blue carton of rice milk that comes with its own straw. I have been looking at a book of paintings by Duccio. Olivia eats. Bits of puffed rice fall to the carpet.

A few hours ago, the 76-year-old woman, missing for two weeks in the wilderness, was found alive at the bottom of a canyon. The men who found her credit ravens. They noticed ravens circling—

Duccio's *Annunciation* sits open on my desk. The slender angel (dark, green-tipped wings folded behind him) reaches his right hand toward the girl; a vase of lilies sits behind them. But the white dots above the vase don't look like lilies. They look like the bits of puffed rice scattered under my desk. They look like the white fleck at the top of the painting that means both spirit and bird.

Olivia, who is six, picks up the wooden kaleidoscope from my desk and, holding it to her eye, turns it to watch the patterns honeycomb, the colors tumble and change—

Today is the 6th of September. In six days, Russia will hold a day of conception: couples will be given time off from work to procreate, and those who give birth on Russia's national day will receive money, cars, refrigerators, and other prizes.

A six-hour drive from where I sit, deep in the Wallowa Mountains, the woman spent at least six days drifting in and out of consciousness, listening to the swellings of wind, the howls of coyotes, the shaggy-throated ravens—

I turn on the radio. Because he died this morning, Pavarotti's immoderate, unnatural Cs ring out. He said that, singing these notes, he was seized by an animal sensation so intense he would almost lose consciousness.

Duccio's subject is God's entrance into time: time meaning history, meaning a body.

No one knows how the woman survived in her light clothes, what she ate and drank, or what she thought when she looked up into the unkindness of ravens, their loops, their green and purple iridescence flashing—

I think of honeybees. For months, whole colonies have been disappearing from their hives. Where are the bodies? Some blame droughts. Too few flowers, they say: too little nectar.

Consider the ravens. They neither sow nor reap, they have neither storehouse nor barn, and yet God feeds them. (Luke 12:24)

The men never saw the ravens—just heard their deep *kaw, kaw* circling.

Olivia & I look down on Duccio's scene. I point to the angel's closed lips; she points to his dark wings.

The blue container of rice milk fits loosely into Olivia's hand the same way the book fits into the hand of Duccio's Mary. She punches a hole in the top and, until it is empty, Olivia drinks.

Another True Story

The journalist has proof: a photograph of his uncle during the last days of the war, the whole of Florence unfolding behind him, the last standing bridge, the Ponte Vecchio, stretching over the Arno and—you could almost miss it, the point of what is being proved—a small bird on his left shoulder.

Above the rubble, Florence is still Florence. The Duomo is intact, and somewhere in the background, Fra Angelico's winged creatures still descend through their unearthly light, and Da Vinci's calm, soft-featured angel approaches the quiet field—

The war is almost over. The bird has made its choice, and it will remain, perched for days, on his shoulder. And though the captain will soon go home to South Africa and then America, though he will live to be an old man, in this once upon a time in Florence, in 1944, a bird chose him—young, handsome, Jewish, alive—as the one place in the world to rest upon.

When Noah had enough of darkness, he sent forth a dove, but the dove found no ground to rest upon. Later he sent her again, and she returned with an olive branch. The next time she did not return, and so Noah walked back into a world where every burnt offering smelled sweet, and God finally took pity on the imaginations he had made.

Some people took the young captain, walking around for days with that bird on his shoulder, to be a saint, a new Saint Francis, and asked him to bless them, which he did, saying "Ace-King-Queen-Jack," making the sign of the cross.

Saint Good Luck. Saint Young man who lived through the war. Saint Enough of darkness. Saint Ground for the bird. Saint Say there is a promise here. Saint Infuse the fallen world. Saint How shall this be. Saint Shoulder, Saint Apostrophe, Saint Momentary days. Saint Captain. Saint Covenant of what we cannot say.

Update on Mary

Mary always thinks that as soon as she gets a few more things done and finishes the dishes, she will open herself to God.

At the gym Mary watches shows about how she should dress herself, so each morning she tries on several combinations of skirts and heels before retreating to her waterproof boots. This takes a long time, so Mary is busy.

Mary can often be observed folding the laundry or watering the plants. It is only when she has a simple, repetitive task that her life feels orderly, and she feels that she is not going to die before she is supposed to die.

Mary wonders if she would be a better person if she did not buy so many almond cookies and pink macaroons.

When people say "Mary," Mary still thinks *Holy Virgin! Holy Heavenly Mother!* But Mary knows she is not any of those things.

Mary worries about not having enough words in her head.

Mary fills her cupboards with many kinds of teas so that she can select from their pastel labels according to her mood: *Tuscan Pear, Earl Grey Lavender, Cherry Rose Green.* But Mary likes only plain red tea and drinks it from morning to night.

Mary has too many silver earrings and likes to sort them in the compartments of her drawer.

Someday Mary would like to think about herself, but she's not yet sure what it means to think, and she's even more confused about herself.

It is not uncommon to find Mary falling asleep on her yoga mat when she has barely begun to stretch.

Mary sometimes closes her eyes and tries to imagine herself as a door swung open. But it is easier to imagine pink macaroons—

Mary likes the solemn titles on her husband's thick books. She feels content and sleepy when he reads them beside her at night—*The Works of*

Saint Augustine, Critique of Judgment, Paradigm Change in Theology—but she does not want to read them.

Mary secretly thinks she is pretty and therefore deserves to be loved.

Mary tells herself that if only she could have a child she could carry around like an extra lung, the emptiness inside her would stop gnawing.

It's hard to tell if she believes this.

Mary believes she is a sincere and serious person, but she does not even try to pray.

Some afternoons Mary pretends to be reading a book, but mostly she watches the patterns of sunlight through the curtains.

On those afternoons, she's like a child who has run out of things to think about.

Mary likes to go out and sit in the yard. If she let herself, she'd stare at the sky all day.

The most interesting things to her are clouds. See, she watches them even by moonlight. Tonight, until bedtime, we can let her have those.

To Gabriela at the Donkey Sanctuary

All morning I've thought of you feeding donkeys in the Spanish sun—Donkey Petra, old and full of cancer. Blind Ruby who, you say, loves carrots and takes a long time to eat them. Silver the beautiful horse with the sunken spine who was ridden too young for too long and then abandoned. And the head-butting goat who turned down your delicious kiwi so afterward you wondered why *you* hadn't eaten it.

Here I feed only the unimpressed cats who go out in search of something better. Outside, the solitaires are singing their metallic songs,
warning off other birds. Having to come down from the mountain this
time of year just to pick at the picked-over trees must craze them a
little. I can hear it in their shrill, emphatic notes, a kind of no, no in
the undertone.

Gabriela-flown-off-to-save-the-donkeys, it's three hours past dawn. All I've
done is read the paper and watch the overcast sky gradually lighten. Breaking news from the West: last night it snowed. A man, drunk, tied a yellow
inner-tube to his pickup, whistled in his daughter, and drove in circles,
dragging her wildly behind. . .

I know. But to who else can I write of all the things I should not write? I'm
afraid I have become one of those childless women who reads too much
about the deaths of children. Of the local woman who lured the girl to her
house, then cut the baby out of her. Of the mother who threw her children
off the bridge, not half a mile from where I sleep.

It's not enough to say the heart wants what it wants. I think of the ravine,
the side dark with pines where we lounged through summer days, waiting
for something to happen; and of the nights, walking the long way home,
the stars so close they seemed to crown us. Once, I asked for your favorite
feeling. You said hunger. It felt true then. It was as if we took the bit and
bridle from our mouths. From that moment I told myself it was the *not yet*
that I wanted, the moving, the toward—

"Be it done unto *me*," we used to say, hoping to be called by the right god.
Isn't that why we liked the story of how every two thousand years, a god
descends. Leda's pitiless swan. Then Gabriel announcing the new god and
his kingdom of lambs—and now? What slouches toward us? I think I see
annunciations everywhere: blackbirds fall out of the sky, trees lift their
feathery branches, a girl in an out-sized yellow halo speeds toward—

I picture her last moments, the pickup pulling faster, pulling rougher, kicking up its tracks in the slush: she's nestled into that golden circle, sliding toward the edge of the closed-off field—

I am looking at the postcard of *Anunciación*, the one you sent from Córdoba in the spring. I taped it to the refrigerator next to the grocery list because I wanted to think of you, and because I liked its promise: a world where a girl has only to say yes and heaven opens. But now all I see is a bright innertube pillowing behind her head. All I see is a girl being crushed inside a halo that does not save her.

This is what it's like to be alive without you here: some fall out of the world. I fall back into what I was. Days go by when I do nothing but underline the damp edge of myself.

What I want is what I've always wanted. What I want is to be changed.

Sometimes I half think I'm still a girl beside you—stretched out in the ravine or slouched in the church pews, looking up at the angel and girl in the colored glass, the ruby and sapphire bits lit up inside them. Our scene. All we did was slip from their halos—

Which is to say, *mi corazón*, drink up the sunlight you can and stop feeding the good fruit to the goat. Tell me you believe the world is made of more than all its stupid, stubborn, small refusals, that anything, everything is still possible. I wait for word here where the snow is falling, the solitaires are calling, and I am, as always, your M.

KING JAMES AND THE PROSE POEM

Mark Jarman

Anyone who grew up reading the Authorized King James Version of the Bible, published in 1611, would have believed that its poetry was written in prose. That is because the poetry of the Psalms, of the Prophets, of Solomon's Song of Songs, of Job, of Jesus, in the KJV are all set typographically as blocks of prose. Take verse 4 of Psalm 23:

> Yea, though I walk through the valley of the shadow of death, I shall fear no evil; for thou art with me; thy rod and thy staff they comfort me.

Hardly a sing-able translation of the Hebrew verse, but for the Jacobean translators of the Hebrew, it was closer to the verse form of the original. In order to make the Psalms available as hymns, at least for Scottish congregations, in The Scottish Psalter of 1650 they were rendered in meter and rhyme, in common measure, in fact, producing gems like the following:

> Yea, though I walk in death's dark vale,
>   yet will I fear none ill:
> For thou art with me: and thy rod
>   and staff me comfort still.

Mark Jarman is Centennial Professor of English at Vanderbilt University. He is the author of 10 books of poetry, including *Bone Fires: New and Selected Poems* (2011). He has also published two collections of his prose, *The Secret of Poetry* (2001) and *Body & Soul: Essays on Poetry* (2002), and a volume of prose poems, *Epistles* (2007).

The only convention of verse missing here is the initial capital in each line. The great eighteenth-century hymn writers, like the Wesley brothers, John and Charles, Isaac Watts, and others, did their best to recast this near doggerel into equally sing-able poetry. In the later American Standard Version or Revised Standard Version, translated between 1870 and 1901, the verse of the Bible was rendered into lines, without any straining at meter and rhyme. The result was a free verse which, in the late nineteenth century, has a surprisingly Modern look to it:

> Even though I walk through the valley
> > of the shadow of death,
> > I fear no evil;
> for thou art with me;
> > thy rod and thy staff,
> > they comfort me.

Reproducing this passage just now I had the uncanny sense that I was simply reprinting a passage from one of A. R. Ammons' long poems. But to return to my earlier point: the seventeenth-century translators of the Bible's poetry for the KJV were actually trying to reproduce the verse techniques of the Hebrew original. These were forms of parallelism, and not metrical and rhyme schemes. In English, then, the result was apparently prose. In the eighteenth century Christopher Smart saw the possibilities for turning the prose into verse in his "Jubilate Agno," and, of course, in the nineteenth century Walt Whitman did, too.

The rhythms of prose have long been recognized as based on parallelism and repetition, even meter, but without predictable patterns, without the formalized stichic and stanzaic patterns, often united by rhyme, which have characterized most European poetry, including English poetry, until the twentieth century. I think it is, in fact, the King James Version of the Bible that provides an original foundation for English prose, and therefore for the prose poem in English. The term "prose poem" is sometimes dismissed as an oxymoron by those who would also dismiss prose poetry, but it is simply an accurate description of the poetry of the KJV. Psalm 23 is a prose poem, like the rest of the Psalms, like the Song of Songs, like Job, like the prophecies of Isaiah and the Beatitudes of Jesus.

When I turned my hand to the writing of prose poems, in the early 1990s, I had spent several years trying to master traditional verse in order to write poems that would not merely be exercises in meter and rhyme. I was especially interested in the sonnet. Having achieved a certain skill with meter and rhyme I began to understand that it was time to do something else, especially since for me the spontaneous act of composition was increasingly coming out in rhyming quatrains and couplets in iambic pentameter. A prose poem in the manner of the prose poetry of the King James Bible seemed to me to be an opportunity to create a hybrid of what I liked in traditional verse—patterns of repetition—and the less predictable parallelism and repetition possible in a prose paragraph or group of paragraphs.

I have been reading the KJV and its adjunct, The Scottish Psalter, since I was a child. My father, a Protestant clergyman, took his family from California in the 1950s to serve a church in Kirkcaldy, Fife, Scotland, for a few years as part of an aid program that our American denomination provided its British churches in the years after World War II. The KJV was the standard text in most Scottish churches, and as soon as I joined the Sunday School in Kirkcaldy, I was given a KJV New Testament, which had as an appendix "The Psalms of David in Metre," a version of the famous Scottish Psalter. As soon as we returned to the United States we returned to the use of the Revised Standard Version of the Bible. That may have resulted in my first recognition of crucial differences in dialects of written English. As a child I believed the KJV was Scottish English and the RSV was American English. Actually, I wasn't far off. But as a minister's son, in a household where the Bible was read daily, I can say that the poetry of the Bible, in both the KJV and the RSV, was as familiar to me as Mother Goose or Dr. Seuss. It took years of writing poetry as an adult before I recognized that the poetry of the Bible's prose and the prose of the Bible's poetry were available to me in the most intimate way for making the hybrid we call the prose poem.

HYBRID WORK
From Epistles

If I were Paul

Consider how you were made.

Consider the loving geometry that sketched your bones, the passionate symmetry that sewed flesh to your skeleton, and the cloudy zenith whence your soul descended in shimmering rivulets across pure granite to pour as a single braided stream into the skull's cup.

Consider the first time you conceived of justice, engendered mercy, brought parity into being, coaxed liberty like a marten from its den to un-coil its limber spine in a sunny clearing, how you understood the inheri-tance of first principles, the legacy of noble thought, and built a city like a forest in the forest, and erected temples like thunderheads.

Consider, as if it were penicillin or the speed of light, the discovery of another's hands, his oval field of vision, her muscular back and hips, his nerve-jarred neck and shoulders, her bleeding gums and dry elbows and knees, his baldness and cauterized skin cancers, her lucid and forgiving gaze, his healing touch, her mind like a prairie. Consider the first knowl-edge of otherness. How it felt.

Consider what you were meant to be in the egg, in your parents' arms, under a sky full of stars.

Now imagine what I have to say when I learn of your enterprising vicious-ness, the discipline with which one of you turns another into a robot or a parasite or a maniac or a body strapped to a chair. Imagine what I have to say.

Do the impossible. Restore life to those you have killed, wholeness to those you have maimed, goodness to what you have poisoned, trust to those you have betrayed.

Bless each other with the heart and soul, the hand and eye, the head and foot, the lips, tongue, and teeth, the inner ear and the outer ear, the flesh and spirit, the brain and bowels, the blood and lymph, the heel and toe, the muscle and bone, the waist and hips, the chest and shoulders, the whole body, clothed and naked, young and old, aging and growing up.

I send you this not knowing if you will receive it, or if having received it, you will read it, or if having read it, you will know that it contains my blessing.

My travels in Abyssinia

My travels in Abyssinia are at an end. I hear three kinds of singing around me at this instant. Each voice (it is night) is pleading. I need a *Dictionary of Commerce and Navigation.* I need silk stockings woven with elastic threads. I need cartridges, fruit pastilles. I need your word. Your solemn touch. A simple answer.

You know what it is like to cease to exist to everyone but yourself. The cyclone that damaged the national art treasure made you homeless. On the day of the spectacular assassination, you discovered the first symptom of your final illness. Indeed, you know what it is like to exist *like* everyone else. And yet you live, your name is official, you can point to the place that says you are who you say you are.

I can see you in a drained tide pool, a grainy lump that closes on the delicate tentacles of the sea anemone. What you wouldn't give to taste the salty mineral soup in which you flower. But the entire ocean has turned its profound interest elsewhere. And whole species die, not to mention those, like you, who thought they were one of a kind.

We are engendered by the same obscurity. And we can imagine that it loves us, as the irrational number loves the infinite places to the right of its decimal point. Buried in the deepest reaches of 22 divided by 7, beyond which lie enormous wastes of energy and perseverance, we can see necessity. The previous number gives birth to the next. That is the reason we live. Let this knowledge cradle you. The lullaby that rocks your heart says you will not be, only because you are.

Now as so often before, I have given when I hoped to receive. I need a manual on irrigation technique. I need tincture of benzoin to harden the blisters on my heels. I need a token of your esteem. Before I board the ferry, I want to see a courier pressing through the crowd, who will reach me as I put my foot on the bow and hand me... But how can you respond as I would have you respond?

You know how it is to set out, laden with all you will leave enroute. To look back and see the years, like chairs and tables, abandoned in the desert. To see days going under like trunks of china in the horse latitudes. Weeks and months jettisoned and floating in the zero gravity of space. You know how it is to take stock by repeating *at least, at least,* until all you have is your life.

Let this be like the prayer that God will always answer. The one that gives thanks for everything and asks for nothing.

We have reached a place where nothing looks back

We have reached a place where nothing looks back except what we know. Those who greet us raise a hand, step back one foot at a time, reflecting our gestures. Nothing looks back from rock face or tree trunk except our words—*face, trunk.*

I whisper this.

A student wrote from North Africa, in the desert he understood why there was only one God. Here I know why there are many.

Eternity

Eternity will be strange at first, because there will be no *at first.*

Still, try this. Think of blank times with other people's habits, when you had to eat with strangers and strange hosts, and follow their customs and rituals at table. A glassy patience took over. Through its panels even watching was a kind of starvation, a sort of drought. The portions lay stranded on large plates. The grace was minimal but stiflingly pious. There was nothing to drink. And the time ahead filled a football stadium.

Then you discovered their peculiar passions—genre fiction, dog racing. Suddenly you were an umbrella stand of questions. Time, almost like the drink you were denied, turned almost sexy. When you left, sated with information, and even a little drunk with a fizzy affection for the plain, stolid family of doorstops, they invited you back.

Heaven may turn out to be one long church service, with everyone in the choir. Or Thanksgiving dinner. You will be one in a crowd, singing Handel. Or stranded forever, eating with your extended family. If what they say is true, you'll be happy just to be there in your seat behind the pillar, near the back. Or at the children's table, in the corner.

Her mother was drying her hair. She'd been sick for two days and was taking medication. I was downstairs, reading, when my wife called and said our daughter had fainted. Our child, in her nightgown, her thick short hair now dry, was sitting on the floor before the sink in the bathroom. Her face was like putty, her pink lips gray, she wasn't wearing her glasses. Her mother remained cool, speaking to her, calling her name. She turned in my direction, and there was such a look of departure in her eyes, I wondered if we'd get her back. Her: our child. In a soft voice she said she couldn't see. She was like a traveller who'd gone to live in another country and stopped writing home. Then she regained her sight, her color returned. Soon she was chattering about how frightened she'd been, but also about what she'd done all day at home in bed—reading, homework, crosswords. The light had become too bright for her, she said, and she felt she couldn't speak, except softly. That was all. The first time she was sick, when she was a little thing, she had become dumb, an empty puppet. We had seen that face again—of a creature who had no earthly idea what had happened. She looked at us, her mother and father, as if we did not exist and as if we were the ones who had done this to her.

And that is how they look at us, both the damned and the saved. That is how they regard the living. And yet we can try to soften the picture. Look at your own hand and try to believe that once this thing grasped the heart of the sun. Look at it and imagine it returning to that heart, thrust there. And you follow it, pulled by the wrist, your body a banner of streaming atoms, signed with an unrecognizable name, which nevertheless is you.

The living will always misinterpret the last look we give them. It does not mean they are nothing. And it does not mean they are guilty. It means they are coming too.

To the Trees

How do you feel as you rear up or hunch over to seek sunlight? When young, as pliant almost as water, when old, second only to rock. I think you must feel that roots are better than roads, that the avenue to the sky is best straight up or crookedly up. That whatever happens around you is no more than rain or snow, even the building that embraces you, even the saw and stump remover that eat up all trace of you.

For the present you are stone, but let the wind rise and you sing and dance like bamboo. Your children are the dapples of sunshine in shade. Your ancestors bask on the mossy facets of your bark. And within is a coming and going of thirst and records of thirst, of flesh that fire would love to taste. You know the math that sends the fire branching upwards. You know the myth that lights the candelabra. Planets and stars gleam on your smallest twig ends.

You have held back the body of the wind. You have held back the onslaught of the heat. You have given me the idea of depth. You have revealed the nesting of microcosms, all while staying in one place. We came down from you and stood upright like you. Because you will not rush along with us we cut you down.

It's what's inside and outside that counts. Hollow with ant meal, your blossoms and leaves still come. Solid as granite, you can stand deadgray for decades. You bleed, you break, you rot. The massive inner framework fades, and there's a limp limb, a branch of brown leaves among green, a bridge across a stream, a back-breaking fall on a ranch-style house. You rot, you break, you bleed. You go up in smoke, sideways in fire, down and down and down.

In my metamorphosis, she appears in the doorway, wet from the shower and looking for a towel. We catch each other by surprise, goddess and little boy, and we are both changed. At times she is a row of eucalyptus, where the trees and the sunlight between them are the same smooth color. It is my fate to hunt for her everywhere except where that tree grows. At times I am pyracantha under her windowsill, burning to speak. It is her fate to believe I have nothing to say.

You are life to those who hold fast to you, but standing apart on the lawn, don't you all long for the forest canopy? To join and blot out the sky, with a dancing floor lifted to the sun for hawks and monkeys and orchids in the higher parts of shadow? Don't you all long to rise up and erect your shade?

Let me be neither branch nor leaf but one facet of your bark, deeply incised on all sides, gray in dry sunny weather, and in rain, showing a face of turquoise.

POINTING AT THINGS
A Short Guide to Writing Photographically

Tung-Hui Hu

Turn, please, to the index at the end of a nearby book. That list of words and numbers is a distant descendant from the first index, the *Index Librorum Prohibitorum*, compiled in 1564 by the Catholic Church to indicate books considered immoral and therefore unfit to be read. Perhaps that's why the index can seem so schoolmarm-ish and bland: tax codes, the Dow Jones Industrial Average, and cost-of-living indexes. An index is a reference, that which points at something else. But press a leaf between those pages or prick your finger and let a spot of blood fall on them, and you have an entirely different kind of index: that of a sign, a clue, or a piece of evidence. This second meaning has mostly fallen out of English usage, or become fused with the first meaning, but French keeps the two words separate: *index*, and then *indice*.

An *indice* is an after-effect, a mark of something that has already happened. It is the berry cobbler stain on a shirt worn at the office, or the haze of smoke after a quenched fire. These clues point backward in time, and connect us, however tenuously, to an original agent or moment, not unlike the way a lyric poem evokes the absent presence of its speaker. "Oh! Look over there," says a friend as he points at a bird flying away; I follow his (index) finger, having missed the bird itself.

Tung-Hui Hu teaches poetry and digital studies at the University of Michigan. He is the author of three books of poetry, *Greenhouses, Lighthouses* (2013), *Mine* (2007), and *The Book of Motion* (2003). His writing has been published in a wide range of publications, including *The New Republic, Ploughshares,* and *Martha Stewart Living Radio.*

These two ideas, bookish knowledge and lingering presence, often encounter each other in the medium of photography. A photograph provides information; it is factual because it is all reference: we are three people wearing brightly colored windbreakers around 4 p.m. on a clear July day, standing in front of this dome-shaped mountain and smiling; see—we are friends who have traveled to Yosemite together. But sometimes, ecstatically, a picture draws the viewer inside its *indice*. If you have ever felt the presence of faces from an old photograph looking back at you, you may have some sense of the past reanimated: a brief movement inside the present.

Could these two estranged modes be called forth at the same time? I resolved to teach myself to write photographically by choosing a subject—a lighthouse called the Smalls—that is also an index in its own right. It points to the location N 51°43'17", W 5°38'47" on a navigator's map, i.e., a reef 23 miles west of westernmost Wales, at the end of a dangerous Atlantic shipping lane. Each lighthouse's transmission is entirely repetitive and data-driven, meant to convey the station's individual signature: a chart of British lighthouses lists the Smalls light as "W Gp Fl (3) ev 15 secs," a white group of three flashes every 15 seconds. And yet out of this endless broadcast comes the pathos of the situation: Is anybody watching or listening? What time did the transmission fail?

Paragraph by paragraph, "Invisible Green" grew around the idea that *index* could set up *indice*, and documentary might house the lyric. Each paragraph resembled a single shot of a camera, whether a single fact or a single moment in time. On my desk I had compiled a stack of cargo manifests, physics treatises, archaeological surveys, and geographic handbooks. In the tradition of John Baldessari's tongue-in-cheek response to criticism that "conceptual art is just pointing at things," most paragraphs point at a document photocopied from the archives. Here the advantage of working in uniform blocks of prose became clear: source documents could be copied wholesale into the text, like any other piece of prose. Prose also allowed me to experiment with the best structure for the piece. Given the tawdry symbolism of my subject—lighthouses too often suggest inspirational posters—I did not, for instance, want to use the "I" voice that often holds a lyric essay together. Instead, I began to group paragraphs into brief sequences—a three-paragraph prose poem about nineteenth-century messages in bottles, for example. As these sequences began to accumulate, I shifted to the larger scale of the essay; the sequences of still images had begun to assemble themselves into a moving picture.

In the middle of the text, I offer the idea of a "determined watcher," someone who watches voraciously and dispassionately, like a surveillance camera, and is rewarded for his or her patience by that flash of green light that sometimes occurs on the horizon. Not long before its writing, I had spent some time with Tacita Dean's short film *The Green Ray* (2001). Working in 16mm, Dean traveled to Madagascar to shoot that "last second of greenness" before the sunset. It's a one-in-a-million experience: for his 1986 *Le Rayon vert*, Eric Rohmer tried for two months to film it, and failing, finally faked it. You can't find a green flash inside any frame of Dean's film, since, as an optical trick, the flash really moves inside your eyes. Her green flash is an apt metaphor for how a mere recording or transcription of an event can produce a momentary sense of presence—albeit one only visible through its afterimage.

So, in this essay about an essay, an afterimage: at the end of a business trip to London, due to a last-minute change of plans, I found myself with an unexpected 72 hours to spare and decided to visit Solva, the remote village where the Smalls lighthouse was first assembled. The poem had already been written, and the original lighthouse long abandoned, but I was intent on seeing the place for myself. The ocean was uncooperative and the boatmen did not think they could take me out to the Smalls. So I walked around on my own and tried to sight it from the shore. Near the harbor, I discovered a few iron bracings and a stone engraved *T. H. 1856*, T. H. being short for Trinity House, the British lighthouse authority. Walking around the peninsula and through St Davids, I stopped to look out every few minutes. I think the locals assumed I was trying to steal their WiFi.

At one grassy field full of cows, I was sure that I stood at the place where the lighthouse had been pieced together onshore. In the corner of the field was, indeed, a plaque with a picture of the lighthouse. I had not found my lighthouse. But I had found its historicity, which is to say its picture.

HYBRID WORK
From Greenhouses, Lighthouses

Invisible Green

> "Commanders of vehicles in distress are desired to make their usual signals. Rooms and bed are provided for shipwrecked seamen... Dead bodies cast on the shore are decently buried gratis."
> *The New Seaman's Guide and Coaster's Companion*, 1809

I

In 1772, the 26-year-old violinmaker Henry Whiteside began to build a lighthouse on a pile of rocks 20 miles off the coast of Pembrokeshire, Wales, called the Smalls. His design was unusual; the light perched on top of eight oak piers like the head of a stiff-legged octopus. Rather than making a solid base, Whiteside reasoned, he would let the force of the waves pass through the structure. But when the waves did so, the living quarters swayed violently; one visitor reported that a full bucket of water was half empty by the time he left. The force of the storm made each thing—bucket, glass, stove, table—resonant; it bent the lighthouse, shaping it into an instrument of music.

The violinmaker began his design by setting his compass point at N 51°43'17", W 5°38'47". Then he drew a circle, three miles out, the distance of cannon shot and therefore the distance of territorial waters. Another circle, four miles out, representing the reach of the Smalls' "pellucid green" beacon: he drew this intermittent light as a series of green dashes. A third circle, 12 miles, thick line: a brighter white light to warn of rocks. A series of concentric circles to represent the ocean, with the lighthouse fixed at the center. But a final circle should be drawn 40 feet out, representing a lighthouse keeper's circuit around the gallery railing in winter. He is at the center of the center; the world comes to him, wrecks itself on his shores.

2

They are out of rations; they are still waiting for lime juice and pickled vegetables. The owners are cheap; the resupply ships are late. Why, then, the rumor that lighthouse keepers "at the last stages of a decline... are prodigiously fat" when they leave their posts? A few years' duty at the Smalls, so they say, wards off consumption, breaks fever, and reverses wasting disease. How can the meanest personalities turn into jolly, good-spirited fellows; how can scrofulous, emaciated men walk in, and corpulent doubles walk out?

As one keeper, formerly a watchmaker, writes, this work is "rusting a fellow's life away." The rotating prisms operate through a clockwork mechanism—he knows how to wind and fix them; the lighthouse is simply a large watch to maintain and repair. But what he belatedly realizes as he is oiling the surface of the gearwork is that he is no longer working on a watch. *He* is the rusted mechanism standing at attention each hour, at twilight and at dawn; in the room full of whale oil and sperm candle, he is the one needing the grease. With no rations left, he eats the oil intended for the candles. Whale oil, rich as cod-liver oil, rich with vitamins, makes the keeper look almost healthy. Food for both stomach and eye. Stink of half-eaten light.

The surface of a glass photograph taken in the village of Solva, where the keepers are based, is pockmarked with white marks that mimic the keepers' vision after repeated exposure to lantern light. These marks seem to float halfway between us and the men on the other side; they are like the translucent deposits that cast shadows as they pass through the eye's vitreous humor. Three keepers gather around an uncomfortable wooden chair for the village photographer. The plate is old and the light unreliable, but none of the men seem particularly fat.

3

"The Smalls, it is said, belong to no parish, nor are they within any county; but they are nearest to the Welsh coast, and the inhabitants of the lighthouse are considered as parishioners of Whitchurch."

   A Topographical Dictionary of Wales, 1845

4

There is no plant life on Smalls reef, with the exception of a few edible algae: oarweed, channeled wrack, and thongweed. The clothes of the men bringing supplies to the Smalls may have reeked of mackerel and pollock, but the keepers instead smelled the roots of new potatoes growing in soil; they smelled flatness and fences and hips and the idea of territory. Money accumulated in bank accounts back home; as with everything else on the reef, it was difficult to see it grow.

5

This despite the fact that, for a time, the Smalls was the richest lighthouse in the world. Bringing in £10,510 a year in 1832 for the two widows who owned it, the Smalls charged light-duties from any ship that passed within 12 miles of the rock, whether or not they ever saw its light. "The waters got crowded daily and hourly with ships of mighty tonnage, / and every ton had to pay." So profitable were the abstract movements of ships on a map that the lighthouse's light increasingly became an afterthought. By the time its lease was repurchased by the Crown in 1836, the Smalls lamp shone at just one-eighth the candlepower of public lighthouses.

The sea, once limitless, was getting crowded. As the need for reliable news grew, insurers at Lloyd's commissioned a network of signaling stations in the Irish Channel. A telescope on the Smalls recorded flag semaphores from a passing ship and forwarded these messages to lookout stations on land. The messages ended their travels in London—first in a newsletter originally titled *Ships Arrived at and Departed from several Ports of England, as I have Account of them in London* and renamed *Lloyd's List,* and later, in a wooden room containing a massive bell salvaged from the HMS *Lutine.* When a missing ship was found, the bellman would ring twice; when a ship was confirmed lost, the bellman would ring once, and the members of Lloyd's, known as the Names, would count their losses.

Draw two compass lines south and southwest; draw a third to make the triangle connecting the busiest ports of the transatlantic trade, Liverpool–Lagos–Philadelphia, or Bristol–Falmouth (Jamaica)–New Orleans. At the vertex is the Smalls. One visitor, after seeing a Liverpool port grown rich from slaving ships, described the oak-timber Smalls lighthouse as a "strange wooden-legged Malay-looking barracoon of a building," a barracoon being a type of slatted cage used to temporarily hold slaves who were to be shipped elsewhere. That cargo was sometimes restrained with the use of ropes interwoven with their hair, and typically insured by Lloyd's from "Averages arising by Death and Insurrection." The Names paid out as long as the ship had been properly hulled with copper to keep out tropical woodworms, and more than 10 percent of cargo were killed.

HOW I BECAME A DETECTIVE
Prose Poetry and Post-Confessional Aesthetics

Carol Guess

The first thing I needed to do was remove my mother.

My mother got in the way of seeing the dead girl.

. . . .

There's a story about my mother being kissed by a stranger, a story I've never known how to tell. She and I were walking in midtown Manhattan when a scruffy passer-by grabbed my mother and kissed her. Then he staggered on his way, mumbling to himself about the Apocalypse.

My mother stood on the sidewalk, crowds swirling around her, and started to cry.

"No one but your father has ever kissed me," she said, sobbing.

. . . .

Before mixing my mother up in a crime scene, I had to resurrect my father's ghost. After my father died, I wanted very badly to write about his research in epidemiology, but couldn't understand it. His scientific writing was crucial to medicine, but when I tried to read it, the words slipped from the page.

Carol Guess is the author of 14 books of poetry and prose, including *Tinderbox Lawn* (2008), *Darling Endangered* (2011), and *Doll Studies: Forensics* (2012). Forthcoming books include *With Animal* (2015) and *The Reckless Remainder* (2016), both co-written with Kelly Magee. She teaches in the MFA program at Western Washington University.

Frustrated with text, I turned to image. While researching medical pho-tography I stumbled on a haunting photo. The image captured the after-math of a murder, parents and child killed in their sleep. Yet the photo was beautiful: a white crib, pink wallpaper, a spray of red above the headboard. Because the spray of red meant blood, the image was violent. But the blood wasn't real and the child was a doll.

· · · ·

The Nutshell Studies of Unexplained Death were created by Frances Glessner Lee during the 1940s and 50s. Born into a wealthy white Chicago family, she inherited endless resources, but because she was female, her parents refused to allow her to attend college. Ambitious, angry, and bored with her husband, Lee began creating dollhouse-style dioramas depicting real crime scenes. Each diorama is littered with clues that may be used to solve the crime.

Lee took her crime scenes seriously; so did police and forensic scien-tists, who realized her dioramas were strikingly accurate. The Nutshells were used as teaching tools; Lee began giving seminars in forensic medi-cine. She's now referred to as the mother of modern forensic science.

After Lee's death, The Nutshells sat gathering dust until photogra-pher Corinne May Botz discovered them. Botz began years of obses-sive research into their creation, culminating in a book of photo essays, *The Nutshell Studies of Unexplained Death*. The book made her name as a photographer. Her photos elevate these practical teaching tools into high art.

· · · ·

I stared at Botz's photos for hours and even naively struck up a corre-spondence with the photographer. I inserted my history into those quiet, fatal rooms. I became obsessed, but at first my obsession was a mirror, a way of using The Nutshells to look at myself. For example, early versions of "The Double Doll" and "Kicks" included the story of my mother and the stranger. The Nutshells were just a vehicle for me to talk about my life.

I collected 15 of these early poems and sent them to the editor and poet Kristy Bowen, who picked them up as a chapbook for Dancing Girl Press. But as I continued to write, hoping to complete a full-length manuscript, I realized my personal life didn't belong in this book.

The Nutshells were not about me.

To really see The Nutshells, I needed to step outside myself. I needed to enter the scene as an observer: to record, rather than elaborate.

In this manner, I became a detective.

· · · ·

This was the process Frances Glessner Lee intended: for bumbling provincial investigators to stop inserting themselves into fresh crime scenes, desecrating evidence. She wanted investigators to see. To stand very still until the truth revealed itself.

When I took myself out of The Nutshells, the dioramas revealed their secrets. Details and plot illuminated the emotion of each scene. I felt terror, grief, and compassion, not for my family, but for the victims Lee memorialized.

In removing myself from the poems, I began to inhabit them. I wasn't in the poems, but I was shaping the poems. I was writing my version of what I observed, not distracting myself with family stories.

Prose poetry seemed a natural form for this new material. Confessional poetry is often lineated, perhaps because line breaks easily echo an author's speech. I wanted to de-emphasize my authorial presence; eliminating line breaks felt like erasing footprints. Persona poems emerged as a result of using prose blocks, not the other way around. While each diorama was distinct, every story ended in death. The rooms I studied were dangerous rooms, claustrophobic cages that coffined their subjects.

· · · ·

The poems took on new urgency. As they widened to include the cultural context of the dioramas, history replaced personal narrative. I began to hear music in those bloodstained rooms. My job was to add sound to Botz's vivid images of Lee's constructions. The narrative voice in most of the poems is an observer, witness, or detective, calm and detached. I also wrote persona poems where the first-person speaker is involved in the crime.

By the end of the manuscript, I fully inhabited the characters. Writing as a doll, I begged Frances Glessner Lee to spare my family's life. I went a little crazy, as artists sometimes do.

I was inside my poems.

Now I needed to get out.

HYBRID WORK
From Doll Studies: Forensics

Aerial Rifle

Here's the dollhouse wife asleep, night's chores finished in miniature. What hangs above the infant's head is red. I mean the way graffiti moves through trains, signaling who's been and when. Her husband sleeps beside her on the floor. This dollhouse lesson has to do with time. I mean the way sound travels through a house asleep. Detectives learn to sweep a story clockwise for detail. Anyone might own a gun. Pink slippers run in place atop a popcorn rug.

Late White

Tuesday detains her among beautiful dresses. She lives in the closet now, sprawl study in beaded slippers and bangles. We don't know what she charged for sex. It's easier to describe a flowered dress. You would like for there to be a rose and there is, in the papered room. Above her headboard hangs a moose. A woman found this woman dead. Each might take the other's place, bonbons in a ruffled box. Merlot coats the glass as it dries, diminishing, as one who leaves a party leaves the conversation stained.

The Double Doll

Frank Harris gets two dolls. Why's he so special? He's sleeping on cement. Beside him in a cell tomorrow's Frank lies dead. Between breathing and dying Frank loses his cap. Dock Street's suspended, waiting for Harvard's pennant. Longshoremen practice stevedore lashing, binding Boston's barrels to barges. Things fall from the sky every day without warning. What struck from above left no trace of blood. Frank returned to stopper knots, no time to nurse a bump on the head. Who doesn't see stars dockside at night on a clandestine run to dump dunnage off deck? Two Franks aligned shims and hoisted rope: visible docker and invisible corpse.

Kicks

You're going to kill her. At least give her legs. She's drinking from a shard of glass, bloomers cycling in rigor mortis. Pink garters chasten knitted stockings. A cake of soap pines for her dirt. Sauced on gin, perhaps she slipped. Stiff legs suggest she stiffened elsewhere. Dinner tasted of its tinfoil cover. Wainscoting grasps the tub in its fist. Gentlemen friends brought gin to her room, but somehow *Dark Bathroom* is the scene of the crime. She's open-ended. You can see up her skirt. No doubt she's finished to the last doll part. She's swimming upside-down in flounces, drunk on water, the last thing she'll taste. She'll never listen to Sousa's opus. *Plessy v. Ferguson* upholds the law.

Headline Red

Lipstick loses face fast slashed on the sash of one wet wrist. Kisses and whiskey: I thought Marie missed me. My step on the stair. My razors and foam. She brought me home for what—to wait? A date with a suitcase fat with excuses. Prissy this and dizzy that. She put up a fight with fists, and bit. The most dangerous knives are dull. No matter; I win what I want one way or another.

Pastoral, with Noose

Hunger was a problem I thought I could solve. It isn't true that farmers want a world where nothing happens. I know the city birds know, violence and passion amid bracken. I never asked buildings to bend to my plow. When the human city came for my farm it came for the land, not the land's bounty. What good is a horse compared to a car? Fat rubber legs run so dirty, so fast. I swear the blight looked beautiful at first: Alternaria, stippled like a Hoover flag.

Petitioner

Linda Mae's black rocking stallion gallops into her cradle from a Cracker Jack box. Must you use that crimson paint? You made us. You gave us tiny Rice Krispies. You could let us sleep; breakfast's already set. Kate's dishrag dries on the edge of the sink. Milk's on the porch, three creamy bottles. Soon Paul Abbott will arrive with his car. Can't you shut the window, seal Bob's gun inside his safe? The telephone echoes. Miniature flashlights illuminate rescue. Can't we leave the house alive?

5

. . . .

Performative

PERFORMATIVE
An Introduction

Riffing, posing, and exploring various kinds of double consciousness, performative works of literature structurally incorporate elements ranging from the imaginative play of childhood to the script of psychoanalysis, from business presentations to magical rituals. Their focus is the *performance* of identity, rather than the construction of identity itself. The precursors to contemporary performative work reach back in time to the ancient court jester, a professional employed by the Aztecs, the ancient Egyptians, the Emperor of Japan, the King of Tonga, and all the courts of Europe. Inhabiting a liminal position vis-à-vis civil society, the jester was allowed to speak truths so obvious they were often invisible, and so they were truths that would otherwise have remained unarticulated. Shakespeare famously made use of the idea of performative speech in *King Lear*, the plot of which depends upon the King's demand that his daughters perform their loyalty through speech, and his incorrectly identifying which daughter was sincere and which deceitful. He called his faithful, truthful daughter, "My poor fool."

The jester is related to the trickster, who figures in mythic, cultic, religious, and folk situations, especially in African-American literature and literary criticism, from Charles W. Chesnutt's *The Conjure Woman* tales to Br'er Rabbit, or from Toni Morrison's *Beloved* to the double voicing of blues songs. The trickster's deceit is salvific. Through the intervention of Prometheus, Coyote, Raven, Eshu, and other such figures, the boundary between appearance and reality, silence and language, human and non-human, the spirit world and the material becomes diaphanous, allowing entire cosmologies, realities, and inventions to come into being, or to pass from one world to the next. A third precursor to such performative works as the ones included here is the play-within-the-play, which occurs notably in Michael Frayn's *Noises Off*, Shakespeare's *Midsummer Night's Dream*, Ovid's *Metamorphoses*, as well as the dance sequences in such Bollywood films as *Dil Se* (1998).

Performative works are most fundamentally poems, prose poems, memoirs, and works of fiction whose distinguishing characteristic is, as the name suggests, their performative element: presentation and audience are built into their rhetorical structure. The excerpts included here co-opt the language and form of plays and performance pieces to expose dualities or multiplicities: the life we live in our own heads and the life we live in other people's heads; the life we live in the physical world and the one we live on another plane. Performative works often articulate that which is previously unstated, reading between the lines of the various kinds of texts and scripts in our social, civic, and private lives. As Jenny Boully says in her process essay, "pretending to be one thing, you can better accept that you are not another thing."

Boully's excerpt from *not merely because of the unknown that was stalking towards them* is an engagement with J. M. Barrie's *Peter Pan and Wendy* that employs literary criticism, fiction, and childhood make-believe. Terrance Hayes' Pecha Kucha selection borrows the structure of a Japanese business presentation to imagine the brothers of Malcolm X watching his funeral on a television screen. In "Non-Sequitur," excerpted from her book *Black Peculiar*, Khadijah Queen uses the form of a theater play, complete with stage directions, to explore the ways we are complicit in, and the ways we perform, social expectations of race. Writes Queen: "being a Black person (both in America and abroad) often demands a certain degree of performativity. Sometimes one's safety is at stake; other times one's livelihood."

Like Hayes and Queen, A. Van Jordan's work in *M-A-C-N-O-L-I-A* is also firmly rooted in questions of race and language, but he turns his focus to the very elements of communication. He examines the parts of speech we normally ignore to bring into sharper focus how we make sense of the hand we've been dealt. "I was conscious of the nouns and verbs carrying both imagery and stresses, but it dawned on me, for the first time, really, just how important prepositions were to the poem as paths to the nouns and verbs; indeed, these seemed to operate like the electrical charge between a proton and an electron in an ion atom," he writes.

Completing the group is the "Santa Lear" chapter of Nick Flynn's memoir *Another Bullshit Night in Suck City*, which depicts the duality of the physical world that the narrator inhabits and the psychological world in which he is experiencing a breakdown. Like Queen's, his play-within-the-story is an absurdist one, but the absurdist element, for him, moves a psychological breakdown "from being enacted through language into being embodied in sensation."

What all of these performative pieces show is that "language's ability to *create* equals its ability to *erase*," as Hayes puts it. This gives Hayes hope: "I love that metaphor means there is no such thing as a pure system of meaning." The performative, then, explores the way we create and inhabit systems of meaning in our own impure experience. It draws attention to the ways we, as artists and consumers of art, are both performer and audience, at once and always.

—*Marcela Sulak*

THE ESSENTIAL YET HIDDEN ARTIFICE

Embodying Sensation in *Santa Lear*

Nick Flynn

The *Santa Lear* chapter of my memoir began with a photograph, or the memory of a photograph—a photograph of my father dressed as a Salvation Army Santa, ringing a bell beside a black pot. The pot was suspended above the snow on a tripod; the bell had a wooden handle that my father held in his fist. This photo came to me in the mail, included in one of the hundreds of letters he sent me over the years he was living on the streets. After I opened the envelope, after I saw the photograph, each Santa I passed that winter—and for the next many winters—could have been him. Now, each Christmas he would be everywhere—disguised, jolly, drunk.

One television show, from my childhood of TV and Pop-Tarts, had a town drunk as a recurring character. The show was *Mayberry R.F.D.*; the drunk was Otis. In my hometown we also had a town drunk; his name was _____. I kept my eye on him. I saw him everywhere. I don't know why. As he walked past our house I'd be at the window; if he was asleep on Front Street I'd notice. He was one of the most consistent presences of my childhood, and when I was older my friends and I would get him to buy

Nick Flynn's *Another Bullshit Night in Suck City* (2010) won the PEN/Martha Albrand Award for the Art of the Memoir, and has been translated into 10 languages. He is also the author of two books of poetry, including *Some Ether* (2000), which won the PEN/ Joyce Osterweil Award. He has been awarded fellowships from The Guggenheim Foundation, The Library of Congress, The Amy Lowell Trust, and The Fine Arts Work Center. His poems, essays, and nonfiction have appeared in *The New Yorker*, *Paris Review*, and National Public Radio's "This American Life." He teaches at the University of Houston.

for us. Otis would let himself into jail each night to sleep off his bender. He would hang the key within arm's reach to let himself out in the morning. I can remember almost nothing else of that show—maybe someone whistling at the beginning.

One of the many jobs my mother had when I was very young was making donuts. She'd bundle my brother and me into whatever shitbox we were then driving and take us to the supermarket in the still dark, prop us up on the red swivel stools of the lunch counter, feed us toast. My favorite part was the little basket of butter and jelly that never went bad, secure in their airtight plastic coffins. While she worked I would wander the dark aisles—aisle of juice, aisle of fruit—and eat whatever I wanted. Years later, up at UMass, after tripping all night, I found myself inside a donut shop I'd walked past many times. It had seven types of donuts, each one more complex than the one beside it, and it was clear that each was the same donut, only further along in time, that the donut from the first day was dusted with sugar the next day, then coated with chocolate the following day, then drizzled with frosting the day after that, then bejeweled with jimmies, and on and on until the final day, the last donut—a baroque monstrosity.

I ate a lot of donuts when I was young, and I watched a lot of television. At college I studied Shakespeare, and then I dropped out and ended up working at a homeless shelter, which is where I found my father, or where he found me. I'd been working there for three years when he got himself evicted and ended up coming through our doors. He ended up sleeping there or on the streets for the next five years—he had nowhere else to be. A shelter is a type of village, yet instead of one town drunk there are many—my father became one more. He turned into Otis, yet the key was always just out of reach. And when he was trying to pull himself out of it—and he was always trying to pull himself out—he became a Salvation Army Santa. All these elements (donuts, *King Lear*, *Mayberry R.F.D.*, a lost father) are woven together into *Santa Lear*, a play-within-a-memoir.

Santa Lear comes about three-quarters of the way through the book *Another Bullshit Night in Suck City*, my memoir about those years, about the trajectory of my life and the trajectory of my father's life, and how those trajectories crossed in that shelter for those few long years. I began the book 10 years after he walked through the doors, and for some of the seven years it took me to finish it, I was living in Ireland, where I was lucky enough to see a lot of good theater. In the narrative arc of the book, in the Aristotelian sense, *Santa Lear* appears at what is known as *the crisis stage*—my father had been homeless for two years; I was manifesting symptoms of some sort of psychological breakdown; my days were becoming more and more surreal. To leap into a play with seven Santas and three donut sellers, to weave in motifs from my childhood (Otis, donuts, Lear), seemed to embody a texture of what those days were like for me. It is disruptive to the narrative flow of the book to leap into such utter abstraction and artifice, and yet it comes closest to my experience of that time. If you want to know how it felt to see my father sleeping outside, read *Santa Lear*. Sometimes artifice can capture the sensation of what it is to be alive more accurately than realism.

Realism moves along an orderly track, and we readers are in a train car on that track, looking out the window as mundane or surreal or terrible things happen outside the window. But we know where we are; we are grounded in time and space, and we trust that the mind of the narrator will translate what we are seeing into recognizable images. Yet in a hybrid text, this grounding is continually subverted. In *Another Bullshit Night in Suck City*, the shift into the play *Santa Lear* punctures the comfortable illusion of realism. Then, by making that play more spectacle than naturalistic, my psychological breakdown moves from being enacted through language into being embodied in sensation. For the reader, the hybrid text has the uncanny ability to disorient, by highlighting the essential yet hidden artifice of all narrative connective tissue, which, until that moment, felt grounding. All art, at some point in the process of creation, takes place within the artist's head, and perhaps it should be unsettling to bring that interior madness into the light.

After the book came out I found the photograph he'd sent me, years before, of him ringing that bell for the Salvation Army. The snow is there, the bell, the black pot, the tripod. The demented look on his face. Except he isn't wearing a Santa outfit—no white beard, no red coat, no black boots, no pointy hat. He is simply wearing a winter coat. For years I looked for him in every Santa, but he was never there.

HYBRID WORK
Excerpt from Another Bullshit Night in Suck City

Santa Lear

Still outside, winter everywhere, snow falls (*Grain upon grain, one by one, and one day, suddenly, there's a heap, a little heap, the impossible heap*), his toes now blackening in his sock.

For the days leading up to Christmas he works for the Salvation Army as a fake Santa—the belted suit, the faux trim, the ringlet beard. Stationed on the sidewalk before a black pot, he rings a bell. I first learn of this when he tells me, one morning at the shelter as I finish the graveyard shift on the Van. I run into him on his way to get into his suit. He even shows me a photograph, and I'll be damned, there he is, one of the downtown Santas. A bell-ringer, my father. Later, walking, I realize I'd never noticed just how many Santas there are. I pass dozens of them, one on every corner, same black pot, same worn suit, but from now on I'll never know if one is my father. The Santa Brigade of the Salvation Army, each face disguised—rosy-cheeked, rosy-eyed, rosy-nosed—each bleating out a bleary, *Ho-ho.* If I look too closely into any one of their faces an eye will wink, or blink, but this doesn't mean it's him. Maybe they all wink, crinkle their eyes, *Ho-ho.* One stands before a Dunkin' Donuts, a pink-glazed monstrosity the size of a truck tire filling the window behind his head.

setting:

A sidewalk outside an urban donut shop. Rush hour. Stage crowded, action frozen. Scratchy Christmas carols play. A slide projection on a scrim of glistening, sick-colored, overlit donuts, 10 times normal size. As lights come up slowly the stage clears, leaving five SANTAS and three DAUGHTERS. DAUGHTERS, dressed exactly alike in white aprons and wearing same black wig, bobbed with bangs, stand in a row before the scrim. SANTA FIVE surreptitiously chases a dawdling BUSINESSMAN, coming up behind him, head low, gesturing wildly, giving him the finger with both hands. BUSINESSMAN looks over shoulder uneasily, but SANTA FIVE straightens and looks down at feet, at walls, seemingly innocent, until BUSINESSMAN turns away. BUSINESSMAN exits. SANTA ONE squats on the floor, holds a close 'n play, playing Christmas carols, oblivious. SANTAS TWO and THREE loll together, before a black pot suspended on a wooden tripod, halfheartedly ringing bells, smoking, murmuring to each other, scratching themselves, bleating out an occasional ho-ho. SANTA FOUR is passed out on a small mountain of shoes. SANTA FIVE now pokes through a trash barrel, paranoid, glancing around. Heavy snow falls, tapers off.

Daughter One: Seven days a week this—

Santa One: (through bullhorn) Snow on! I will endure, on such a night as this!

Daughter One: (annoyed)—is the process.

Santa Two: (gestures to SANTA ONE) His wits begin t' unsettle.

Santa Three: Canst thou blame him?

Daughter One: Monday. Day One—plain, the classic donut. God's gift— flour, eggs, milk, butter—good, clean, all-natural ingredients.

Santa One: (bullhorn) The ha-ha, the ho-ho,

Daughter Two: (ignores him) Those that do not sell on Day One move into Day Two, where we glaze them. Honey-dipped, we call it, though we use no honey. The same donut as Day One, now transformed. Many people wait for Day Two, the shiny donut.

Santa Three: (grabs bullhorn, to DAUGHTERS*)* Is there a point to this?

SANTA FOUR *rises. Appreciative applause heard over the sound system, perhaps an electronic applause sign overhead.* SANTA FOUR *steps out of character for just an instant, acknowledges the applause, tiptoes behind the counter and swipes a donut, then continues stumbling over to the jail cell, which he lets himself into using the oversized skeleton key hanging beside the bars. At the door he turns to the audience.*

Santa Four: (holds up donut) Do you realize that the latest theory of the universe is that it's shaped like a donut? Fucking amazing. (*He enters cell, curls up and snores loudly over the rest of the donut-process recitation.*)

Daughter Three: Day Three we dust the remaining honey-dipped with confectioner's sugar—it is now a sugar donut. The faux honey has begun to skin over like a caramel apple—it has some bite now, the sugar floating upon the surface like pollen dusts a pond in spring.

SANTA FOUR *takes his pillow and covers his head, attempting to block out the sound. Muffled curses.* SANTA FIVE *stands before* DAUGHTERS, *motions for a cup of coffee.* DAUGHTERS *ignore him. When they look away* SANTA FIVE *gives them the double finger.*

Daughter One: Day Four—

Santa Three: (bullhorn) For the love of Christ can't you move this along?

The SANTAS *adjust the pillows that make up their bellies.*

The projection on the scrim flickers, becoming the wall of a morgue, small stainless freezer doors stacked five high, maybe eight across, lit in the same way as the donuts. The DAUGHTERS *exchange their flour-coated aprons for black industrial rubber aprons. Each rolls a gurney beside* SANTAS ONE, TWO, *and* THREE, *who climb aboard and are covered with a white sheet. All barefoot, we now notice, with a tag hanging from their big toes, now revealed in their prone positions.* SANTA FOUR *stays in cell,* SANTA FIVE *huddles along left wall. The* DAUGHTERS *wheel the bodies into position, lined in a row, feet forward. One* DAUGHTER *stands behind each head. A blinding overhead light lowers over each body. One by one* DAUGHTERS *read the vital stats off each toe tag, and as they read each* SANTA *sits up briefly, winks, tells story, lays back dead.*

Daughter One: Fell on a broken bottle and bled to death—his last words were about robbing a bank.

Santa Two: The whole enterprise—the hoo-hoo, the ha-ha, the goo-goo, the ga-ga—my idea, my brainchild. Those other morons did what I told them. Dippy-do Doyle? Couldn't find his way out of a paper bag. I made millions, kid, millions. Lived well, drank in Joe Kennedy's hangout in Palm Beach. I walk in, bartender throws me a Johnnie Walker Black, asks, What're you writing these days? Mostly checks, I tell him, ha ha.

SANTA FOUR *exits cell, again to applause, picks up the bullhorn, coughs into it, rubs sleep from his eyes. He sits on the floor, begins to play close 'n play Christmas carols quietly, experimenting, scratching a song. It begins to snow lightly.*

Daughter Two: Froze to death, couldn't pry the bell from his hand.

Santa One: I was a goner from the first moment, the first check. Doyle set me up. He knew about you kids, knew where you lived, threatened to kill you both and Taddy-tu-tu if I didn't keep going along with it. Said he'd kidnap you, for chrissakes, what was I supposed to do? I only got a few thousand out of the whole gig, nothing, really.

Santa Three: (sits up suddenly, speaks to SANTA ONE) Now, wait a minute, dryballs. There I was, in front of the Great God Giggles Garriity, the greatest judge in the U.S. judicial system... *(to DAUGHTERS)* Write it down, dryballs, it's classic.

DAUGHTERS *look at each other, confused, mouthing the word "dryballs?"*

SANTA FOUR *stands up and attempts to hold bullhorn before* SANTA THREE.

Santa Three: He never smiled until the day he sentenced me. *(bullhorn to* DAUGHTERS*)* Turn the page, dryballs, you need a new page.

DAUGHTERS *slowly begin transcribing on clipboards.*

Santa Three: Six U.S. marshals brought me in, in shackles, penis included. (DAUGHTERS, *confused, mouth the word "penis")* A two-million-dollar case. I was arrested going into the Breakers with a beautiful broad. *(through bullhorn to* DAUGHTERS*)* Hey, numbnuts, you don't write fast enough, you're all losing your brains. I was in love with the broad, said I'd be right back, after I spoke with the police. Dumb bunny's probably still waiting for me, ha ha.
Santa Four: Any donuts left?

Lights flicker.

Daughter Two: We drove at night, the city locked, subdued, steam breathing from the sewers, steam from the sides of buildings. The steam drew him to it, a cipher until he spoke, a shape, the shape of a man asleep. I am here to check his breathing, to watch the blanket rise and fall.
Santa Four: (through bullhorn) When the mind's free the body's delicate.
Daughter Three: The wind means something here, the snow means something. Footprints in the snow mean something. No footprints lead to this man. The snow began falling at midnight. He lay down before then. This means something.
Santa Three: Buried most of it below a tree—I'm not telling you where, you bastard—but know it's waiting, waiting for the dust to settle.

Daughter One: The engine running, hot air blowing on my legs. Art cold? Thou art the thing itself, methinks. Inhale, exhale, the body's steam, the engine inside, the soul manifest, the dream's white cloud. I am cold myself.

Daughter Two: For a few months after I got back from Mexico I seriously considered buying him a one-way ticket to Mexico. Get him drunk one night and put him into a bus while he's passed out.

Santa One: (morose) If there was any way I could snap my fingers and bring your mother back into this room...

Daughter One: (touching SANTA TWO) We got a live one here, I tell Jeff if it's the first. I reach out and touch the shoulder, only after having whispered near, Hey, you need anything—

DISCRETE CONNECTION/
FALSE ISOLATION

On Hybrid Structure in *Black Peculiar*

Khadijah Queen

Black Peculiar, my book from which the verse play "Non-Sequitur" is excerpted, is a three-part, hybrid, multi-generic whole that examines the way we speak about (or don't speak about) race, power, and gender in the United States and abroad. The book's title gestures toward a euphemism for slavery ("that peculiar institution"), highlighting the way in which what is omitted from our language is the basis upon which our reality takes shape.

I wrote "Non-Sequitur" while thinking about how being African-American (both in America and abroad) often demands a certain degree of performativity. Sometimes one's safety is at stake; other times one's livelihood. Cultural assumptions and social expectations for most people in general can create situations that require intellectual, physical, and psychological acrobatics, but not everyone's survival depends on it. The absurdity, the violence, and the difficulty of such performance, particularly with regard to the experience I can speak to as a heterosexual Black woman, is both laughable and uncomfortable, and the stage play format encourages more awareness of (unconscious or conscious) participatory roles we all may take on in our own lives in order to incite both empathy and an acute awareness of the fallout of such participation.

Khadijah Queen is the author of *Conduit* (2008), *Black Peculiar* (2011), and *Fearful Beloved* (2015). Individual poems appear in *Fence, jubilat, RHINO, Best American Nonrequired Reading, The Force of What's Possible*, and elsewhere. She is the 2014 winner of the Leslie Scalapino Award for Innovative Performance Writing, which includes a staged production of her verse play "Non-Sequitur" in 2015.

In *The Night Sky: Writings on the Poetics of Experience,* Ann Lauterbach writes:

> Perhaps the reason that poetry is mostly ignored in our time
> has to do with its assertion of combinatory and coincidental
> experience, its desire to refute the various ways in which
> modernity has contrived to separate us from the authority of our
> existence, real and imagined, separately and together, to make
> the dark glass darker as the [computer/TV/mobile phone/tablet]
> screen is more and more illuminated.

Looking at Act II in "Non-Sequitur" in particular, we can discern conscious and subconscious acts via setting and dialogue: amid the wildness of a desert in Scene 1, a dinner party in Scene 2, the stage itself in scene 3, a meadow that is interchangeable with a meat freezer or a strip mall in scene 4, and a sensual video during the interlude. The juxtapositions of violence and beauty, the natural world and the contrived world, all stand in for thought. How often do we replay images in our minds, how often do we hear the voices of others as background to thought and memory, affecting choices we make in the present? We bring to any environment our full selves including those thoughts, memories, pasts, bodies, scars, hopes. The multitude of characters in the play hints at the seeming infinitude of players in our lives, and the sometimes absurd, sometimes abject process of sifting through such influence. Since most of these characters do not interact with one another, the reader doesn't get drawn into fictive action. Rather, s/he or ze is asked to create or co-construct with the text a possible container for these scenes and acts and words within which an understanding about the said infinitude of pronouncements and behaviors can be examined on the reader's terms. By incorporating a fragmentary poetics into a dramatic structure, my hope is to have pointed out and challenged ways of seeing that defer to the obvious, and to have expanded ways of seeing into the underside of what's said and done in the play. "Non-

Sequitur" privileges the unsaid, inspiring discomfort by clearly marking with language (and humor) the outrageous absurdity of often very painful cultural norms and practices, as the READYMADE BRIDE character in Scene 4, for example, mentally breaks down under the pressure of fulfilling expectations.

. . . .

Not a one of us is pure or singular. We are genetic amalgamations, collages of remembered landscapes, and ideological gumbo. The struggle for purity can be destructive and dangerous madness, and an excuse for exclusion. *Black Peculiar* reminds the audience that purity is a myth, that simplicity is a myth, and that complexity is just as normal and natural as breathing, which exercises the lungs, amplifies perception, and keeps us alive—an intricate process that is automatic for most of us, though not even breathing is an absolute to be taken for granted.

And if I look at a leaf, for example, not even to draw it, but to just really look at it, I see there's nothing simple about it. It is a complex and unique creation, veined and striated, shaped subtly or dramatically differently from its cohorts by chance and the elements, as are we all. *Black Peculiar* reacts against simplicity and easy packaging. It presents a multifaceted view that can be interpreted and applied individually.

I've talked in the past about jazz being an influence, and that kind of electric, spontaneous, and audience-engaged process of creation is certainly inseparable from the hybridity of *Black Peculiar*. Also inseparable: Lucille Clifton's dense, rich poetic economy; Jacques Derrida on *différance* and the oppositional qualities of language; Hélène Cixous on the body and identity and dreams and the abject; James Baldwin on boldness and the countless difficult aspects of being Black and creative and aware; the unflinching performances of Marina Abramović, particularly the bone-cleaning in *Balkan Baroque*; Lorna Simpson's photographs that are accompanied by text, especially *Waterbearer*; and Aphra Behn's bawdy and ahead-of-her-time depictions of female empowerment, just to name a very few literary, artistic, and philosophical referents. But underneath the work, informing the choices and the results, for the most part lies the unruly and disjointed process of living, and thinking about how best to capture the varied machinations behind the apparent chaos.

HYBRID WORK
Excerpt from Black Peculiar

From "Non-Sequitur"

ACT II
Internalizing externalities and vice versa

SETTING: A desert. Lights are red. Fierce wind sounds play. A black & white video of feathers falling is projected on a large screen off center, like a square of burned out sun.

SCENE 1
(Three spotlights come on. PLAYERS enter from right and line up evenly spaced downstage center into the spotlights)

THE MILD EX-PRISONER
I didn't sleep well last night.

THE KILLED ROACH *(rubbing stomach, picking teeth)*
Yeah, I've crawled across many a pillow in my day.

THE SHRINKING ELITIST
My grandmother would call us a bunch of wild Indians if we acted like that.

THE MILD EX-PRISONER *(sighs)*
I didn't eat very well either.

THE KILLED ROACH
Took a dump in 1,000 breadboxes.

THE SHRINKING ELITIST
Do you mind if I take a shower first?

THE KILLED ROACH
Now *(sighs slowly, dejectedly)* I'm dead.

THE SHRINKING ELITIST
You've got to call the front office if you need help.

THE MILD EX-PRISONER
The man on top of me snores all night.

(PLAYERS exeunt)

INTERLUDE
(VIDEO of thighs opening and closing projected on screen. VOICES heard
offstage, speaking slowly)

THE SHOE FETISHIST
I might make beauty behave as a whip.

THE SOBER CONSERVATIONIST
Intelligence is a kind of violence.

(pause for imagined effect)

SCENE 2

SETTING: A dinner party. Each player has a wine glass or champagne flute. Various snacks on the table. (PLAYERS enter from downstage right and line up in a loose circle center stage)

THE ROCK KICKER *(singing Faith Evans mournfully, rocking to imagined beat)*
You used to love me every day, hmmm-hmmm love has gone away...

THE SHIT TALKER *(smoking hookah)*
Congratulations! You didn't slap the person who told you that shit.

THE MATHEMATICIAN
It's a microbe trick. I made up an equation.

THE ROCK KICKER
Can't you hear me...hmmm-hmmm-hmmm... not what love's about...

THE SHIT TALKER
Oranges don't come from apple trees.

THE MATHEMATICIAN *(takes off glasses, cleans them slowly with a soft cloth)*

THE ROCK KICKER
You let me walk around... hmmm-hmmm...it's all right....to let me down – *(pause for a choir of pre-rehearsed members of audience to sing the refrain: "I remember / the way / you used / to love / me")*

THE SHIT TALKER
Amen! Praise Barack!
(several pre-rehearsed members of the audience also shout, "Praise him!")

THE MATHEMATICIAN *(takes out a huge calculator, starts furiously making calculations)*
(Lights fade, PLAYERS exeunt)

SCENE 3
(Four spotlights come on. PLAYERS enter spotlights from downstage right and line up, evenly spaced, center stage)

THE VOICE OF MALCOLM X *(offstage recording plays)*
I said he loved the master better than he loved himself!

THE INVISIBLE INSTITUTION
Playing with children, playing with adults—same thing.

THE BROWN VAGINA *(points to a door)*
Somebody left the door open—

THE ONLINE PAYMENTS
Reminder: please send payment by the due date.

THE VOICE OF MALCOLM X
My original name was taken from me when my ancestors were brought over in chains.

THE INVISIBLE INSTITUTION *(in a baby voice)*
Oh. Look at all the misdemeanor contraventions. How cute!

THE BROWN VAGINA
Yes, I know you'd like me better pinked.

THE ONLINE PAYMENTS
We have the right to file a judgment against you.

THE INVISIBLE INSTITUTION
I love my assumptions. They make other people think I'm *(uses air quotes)* "down" with them.

THE VOICE OF MALCOLM X
Power never takes a back step—only in the face of more power.

THE BROWN VAGINA
I really don't appreciate your microaggressions.

(a chorus of 10 people dressed like ONLINE PAYMENTS enter from upstage left and line up pyramid style behind him/her. All spotlights shift to them)

THE ONLINE PAYMENTS
I'm sorry. Your payment did not go through. Please try again later.

(Lights fade, PLAYERS exeunt)

SCENE 4
SETTING: Projection of a meadow of poppies, a strip mall or a half-empty restaurant meat freezer, all meat freezer-burned. (PLAYERS are already onstage, each engulfed in a spotlight that fades in as projection shrinks)

THE READYMADE BRIDE *(frowning, bending over and walking around as if looking for something)*
Where's the kitty? Kiiiiiiittttyyyyyyy!

THE PREHEATED OVEN
I'm never empty for long.

THE 40% DISCOUNT *(mopey-faced)*
I'm messed up. Or I messed up.

THE PREHEATED OVEN *(picking at fingernails)*
Don't these people believe in cleaning?

THE 40% DISCOUNT *(looks at outfit, smoothes fabric)*
Then again...

THE READYMADE BRIDE *(stomps foot)*
I can't get married without the kitty!

THE PREHEATED OVEN
I could have sworn I was hot enough already.

THE 40% DISCOUNT *(sighs)*
There isn't enough money in the world.

THE READYMADE BRIDE *(runs offstage, sobbing)*

(lights fade, PLAYERS exeunt)

DISCOVERING THE DEFINITION POEM

Prepositions and Performativity
in *M-A-C-N-O-L-I-A*

A. Van Jordan

Image gets privileged in the poem, and image carries privilege in the world around us. The image of a young black girl in 1936, however, wanting to be acknowledged for her brilliance carried no privilege; it was perceived as a problem. How does one convey this image to others? The conveyance of the image on the page often comes attached to the preposition as conduit. The preposition often works to hedge the language around the image, to soften the chord struck by it, or to make sense of its context. The question then is who will be the preposition, the conveyor of image, in the world. Too often, the answer is media. Ideally, the image of ourselves can stand alone, but too often it needs to be qualified to placate others: an *articulate* black male; a *well-mannered* black girl. Our images need modification as we cross racial lines or gender lines or regional lines in order to find acceptance. This is the social performance we enact in our daily lives, and this is what I attempted to capture on the page.

Beginning in 2000, I set out to write a collection of poems about MacNolia Cox, who was the first African American to get to the final round

A. Van Jordan is the author of four books: *The Cineaste* (2013), *Quantum Lyrics* (2007), *M-A-C-N-O-L-I-A* (2004), which was listed as one of the Best Books of 2005 by *The London Times*, and *Rise* (2001), which won a PEN/Oakland Josephine Miles Award. Jordan has been the recipient of a Whiting Writers Award, an Anisfield-Wolf Book Award, and a Pushcart Prize. He is a recipient of a John Simon Guggenheim Fellowship and a United States Artists Fellowship. He is the Henry Rutgers Presidential Professor at Rutgers University-Newark.

of the National Spelling Bee. While I wrote *M-A-C-N-O-L-I-A*, I think my mind was determined to look up as many words as possible from that 1936 Bee, but I soon realized that this was simply a method of procrastination.

At the time, my idea was that I would tell the story of how this girl won spelling bees in her school; her city of Akron, Ohio; her county, Summit; the state of Ohio; and, ultimately, all rounds of the national competition until that tricky final round when the southern judges got nervous, seeing that she was going to win, which prompted them to pull a word not on the list but that had come into common usage: nemesis. (No, I'm not making this up.) The words on the list were quite formidable, both much longer and less common than nemesis, but the judges could see that MacNolia had memorized all 100,000 words; she was the only contestant left in the final round who had not gotten there on a technicality; she spelled every word correctly, without variation. She had also endured the trip to the competition: crossing the Mason-Dixon line on the train and she and her mother having to get off and re-board in the "Colored" car; she endured getting to D.C., a segregated city at the time, and staying at a "safe house" because she and her mother weren't allowed to stay at any of the hotels; she endured making it to the competition to find that she had to enter through the back door of the armory, the back door being the colored entrance, and, subsequently, climbing the stairs to the ballroom in which the competition was held; and, once she made it to that ballroom, she also endured being sequestered off to a card table—she and Elizabeth McKinney from North Carolina, the only other African American in the competition—away from the other contestants. Indeed, by the final round of the competition, it was clear that MacNolia Cox was unflappable.

So, with this rich material, the artistic problems started to emerge: How do I represent both this level of resilience and this degree of precociousness in an adult? When children are this precocious and charismatic, what are the vestiges that remain in the adult who hasn't quite lived up to their expectation?

Of course, the answer to these queries will differ from subject to subject. MacNolia became a domestic in the home of a doctor, married a streetwise fellow who went from job to job, and then she died of breast cancer in her early 50s. With that kind of a trajectory, we have to look at the ways in which her intelligence peered through her day as she performed more quotidian tasks.

I thought that maybe she could use some of the big words from the spelling bee in her daily routine; of course, this is an embarrassingly bad idea, but it was my idea, nonetheless. It was also just another excuse to procrastinate: I started spending even more time with the *Oxford English Dictionary* (*OED*). As I luxuriated on the pages, while I looked up words that no one who had any common sense to couple with their book sense would use in their day-to-day conversation, I would stumble upon definitions of prepositions and conjunctions, small words with pages and pages of definition.

While I was struggling to write a narrative poem, a poem that was coming to me in prose, about the first night that MacNolia spent with John Montiere, the man who would later become her husband, I found myself trying to shoehorn in larger words from the spelling bee (still in bad idea mode) and then, procrastinating further, I started becoming obsessed with the ways in which I was using the words "from" and "to" in the poem. I ran across the definitions of these in the *OED*, and I thought, *Do I even really know all the variations on the usage of these little words?* I found myself going back and forth between the definition and the narrative poem. And then it was as if the structure of the poem lifted off the page, as if it were a hologram, and all I could see were the prepositions and their definitions.

I was conscious of the nouns and verbs carrying both imagery and stresses, but it dawned on me, for the first time, really, just how important prepositions were to the poem as paths to the nouns and verbs; indeed, these seemed to operate like the electrical charge between a proton and an electron in an ion atom. If I privileged the prepositions, I might be able to see the connections that were being made between the images more sharply. Using the definition structure from the dictionary allowed me to lay the definition over the narrative like a pattern to follow. The strange thing about reading definitions in the dictionary is that they already feel like you're reading a narrative poem with surprising lyrical moments. The structure is set in the fully fleshed out definition of the word.

The hybrid of the narrative poem and the dictionary definition is something that I doubt I could have come up with by thinking of making the form itself. My first thought was how could I convey some semblance of MacNolia Cox's childhood precocity in her adult self. That is to say, the content and subject *must* dictate the shape of the poem; the shape needs to complement the subject, not the other way around. Sometimes the lyric poem could work in this form even better, and I've tried this as well, but it really depends on the subject of the poem. The definition—the defined word that shapes the form itself—should reveal itself later.

HYBRID WORK
Excerpt from M-A-C-N-O-L-I-A

MacNolia

from (→) *prep.* **1.** Starting at (a particular place or time): As in, John was *from* Chicago, but he played guitar straight *from* the Delta; he wore a blue suit *from* Robert Hall's; his hair smelled like coconut; his breath, like mint and bourbon; his hands felt like they were *from* slave times when he touched me—hungry, stealthy, trembling. **2.** Out of: He pulled a knot of bills *from* his pocket, paid the man and we went upstairs. **3.** Not near to or in contact with: He smoked the weed, but, surprisingly, he kept it *from* me. He said it would make me too self-conscious, and he wanted those feelings as far away *from* us as possible; he said a good part of my beauty was that I wasn't conscious of my beauty. Isn't that funny? So we drank Bloody Mothers (Hennessy and tomato juice), which was hard to keep *from* him—he always did like to drink. **4.** Out of the control or authority of: I was released *from* my mama's house, *from* dreams of hands holding me down, *from* the threat of hands not pulling me up, *from* the man that knew me, but of whom I did not know; released *from* the dimming of twilight, *from* the brightness of morning; *from* the love I thought had to look like love; *from* the love I thought had to taste like love, *from* the love I thought I had to love like love. **5.** Out of the totality of: I came *from* a family full of women; I came *from* a family full of believers; I came *from* a pack of witches—I'm just waiting to conjure my powers; I came *from* a legacy of lovers—I'm just waiting to seduce my seducer; I came *from* a pride of proud women, and we take good care of our young. **6.** As being other or another than: He couldn't tell me *from* his mother; he couldn't tell me *from* his sister; he couldn't tell me *from* the last woman he had before me, and why should he—we're all the same woman. **7.** With (some person, place, or thing) as the instrument, maker, or source: Here's a note *from* my mother, and you can take it as advice *from* me: A weak lover is more dangerous than a strong enemy; if you're going to love someone, make sure you know where they're coming *from*. **8.** Because of: Becoming an alcoholic, learning to walk away, being a good speller, being good in bed, falling in love—they all come *from* practice. **9.** Outside or beyond the possibility of: In the room, he kept me *from* leaving by keeping me curious; he kept me *from* drowning by holding my breath in his mouth; yes, he kept me *from* leaving till the next day when he said *Leave*. Then, he couldn't keep me *from* coming back.

MacNolia

with (=) prep. **1.** Against: It started in the fall of 1950, a fight *with* my husband John. He could not accept my being pregnant. But, as I told him, he didn't have a problem when we were conceiving it. **2.** From: It was like parting *with* a friend, being pregnant. John became distant: distant lying next to me in bed, distant inside me in bed, distant walking out the door in the morning. **3.** In mutual relation to: He talked *with* my brother, who had always been a friend to John. On that day, they were just two men talking. Brother's language was plain. "You do good by my sister." After that, we changed the way we talked *with* each other. 4. In the company of: The next Friday, I went to the movies *with* him. He helped me climb the steps to the balcony, that nigger heaven, which I didn't feel like climbing to; I was as big as the movie house itself, eight months pregnant. He held my hand in the dark, fed me popcorn. He held my hand all the way home, and I knew again why I was *with* him. 5. As regards, towards: John is not a patient man. And I wondered: Could he show patience *with* children? 6. In support of: I wanted to hear him say he was *with* me, even when I looked one pillow down and saw him lying next to me. For once, I needed to hear a man say what his actions were already telling me: he was *with* me and he wasn't going to leave. 7. In the presence of or containing: I needed to know we were like Lipton tea *with* sugar: better together than apart. 8. In the opinion of or judged by: I couldn't take it if we had another argument, not in my ninth month; these moments had weight *with* me. 9. Because of, through: I could tell John was going to be blue *with* pride, especially if we had a boy—as if this were all his doing. And I'd be happy *with* that. 10. Despite: Even *with* all his earlier protests, he kept a smile on his face when our son, Darrell, was born. 11. Given, granted. *With* his blessing, we baptized our son, and they both cried, both like grown men, for a man never changes the way he cries, always as if he were the coming of spring.

Mrs. Alberta Cox, MacNolia's mother

to (▯) **1a.** In the direction toward so as to reach: As in, when we went *to* the picnic, I saw how the men didn't look at you, how when they walked *to* you, it was only because you were in my orbit, how when you walked *to* the table where they drank and sang and licked their fingers of food, you didn't look at them either, how when you skipped over *to* the lot where the boys played, they simply played and you played with them till it got dark and then you simply stopped playing, without my saying a word, which made me smile. **b.** Toward. And you turned to me, and I told you the heavy truth: you'll get through this life on your spelling, not your smile; on your math, not your legs; on the many sciences of life, not your sex. And this, my dear, is when you were born a woman. **2a.** Reaching as far as: Then I didn't feel like a mother. I looked into your eyes; water was clear to the bottom, the loose steel that hardens us from girlhood through womanhood was already damn near *to* the base of your skull. **b.** To the extent or the degree of: I loved your father *to* distraction, which drove me *to* grief, which, I guess, drove him *to* a younger woman, who hadn't learned this much about men. Which is why I tell you now, I love you. I love you all the way *to* your next life, which should get you, at least, halfway through this one. **c.** With the resultant condition of: When you were born the first time, you came early and weak and near dead and I prayed you back *to* life. **3.** Toward a given state: Your hair in a ponytail, the white satin strap of your slip slung over your brown shoulder, the crescent moon of your foot from which a red shoe dangles in mid-July—girl, none of these will help women *to* equality. **4.** In contact with; against; When the Ohio snow came *to* our eyes, when the sun came to the eastside steaming off the sidewalks, when the leaves came *to* the ground, when your father left, before we tired of waiting, we pressed our faces *to* the window. **5.** Opposite; near or in front of: And when I finally saw you chest *to* chest with a boy, I reminded you of the year of your father's leaving. I held you *to* my breast. I warned you: don't place a great deal of importance on holding a man close *to* your heart. **6.** Used to indicate appropriation or possession of or belonging with: Being a wife *to* a man is like being a lid *to* a jar: if she doesn't fit, he'll simply try another lid. **7.** Concerning; regarding: As *to* your father, after many years had passed, after your winning the local spelling bee, after your picture appeared on the front page of the paper, after you were a finalist in the national competition, after we came back and the city threw a parade in your honor downtown, did I tell you, I never gave an answer *to* any of his letters? Never. **8.** Used before a verb to indicate the infinitive: There are women who will never get *to* know their fathers and won't get over it. There are women who have had *to* know their fathers and won't get over it. There are women who know what it is *to* live with a man, but who will never know what it is *to* marry a man; and there are women who know what is *to* marry a man, but who will never know what it is *to* live.

WRITING BETWIXT-AND-BETWEEN

Performative Spaces in
Real Life and Make-Believe

Jenny Boully

In J.M. Barrie's *The Little White Bird* (1902), Peter Pan is referred to as a "be-twixt-and-between." It is in this book that Peter makes his first appearance in the works of Barrie. We will see him again, each time a bit different, in several more texts. How Barrie delivers the Peter story to us is already, in its nature, hybrid: Peter exists as a beginning in *The Little White Bird*, a play in *Peter Pan* (1904), a new beginning in *Peter Pan in Kensington Gardens* (1906), and finally as a novel in *Peter and Wendy* (1911), which happens to be my favorite. In all of these Peter texts, what I adore is the intermingling of fact and fantasy, real and pretend. Dream-life, death, existence, play, and make-believe all comingle, and one's position in any of these existential states is of grave and serious importance. In Neverland, death can be performed, but is it also very real. By way of illustration, the narrator of *Peter and Wendy* reminds us that Hook can kill a pirate just to show us, the readers, how easily death is done on the island: poor Skylights hardly lives through the span of a sentence. And so many other deaths abound. Tinker Bell will hardly live for a year, and Wendy Darling, we know, gets too tall to fit in Peter's world and goes on to have children and grandchildren with whom Peter replaces her.

Jenny Boully is the author of five collections including *of the mismatched teacups, of the single-serving spoon: a book of failures* (2012), *not merely because of the unknown that was stalking toward them* (2011), *The Book of Beginnings and Endings* (2007), *[one love affair]** (2006), and *The Body: An Essay* (2002). Her work has been anthologized in *The Best American Poetry*, *The Next American Essay*, *Great American Prose Poems: From Poe to the Present*, and other publications. She teaches at Columbia College Chicago.

My fascination with *Peter and Wendy* grew out of my fascination with Wendy. She was in love with a betwixt-and-between who was forgetful, disloyal, and refused to ask her parents a question on a "rather sweet subject." I was in love. I was in love, and I too felt as if I were a wee child playing house and marrying pretend. Because I still felt like a child—I still do— my love existed in the realm of performance. I played the good housewife and wanted children to mother. I was trying to have a baby at the time and could not have a baby, and so I felt Wendy's want of children and her performance of mother to the Lost Boys most poignantly.

I did not intend to, but I was so captivated by Wendy, so enchanted by her multiplicity, that I wrote a whole dissertation chapter on the uses of make-believe in *Peter and Wendy*. Role-playing and trying on different guises aids in assimilating real life, its successes, its failures, its happenstances and all. By pretending to be one thing, you can better accept that you are not another thing. And perhaps that is where my love of possibility in form and for Wendy begins. My writing was hybrid insofar as the writing itself took on the guise of both a critical essay and the experimental creative work *not merely because of the unknown that was stalking toward them*. The book is the creative outgrowth of my research on the Peter texts, yes, but it is also critical theory and a theory on reading insofar as it suggests, albeit in an experimental way, an alternative to the traditional academic essay on literary interpretation. However, it can also be classified as prose poetry because of *how* it is written, as veiled memoir (I wrote myself into this), and—due to my building on Barrie's story—fiction.

It is also hybrid, however, in *how* it appropriates space. The bisected page, relying on the *Home Under Ground* sections to contain those moments that center on decay, death, and passing out of existence, acts as a casket of sorts, a memento box. The bisected page also interrupts or disrupts the act of reading. So in a text that presents a multiplicity of voices and points of view, there is also a multiplicity of reading experiences.

I could say that my work is not so easily demarcated because its sub-jects, Peter and Wendy, are also not so easily demarcated, but I find that I often rebel against boundaries, preferring instead to envision, to test, to experiment, to practice, to pretend, to fracture and then to make anew. The text could only be subversive; that is, it could only exist as complicated, as yearning, as multifaceted as Wendy Darling—the girl who, as I see it, fell in love with the bad boy, ran away with him, wanted to delight in adult games and desires, to have fantasy cross over into real life. It could only be its best while playing at its own brand of make-believe. That is, the text is only successful if it truly believes the story it puts forth: that what its author has read between the lines in *Peter and Wendy* is the truer story.

HYBRID WORK

Excerpt from not merely because of the unknown that was stalking toward them

Oh, what, oh what *can* we do if we haven't got a thing to do? Why, you can help me wash your bearsuits, says Wendy. But the lost boys protest: they haven't taken off their bearsuits since. Don't you think, says Wendy, don't you think there is something strange and cruel about Peter making you. Wear them? Especially in this here August heat? But the lost boys, what can they say? They haven't known; they haven't ever known. They only do what Peter says. And Tootles, poor Tootles, who always misses an adventure, Tootles, we all know when his belly has a little grown; his bearsuit fairly stretches tightly over his tummy. I complain of Peter, he says, who makes us wear these bearsuits, but none of the other boys join in.

––––––––––––––––––––––––––

The Home Under Ground

Do you sense, dear, a certain *something*? Like a hand that keeps? That keeps on *interfering*? I wonder what would happen if not. Would we still all be here, free to do and choose? Then, I choose you, Peter, you of the pearl teeth, you of the skeleton leaves, you of the mourning doves. See, Tootles has to go. He has to go peepee, and that isn't, I daresay, *in the story*. He'll not climb out of the house under ground, but rather he'll just pee in that ole corner there and some of the pee will come and splash up on his feet and then he'll just return to bed and go to sleep as *if*, as if he didn't just pee on his floor, as if he didn't have any pee on his feet. Or take the baby— Michael lately has taken to sticking his finger up his pooper hole and then up his nose: that certainly isn't going to make it *in*. I daresay: there *is* a certain hand *intervening*.

(And how many children has she, has she? Let's see, there's Tootles and Nibs and Slightly and Curly and then the Twins. And Peter is the daddy and come lately are Michael and John, with Michael being the baby. And the tree underneath which they sleep curls and curves like an English sycamore, but not really. Not really.)

How cruel, how cruel he has been to Nana. He has placed the whole of his medicine in her drinking pan, and she will have to drink lest she get thirsty and what then? Mr. Darling: all in a flummox simply because, well, of *anything* really. (My dear, says Mrs. Darling, I just don't think I would like to, here, incorporate *anything* that the critics have got to say.) Mr. Darling: all in a flummox simply because.

The Home Under Ground

Don't let the Peter bird fool you (*fool you!*): he indeed knows how to read. A *certain code*. There are *certain books* for the learning in *his library*. But you haven't the key; you haven't the right words. Don't let the Peter bird fool you: he already knows that you will end in a realm of forgetfulness. You, the girl Wendy, no more useful than the rings on a Never tree, the rings on the oldest of the oldest Never tree even; you, the Wendy girl, no more useful than the layers of Never sediment, the husks of Never lobsters, the new year conch shell grown a little larger now. The little hermit crabs say that they too have buried themselves below ground; they too have peeled off an old skin; they too will need a new home now that they too done grown, done grown. The old fur doesn't fit; doesn't fit anymore, Wendy girl. And all your books and all your stories, why mother is taking them; she's taking them to some orphanage for girls. And Peter loved you for them and for them only. Somewhere in the Never trees: your old skin, your old skin in the wind done blown.

Some men would have resented her being able to do it so easily, but it was all a bit second nature to Mrs. Darling, all this knot tying: thirteen types of knot tie could she: the reef, the figure eight, the bowline, the sheet bend, the clove hitch, the common whipping, the butterfly, the eye splice, the oysterman's stopper, the single hitch, the thief, the thumb, the true lovers. She had, after all, learned how to do so from a certain sea cook, a Jas Hook, who she simply, as time wore on, called James. James, James, Darling James. James, James who didn't seem to mind it too much when her nightgown outgrown. *This* man now: all a sorry excuse for one. His tie won't tie he says and if his tie won't tie well then he simply won't be able to go to dinner tonight

---

The Home Under Ground

The girl's hair now so wild, all a mess of corn silk from a baby corn flush plucked. They've stolen a mess of them yesterday from the field of braves. Ole Tootles having a time. And the cow that lately wandered here being whetted for milk, and the twins turn-taking with the butter churn. Ole Tootles having a time with so much crème. He thinks he remembers something now about mothers. I do believe, Wendy, says he, pulling down on a teat, I do believe that I recall something about mothers; his bearsuit all foamy. But Wendy doesn't dare tell him; leaves him to quite believe what he pleases. The milk pail all salty and frothy by now. I do say, with all this teating and butter pounding that we've all taken on a rosy complexion; why our cheeks are quite the picture of strawberries and crème, which reminds me. Better take care of that skin, an old lady once told me. Someday, the girl Wendy's hair taking on a dried brittle cornhusk quality; the sun a big, burning something sunk down in the corn field; a Never piglet lost its mother, and a Never locust and a Never katydid circling something fierce; a dark pirate song miasma creeping in. It's about time. It's about time, says the girl Wendy, that we go in.

and if he isn't able to go to dinner tonight well then he won't be able to go to the office and if he isn't able to go to the office well then he'll lose his job and if he loses his job well then we'll all be out on the streets and we will all starve. All of this, to him, is a great *adventure*. And that is why, to him, Nana simply can't be nurse, can't any longer at night be brought in. With the children, he will try to play about in the nursery; he'll hoist young Michael on his back and play at sailing through the air, but that has, to the children, who lately have learned to fly, become oh-so-boring. But we are romping! We are *romping!* says Mr. Darling. Oh dear, oh dear, thinks Mrs. Darling, perhaps *ever after* should not happen, should never have happened *here*. She will show him the shadow; she will keep the shadow to her bodice pinned. He looks rather like a scoundrel, Mr. Darling says. He has the look of a scoundrel about him. Uh huh, says Mrs. Darling, that's him! That's him!

Something surely turning out strange with the formatting. Can't quite seem to get the space just right. The spacing quite off and

---

The Home Under Ground

Skylights: he didn't *last* long. How long was he there? I think it must have been the space of three sentences. But that is the storyteller's way— to kill simply to show you how it is done. The body kicked aside, the cigars unmoved, and the pirates simply keep on, keep on. That is what the storyteller has done, Wendy. (You didn't last *long*: the space of a *story*. If ever you think that the Hook is doing something or that Peter is doing something, you must remember that it is the storyteller who is doing something.) Morgan Skylights: we don't quite know anything else. And the pirates and the storyteller move on, move on. Skylights: he gave one screech.

these two stars here too far apart, not quite where they should be. It's happening all over I do believe. But do not despair—do not ever despair. If this here storyteller isn't quite right, why then, another, I do believe will shortly come. It's been known to happen. It's been known to happen, my dear. That's great, Wendy, because I do believe that I don't quite like *this* storyteller. I do think, Wendy, that I would like to hear one of your stories. Make it a story with *us* in it, something that I can't quite remember. Make it an *adventure*, Wendy.

Do you know the difference between real and make-believe? The Peter bird does not. He can have make-believe sex and think he's having real sex, and that is what is so great about the Peter bird. You haven't to worry about all that chafing. And that, I think, is why the

----

The Home Under Ground

The crocodile too, passes, passes, moves on. You could, you know, smother. The tiny sound with leaves. That's how quiet the sound of it was on the island. That's how come the little peas kept *disappearing*, and why, and why each new leaf showing on the Never trees were carrying a semblance of *just having been there all along*. (Why? Why don't you talk, Peter, about your dead brother? I think that's the story *we would like to hear*! And see how you've even adopted his stance, his gait, his habit of playing pipes, that certain twitch in your ears.) Wendy will find her way by *following*. The beast will lead her to Jas. Hook, always. He will call her *my beauty*. But it is much more interesting to think of the gagging: *he was so frightfully* distingué, *that she was too fascinated to cry out. She was only a little girl.* Hook fingering a stack of cards; Wendy's finger on the dirty glass, inscribing: *dirty pig, dirty pig.* She, like her boys, staring only at the plank. Give them, Wendy; give them a mother's last. Wishes.

Tiger Lily has never gotten. Their make-believe is pretty amazing, but don't tell Peter that I told you that. What's that you say? He doesn't do it to you *make-believe?* Well, then, that would explain it then; that would explain *many* things. Attachment, for instance.

Did you know that the little shells are breaking? It's about that time when the shells start breaking. New birds done hatched, done grown, done flown. They've hardly anything in their newborn food sacs; they're still waiting to grow a belly. Here too, a gale that will come and kill them. All. Tomorrow, we'll find them all crushed on the Never ground, and Nibs can calculate how many, how many. Perhaps we'll take to playing doctor and stick a glass thing in. Glass thing will say they're dying. Or about to. Too dark, today even, for the tulips to open.

The Home Under Ground

You see, Wendy, I can take you part of the way, but I won't go *all the way.* With you. I will do this so that you will be *less afraid.* There will come a time, Wendy; there will come a time when even father will talk less and less to you, but you needn't sulk and hide in your room all day. That will just be the way it is; that is just his way. You needn't wait for me anymore all day. Oh, yes, you see, it is quite *dense,* but haven't you? Haven't you a good writing day, Wendy? I am only *quite sorry,* so sorry that this drawer won't open anymore. I daresay that something of me is tucked up inside of it. And I know. I know it isn't a matter of having a key or prying.

PICTURE (ピクチャー)

Performing Chit-Chat

Terrance Hayes

1.

In 2008 the Carnegie Mellon University School of Architecture invited nine or 10 people from different fields to talk about what the term "open systems" meant to them. The presenters included an architect, an urban planner, a jazz bass player, and me, a poet.

2.

"Each person shows 20 images. You have 20 seconds to show each image. You have no control over this. It will be programmed on a computer, so you should be fast. It will be fun and filled with ideas! Have fun, remember that you only have 400 seconds on stage!"

3.

I combed the internet for definitions of "open system." And for images (images?) that might have something to do with the term. According to Wikipedia: "an open system is a system that continuously interacts with

Terrance Hayes is the author of *Lighthead* (2010), which won the National Book Award for Poetry; *Wind in a Box* (2006), named one of the best books of the year by *Publishers Weekly*; *Hip Logic* (2002), which won the 2001 National Poetry Series; and *Muscular Music* (1999), winner of the Kate Tufts Discovery Award. His honors and awards include a Whiting Writers Award, a Pushcart Prize, three *Best American Poetry* selections, a National Endowment for the Arts Fellowship, and the Guggenheim Foundation Fellowship. He is a professor of creative writing at the University of Pittsburgh.

its surroundings via information, energy, or material transfers." I recall myself uttering a long, perspiring "Huh?"

4.

The jazz musician played audio of a looping drum solo while improvising 20 different 20-second bass lines. No, maybe he played a dozen or so 20-second riffs. He used the other segments to explain what "open systems" meant to jazz musicians like him. "Music is an inherently open system," I think he said.

5.

One wall of the room was made of glass blocks. The students, audience members, and presenters milling on the other side were a blur, a manifestation of my own blurry notion of our purpose that night. My wife patted my knee intermittently. I ruffled my paper, a poem made of 20 different fragments of 20 poems I loved.

6.

"Pulse and vein, cord and wire, if language is an open system, is it mostly an animal or a machine system?" That was my second question. "Would these fools play my slides in the appropriate order?" That was my first. I was sweating more than usual.

7.

Pecha Kucha graced Carnegie Mellon with neither signs nor publicity materials. (The organizers had not gotten permission to use the term.) Standing near the chips and dip, the architecture student (a closeted poet) who'd invited me whispered the word: "Pecha Kucha." I know a little Japanese, but it didn't sound like any Japanese I knew.

8.

"There are many kinds of open / how a diamond comes into a knot of flame / how sound comes into a word, colored / by who pays what for speaking," I began. An excerpt from "Coal" by Audre Lorde accompanied by an image of Lawrence Weiner's text-art: "Bits & Pieces put together to present a semblance of a whole."

9.
Bits of Adrienne Rich, Jack Gilbert, Amiri Baraka, Dean Young: my poem and slides were a collage of intensities. The architect's comments and slides were orderly and sensible. "Open systems architecture is a standard that describes the layered hierarchical structure, configuration, or model of a communications or distributed data processing system," the architect said.

10.
At home that night my wife convinced me the audience was hushed when my 400 seconds were done because they were bewildered, blown away, floating. Reading the poem made me sweat. No poem had ever made me sweat. I wanted to reproduce the feeling in my own work. I went to work.

11.
For two years I'd been working on a poem (it was maybe 100 pages of failure) about meeting my biological father in 2006. Also, during a trip to New York, I'd encountered the wood sculptures of Martin Puryear. I decided to set 20 Puryear works in conversation with 20 fragments of my writing.

12.
Later I decided to try using 20-second snippets of Fela Kuti songs to frame 20 poem fragments exploring American warmongering, indictment, and self-indictment. For a moment there, I wanted to squeeze everything I wrote/thought/heard/saw into 20 20-second boxes. My ambition, now and then: to make unity out of collage.

13.
Malcolm X's assassins were never caught. "Someone should write a detective novel about Malcolm X's brothers; I bet they know who killed

him," I said to a novelist at a party. "You should write it!" he exclaimed. "My prose always winds up chopped up and screwed," I said. "Any time I tell a story, I resort to metaphor," I said.

14.
Sometimes I think all my poems are about brothers. Two boys on an adventure. Two boys separated, but bound by blood, just as my half-brother and I are separate and bound. Whenever I write about two boys, I am, I guess, writing about us.

15.
"*Pecha Kucha* is," the format's inventors told me when I met them in Tokyo in 2010, "Japanese slang for *chit-chat*." I prefer to think of its primary origin as a Japanese loan word for *picture*. "Pikcha." May I take your pik-u-cha.

16.
Language's ability to *create* equals its ability to *erase*; it can insult or offend and simultaneously humor or praise. I love that metaphor means there is no such thing as a pure system of meaning. The whole world is always on fire, and we are always to blame.

17.
"For Brothers of the Dragon" is a hybrid of fiction and poetry. After writing pecha kucha poems using image (pecha kucha's original intention) and music, I wanted to collage elements of the novel I could not write and the poem I also could not write. Part detective novel, part personal investigation of brotherhood.

18.
However else fiction functions, it fills you with the sound
of crows chirping, *alive alive alive*. But that's temporary too.
Tell my story, begs the past as if it was a prayer
for an imagined life or a life that's better than the life you live.

19.

I am, I suppose, too restless to commit exclusively to the pecha kucha poem. But the lessons inherent in the form—chiefly that it is possible to sing and tell a story simultaneously—have become an aesthetic philosophy. That is to say, the form has made me irrevocably attuned to the hybrid nature of poetry, of narrative, of thinking.

20.

If language is an animal, it is hybrid by way of nature. We struggle heroically, tragically, to make it one thing, though, thank goodness, it can never be a "be," only a "being."

HYBRID WORK
From Lighthead

For Brothers of the Dragon
a pecha kucha

[PREMONITION]

I dreamed my brother said I'd live with the feeling
a child feels the first time he sees his brother disappear.
I went down on my knees and sure enough, I was the size
of a boy again. With my shins like two skinny tracks in the dirt,
I could almost hear a train carrying its racket up my spine.

[OPENING SCENE]

The day Malcolm X was buried, his brothers were in a motel
watching the funeral on a black-and-white TV. If I were in their story,
I would have run down the assassins and removed their eyes.
It does not matter if this is true, only that it can be conceived.

[HOW FICTION FUNCTIONS]

However else fiction functions, it fills you with the sound
of crows chirping, *alive alive alive*. But that's temporary too.
Tell my story, begs the past, as if it was a prayer
for an imagined life or a life that's better than the life you live.

[SCENE AT THE GRAVE]

I am considering writing a story about the lives the brothers lead
afterward. They will change their names a third time and abandon
their families. They will visit their brother's grave at Ferncliff.
They will be poor and empty. One will bag the dead man's bones
while the one holding the shovel begs him to hurry.

[FORESHADOWING]

I keep thinking I'll have a dream about the smoke clouding
the bar my brother and I used to haunt. We spent hours saying
nothing. He pretended he didn't know the man raising us was
his father but not mine. Instead I dream about the mouth
of a dragon, the smoke of a train vanishing into a mountainside.

[DRAMATIC ARC]

One brother will want, at first, redemption; one brother will want,
at first, revenge. Their story will be part family saga and elegy,
part mystery. What changes them before the story begins will be,
at first, more important than what changes them when it ends.

[IMAGERY]

I have no problem with the flaws of memory. The bird carcass
stiff as the shoe of a hit-and-run victim on the side of the road
might just be a veil the wind pulled from the face of a new bride.
Why was the imagination invented, if not to remake?

[OPENING DIALOGUE]

The motel's twin beds will be narrow and dingy. On each pillow
will be a sweating peppermint candy left by a desk clerk
who will sigh the way my mother sighs. "Y'all look like the ghosts
of Malcolm X," I'll have her think, carelessly. "Y'all smell
like men who slept all night in a boxcar or on a roadside."

[SYMBOLISM]

However else fiction functions, it fills you with the sound
of running away. The dirt, the smudged mirror, even the silences
between speech have something to say. In novels
there is no such thing as a useless past or typical day.

[FLASHBACK]

I'm thinking of black boys in the countryside with a white boy
who'd seen, only a summer before, a black man strung up
at the edge of town. They'll be singing when they drag the white boy
to the river and throw him in. They'll be singing when they
dive in and drag him back to shore before he drowns.

[STATIC CHARACTERS]

In my novel all the minor characters will look like various friends
and family: Blind Vince Twang, BlackerThanMost, Deadeye Sue,
Lil Clementine. They will be more human than my protagonists
because they will be left with lives that do not change.

[POINT OF VIEW]

The chin of Malcolm's widow will quiver below her veil.
Where is home now? she'll think. It will be the wind
or her trembling that moves the veil. I am not going to describe
her face because I want you to think of her as a bride.

[SETTING THAT ILLUMINATES CHARACTER]

When I try remembering dirt, I remember my mother's pale carpet
stained by mud and my brother on his knees with a hairbrush
and bar of soap, scrubbing before school. I do not remember
the names of the birds who lived outside our house,
but I know their music was swallowed by the passing trains.

[ALLEGORY]

One brother will tell the other a story: *Once, in the shadow of a tree
lit with song, when a black woman unbuttoned her blouse,
all the birds came to dine.* It will mean there are people who root
and people who roam; people bound to a place
and people bound to an idea, whatever the idea may be.

[CONNOTATION]

I wish I was not the kind of man who abandons
those who love him repeatedly. My brother must be
one hundred pounds heavier now than he was
all those years ago. Because growing old is like slipping
into a new coat without taking the old coat off,
I think of him bearing the weight of our family.

[DELETED CHAPTER]

You'll find salt in the eyes of anyone who kneels too long
with his head in the dirt. I should say what happened
to my brother when he was sixteen. My mother found him
naked and weeping to himself in the closet. Because
I wasn't there, there is no suitable place in the story for this scene.

[FALLING ACTION]

Later both X brothers show up at the widow X's door and miss
the softer woman she was before. Here, I am not going to say

she forgives them. When she turns them away, I imagine
the sunlight bleeding its heaviness upon their backs.

[METAPHOR]

Because I am a brother of the dragon, call me Dragonfly.
When I dream of the train riding our parallel spines, carrying
our history, the weight that turns my brother into fire, makes me
scattered light. In my story the X brothers will live
without their brother, but that doesn't mean they'll survive.

[ALLUSION TO THEME]

It's all true: the pair of tracks through the darkness,
men who look like me, disguised. The bewilderment
that cannot be described. What I feel is *Why*. In fiction
everything happens with ease, and the easefulness kills me.

[RESOLUTION]

I am full of dirt sometimes. I am trying to tell you a story
without talking. I promise nothing I write about you
tomorrow will be a lie. Instead of fiction, brother,
I will offer you an apology. And if that fails,
I will drag myself to your arms crying, *Speak to me*.

6

. . . .

Short-Form Nonfiction

SHORT-FORM NONFICTION
An Introduction

Combining the concision of poetry and the expository nature of the personal essay, short-form nonfiction offers both immediacy and intensity—giving the reader brief but compelling access to the writer's quick, powerful, and true thoughts and discoveries. In his introduction to *The Rose Metal Press Field Guide to Writing Flash Nonfiction*, Dinty W. Moore locates the beginnings of short-form nonfiction with the Greek philosopher Heraclitus, circa 535 to 475 BCE. John D'Agata makes a case in *The Lost Origins of the Essay* that the short essay dates even further back to find its origin in the brief statements in the *List of Ziusudra*—observations, advice, and musings compiled by the Sumerian king Ziusudra some 5,000 years ago.

Michel de Montaigne, the meditative founder of the traditional essay, includes numerous brief essays in his *Essais*, first published in 1580. And the English essay, as practiced by Addison and Steele in the early 1700s, and later by a diverse range of nineteenth-century essayists—among them Matthew Arnold and Oliver Wendell Holmes—was often necessarily short to meet the requirements of daily newspaper printing. Even as printing became easier and cheaper and magazines grew more sophisticated, columns like *The New Yorker's* "Talk of the Town" have given and continue to give such prestigious writers as E.B. White, James Thurber, and, more recently, Ian Frazier, a tight space to pack with pithy detail. Since the 1990s short-form nonfiction has been on the rise again, popularized first in a series of anthologies including *In Short* (1996) and *In Brief* (1999), edited by Mary Paumier Jones and Judith Kitchen. The genre continues to grow under the innovative editorial watch of Moore, whose online nonfiction journal *Brevity* publishes pieces of 750 words or less. The pieces anthologized in this chapter extend to the roomier 1,500-word limit.

While the brief essay can still be ruminative, exploratory, lyric, or meandering like its long-form cousin, it must make its discoveries quickly, starting the reader as close to the intellectual and narrative action as it can. Every word counts—will literally be counted—in the short form, so there is tightness to the language, thereby ensuring that it can hold up when the words keep company in such close quarters. This means that the brief essay can better encapsulate an individual moment or a solitary thought. It often tries for a single, beautiful image or one profound idea. To make these moments shine, short-form nonfiction relies heavily on rhythm, tone, image and language.

The relationship of short-form nonfiction to poetic language and technique is embodied in Sarah Gorham's *Study in Perfect*. Of "Perfect Solution," "Perfect Heaven," and "Perfect Sleep," she writes, "All three mini-essays could have been poems." But the pieces became essays because they favor memory and narrative, as well as using the essay's lyrical mode to engage pieces of forgotten personal history, to create a sort of elegy between the spaces, spaces that Gorham makes as much a part of the essays as the rest of the text.

Brenda Miller's "An Earlier Life" also engages the brief, episodic style of the essayist while "relying on language, rhythm, and image much as poetry does." Here she brings vignettes into dialogue so that they float together, arranged to tell a story composed of many memories. This, too, is one of the joys of the short form: that one person's small, minute, private details can stand in place for anyone else's, and that these quotidian details can be as powerful as the grand or the heroic.

Because essays often focus on the day-to-day, short-form essays are likely to concentrate on one scene or event, as Bret Lott's "The Importance of Story" does. Lott writes, "If you want to write, you must be a kind of story mercenary. You must always be on the prowl in your life for stories." Lott's piece, a single narrative arc, serves as an example of the narrative structure nonfiction can have, a style that makes more borders fluid, bringing memoir closer to short story.

Patricia Vigderman's essay "Sebald in Starbucks" also starts by obliterating borders, and she mentions that she doesn't even know quite what to call the pieces she writes—that she is less interested in calling them anything and more interested in letting them take shape. Her work shows that boundaries can be crossed and re-crossed, especially when an author is meditating on the ideas of another writer—in this case, the German intellectual and literary critic W. G. Sebald.

Similarly, Ander Monson in "Burn This First/Unison Device" and "Dear Sepulcher, Dear Bless Your Heart" decentralizes narrative, bringing the short form ever closer to the line of lyric. He speaks in his contributor's essay of the white space an essay exhibits, especially the short essay, and shows how a short essay can "accelerate through its last line into air and suspend there."

This idea of accelerating recalls the other name short-form nonfiction sometimes goes by: *flash* nonfiction. As all the pieces in this section show, there is a momentum in the brief essay that is generally unmatched in longer forms, and which gives the short-form essay its particular pleasure and power.

—*Scott Russell Morris*

CABLES, CHAINS, AND LARIATS
Form as Process
Brenda Miller

It's Monday morning, and I'm where I usually am on Monday mornings: writing with my practice group in my friend Nancy Canyon's art studio in Bellingham, Washington. We've been meeting for years, sometimes in a café, but lately we've settled into the studio where we're surrounded by Nancy's paintings: lush colors that form images of watery reflections.

We settle in quickly, using a formal writing practice technique that Nancy has taught us: We each write words or lines on scraps of paper—sometimes grabbing whatever book or brochure is handy—and toss these scraps into a porcelain dish, to be chosen at random at the beginning of each writing segment. These lines or phrases act as triggers for the writing to come; whatever we choose starts us off for that segment, but the writing can veer wildly from there. The first exercise is five minutes of writing very short sentences. The second is 10 minutes of chaining sentences, where the end word of a sentence becomes the beginning word of the next. The third is writing one long sentence for 20 minutes. These technical restraints give the intellect something to focus on, while the subconscious mind comes forth to fill in the content. Each writing segment can focus

Brenda Miller directs the MFA in Creative Writing and the MA in English Studies at Western Washington University. She is the author of four essay collections, including *Listening Against the Stone* (2011), *Blessing of the Animals* (2009), and *Season of the Body* (2002). She also co-authored *Tell It Slant: Creating, Refining and Publishing Creative Nonfiction* (2012) and *The Pen and the Bell: Mindful Writing in a Busy World* (2012). Her work has received six Pushcart Prizes.

on different material, or if we find ourselves "on to something" we can continue with that theme or scene in the next segment, turning whatever the start line might be toward that topic. In between each timed writing, we read what we've written aloud, with no response from the listeners. At the end of the whole writing practice, we "speak back" to each other the images or phrases that resonated with us.

It's a simple but powerful practice. And while not everything I write will make it into finished work, it's the practice itself that becomes essential, keeping the writing mind well oiled and ready. Since these women and I have written together for so long, we're able to enter quickly into a deep space: a space in which we excavate memories and scenes and images that would not have come forward on their own. The formal constraints—and the random start lines—demand that we let go of preconceived stories and follow the rhythm and waves of language wherever they might take us.

Today, as with many days, I find myself writing about the few months I spent in the Arizona desert as a young woman with a man who was bad for me. I've tried to write about this time before, with no success. But in the confines of this room—surrounded by art, by other women writing—and subservient to the assignments, fragments of this era emerge quickly on the page, no matter what start line triggers them. I'm writing fast: no time to censor or pretty up, no time to hesitate. And different voices will speak, depending on the form.

The short sentences sound like urgent telegraphs: cables from the past that necessarily must give only the important bits of information. It's a solemn voice, with no patience for hedging or clearing the throat, but a compassionate one as well, striving to deliver the news gently.

The chaining sentences coil together, forming a rhythm that captures the narrator in their own momentum. The pattern demands that she keep going forward, each sentence leading inevitably to the next, just as this girl's life back then seemed inevitable, carried by a force she couldn't control. Sometimes, these chains seem heavy and metallic, jailing the narrator in the story with no way out; but sometimes they remind me of daisy chains, or the small loops of colored paper we made as children, chained together to form a garland. Something that is light and transient.

The long sentence is the most demanding and the most urgent. We have to breathe as we write, and use lots of conjunctions, and keep up our stamina; we can't stop even when we've reached a dead end; we have to keep moving, keep searching, riding the galloping horse of the sentence with a lariat in hand, seeking out the image, the scene, the story that will get us out of here in one piece.

Later, in my own writing space, I'll be able to turn to the notebooks and see what I've written. I always have someplace to start, my handwriting like tracks I follow in the sand. I have to make some decisions about what gets typed up and what does not. I'll need to decide whether I can keep the fragments in the form that triggered them, or revise so the prose makes more narrative or aesthetic sense. But still, the forms will continue to infuse the pieces with a particular tone that contributes to the essay's meaning.

Since we are writing in short bursts, this practice lends itself to the short short form, relying on language, rhythm, and image much as poetry does. Sometimes I wonder if these fragments can add up to anything, but once I've assembled dozens of them together, I can see the patterns emerge. I arrange and rearrange, notice repeating imagery, combine and cut apart. The story that develops is one that follows a logic beyond the intellect, beyond the mind itself; this story exists in the intuitive gaps between thought and intention. The fragments say what they need to say, and I watch. They are cables, chains, and lariats: each one leading me carefully to a place that requires such sturdy and lovely support.

HYBRID WORK
From An Earlier Life

Groceries

We always got the battered cart with its stuck wheel limping up and down the brightly lit aisles full of canned vegetables, boxes of cereal, flour, milk. Milk and Kool-Aid and hominy, a little bit of tough pork—that's what we'd buy, though I'd thrown a fit over the cost of the Kool-Aid, calculated the price in my head, weighed the few bills in my pocket over the promise of sweetness to the water. The water at Wahweap Marina tasted metallic, and all he wanted was something to make it bearable, but I said no to the Kool-Aid, said it was a luxury we couldn't afford. (*Afford?* How did one calculate such things—I was only 23, had never run a household, knew nothing of budgets, remembered only my mother and her fan of coupons in hand at the checkout line, the careful way she counted up how much she had saved.)

Saving as much as I could of the seven dollars in my pocket, I said no to the Kool-Aid, and we fought right there in the soft drinks aisle—the Navajo shoppers knew to look away, familiar with fights held out in the open, hiding their disapproval of this white girl and Indian man duking it out over the Kool-Aid—while the white shoppers stared openly as they pushed their carts by us, until he finally threw 10 packs of the powder into our cart—berry, lemon, lime, orange—while I slunk behind him to the checkout counter; we placed on the conveyer belt our cans of hominy, our Wonder bread, our little bit of pork, our white flour, and salt.

Salt at least made things taste better, and I watched it slide by, while I glanced at the magazines holstered in their racks—*Good Housekeeping, Better Homes and Gardens, Women's Day*—then we bagged everything up, took the lone sack back to our trailer, where I doled out salt into the *posole*, measured with the cup of my palm, the skin there red and cracked from the cold.

Mirror

In the mirror, I see him sitting on the bed. On the bed, he lies back, hands behind his head, belly bloated above his belt. His belt is loosened, his mouth slack, his dark hair smooth, save for one cowlick at attention. On top of the dresser sits a bowl of change, a set of car keys, a pipe, a pouch of tobacco. This tobacco feels smooth against my fingers, leaves them smelling sweet. I bring the pouch to my nose, sniff deeply—tobacco mixing with leather—and I can even detect the smell of turquoise, if turquoise had a scent. There's the smell of beer, too, and gin, underlying the air in that room.

In that room, he's asleep, but not at rest, only the deep sleep of obliteration, a blackness in which the body shuts down, tries to recoup, circulates the poison through and out. Outside, ravens and hawks circle the campground, on the hunt for anything that moves, and I don't look at myself when I take the tobacco, the coins, the car keys, and walk outside into the dusk. Dusk in the desert: the segue between glaring light and total darkness—a forgiving time, when anything might still be possible.

Beloved

On Lake Powell, the silence grows so deep it pulses against your ears, and you sit alone, rocking in the motorboat, your boom box tinnily playing Fleetwood Mac; it's the only thing here that's truly yours, while you watch the dock, waiting for him to emerge from the store. This store carries bait, motor oil, potato chips, Fritos, Styrofoam coolers, and drinks, lots of drinks: water and Pepsi and Gatorade and beer.

Beer, you know, is what he'll emerge with, a case of something cheap, and he'll carry it with a swagger: hiding it and flaunting it at once. Your neck prickles as you wait, the boat rocking, the water slapping the sides of the deck, Stevie Nicks singing of leather and lace, her voice barely denting the silence of the high desert—absorbed by the high red rocks, the unreal blue, the light bright and subdued at once.

This cool air in the desert, over the water: it's a land of contradiction: deep blue, bone cold, desert sun, red cliffs, and the drowned trees beneath them. You can motor along the wide expanse of the lake, find a small canyon to enter, look for the hanging gardens: plants growing high above the water line, gaining foothold and flourishing on bare rock, while beneath you—far beneath—the drowned trees, the flooded caves. A ghost garden mirroring the one above.

You thought you were going to Rainbow Bridge, where all the tourists go, that huge arch spanning the sky. A place, they say, that is full of spirits, and the natives here say it is a bridge to the afterlife—or used to be anyway, before all the tourists came, before all the boats broke the silence and everyone was so eager to set foot on sacred soil.

But it turns out you're not going to Rainbow Bridge after all; he shoves the beer into the boat's stern, doesn't look at you, moves quickly to untie the boat and steer you out in the opposite direction: away from the shoreline with its many attractions, but instead into the flat wide expanse of water unbounded by anything. Water that looks blue from a distance, but close up becomes black.

You know you should remain quiet, just sit back and admire the stark beauty all around you—the smooth granite of Gunsight Butte, the water snaking its way through the wide river canyon—but you get out into open water, and he cuts the engine. He cracks the first one open, the pull tab creaking loudly against your ears. He drinks long and hard, the way men do who are this kind of thirsty.

Your hands gripping the gunwales, and you can't help it, you say, *I thought you weren't going to drink...* but your voice is insubstantial, weak as Stevie Nicks who sings from far inside the boom box. He throws the empty overboard, and you watch it bobbing, *Budweiser* in blood-red letters curling against the black. And you see now you're really far from shore, and you're starting to burn in that exposed area of your neck, that little strip your shirt fails to cover.

He says nothing, but leans toward you, another beer in hand. He picks up the boom box by its handle and looks at it appraisingly. Stevie Nicks keeps singing as it sways in his hand. You spent more money than you had on that tape player, and it traveled with you from California to Arizona, keeping you company on all those nights alone. Your stash of cassettes is well worn—full of hand-lettered liner notes that have faded to barely distinguishable words. You have lots of bootleg Grateful Dead tapes you listen to over and over, remembering yourself when you could dance with abandon. Many of the tapes have broken, but you keep them anyway, as reminders.

I could throw this thing in the lake right now, he says, his voice soft, but his eyes hard. He holds it a few moments longer, then drops it on the seat, and the music clatters to a halt. Stevie Nicks shuts up, the way you should have done, should have just kept quiet. You imagine you and Stevie in this boat together, huddled against one another, groping for each other's hands.

Or I could throw you overboard, he says, not really to you but to himself. A threat but not a threat, just a statement of fact.

He puts his free hand back on the rudder, drinks his beer while turning toward a side canyon, toward a cove with a beach of white sand. A place that in any other time, with any other person, would be a romantic picnic spot—the water lapping, the rock sheltering—and you putter in, anchor the boat, slosh your way toward shore. He has cans of beer stuffed in every pocket. You don't know what will happen next.

You're not lost: that will happen later, when he begins walking up a trail to the mesa, and you'll follow because what else is there to do? You'll climb in the hot sun (no cool air now, no breeze, no comfort) until you reach the top, where you'll be able to see now—in a way you never could from below, when you're immersed in it—the expanse of this land, cracked and broken. No straight line between here and there, between past and future; instead, many small rifts open between where you stand now and where you are trying to go.

Box Canyon

Sometimes there's no road at all—just a game trail through the desert, a faint track that leads past piñon pine and prickly pear, zigzagging across the rust-colored dirt, always heading toward water, perhaps just an underground spring emerging as a damp trickle under a green bush. You sniff it out, the sky wide overhead, a breeze you can't feel moving the spare branches against the canyon walls. You keep following it until you come to a dead end: the box canyon, a place where the Indians used to drive wild horses, knowing there'd be no way out, the wild ones snorting and snuffling against the cliff, while the tamed horses grew inflamed with the hunt, sweat on their flanks, high-stepping sideways. The Indians threw their lassos, caught the horses by their necks, coaxed them out of the canyon and into the fold, thundering out of the desert. Sometimes you think you still see wild horses on the ridge, their small backs, their heads turning to watch you as you make your way along the watershed, watched, too, by coyote and rattlesnake, jackrabbit and scorpion, as you zigzag across the desert, the vultures overhead, but you make your way out, you find the familiar stones, the ones that can lead you home.

An Earlier Life

In an earlier life I was a baker, in a bakery on a cobble-stoned street. I woke early, in the dark, to do my work. Before the birds. Before the music of the world commenced. In the quiet, I brought something to life. In an earlier life I proofed yeast in large bowls, or I coddled the sourdough mother, urging it to grow. Only the scrape of my spoon against the bowl. Only the smell of yeast and flour, honey and egg. My wrists were strong. My back, strong. I knocked a Morse code on the undersides of loaves to test if they were done. Children pressed their noses to the glass, begged for tiny morsels to fill their mouths. I made special loaves for them, swirled in cinnamon and sugar. It was my only kindness.

THE ESSAY IS THE EGG

On Shortness

Ander Monson

> *"Don't want no short dick man."*
> —20 Fingers featuring Gillette

In America we admire the large, the supersized, the tome, the megaboob, the trente, oversize, the Escalade, the epic sprawl, Supra Extra Nacho Cheesier Doritos, everything embiggened.

Bigness leaves me breathless. As an asthmatic I'm aware of the usefulness of breath. As a fiction writer and a poet, my unit of meaning is always in some way the capacity of the human breath, the sentence, more or less. My tool: the human voice (I thought grandly of and to myself). But, oddly, until recently, not in nonfiction. My essays used the page, not the breath, as their natural habitat. They were visual like that, hard to read aloud.

The whole point of essays, I thought then, was to connect and keep connecting: it's what I loved about them, essaying as networking: essay as conversation, as aggregation, as pathogen vector, or maybe just books rhizome on library shelves, one essay echoing after or referencing another.

Ander Monson is the author of six books of poetry, fiction, and nonfiction, most recently *Letter to a Future Lover* (2015). He edits the magazine *DIAGRAM* and is the editor and publisher of New Michigan Press. He teaches in the MFA program at University of Arizona.

My sentences began stretching longer, containing more. Essay as collection. An idea sparked another. A research move dominoed a dozen more. It all fits, I'd say, so leave it in. I essayed like *Katamari Damacy*, kept rolling stuff into my katamari, kept collecting.

But some of my favorite essays were more superdense star than lip-glossed suburban teen mall sprawl. I read the occasional iteration of Dinty W. Moore's *Brevity*, an entire magazine devoted to nonfiction pieces of 750 words or less. Sean Lovelace, an auteur of the short, schooled me by going short about a short—specifically Augusto Monterroso's eight-word story "The Dinosaur"—in the December 17 entry of the Essay Daily 2012 Advent calendar.

Something changed. Like a blog or blob I kept getting bigger but more dilute. I missed my constraints, Oulipian or otherwise imposed.

If we can do anything, Bruce Mau told me, *what will we do?*

So I quieted down. Spent days in libraries, reading and writing actual books, you know, the kind that smell of paper, that you can drop in water and keep reading. I started finding weird stuff in them: marginalia, inscriptions, a human hair. I wrote about it. And I wanted to publish the weird stuff I wrote about the weird stuff I found back in the book where I found it as a way of messaging a future reader of the book. This meant 6x9 cards, double-sided. This meant they'd max out at 750 words.

I had to learn to write short. Was hard. Changed my brain.

Recently I read Patricia Vigderman's essay collection *Possibility: Essays Against Despair,* which features quite a few short essays, including at least 10 of four pages or less, including "Eggs," most briefly and amusingly, clocking in at 509 words.

Short is hard but powerful. The poet knows this well, aware as she is of the dialectic between the textshape and whitespace. Compression and suggestion make the muscle stronger. It's what's best about the fragment: the reader's asked to do more lifting in the reading. She's supposed to process more what's there.

Of course it should all be compressed: prose, as we sometimes disparagingly call it. Otherwise it just runs and runs and breaks where it breaks until it ends. But prose has a tendency to get prosy if you let it.

I'm running out of words (not a problem unless I make it one: I'd rather my flaw become a feature), so back to Vigderman. "Eggs" begins: "Peter is trying to figure out how to create a structure in which to drop an egg from a fourth story window without breaking it." Who's Peter? Doesn't matter. Where we at? Whatever.

I'll get to it quickly: the essay is the egg, though it wouldn't be so gauche as to say so.

From this scenario we go to dream, to anecdote, to metaphor, to "the art of boiling an egg, while perhaps entirely off-message and perfectly unspectacular, is nevertheless a useful application of physical principles." Liquid becomes a solid, more easily manipulated. The essay admits it's straying here, but lies. It's not straying: instead it's leaping from a window, four stories above, hoping not to crack.

Flashback: "What makes an egg crack [...] is that when the bottom of it hits the ground the top is still falling." There's something resonating here. Can you feel it? It's what we want from the whitespace an essay (poem, story) exits into at its end: a question mark, a little wonder. Art should accelerate through its last line into air and suspend there.

HYBRID WORK

From Letter to a Future Lover: Marginalia, Errata, Secrets, Inscriptions, and Other Ephemera Found in Libraries

Dear Sepulcher, Dear Bless Your Heart,

ptu·ncial, *a. Obs.*—⁰ [ad. late L. *sep-tis*, f. L. *sept-em* seven + *uncia* OUNCE¹.] BLOUNT *Glossogr., Septuncial*, of seven ounces, or arts of the whole.

tuor (seʹptiⁿⱥı). [a. F. *septuor*, f. L. *sep-*ter *quatuor* quartett.] = SEPTET. LONGF. *Life* (1891) II. 177 The first and longest a ny..the last a Septuor, very beautiful. 1873 'OUIDA' *I*. 111 Phrase after phrase, chorus on chorus, solo tuor, and recitative.

tuple (seʹptiuⱥpʹl), *a.* and *sb.* [ad. late L. *lus*, f. *septem* seven : see -PLE.] **A.** *adj.* venfold.
'*ait's Mag.* I. 456 The ' quadruple ' alliance will very :..a ' septuple ' one. **1868** LOCKYER *Guillemin's* s (ed. 3) 350, θ Orionis is a septuple star. **1882-3** in *Herzog's Encycl. Relig. Knowl.* I. 49 The sep-lness of the Holy Spirit.
'*us.* Having seven beats in a bar.
rove's Dict. Mus. IV. 120/1 There seems no reason Composer, visited by an inspiration in that direction, not write an Air in Septuple Time, with seven beats

:*b.* The seventh multiple.
apt. *Smith's Seaman's Gram.* II. xv. 173 The Cube Septuple thereof is 1·913. **1755** JOHNSON, *Septuple,*

chre ; *pl.* the church of this order. Cf. SEPULCHRINE. **1844** A. P. DE LISLE in E. Purcell *Life* (1900) I. 130 Mr. and Mrs. Craven met us at Mass at the Sepulchran Nuns. **1857** G. OLIVER *Coll. Cath. Relig. Cornw.* 30 The English Sepul-chran nuns had determined to emigrate from Liege.

Sepulchre (seʹpɪlkəı), *sb.* Forms : 2-7 sepulcre, 4 sepulchur, 5 scepulcur, sepulkyr, 5-6 sepulcur(e, 6 sepulcor, sepulcar, sepulcer, sepullcre, sepullcur, (sepulchree, sepulchrie, sepulcrye), 6-9 (now *U. S.* sepul-cher, 3- sepulchre. [a. OF. *sepulcre* (11th c. in Hatz.-Darm.), ad. L. *sepulcrum* (less correctly *sepulchrum*), f. root of L. *sepul-tus*, pa. pple. of *sepelire* to bury ; cf. Sp., Pg. *sepulcro*, It. *sepolcro*.]
1. A tomb or burial-place, a building, vault, or excavation, made for the interment of a human body. Now only *rhetorical* or *Hist.*
*c*1200 *Trin. Coll. Hom.* 101 Oðer is þat bitweuen his browenge and his ariste he lai on his sepulcre. **a 1225** *Ancr. R.* 170 Uor ȝe beoð mid Iesu Criste bitund ase ine sepul-cre. *c*1390 *Holy Rood* 400 in *S. Eng. Leg.* 13 And þo he cam to Ierusalem of þe sepulchre he hadde doute þat ore louerd was on i-leid. **1340** HAMPOLE *Pr. Consc.* 5188 Par es þe mount of calvery, And þe sepulcre of Crist fast þarby. *c*1386 CHAUCER *Wife's Prol.* 498 The sepulcre of hym Daryus Which that Appelles wroghte subtilly. *c*1440 *Gesta Rom.*

The Compact Edition of the Oxford English Dictionary, Oxford University Press, 1971, Personal Library

Sepulcher. Alabamian. Kennel. Papeete. Retaliate. Like all words, these are doors to open up new corridors, leading to another dozen doors, then each leads back into the labyrinth, a familiar wind through books and stone. I've been caught in ruts like this, in stacks like this, among the casks, the tuns, the old amontillados, underneath the clockwork and the slow work of hearts a floor or two above us, still broadcasting/telltaling from the past. Some words have freight, are freight—when pressed they spring back, retaliate, they bring a fright, bring fight to nights otherwise loose with dreams. You roll over in the bed; I am still awake. The crosswalk sound from a mile away propagates through nighttime air and open door: *walk, walk, walk, walk, walk, walk, wait.*

If the stacks collapsed, would we be entombed here in this library together, you and I, pressed flat by dictionaries that are no longer current, to the extent any dictionary was ever current (these things are not electricities: they just describe how power works, how we used to say it worked)? Isn't this book just an echo of the past, receding, echo, acceding to distance, pebble down an empty well, an overheard moan in the library stairwell a floor above—descriptive of a love affair or something over? Who knows how far away it was from us when we finally picked its frequency up, given interval of starlight light and great distance, Doppler effect and parallax, nerve delay and lag in comprehension, rendering everything finally salient just on the other side of now?

You found me or I found you or somehow we found each other. Some nights this library echoes like a tomb. Other nights: a bomb ticks a floor below, waiting to shrapnel out your heart. Other nights: a kennel. The sounds of dogs. I have things to say about Alabamians, though I can't count myself among them, having only lived there for four years. Mostly I remember people saying *bless your heart* to me, only realizing a year later (another dictionary echo, that lag in understanding) that this was not meant as compliment but blessing, offered on the heart of the deranged, profane, foolish, strange, disabled, or touched, so as to prevent damnation and confer protection. When spoken, some words confer protection: these are spells. Learn to spell them well and mind what they say of you.

Alabama, sepulcher of a state, houses revenants of warlost dead. At night they fight their war against the waking world again. Everything is overgrown, blown-up, and over: the kudzu creeping into the tornadoed swath; the Bellefonte Nuclear Generating Station mostly built but sitting idle in Hollywood, Alabama, still owned by the TVA; the lake left when the Martin Dam erased the town of Irma. So I imagined history like this, submerged like *Waterworld*, and skimmed the surface thinking *water moccasin* but never dipped a toe or thought of the forgotten dead. You hear stories. You read stories, *Deliverance,* for instance, and wonder about the darkened wooded spots that cameras and sentences rarely see. These too are echoes, in which we might hear our fears and confront them there. Look long enough to find the order in the orderless, conscious in the subconscious, waking life in dream, in dictionaries that network language between generations.

These books say: here's what we thought before, as recently as 1971. The *OED* omits place-names like *Papeete,* on another island I will never visit, named for a basket designed to carry water. Reader, put all your water in a basket. Note where it leaks out, and when. We call those leaks a tell, a frozen sea or margarita waiting for an axe to open it, maybe a martini in Tahiti surrounded by bikinis, thinking of another blown-up atoll a century of nuclear decay away. This is another echo, meaning single heart as solo moan. When I'm at home I think *away;* when away I think of home.

Memorial Day, 2012

Burn This First/Unison Device

> *"Over coffee one afternoon in the summer of 2001, András reminded
> me of another way to burn books, explained to him by a colleague who
> survived the siege of Sarajevo. In the winter, the scholar and his wife
> ran out of firewood, and so began to burn their books for heat and
> cooking. "This forces one to think critically," András remembered
> his friend saying. 'One must prioritize. First, you burn old college
> textbooks, which you haven't read in 30 years. Then there are the
> duplicates. But eventually, you're forced to make tougher choices. Who
> burns today: Dostoevsky or Proust?'"*
> —Matthew Battles, *Library: An Unquiet History*

If you are in duress, burn this first. I give you my permission. My position
is that this is disposable, like electronic text, like ticker tape, track for news
of stocks, the earliest digital electronic communications medium. The first
invention Edison sold, his "Electrical Printing Instrument," was patented
Nov. 9, 1869. It was not the first stock printer, though Edison's remains the
best known. 1867 saw E.A. Calahan's first machine. 1871 introduced the
"Unison Device," which would "stop the type-wheels of all the printing-
instruments in a circuit at a given point, so that they will all print alike
when in operation"—which would bring all the tickers on a network into
unison, so that information would synchronize and propagate. There's that
moment in which what seemed like chaos is no longer, and things align,
a structure's found. Impossible, perhaps, to overstate how significant this
concept was: networked machines, distributing simultaneous information
a century before the Internet.

So read this once then secret it away for the next to troll these pages: this is
meant for obsolescence. Maybe these sentences are already obsolete. But in a
pinch it can be burned. This is not a sacred text, unlike the Quran, the word

of God, which "does not include instructions for its own disposal," and should be buried, erased, or stored indefinitely; alternately, "desanctify the book by removing the text from its pages. Some medieval scholars recommend wiping off the ink and disposing of the paper by ordinary means. A more modern and practical alternative is to tie the book to a stone, then drop it into a stream to symbolically achieve the same effect" (these quotes via *Slate*, and for all I know (the scholar sighs (these eddies within eddies) the article might already have disappeared). Sacred Jewish texts should be placed into a repository to await mass burial. Though a Bible has no built-in disposal ritual, and thus it can be burned, one should generally avoid burning sacred books because of fire's association with the devil and the underworld.

While you can't hold on to everything forever, you're a fool if you sell back your college books at semester's end: have you learned nothing of this life? Reread that book you disliked in ninth grade and see how it sings to you now: you understand the story differently because your own has changed. To celebrate your growth, throw yourself a ticker tape parade for and of your disposed-of books—confettied by clouds of shredded pages, call yourself a nebula of assorted information. In bits they are much easier to burn, though the flame won't last as long.

Though we call it that, we haven't used ticker tape in ticker tape parades for years: now it's all confetti, shredded financial documents shotgunned out in clouds over Broadway as whoever passes now for heroes processes below. For the last ticker tape parade, 2012, celebrating the New York Giants' Super Bowl win, a half-ton of confetti was distributed in 25-pound bags to the buildings all along its route.

What else we drop: calls, balls, 7 in handheld smartphone games, in certain cases walls, ceilings filled with secrets we stashed as adolescents above the chewy tile: all of these literally, even how we say "literally" now, meaning its opposite, *metaphorically*, trying to redirect our attention to the figure of speech, to refresh and amp it up.

I hope you are lucky enough not to have to burn your books for fire or food. Reading networks sentences, memes them, beams them between brains in surprising ways: what's kept, what's stuck there, what's lodged in a cul-de-sac after the rest has left. It's like a game, a labyrinth. Everything in time becomes a trivium—in the latter half of the twentieth century, "knowledge that is nice to have but not essential"—originally *trivium* referred to one of the three topics of basic education (grammar, logic, rhetoric), though now it's for those inclined to marginalia, cultural crud that cakes the brain, knowledge acquired at random, obsessively, used in games like *Pursuit* or in game shows, or to impress those you meet at parties, papering over your lack of actual classical learning like a defiant slap across the bow of those who tried to educate you. Your meanders in the shredded trenches of Wikipedia minutiae and rarely-visited library stacks have to pay off eventually. They will, won't they? Please say they will. If we say these words out loud together, we will be as one, in unison, synchronized with this device, the page.

A NET YOU CAN BREATHE THROUGH

Digressing into Form

Patricia Vigderman

Don't call it fiction or nonfiction or poetry—don't even call it *creative*. The business and pleasure of writing is finding a form that can contain more than one register at a time: humor with loss, or admiration with exasperation, or awe with ordinariness—or all of those at once. The real work for me has always been to speak clearly, and the improbably difficult task of finding my own voice has, paradoxically, always included discovering it as part of reading the work of others.

George Eliot wrote her great novels at the height of fiction's historical moment, but they are also hybrid creatures of moral philosophy. Her digressions work their way into plot, but plot is not what makes her novels matter so much, or what draws readers back to them. Their close observation of social and emotional behavior offers the companionship of her imagined characters within the intimacy of her particular voice. Leo Tolstoy used history as a great screen on which to project the drama of human character; Vladimir Nabokov's carefully plotted series of essays in *Speak, Memory* creates the lost world of his own past in a voice that enchants like a lover, suggesting only parenthetically how history might have unfolded quite differently.

In my experience, then, form is the challenge, not genre: form as structure or shape, and expression. It's the challenge of weaving moral, social,

Patricia Vigderman is on the English faculty at Kenyon College. She is the author of *The Memory Palace of Isabella Stewart Gardner* (2007) and *Possibility: Essays Against Despair* (2013). Her writing has appeared in many venues, including *Harvard Review*, *The Nation*, *The New York Times*, and *Raritan*.

emotional, and aesthetic responses to the world into a net fine enough to hold and loose enough to breathe through. When I first encountered the work of W. G. Sebald, in his short four-part novel *The Emigrants* (1992), I had no idea what I was reading about. It was so subtle, so gentle, so quietly done that I only gradually apprehended the shadow of the Holocaust. I was intrigued but puzzled by the little photographs scattered throughout the text. The night I finished it, I turned back to page one and started over. Later I read *Rings of Saturn* (1995) and with it, too, I have found the book's riches compounded on subsequent readings, its mysteries more resonant, its breathless sentences breathing more deeply. Open it anywhere: the infinitely digressive style draws catastrophes into marvelous and horrifying and suddenly funny shapes. His history moves like the unraveling heraldic dragon he describes, half faded from the side of a miniature railway car, a remnant of imperial China inexplicably running now across the English river Blyth.

Sebald left his native Germany for England as a young man because he was unable to get the truth about the Second World War from the adults among whom he'd grown up. His books are classified as fiction, but they are driven by that parched necessity to know what's true. The form he created to hold this need is one of long drafts and enormous gulps, one swallow leading unstoppably to the next, and this pleasure of slaking thirst is communicated to the reader over and over, again and again. For me, that relief included recognizing the real thing—real art—which is what my essay excerpted below is actually about.

Toward the end of the essay, after I describe the ordinary and peaceful public circumstances in which I am reading Sebald's *Austerlitz* (2001), there is a paragraph of homage: it's one long sentence that begins with the use of his first name and ends with the *long drawn out scream* of a line from the book. I love Sebald's long sentences, as I love Proust's, because they gather lost and unstoppable time into the reading present, as notes in a musical score suggest the unheard present within the time-based melody. In my essay I've folded experiences of disparate places over my sense of disparate times—West Texas emptiness; the busy coffee bar in Cambridge; the early death of Fyodor Dostoevsky in 1881 and that of Sebald 120 years later in 2001. And over that is the miracle of what language can do with time and space, and of my own mind's being part of that in this unfolding moment of all that has vanished, like a great sentence carrying the freight of lost experience through the dark.

HYBRID WORK
From Possibility: Essays Against Despair

Sebald in Starbucks

Marfa, Texas. Dry grasslands, desert and mountains. The western corner of Texas wedged between Mexico and New Mexico, where the hot emptiness of the Chihuahuan Desert obliterates the border, keeping the Border Patrol wired and alert. The railroad runs through it; the railroad put it on the map; the railroad is still hauling freight from the California coast to the Gulf of Mexico, almost 800 miles across Texas. The trains run through all day and all night, hooting, calling, sometimes a hundred cars long, moving across the high desert. At night the great eyes of the engine lights move east, move west, through the darkness. Under black skies, or moonlit ones.

Marfa is a funny sounding name. Like a child's lisp, or a foreigner who can't get that troublesome English *th* sound. Or like a brand name cobbled together out of two people's names—Marfa Delivery, maybe, or Marfa Soap, recalling Marv and Fanny, or Martinez and Farrell. As it happens, this little whistle stop, founded to accommodate the railroad in 1881, was named by a Russian, a woman, a frontier wife brought to the wide views of the Chihuahuan Desert and the long view of the iron rails cutting through it because her husband was a railroad overseer. So, one important thing to know is that in Russian that Cyrillic *f*-sound is perfectly acceptable. A literate woman, reading *The Brothers Karamazov* by Fyodor Dostoevsky, provided a name for the place, from the Karamazov family servant, whom nobody remembers, but to whom Dostoevsky gave the name Marfa. And if you think about it, Fyodor has the same problem of the lispy-sounding *f* instead of *th*.

What seizes the imagination here is the woman reading a recently published novel, something just out from a contemporary writer from home. She was on the other side of the world from Fyodor and his Karamazovs, the dysfunctional relationships, unholy and holy desires, the exploding sentences. Possibly for her it was a link to home, possibly it was a way to while away the long hot days in the desert, a way to defeat the interminable space and the bright eye and lonely hooting of the trains. Did she know that she was reading Russian Literature? (Dostoevsky: Isaiah Berlin's great example of the literary hedgehog, the thinker who knows One Big Thing; outsider, epileptic, prophet; in 1881, just dead in St. Petersburg.) She was reading a novel published the previous year and brought along to Texas, where she, nameless footnote to America's Manifest Destiny, dropped the simple and rather foolish name of one of its minor characters.

In Marfa for a quiet month of work, I began reading *Austerlitz* by W. G. Sebald. I have read other books by this same author, and of course many other books by authors both dead and alive. So many authors are alive in my time with their names before the public, but some of them you can read very quickly. Now I am reading Sebald's book, also a recently published work of fiction, in a Starbuck's in Massachusetts, and I find I am reading very slowly, almost word by word, following its winding sentences and paragraphs, and looking at its strange photographs (all Sebald's books scatter photographs, black and white snapshots without captions, that illustrate not so much the story he is telling as the difference between his precise text and the camera's casual glance), and sometimes going back and rereading pages or looking at how many pages are necessary for one paragraph (25 is not unusual).

I would say the effect is dreamlike, entrancing, except that the associa-
tiveness, the quiet shifts and turnings are also keeping me alert—to time
and place and simultaneity. This author now is pulling me through cities
and vistas and time, down through layers of narrators (but always reminding me, in the gentlest, most rhythmical way, who is speaking) into his
story and around it and behind it. I am moving into the past with him, but
like the railway overseer's wife I am also moving into the future, because
with this book in my hands I am connected to those who will read this
same book in the future and know this author's name as part of Literature.
My immersion in the mental world of *Austerlitz*, my meaningful now, does
not undo the strangeness of this object, bought in a bookstore in Ohio and
carried to Texas and then to Massachusetts, where I am now reading it just
as I read the other books I have on my desk or by my bed or waiting for me
elsewhere in my restless life. Only unlike most of those, I am pretty sure,
this book in my mortal hands has the uncanniness of its life in a future
when I am long dead.

Sebald himself has recently died, like Dostoevsky back then, though a
few years younger. By doing so he has turned himself into an untimely loss,
an example of the senselessness of things. Sebald writes without drama of
horror and loss, of the sudden incursion of unreality into the real world, of
the possible co-existence of all moments of time in the same space. Loss
of family, of country, of mind share in his sentences unsensational space
with sunlight coming through the feathers of a bird's wings, or a perfectly
appointed billiards room left shuttered and untouched for 150 years.

In this quiet way, on an unperturbed Monday morning, he is describing for me a Nazi prison in Belgium called Breendonck, and a particularly
horrible Nazi torture. I am sitting in Starbucks and the woman at the next
table has a drink topped with a mound of whipped cream under a plastic
bubble. And music is quietly bubbling around the readers and writers and
talkers at the other little tables. Everything is easy and safe: the friendly
guys at the counter, the sweet and pungent coffee smell, the busy brains

of Cambridge in here and walking by outside. Across the street the little green box of the ATM kiosk, a corner in a familiar world, unruffled sunlight of late winter.

Into all this Sebald, known as Max to his friends when he was alive and writing the words I am reading, brings that other world so gently, in one long sentence, a sentence like a distant line of freight cars across the high grasslands, with the irony only of its unexpected appearance in a passage about a seemingly random memory of the laundry room in the narrator's childhood home, an image connected to the Holocaust only by the fact of its invoking a German word his father liked and he didn't—*Wurzelbürste*, the word for scrubbing brush—but slipping on the soft soap smell of its umlaut into a story of a prisoner at Dachau who, upon his release, left for the jungles of South America, a self-exile that leads the section of the book I am holding to end with three lines of capital As, *like a long drawn out scream*, says Sebald.

So it becomes afternoon in Cambridge, the sun slipping farther across the street. The outsized Flemish fortress of Breendonck proved a useless defense in the First World War, and again in the second one. Its history and the cruelty practiced therein are an hour further away, as Sebald tells it first in English, and then repeating the original French of another writer's memories, and then giving more details about the Frenchman's intention to put distance between horror and himself (a green jungle, a painting that repeats and repeats the letter A) so this telling over in unwinding sentences of a past is now part of the daily peace of my small city on a Monday. A city full of my own past and my own mysterious brain, so many Mondays thinking and beginning again and drifting in long winding sentences to maybe just the repetition of the capital letter A.

I think his endless unruffled paragraphs show how reading works, how the mind moves from observing swallows in Wales to a cleverly contrived suicide in Halifax to the Royal Observatory in Greenwich, the Border Patrol of time, where they calibrate with instruments as beautiful and mysterious as his sentences. It is my good fortune right now to be reading this and going into it and being part of it, an early reader, a contemporary reader, a person in its world—as the woman who named Marfa was in the servant Marfa's, and also in Dostoevsky's. That world of calibrated and timeless language does not seem to be part of this transient sublunary Starbucks at all, but mine are the nameless hands and eyes and brain it is passing through while all the moments of our lives, Sebald says, are occupying the same space. Time is going through me and all around me and I am sitting in a chair with a book in my hands. Entirely lost but still there, like the wife of the railway overseer, like the Russians in Texas, like the tumbleweed along the tracks and the long hooting of the train in the dark Texas night.

IDEA AS SCULPTURE

Exploring a Subject in Three Dimensions

Sarah Gorham

I began my writing life as a poet and spent more than two decades happily composing tight imagistic poems with sharp turns and small flashes of insight. I adored the compression of Louise Glück and Zbigniew Herbert. But I also inhaled and was equally inspired by prose—Vladimir Nabokov, Günter Grass, Marilynne Robinson's *Housekeeping*. My reading mind was equal opportunity and made no distinction: all was grist for the mill. The first hybrid I remember reading *as hybrid* was Michael Herr's *Dispatches* (1977), a frightening, telegrammatic set of imagistic scenes from Vietnam. This was long before I attempted mixed genre myself.

We now find numerous dazzling examples of hybrids in our literature—Lydia Davis' *Varieties of Disturbance,* Anne Carson's *Autobiography of Red* and *Short Talks,* James Richardson's *Vectors,* and Geoff Dyer's *Out of Sheer Rage: Wrestling with D.H. Lawrence,* among others. I discovered a little book called *The Logia of Yeshua,* the sayings of Jesus translated by Guy Davenport into poetic fragments that allow a more ironic, sometimes harsh, and I think more believable interpretation of Jesus' words. Previously underemployed genres are also being adapted for literary purposes: lists, office memos, recipes, radio schematics, games, bumper stickers, the 12 steps of Alcoholics Anonymous.

Sarah Gorham is the author of four collections of poetry: *Bad Daughter* (2011), *The Cure* (2003), *The Tension Zone* (1996), and *Don't Go Back to Sleep* (1989). Her recent essay collection, *Study in Perfect* (2014), was selected by Bernard Cooper for the 2013 AWP Award in Creative Nonfiction. She is the co-founder and editor-in-chief of Sarabande Books.

Each genre has a particular flavor. But really, aren't they in the end all made of words? And isn't this the reason we love them? Words: So infinitely flexible, expansive, adaptable, and above all, *stimulating*.

All three mini-essays excerpted here could easily have been poems. But by the time I arrived at my subject—the multifaceted notion of *perfection*—my writing process had evolved; it had loosened. I gave myself permission to proceed without editorial nay-saying. I filled up the page instead of crafting one skinny line at a time. My scribbling stretched into and over the margins. A sentence could be a long exhalation *or* a short burst. It could chug along with repeating consonants or off-rhyming verbs. It felt natural, finally, and more like the way I thought and sang.

A novel or nonfiction work can be likened to a documentary film, which may contain a discursive narrative with multiple characters, sketches, and digressions. It relies on an accumulation of information and sensory detail absorbed *over time*. In the short-form essay, I limit the questions posed to those that can be examined all at once, in one gestalt glance, like viewing a sculpture instead of a film. I can zoom in on details etched in this or that outstretched hand. I can walk around the sculpture and examine it from every angle. Yet it remains one object, frozen in one place and one moment in time. The sculpture itself does not change. However, it is *enriched* because seen from many perspectives.

"Perfect Sleep," "Perfect Solution," and "Perfect Heaven" are excerpted from a series of 12 short essays called "Study in Perfect." Others include: "Perfect Paper Towel," "Perfect Barn," "Perfect Being," "Perfect Flower," "Perfect Tea," "Perfect Word," "Perfect Conversation," "Perfect Binding," and "Perfect Tense." *Study in Perfect* is also the title of a full collection, which contains longer pieces based roughly on the same theme.

All sorts of moves and exchanges are taking place at whatever level I'm working within this series. The essays employ several types of parallel structure: Sentences might contain lists, themselves a series. Words within those lists are linked by sound or image. Indeed, it's impossible to focus on one essayistic feature without simultaneously engaging them all. Examine the insides of "Sleep," "Solution," and "Heaven," and you'll notice many of these elements operating together. *What is the perfect solution but a pair of disappointments, two less-than-perfects, a middle-making. I stroked and coasted, sculled and skidded. Burn her sweaters, party shoes, and skirts so she can wear them if she wants.*

We are sometimes drawn to large subjects, which bridle at any kind of containment. We write one poem or story or essay, successful on its own, but we want to go on. Perhaps it's the same instinct that led Wallace Stevens to his famous poem "Thirteen Ways of Looking at a Blackbird." There's so much to say! Or, we didn't say it perfectly the first time and want to re-emphasize, magnify. Or we want to show off our imaginative powers. I can do this, and that, and this too!

There are dangers though. We run out of steam and the language grows slack. We find ourselves writing multiple versions of the original, second or third glances that don't carry forward the surprise and delight of first sight. What I learned in writing the short-form essay is to have patience. I spent a year on the project, every one of the pieces composed when I was bursting with energy, primed with reading and thinking—desperate, in fact, to get something down on paper. There were month-long gaps. Each subsection had its own birthplace—"Perfect Barn" grew from a careful description of just that, a barn I'd seen on Wolf Pen Branch Road in Kentucky. "Perfect Paper Towel" was driven by sound and an imitation of the Bounty television commercial ("The Quicker Picker Upper"). "Perfect Sleep" was an extended recurring dream.

In "Perfect Heaven," I had been reading the sermons of C.S. Lewis, whose theology deepened my thinking on the idea of heaven. Also, the modernized ghazals of Agha Shahid Ali. As most people are aware, a ghazal is an Arab "poetic expression" that focuses on loss and beauty, but does so through unrelated couplets. There are other strictures to the form, but this element interested me most. Ali described each couplet as "a stone from a necklace," which should continue to "shine in that vivid isolation." I wrote these long-lined "couplets" in the wake of my mother's death, which I had been circling for three decades. Not unlike that walk around a sculpture, with its multiple viewpoints.

Note that I began each piece with something specific, rather than trying to define a broad term. An abstraction can steer our writing as well, but not overtly. That would be too much to bear. Instead: break it down, sneak up on it, and assemble the whole by accretion. We often find that what we have done is not just explore the *subject*; we have also experimented with various *formal means* to get at the subject. Finally, when I pulled all the "perfect" sections together I found they described imperfection as much as perfection, which then became the understory of my full collection.

HYBRID WORK
From Study in Perfect

Perfect Solution

A toddler's pink and white striped dress, with gauzy apron, and purple ribbon tie-backs. Hand-me-down from her cousin, already well-worn, nevertheless worn everyday whether or not her mother would allow it. The dress had a name—"Pollo," like "Paulo," a close derivative of "pillow," for she slept inside the dress, not needing a pillow. On the yoke, two oval strawberry stains and one long drip of indeterminate origin. Apron semi-detached in places, where she stepped on it while attempting to rise from a sitting position.

It was a slip of mother, like her mother's slip, a second skin without the hurting patches. She lifted the dress over her face and her stomach calmed. She lowered it and knew what to do next. Could you wear a pillow, a glow-worm, a blanket? The dress was her forest place without the scary journey.

She listened to the dress and, in time, refused to wear anything else. In her parents' world, this was impossible. What would people think—that she was poor, unbeloved? They cajoled, distracted her with party shoes, firmly enforced time-outs when the battle grew intense, and still the child would not take off the dress.

What is the perfect solution but a pair of disappointments, two less-than-perfects, a middle-making. Not throwing the dress away, not wearing it forever. What, said her father, if Pollo were a pet, like a parakeet or fish? Would you crush it in your sleep? Wouldn't you want to pat, preserve, and keep it happy?

She could have her dress, but only if she carried it in a brown paper bag. And so she did for five years, and then some.

Perfect Sleep

I remember only one such sleep following my firstborn's delivery by C-section. I was under the influence of morphine and a pure, thorough body-exhaustion. The first course was upwards, a mix of things half-heard, only partially understood, and so wrapped in imaginative ribbon. The rattle of a blood cart became a tree with spoons in place of leaves. A nurse became a lifeguard with layers of zinc on her nose. Her announcement over the intercom, the answer to all those dream-exams.

I say upwards, because so much sleep is depicted as falling. Mine was not so. The room with all its detail receded, and I rose with a slight toiling up up up into the sun, to the second course, a kind of plateau. This was new land, very flat, very white, a salt field or desert made of chalk. Patches of dream flew against the sun: a miniskirt, some costume jewelry, but they didn't engross me. When I was hungry, I ate coconut. When thirsty, I drank the milk. This went on for hours, this perfect sleep.

I reached the end by backstroke, the mind carving shoulder blades and wings in the sand. I stroked and coasted, sculled and skidded. Soon I began to wake, down into the township, the atrium, the bed, then lower into a squalling sound. I found the baby's face in mine: *Oh, there you are.*

Perfect Heaven

When my mother died, I began to smoke Kents, as *she* had during difficult times.

It didn't last long.

If only I knew her intimate habits and feeling. Then the space she left behind would not seem so stark.

I tried to pray with absolute attention. I enjoyed the "Our Father" for its symmetry: *on earth / as it is in heaven,* and *Forgive us our trespasses / as we forgive those who trespass against us.* But my mind rambled. By *now and forever,* I was making a list for the hardware store, wondering which fertilizer would save the Japanese maple by our front porch. A different sort of consolation.

I pictured her figure open to the elements, birds plucking bits of cotton, skin, hair, carrying them off to line their nests. Rain drawing her blood into the soil; tissue, tendon, and muscle battered with air. Finally bone, returned to its chemical components and scattered like microscopic hail.

Perhaps a body is perfect, not when it is complete, but when there is no longer anything to take away.

I can't recall my mother singing. Not a robust coughing or sneeze either. Was she preoccupied by minute workings of blood through her temples, an ear filament flaring out, or cells turning mean, flipped over to their dark side like microscopic playing cards?

When I think of my mother's inner life, I see a Kleenex, its powdery edges twisted into sculpture. She gripped it while the party wound down.

After she died, I removed a crumpled one from her purse. Dry, but sudden too, as a splash in my hand.

Maybe heaven is textured like a river after it falls over rocks. Maybe it is nothing. Perhaps we are suppressed or super-real. Unaccompanied, or linked by our hair to everyone who's died.

My mother was given 12 baby-shaped beans to hold tightly as she went over, the grandchildren she would not meet in this life.

Burn her sweaters, party shoes, and skirts so she can wear them if she wants.

SMALL WINDOW, BIG VIEW
The Short Essay and the Wide World

Bret Lott

I have wanted for years to write the story of the event described in "The Importance of Story." It was a strange—very strange—occurrence, a small pocket of time that played out in front of me and that seemed to call to me, all the while it was happening, to record it, put it away, and hold it in reserve.

This is because story is the engine and vehicle and highway of what matters during the brief lives we have been given. Indeed, story is so important and all-encompassing that the disassociation *from* the narrative arc—the story—of our lives is always seen as a malfunction: on one side of the coin are amnesia and Alzheimer's, the loss of one's memory, one's own history; on the other lies antisocial personality disorder, hallmark indicators of which include "the incapacity to experience guilt and to profit from experience," and the "callous unconcern for the feelings of others and lack of the capacity for empathy." In other words, the disengagement of self from the story of oneself in relation to others; either way, whether we have forgotten our story or become physiologically and/or psychologically unhinged from it, we are adrift without it. We are lost. We are not who we are.

Bret Lott teaches at the College of Charleston, and is the nonfiction editor of the journal *Crazyhorse*. He is the author of 14 books of fiction and nonfiction, most recently *Letters and Life: On Being a Writer, On Being a Christian* (2013) and *Dead Low Tide* (2012). He has served as Fulbright Senior American Scholar and writer-in-residence at Bar-Ilan University in Tel Aviv, spoken on Flannery O'Connor at the White House, and was a member of the National Council on the Arts from 2006 to 2012.

Here is a paradox, and the truth, of the all-encompassing power of story: even when we lose our history to Alzheimer's, our story becomes one of that loss; one's story is, if one gets amnesia, the story of someone who is set adrift from his or her own story. Story expands to include even its own break with itself.

This is why I believe that if you want to write, you must be a kind of story mercenary. You must always be on the prowl in your life for stories. You must ruthlessly pay attention to what is going on around you, and then be willing to use what you find in order to tell the story.

But the problem with what happened on that road in Jordan was that later I couldn't quite see how this might be used; it seemed somehow more an anecdote and not its own moment of self-recognition that I believe every short essay ought to be. I ended up using a reference to the event in an essay I published a few years ago called "Writing with So Great a Cloud of Witnesses," but only to help enhance the portrait of Jeff, my friend, about whom I was writing; the experience ended up being a clause within a sentence, not even rating a complete sentence of its own. But the experience stayed with me, some kind of pointless arrow in the quiver I am always refilling as I prowl for more writer ammo.

It wasn't until I was asked to contribute a piece to this anthology that I finally worked up the nerve to try and see if the event could stand on its own, and to do so in the shortest form possible. Once I'd written the story out in its entirety, I realized my problem with the event wasn't that I hadn't had enough trust in the *event itself*; rather, I was tentative in what I believed about *the weight* of this moment. Only after I'd bracketed the entire thing with what I'd understood about the whole of what had happened was I able to see that the short-form essay, in its simultaneous brevity and call for scope beyond that brevity, was the best way to give a window onto a view so very much larger than the one from the King's Highway that snowy day.

Our being stuck in the snow in a foreign country and being saved by the Jordanian Army and then given hot cups of tea wasn't so much about the adventure, I recognized, but about our desire *within* the story of our lives to tell that story. What I saw, in writing this out and giving it the bracket it has, is that our stories, and our sharing them, are who we are. Without them, and without sharing them, we are nothing; we are adrift and alone. Our story *is* what it means to be a human and, like peering into the smallest of apertures at the viewing end of a telescope and finding inside an entire planet right there, so too the short essay ought to serve its readers. We don't read small things for small things. We read them because we hope they will offer a far greater return than what they might seem, in their few words, to offer. Think, if you're old enough, of the urgency and concision of the telegram—its portent made all the more pronounced because of its being stripped of adornment—and you'll begin to understand that paradox of brevity and scope.

So, be the ruthless mercenary you are called to be as a writer, and understand that brief can be better, that concision and exactness always rule the day. Understand, too, that you are living within those experiences you are stowing away for later use. They have a power of their own. You are here to tell these stories, you are here to be their caretakers, you are here to be their servants. Be brave and know they matter whether you are tentative as to their value or not. Stories are all you have. And, like a tiny cameo inside a locket, sometimes the ineffable soul is best rendered smally.

HYBRID WORK
The Importance of Story

Here is a story:

In the fall of 2006 into winter 2007, my wife and I lived in Jerusalem. I was a guest professor at a university, and while we were there plenty of friends came for visits, giving us more than enough reason to see pretty much all the holy sites in Israel. But in January and nearing the end of our stay, we decided we wanted to see Petra, the ancient city carved into sandstone canyons, over in Jordan. Our friends Jeff and Hart from here in Charleston were visiting us then, and we spent one cold and sun-drenched January day hiking the bright and towering red stone ghosts of the ruins.

But on our way back the next morning there came a snowstorm, and we found ourselves snowbound in a taxi at the crest of the King's Highway between Petra and Aqaba, elevation 5,000 feet, hours and hours from our home in Jerusalem. Forty-five minutes after the driver called in our predicament, members of the Jordanian Army—yes, the Jordanian Army—emerged from the white all around us, having driven their emergency response truck as close as they could to us, then hiked up the highway to the cab. Jeff and I helped the soldiers push the taxi out of its snow-mired fix, the driver pulling away and driving off—he couldn't park and wait for us to climb back in, because we'd get stuck in the snow again, of course.

That left Jeff, me, and five soldiers to walk a mile or so through a blizzard back to their rescue truck. Along the way we pitched snowball fights, America versus Jordan. I actually yelled that out as I reared back to launch a snowball, and was nailed in the shoulder before I could even let go. All of us were laughing, talking—they all spoke English—and trying our best not to think of the cold. Then here was the rescue truck, emergency yellow, sharp and big with its pug-faced grill and running boards two feet above the snow-packed road. We all climbed into the warm quad-cab, the driver inside and ready for us. Eight of us jammed inside, Jeff and I in the back seat in the middle, a soldier on either side of us.

Then one of the men in the front seat pulled from the floorboard a battered Thermos, another soldier produced from somewhere a stack of four thick glass tumblers, the one with the Thermos poured out steaming hot tea, and Jeff and I were given the first two glasses.

I don't even like tea, but I cannot remember tasting anything as perfect as that sweet and strong hot tea, its steam immediately clouding over my glasses.

That was when Jeff, glass in hand, turned to me and said, laughing, "This is going to be a great story."

"Yes it will," I said.

We weren't even warmed through yet, not even reunited with our loved ones and that cab—the story of our being saved in a snowstorm by the Jordanian Army wasn't even over yet—and already we both were thinking, *We have to tell this story.*

That's how important story is.

7
. . . .
Flash Fiction

FLASH FICTION
An Introduction

In France it's known as the *micronouvelle*; in Latin America, a *micro* or *minificción;* in China, the pocket- or palm-sized story and also the smoke-long story (the same duration required for smoking a cigarette). In the U.S., it's been called everything from the skinny story to sudden fiction. Instead of the traditional short story's gradual unfolding, in the flash form plot might manifest itself quickly through discrete elements such as character, point of view, setting, structure, and image. At usually 1,000 words or less, a flash's language can be as highly inflected as poetry, and it excels at illuminating the quotidian, the subtle, and the seemingly insignificant. "The rhythmic form of the short short story," Joyce Carol Oates says in *Sudden Fiction: American Short-Short Stories*, "is often more temperamentally akin to poetry than to conventional prose, which generally opens out to dramatize experience and evoke emotion; in the smallest, tightest spaces, experience can only be suggested."

Flash fiction as we know it today derives from the nineteenth century trend toward shorter fictional pieces known as "tales," "stories," or "sketches." Early practitioners include Louisa May Alcott, Kate Chopin, August Strindberg, Guy de Maupassant, and Franz Kafka, nearly all of whom were also working in the short story, which was simultaneously gaining in popularity, thanks in part to well-paying opportunities offered by syndicated newspapers and magazines. O. Henry, writing in English, and Yasunari Kawabata, in Japanese, did a great deal to further the very short story's popularity. From 1903 to 1906, O. Henry published a weekly story about ordinary city dwellers in the *New York World* and other periodicals; his renown prompted other writers to emulate his style. Whereas O. Henry leaned toward plot-driven pieces with surprise endings, the more lyrical Kawabata drew inspiration from his work as a painter influenced by such Euro-stylistic movements as Expressionism.

The term "flash fiction" was coined in the 1990s with the publication of *Flash Fiction: 72 Very Short Stories* edited by James Thomas, Denise Thomas, and Tom Hazuka (1992), who required the story to fit on two facing typeset pages. Since then, the flash form has become ever more prevalent, perhaps because of the realities of less reading time and the greater likelihood of interruption. One main reason for the form's popularity is its compression; flash fiction is tense and packs a punch, one that stays with the reader long after she has laid down the story. In *Sudden Fiction*, Grace Paley points out flash's affinities with poetry, stressing that "when it is very short—1, 2, 2½ pages—it should be read like a poem. That is, slowly."

Slowness and attention hearken back to an earlier time, one in which airplanes, Walmart, and iPhones were not the status quo. This may be part of the reason why so many flash pieces borrow from such genres as myth, legend, and fable, though these older forms simultaneously allow the writer to explode what may seem like an outdated container to create something radically new.

Speaking to the influence of the fable, Etgar Keret says of his work: "My stories have been called fables that don't teach you anything except how complicated it is to be human." Keret, like other writers who draw upon fable and fairy tale, inevitably foregrounds narrative as an object of study by drawing attention to the elements or cues of these older forms, as in "Once upon a time..." Instead of the "happily ever after," or a conclusion where the villain receives his "just desserts," the endings in flash fiction resist neat closure.

As Keret says, being human is complicated, a fact that Katie Cortese's scintillating "Sum of Her Parts" recognizes from its opening sentence: "My sister Jenny was always skinny, but now she is a waif." Instead of focusing on Jenny's anorexia, as one might expect, Cortese eschews character development and a big narrative arc, focusing instead on shifts in perception.

Robin Hemley's "Riding the Whip" returns to the outing Hemley's fictional teenage self made to an amusement park on the night before his suicidal sister died, revolving around a defining moment from the character's history—the point at which he resolved not to suffer the same fate as his sister. The flash form surrounds that moment, and in the process prolongs it.

Throughout her story "The Bridge," Pamela Painter creates a state of suspense, one that she leaves open when the story ends. "I wanted that uncertainty to provide tension but not direct or prolonged conflict," Painter writes in her process essay, "and I wanted the story to end in that unnerving state of apprehension." From the Old French *aprendre*—to teach, learn, or grasp—apprehension foregrounds a discovery that is not necessarily wedded to an elaborate plot. Flash captures the lingering aftereffects of a defining moment or event.

Julio Ortega locates "Melodrama" in the imagistic landscape of dreams and explores the possibilities of multiple points of view, as he literally switches pronouns throughout the piece, thereby illustrating the role of character as a tool, a means of transforming experience into art. His most seductive statement about his hybrid story reaches out to embrace the myriad stories anthologized here: "You and I wake up to each other on the page." Evocatively, he encapsulates the ways in which art trains us to interpret our day-to-day reality; it is a method shared by many skilled practitioners of the flash form.

Despite the brevity of the form, flash fiction offers the writer a tremendous amount of range. The short word counts and condensation of language, magnified by the importance of tone and rhythm, provide the writer with specific criteria within which to work with both great freedom and precision.

—*Jacqueline Kolosov*

JANET JACKSON, ARISTOTLE, AND FRANKENSTEIN'S MONSTER WALK INTO A BAR

Humor in Flash Fiction

Katie Cortese

As a kid I was haunted by the rumor, now debunked by Snopes.com, that Janet Jackson had removed her lower ribs to appear slimmer. The rib story seemed possible, and efficient. People had noses pared, teeth straightened, and butts lifted, so why couldn't someone with the financial resources snip out those vestigial arcs of bone? It seemed an appropriate response to the pressure I imagined Ms. Jackson must have felt to look perfect.

As a chubby kid, there's no question that I would have sacrificed a rib to be beautiful. If it would have guaranteed that my male classmates in their MC Hammer pants and rattails and pump-up Nikes liked me, I would have given several. When I coolly made this calculation, I was in the fourth grade.

Twenty-five years later, I've learned to love my body with its full complement of ribs, and my drastic childhood imaginings seem ridiculous, exaggerated, the stuff of an 80s sitcom with a laugh track. But as with a clown whose smile is only paint-deep, there's a current of something awful underneath the humor. Shame. Self-hatred. The potential for self-harm.

Not all humor treads the knife edge between laughter and tears—otherwise, how to explain knock-knock jokes and Monty Python?—but plenty does. Certainly most of the sort found in literary flash fiction. The

Katie Cortese is the author of the forthcoming book *Girl Power and Other Short-Short Stories* (2015). Her stories and essays have appeared in *Blackbird, Gulf Coast, Carve Magazine, Smokelong Quarterly*, and elsewhere. She serves as the fiction editor for *Iron Horse Literary Review* and teaches in the creative writing program at Texas Tech University.

link between humor and pain is well established, especially if the pain belongs to someone else. If our friend slips on a banana peel, it's hilarious, but if we ourselves slip it becomes no laughing matter. And if someone else, even our worst enemy, falls on that peel, hits his head, and incurs permanent brain damage, then we're squarely in the realm of tragedy (after an initial, involuntary chuckle). Dark comedy, satire, and tragi-comedy tread this line, often to address a societal problem. Think of Jonathan Swift's "A Modest Proposal."

There's nothing less funny than trying to explain a joke, so I'll keep the anatomy lesson brief. Most jokes contain the following: a catchy opening that presents an incongruous situation (questions about chickens are gimmes); a build-up of expectation; and a punchline that resolves the tension in a surprising way. Lots of factors can throw off the formula—timing, subject, audience—but according to an NPR interview with cognitive neuroscientist Scott Weems, author of *Ha!: The Science of When We Laugh and Why*, when a joke works, something special happens in the brain: the anterior cingulate lights up, the area responsible for processing conflict.

So what makes a good joke is an intriguing beginning, sustained tension, surprising resolution, and conflict; the same elements that make a successful literary story. I'm not suggesting that all stories are jokes at heart, but the two have a lot in common. Jokes and stories both present a world with set rules—whether familiar or strange—attempt to draw listeners in, and present a shift in the world by the end of the arc—whether slight or gaping—that ensures the audience sees the scenario and its characters in a new way. Our re-visioning of the world can come through one of many filters. Irony. Juxtaposition. Reversal. Surprise. Aristotle called such shifts *peripeteia*. And both jokes and stories seek to elicit an intellectual, emotional, and ultimately visceral reaction.

Mike Broida's *Washington Post* review of Stuart Dybek's new flash fiction collection, *Ecstatic Cahoots*, claims that short short stories, as a form, call for a "kind of pun or twist to make up for the lack of substance." Essentially, he likens a flash's ending to a joke's punchline. But this is oversimplifying.

Every successful piece of fiction ends in a different place than it began, even if it's just slightly to the left or right, because stories are about the decisions characters make that affect them and others in their world. One main difference between a story of 15 pages and one of 1,500 words, or 150, is that flash starts much closer to its inevitable point of transition. Another is that the literary story, no matter how short, always works toward generating empathy, which is not required of puns or jokes. Some flash fictions comprise little more than a significant moment of transformation. While the sheer speed with which a flash narrative must unfold may seem funny at first, the best short short stories reveal the tip of a terrifying iceberg, and humor, according to Weems, is often the best or even the "only way to deal with a life in turmoil." Ultimately, the best examples of flash are never *just* jokes.

The spark for "Sum of Her Parts" was an image that I found simultaneously hilarious and strange and disturbing: living body parts in jars for mayo and pickles and jam. Some hybrid of bio lab, Mary Shelley's *Frankenstein*, and that old false story about Janet Jackson's missing ribs. Unscrewing the jars let a few demons into the room though: anorexia and obesity, sibling rivalry, parental and societal pressure, the way people are sometimes compelled to hurt themselves, and the silence—and stigma—that can result.

Flash fiction requires nods to character, setting, plot, and resolution, like any story, but flash's concision releases the author from the responsibility of engaging in extensive exposition, back story, logical progression, and even the laws of physics. In "Sum of Her Parts," the humor—Jenny turning sideways and all but disappearing, a leg of nylon that works as a dress, breasts that live most of the day in a foam-lined box like expensive jewelry—are the greasepaint that gild the clown's monstrous face.

The goal, then, is for readers to swallow the hook, feel a tug in the belly, and be carried away to a new understanding of the world before they realize their feet have left the ground. If they laugh along the way, so much the better.

HYBRID WORK
Sum of Her Parts

My sister Jenny was always skinny, but now she is a waif.

"It's not a diet, Diana," she says. "Just priorities."

I'm back in Tallahassee for Thanksgiving and in the three months since I've seen her, she's grown paper-doll thin. When she turns sideways in front of a broom in the corner, I can see the green wooden handle on either side.

"Liquid meals," I guess. "Buddhism?"

"Better," she says. "Follow me."

Her room is neat and spare as I remember it. My room is an office now.

There's a row of jars on her dresser that used to house mustard or relish, marmalade, diced garlic, non-fat mayo. In their murky depths float fistlike chunks of human tissue.

"I just wear my stomach at mealtimes," she says, tapping a Mott's Applesauce lid. "And if I'm not digesting, the gall bladder and pancreas come out, too."

Oversized plastic tubs are stacked on the floor for her large and small intestines. Some jars are empty, like the large one Sharpie-marked "brain."

"This is healthy?" I ask, planning my own collection of jars and labels, picking out evening dresses for my new, slimmer life.

"Healthier than smoking," she says, one sharp finger stabbing me in the chest.

At dinner, over cranberry sauce and dry turkey, our mother raises a toast to Jenny's twiglike limbs. "May it rub off on the rest of us," she says, but points her fork at me.

My father's cheeks burn while he spears his peas, and I study my plate where my reflection is pale and gravy-streaked. In three days I'll be back at M.I.T. and the rainbow-colored brains on my printouts won't care about my jeans size.

Meanwhile, Jenny blushes and squirms, speechless. After dinner she shows me why, holding up her larynx in a baby food jar. She faces the mirror and pops it back in discretely.

"Don't listen to Mom," she says. "It doesn't work for everyone."

"Don't you ever need all your parts at once?" I ask. Her clothes are all size -10.

She sits on the bed without creasing the comforter, ghostlike. "Not so far," she says. "The brain comes out during sex or chick flicks. The heart during algebra."

"Sex?" I say. She is two years my junior and I've never had a boyfriend.

"Oh, Diana," she says, pulling me onto the bed, riding the resulting jounce. "You're so beautiful on the inside." She taps my head, which has been compared to a graphing calculator, an almanac, the entire Encyclopedia Britannica, but never once to a summer's day.

My heart is heavy, my stomach full. "Show me," I say. "Call it professional curiosity."

"I don't know. You have to have the stomach for it."

"Or not," I say, to make her laugh, which she does, holding her empty middle.

But maybe she is right. The science I study deals with pictures and graphs, not bodies and all their messy possibilities. I get lightheaded at the sight of blood.

Jenny squeezes my hand and goes to her closet, sifting through skinny jeans and sheath dresses until she emerges with something slinky and green. It looks like one leg from a pair of nylons, and as she shimmies into it, I see that's what it once was.

"Thin isn't all it's cracked up to be," Jenny says, smoothing non-existent wrinkles over what's left of her hips. "You wouldn't believe the trouble I have finding clothes."

"Try me," I say, but after telling me to turn around so she can take her boobs from their foam-lined lockbox and slip them on one at a time, she is already on the way to her date, promising to answer all my questions in the morning.

With Jenny gone, I join my parents in front of *Everybody Loves Raymond*. In this one, Ray can't tell his wife he loves her. He tries, but the words just won't come out.

"I'm going to bed," I say before the show is over.

"Goodnight," my mother says, though it's just past 8 o'clock.

In my old bedroom, I plant myself in front of the mirror stuck to the wall it used to share with a lifesize Eddie Vedder. My face is round and full as a moon, but if I smile with my jaw held up, I can sort of hide my double-chin.

A good scientist needs all five senses, so I need my ears, eyes, tongue, and nose. Brain too; its 1,400 grams are mostly water anyway, and everyone knows water weight won't stay off.

It's the redundancies that make me a coward, though: my useless appendix, full set of kidneys, both tonsils, and all four of my wisdom teeth. Even these spare parts I can't let go of.

"It's mind over matter," Jenny says the next morning. Her speech is slushy since she hasn't put in her tongue.

We sip steaming cups of her favorite breakfast—hot water spiked with Splenda. I take a sip to be polite and lick the sweetness from my lips.

"Brainpower," I say, tapping my head, worried she'll pull a muscle trying to heft her mug. She nods as if she's heard me, but I can see by the smooth fall of her hair that her ears are missing, too.

With that same crooked smile, though, and the same lovely laugh, it's hard to believe that most of her isn't even here in front of me, and that back in her room, hundreds of firing synapses light up an industrial pickle jar as her brain plans the day's organ rotation without her. If I thought she could hear me, or that hearing would make any difference, I would ask her why she really wants to disappear. Instead, we sit across from each other at a table bare of food and fill ourselves with nothing, swallowing everything we really want to say.

OVERLAPPING TIME AND SYNTAX

What to Do with a Dream?

Julio Ortega

I

Probably, this is the impossible question for a writer. I doubt that anyone will have an answer. That is, a writer most of the time doesn't know what to do with a dream.

Write down your dreams, on the other hand, is probably the worst advice to give to the aspiring writer.

Nevertheless, the fact is that Jorge Luis Borges wrote a good number of his stories after he woke up from dreaming. María Kodama, his widow, told me that she remembers Borges waking up and announcing that he'd just dreamt a complete story. But more surprising, she added, was that Borges was able to remember the full story as he moved through his day. All he had to do was dictate the whole thing, with minimal revisions. Of course, you don't need to be blind, as Borges was, to follow Borges too far.

More intriguing is the case of Julio Cortázar. In a dream, he saw a man and a woman leaving their home, closing the door, and walking away. He woke

Julio Ortega is a professor of Hispanic Studies at Brown University. A native of Peru, his work has been translated into most of the modern languages and also into Farsi, Arabic, and Quechua. He is the author of *Poetics of Change, Gabriel García Márquez and the Powers of Fiction*, and *Transatlantic Translations*. Along with these critical studies, he has published *Ayacucho, Goodbye*, a novel, and *Emotions*, poems. His stories have appeared in journals including *Antaeus* and *Sudden Fiction International*.

up and started to write "Casa Tomada" ("House Taken Over"). Borges, of course, liked the story a lot and published it in *Revista de Buenos Aires*.

Cortázar also started to write his novel *Hopscotch* from a dream. He dreamt that he was in his flat in Paris, but his flat was part of a street in Buenos Aires. Both places appeared in his dream, a common experience among migrant people.

This mapping produced by a dream announces an open territory for stories that could happen without a place. It is the map of a place still under construction.

2

My story "Melodrama" was also born from a dream. Or from a nightmare. I was in a little plaza among people who were looking at a sort of trial taking place on a dark stage. I recognized the woman being prosecuted. I felt guilt, pain, horror.

Waking up, I understood that my dream didn't articulate the two spaces— hers, mine. Therefore, writing is the true dream—it explores the possible mapping of a non-existing territory.

Because of that, my story begins once and then again. This is not exactly a dream written down, but a dream re-written once and again.

Guilt reveals itself, perhaps, through the logic of dreams—duplicating the characters, the idea of a trial, names, and two different lives.

3

My little story is, thus, an exercise on what to do with a dream. It looks to answer the first question: how to write down in a sequence what is, in the dream, a simultaneous or, at least, an overlapping series of images. I tried to move from the second person (you) to the third person (she) to talk to and about the same woman. I found that by moving between "you" and "she," the woman of the story is free from my relation to her, and that I am, by switching the pronoun, less guilty of her suffering.

4

At the end, the syntax of a hybrid story can be not only dream and fact; it can also be the crossing of pronouns. You and I wake up to each other on the page. That is, on a short page! There are no novels about happy dreams, but unhappy dreams are the stuff of flash fiction. In a short story a writer needs to break a code to produce surprise and change. Flash fiction is fact fiction—you cannot break the rules of representation—which are based in the story told by a credible narrator—but you can cross, instead, the syntax between "You" and "I," and break up the order of the world in the sentence.

HYBRID WORK
Melodrama

The dream

The deranged girl being brought into the plaza to confess her sin is you.

I recognize you despite her pallor and the prisoner's uniform she wears because you stare straight ahead with the same genteel lucidity. But who, I ask myself, not understanding my place in that audience, is dragging this girl here to be made an example of? She has the open look of truth, but if you reveal me to these people, I will have to flee. I want to embrace her if only to convince myself that I am not the proof of disaffection.

I am a witness of this woman, an unknown part of me. Perhaps I am the part of reason that she still awaits.

Now I look for your eyes and say it: You are myself without me.

This is the enigma of my dream. The verb enunciates her, the pronoun reiterates me, but language excludes us from being able to define each other. She, I insist, is what I am not in myself; in her I am someone who eludes me.

Surrounded by triumphant doctors and lawyers she steps onto the platform to confess her guilt. The mob looks for stones, but there are none, and their anachronism is as crude as their resentment. They demand that the wound be opened in public so that the patient will purge her own misery. I, her secret lover, am here to recognize her, but I can do nothing but follow the events that rush with clinical logic.

With her long hair and torn clothing, she seeks with her eyes, and looks at me with pain and does not understand my silence.

The tale

How can I say I am calling you after all these years to tell you a dream?

It would be better to ask if she had dreamed about us as well; at least she would laugh and say, "You're trying to share the luxury of guilt, but let me light a cigarette. You wake me up at this hour instead of remembering my birthday and sending me flowers, or at least an Italian opera."

But I am not calling her, I would not know how to tell her a dream in which she appears like some soft-Freudian madwoman and I, her lover, as the witness of her high, tumultuous bed.

The confession

We finished the way couples finish, divided between guilt and laughter. Then she married. As in an American novel, we get along again. She demanded the stars from me ("The stars, wait, let me see them!"); and we play to extinguish them with our own hands.

The sequel

She finally enters the defendants' box with the integrity of her youth, impelled by the impatience of the judges and the rush of the mad crowd. She looks at all of us, resigned to her clinical death, and says: "Love would save me, even if it is too late." I expect the huge spotlights of yet another chapter of the national melodrama about the couple without a future. But from her sentence I only understood my name.

Should I leave? Or should I overwhelm the enemy and rescue her? How might I interrupt the ceremony (dream, sofa story, operatic chapter), take her by the hand and escape? When irony comes to save me, I resist it: I prefer the twist of remorse.

But emotion hampers us and makes us awkward. One should allow the tears to speak—so to speak.

The dialogue

After all, perhaps you went with me, and then left me forever. We are that slight disagreement.

Every time we met you would pass me a slip of paper with your telephone number on it, remember? First your parents answered, then your husband, and not long ago your daughter.

This time I myself answered: "She is not here," I said, "she has left."

The good-byes

Why don't you leave me in peace? I am not asking you for anything. What more do you want?
One day you wrote to me, and I answered immediately.
Then you turned your back and went to sleep.

There you have it, another star.

MIND THE GAP

Creating Tension through Omission and Absence

Robin Hemley

At the age of 25, I lived in Chicago on Roscoe Ave., the little study where I wrote no more than 150 feet from a bend in the tracks of the Ravenswood El. Every 10 minutes or so, an El train would screech around the bend, constantly threatening my concentration. The window in front of my writing desk looked out onto a deck, and without warning, my upstairs neighbor Dan would let out his two ferocious German Shepherds, Paco and Charlie, and they would bound down the stairs to my level of the deck. Whether my curtains were shut or not, they always sensed me, sent, it seemed, by some malevolent force that wanted nothing else but to see me fail. Teeth bared, they'd bark loudly and incessantly, pausing only for bathroom breaks, until Dan felt like letting them in again.

This was not an ideal situation for an aspiring writer. But I've always felt that you're going to write, if you're going to write at all, through the distractions, and I took the El and Paco and Charlie's malevolence as challenges, as dues to pay. And these distractions forced me to write in short bursts, funneling my creative energies into shorter forms. That was a pe-

Robin Hemley directed the nonfiction writing program at the University of Iowa for nine years before moving to Singapore to direct the writing program at Yale-NUS College and serve as writer-in-residence. He is the author of 11 books of nonfiction and fiction, most recently *Reply All: Stories* (2012) and *A Field Guide for Immersion Writing: Memoir, Journalism, and Travel* (2012). His awards include a Guggenheim Fellowship and The Independent Press Book Award.

riod when I wrote a lot of flash fiction and prose poetry. So perhaps I owe Paco and Charlie a debt of gratitude.

One evening, I thought I'd write something about my sister Nola's death, something I had never succeeded in doing in the 10 years since her passing. A diagnosed schizophrenic, she had tried to kill herself a number of times, but in the end, she died of an accidental prescription drug overdose, a pharmacist's mistake. She had only been 25, the same age as me when I sat down to write about her. A brilliant woman, a polyglot, and a talented artist, her illness had forced her to drop out of a PhD program in philosophy at Brandeis, and within two years of that, she was gone.

The story I wrote would have to be a flash piece (though the word "flash" wasn't widely used, if at all, then), something under 1,000 words. This particular constraint wasn't something I'd arrived at naturally. The word restriction was the major ground rule of a contest I wanted to enter—all submissions had to be under 1,000 words. I accepted the challenge and decided to focus on the night before my sister died, when a woman named Norma, a friend of my mother's, had taken me and her niece to a carnival to "get your mind off things." A kind gesture, but misjudged perhaps, as you don't necessarily want to have fun while your sister is dying in a hospital. I not only felt concern for Nola, but also for my mother, who had flown from South Bend, Indiana, where we lived, to the East Coast to be with my sister. I didn't want to be at a carnival, but I was 15 and didn't seem to have much of a choice. But when I got there, Norma introduced me to her niece, who was my age, pretty, and seemed to like me—the only prerequisites I needed for a crush. To say that conflicting emotions raged within me would be an overstatement. I felt tides of grief, an underground river of anxiety and fear coursing through me, tamped down by Norma's directive to have fun and my own intoxication with her niece. All that's to say, I acted like a normal boy that evening, but I felt anything but normal.

I can't say for sure whether Norma's niece said the line to me that I wrote, which I think is pivotal, "Your sister's crazy, isn't she?" But I'm pretty sure she did. I remember around the age of 25 telling my friend, the writer David Shields, that I once made a conscious decision not to "go crazy, not to be like my sister," and David thought this was a remarkable directive. David's attention made me more attentive, made this moment in the history of my consciousness—when I in effect decided to be sane— stand out.

So what I wanted to capture was the sense of that night before Nola died. I went to my writing desk and started to recall that night. I also recalled favorite stories that had a similar mood, to help bring me into the state of mind I needed to write. I recalled James Joyce's classic story "Araby," from his collection *Dubliners*, in which a young boy foolishly pines over a girl older than him and out of his league. The two stories, his and mine, are quite different, but the settings are somewhat similar, bustling public places where people go to have fun.

No sooner had I sat down than Paco and Charlie thrust themselves at my window, enraged, it seemed, that they couldn't tear into my throat. I parted the curtains to look at them, but already I hardly saw them. The Ravenswood El, shooting sparks and shrieking, rounded the corner. The phone probably rang. But I was back in 1973 by then. The flash form seemed perfectly suited to recreate flashes of memory and the kind of disjointed and displaced feeling that I wanted my young narrator to experience. I kept the majority of my sentences short, the images following quickly one upon the other to create a sense of confusion and slight menace that a carnival fairway possesses. But I only needed the barest nods toward detail, as pretty much everyone who might read my story would know what a carnival looks and sounds like. I only needed to hint, and the reader could fill in the rest.

I combined two events—the night with Norma and her niece and another time in sixth grade when I visited, along with my grandmother, a ramshackle theme park in Florida called "Pirates' World" where I rode a mini roller coaster and my head kept grazing a pipe. When I got off the ride, I stayed off. I didn't go back on, but when I showed the first draft of the resulting story "Riding the Whip" to my friend Sharon Solwitz, she thought my ending was weak and that my protagonist, Jay, needed to go back on the ride again. This was one of the best pieces of advice I ever received and I took it immediately.

The reason why this story works, I think, is closely linked to its brevity—the flash form makes it entirely. Writing this story taught me everything I know about narrative tension, tension in language, and revision. The narrative tension and the tension of the language in "Riding the Whip" are closely linked. Told from the point of view of a boy who doesn't know what he's going through, who can't comprehend the trauma of losing his sister, and the guilt he feels made me rely on evoking emotion through salient detail. I had to find a way to make him articulate his trauma without being able to comprehend it, and the best way to do that is through absence, through gaps in language, through silence. The fact that I had only a few words to use worked in my favor, as I had to find substitute details or actions that would stand in for his emotions. The memory of the painting he bought with paper money from his sister is one. His betrayal of his sister by saying nothing in her defense and agreeing she's crazy is another. The self-flagellation inherent in the bar striking him is yet another. And finally, there's the last image of the violence of the slashed seat. I don't explain how his sister killed herself. I don't need to do that. The tension created in me as a writer unable to say exactly what I meant produced both a narrative tension and a tension in the language that hopefully the reader feels in every line and beyond the last line of the story.

HYBRID WORK
Riding the Whip

The night before my sister died, a friend of my parents, Natalie Ganzer, took me and her niece to a carnival. I couldn't stand Natalie, but I fell in love with the niece, a girl about 15, named Rita. On the Ferris wheel, Rita grabbed my hand. On any other ride I would have thought she was only frightened and wanted security. But this Ferris wheel was so tame and small. There was nothing to be afraid of at 50 feet.

When we got down and the man let us out of the basket, I kept hold of Rita's hand, and she didn't seem to mind.

"Oh, I'm so glad you children are enjoying the evening," said Natalie. "It's so festive. There's nothing like a carnival, is there?"

Normally I would have minded being called a child, but not tonight. Things were improving. There was nothing to worry about, my mother had told me over the phone earlier that evening. Yes, Julie had done a stupid thing, but only to get attention. Still, there was something wrong, something that bugged me about that night, where I was, the carnival and its sounds. I was having too much fun and I knew I shouldn't be. Already, I had won a stuffed animal from one of the booths and given it to Rita. And usually I got nauseated on rides, but tonight they just made me laugh. Red neon swirled around on the rides and barkers yelled at us on the fairway. Popguns blew holes in targets, and there were so many people screaming and laughing that I could hardly take it in. I just stood there feeling everyone else's fun moving through me, and I could hardly hear what Rita and Natalie were asking me. "Come on, Jay," shouted Rita. My hand was being tugged. "Let's ride the Whip." The whip. That didn't make any sense to me. A whip wasn't something you rode. It was something to hurt you, something from movies that came down hard on prisoners' backs and left them scarred.

"You can't ride a whip," I shouted to her over the noise.

She laughed and said, "Why not? Don't be scared. You won't get sick. I promise."

"Aren't you having fun, Jay?" Natalie asked. "Your parents want you to have fun, and I'm sure that's what Julie wants, too."

I didn't answer though I was having fun. Things seemed brighter and louder than a moment before. I could even hear a girl on the Ferris wheel say to someone, "You're cute, did you know that?" One carny in his booth stood out like a detail in a giant painting. He held a bunch of strings in his hand. The strings led to some stuffed animals. "Everyone's a winner," he said.

The carnival was just a painting, a bunch of petals in a bowl, which made me think of Julie. She was an artist and painted still lifes mostly, but she didn't think she was any good. My parents had discouraged her, but I bought a large painting of hers once with some paper money I cut from a notebook. A week before the carnival, she came into my room and slashed the painting to bits. "She's not herself," my mother told me. "You know she loves you."

Now we stood at the gates of the Whip. Rita gave her stuffed animal to Natalie, who stood there holding it by the paw as though it were a new ward of hers. The man strapped us into our seat and Rita said to me, "You're so quiet. Aren't you having fun?"

"Sure," I said. "Doesn't it look like it?"

"Your sister's crazy, isn't she?" asked Rita. "I mean, doing what she did."

I knew I shouldn't answer her, that I should step out of the ride and go home.

"She just sees things differently," I said.

"What do you mean?" Rita asked. She was looking at me strangely, as though maybe I saw things differently, too. I didn't want to see differently. I didn't want to become like my sister.

"Sure she's crazy," I said. "I don't even care what happens to her."

Then the ride started up and we laughed and screamed. We moved like we weren't people anymore, but changed into electrical currents charged from different sources.

In the middle of the ride something grazed my head. There was a metal bar hanging loose from one of the corners, and each time we whipped around it, the bar touched me. It barely hit me, but going so fast, it felt like I was being knocked with a sandbag. It didn't hit anyone else, just me, and I tried several times to get out of the way, but I was strapped in, and there was no way to avoid it.

At the end of the ride I was totally punch-drunk and I could barely speak. Rita, who mistook my expression for one of pleasure, led me over to Natalie.

"That was fun," said Rita. "Let's go on the Cat and Mouse now."

My vision was blurry and my legs were wobbling a bit. "I want to go on the Whip again," I said.

Natalie and Rita looked at each other. Natalie reached out toward my head, and I pulled back from her touch. "You're *bleeding*, Jay," she said. Her hand stayed in mid-air, and she looked at me as though she were someone in a gallery trying to get a better perspective on a curious painting.

I broke away from them into the crowd and made my way back to the Whip. After paying the man, I found the same seat. I knew which one it was because it was more beat up than the rest, with several gashes in its cushion, as though someone had taken a long knife and scarred it that way on purpose.

WHEN THE UNTHINKABLE IS THOUGHT

Turning Speculation into Story

Pamela Painter

As writers we wonder *What if?* And then we allow ourselves to imagine the horrific, the unthinkable, and to write it into story.

One sweltering summer day, I was pushing an empty baby carriage across the Longfellow Bridge that spans the Charles River and connects Boston and Cambridge. The carriage was empty because my friend, Lilian, was carrying her baby daughter and strolling along in front of me. Lilian's dark hair was a gleaming helmet of heat above her thin cotton dress. We were going nowhere in particular—hoping for a breeze, our real reason to be on the bridge on such a hot afternoon. A third of the way across, Lilian stopped to point out the tiny, white sailboats tilting and gliding on the river below. Her grip on her daughter was firm, one arm around her sweet round tummy, the other supporting a thick, diapered bottom. She held her daughter only high enough to allow her to peek over the iron railing. My friend and I saw sailboats, duck boats, and a swift current, while her daughter saw white triangles, shapes that swung in reds and blues and yellows above her crib.

It was then that I thought the unthinkable: what if my friend threw her baby over the bridge?

Pamela Painter lives in Boston and teaches in the Emerson College MFA Program. She is the author of three story collections: *Wouldn't You Like to Know* (2010), *Getting to Know the Weather* (2008), and *The Long and Short of It* (1999). She is co-author of the fiction-writing handbook *What If?* (1991). Her stories have appeared in *The Atlantic, Five Points, Kenyon Review, Missouri Review,* and *Ploughshares,* and in numerous anthologies, such as *Sudden Fiction* and *Flash Fiction.* Painter's new collection *Ways to Spend the Night* is forthcoming from Engine Books.

This question had nothing to do with my friend's character and only to do with mine. I like to think that if I were not a writer this thought would not have occurred to me, but I will never know the answer to that. But what about you? Do you have thoughts like that: *What if?* Do you posit situations you will never encounter, actions on your part or someone else's that you will never move to carry through, but actions you might put in a story?

I was enormously relieved when my friend grew weary of her daughter's sticky weight and returned her to the safety of the carriage, then took over the task of pushing it along in front of me. I was left with nothing to carry, push, or even throw, but I was left with the kernel of a story. We stopped for iced tea on Charles Street, where I didn't tell her what I was thinking, but I was already wondering about my story: the story of a woman throwing something—perhaps a baby—over a bridge.

Sometime in the next few days I began to write it. I knew from the beginning that it was going to be short. It was not going to answer to the elements of the traditional short story—characterization, back story, conflict, rising action, epiphany, and so on. You see, perhaps it was squeamish of me, but already I had retreated from the certainty that a woman—perhaps a mother—might throw her baby over the railing of a bridge to the dark water below. I had moved it back to the realm of conjecture, of possibility. The story needed to be very short to tolerate that uncertainty—on my part, on the part of the narrator, and also for the reader. I wanted that uncertainty to provide tension but not direct or prolonged conflict, and I wanted the story to end in that unnerving state of apprehension.

Another reason I chose the short short form was that I wanted to stay with the point of view of the bystander, the outsider. If the narrator telling the story was the young woman—a mother, a nanny, a kidnapper?—the mystery would be gone. She, and therefore the reader, would know what was being thrown over the bridge and, if it were a baby, the question would then be *Why?* An enormous *Why* requiring a back story, an exploration of motives, and, yes, somewhere an acknowledgment of the father. And what might the father's role have been? Lover? Husband? Was the baby a manifestation of incest? Or the result of an act that was impersonal, perhaps brutal, yet resulting in the birth of a child whose father was unknown? It was my story and I did not want it to go in any of those directions.

By choosing to have an outsider tell the story I could keep the bystander at a distance from the woman ahead of her on the bridge, from the woman's action, and from any certainty that it was a baby that she had thrown over the railing. My bystander, however, isn't entirely inactive. She does scream to passing cars, but no one hears her and no one stops. And when she imagines what she might do if it is a baby, defeated, she admits she will not jump. This admission makes her partially complicit with what has gone before.

The characters finally do engage, but only toward the story's end. First the bystander merely *tells* the young woman what she has witnessed, which causes the young woman to misinterpret her concern and to ask the bystander, "Are you all right?" When the bystander finally *asks* the young woman "What did you throw into the river?" the young woman evades her questions. The bystander never accuses the young woman of the act she herself has posited. It is unmentionable. The reader knows the suspicions those questions are masking, but the young woman's actions and her response that the "rain has ruined everything I planned" give nothing away. Thus the story is not complicated with allegations, perhaps a call to 911, or even an heroic gesture to save the child. Nor does the narrator's act at the end of the story illuminate the story's situation. The story's short form supports the reality that no answers are forthcoming. Both the bystander and the reader are left with the anguished question, suspended in time, and still listening for a cry.

HYBRID WORK
From **The Long and Short of It**

The Bridge

A bicycle whizzes past her from behind just as she steps onto the pe-
destrian walkway of the bridge. It startles her. It also startles the young
woman who is walking slowly 50 feet ahead of her, cradling a bundle of
something—a potted plant, flowers, a baby—she can't tell what. Belatedly,
she has the impulse to call something nasty to the young man on the bicycle, but he is moving away too fast, head low, legs pumping hard. Anyway
the young woman must have said something to him because he swings
his head around to her, slowing down just slightly, before he zooms away
more dangerous than ever. He could have injured them both. The mother
and the baby. Or crushed the flowers.

· · · ·

She carries her purse slung over her shoulder on a long strap and in
her left hand a bag of groceries—no jars or cans to make it heavy. English
muffins, tea, two lamb chops, a bottle of red wine, a ripe cantaloupe. The
wind from the bay is brisk, cool. Below and behind the bridge, the ribbon
of water reflects the fall's gray-white sky. She stops to button her jacket, wrap her scarf smartly around her neck. The scarf matches her skirt,
which pleases her. The young woman ahead has also stopped. She doesn't
know why she says "young woman" because she might be a grandmother
out for a stroll or a volunteer for the elderly on her way with bright flowers and a lot to say. Squinting the young woman into sharper focus brings
no more illuminating details than a scarf that matches nothing else she
wears. She has changed the bundle from her left to right arm.

If she catches up to the young woman, and if there is a child bundled
into a blanket, perhaps they might chat for part of their trip across the
long bridge. For instance, they might exclaim about the rudeness of the

boy on the bicycle. Or she will smile at the baby, admire its hair or eyes or nose, or if nothing warrants, the charm of children. "How old?" she might ask. "Is it a boy or girl?" "The name?" Or perhaps "What lovely flowers," although she can imagine that people might not respond to this beyond a polite murmur of agreement and downcast eyes. Perhaps because they have nothing to do with making flowers.

· · · ·

Ahead of her the young woman stops again and leans over the heavy iron railing of the bridge. She is looking down into the water as if something has caught her eye, something worth the pause. She too stops, torn between catching up to the young woman and wanting to see what holds her interest in the water. She sets her grocery bag down between her feet and peers over the shoulder-high railing into the river below the young woman. There are no barges or colorful sailing boats, no sight-seeing cruises with loud speakers blaring the bored voice of a guide. So what can it be? As she looks back up again, in a graceful curve as of a ballet gesture, the young woman throws her bundle over the side of the bridge.

· · · ·

She strains against the railing and tries to guess the weight of it, the drift of flowers or the downward spiral of a helpless infant, but she cannot. It lands with a soft plop (like a tire puncture), floats an instant then disappears with tiny bubbles. Paper of the kind from a florist's long roll or a small square of blanket drifts past the original spot until it too has gathered enough water to sink. There has been no color, only white paper around flowers, or a baby's white blanket.

· · · ·

She screams, whirling around to passing cars, but they are traveling by too swiftly. She turns back to the young woman, turns toward the young woman whose coat is blowing open in the breeze. She realizes immediately that if it was—or rather—is a baby, what would be the difference? Would she throw down her groceries, tear off her jacket and scarf leaving them draped over the railing, kick off her shoes? Would she call to anyone to witness her leap, even the young mother who now stands motionless, her arms withdrawn from the graceful arc of her throw? And then after the climb onto the iron railing higher than it looks, the leap into the water? The cold high shock of the water. Even now, half-believing, something has died. She does not jump.

. . . .

She hurries toward the young woman, heels clicking like a mugger sure of his prey and silence no longer necessary. She half expects the young woman to hear her footsteps, turn toward her and then run. Another bicycle passes and she wants to cry out, send for help, but she can't find the words. What can she tell even her husband later, as they sit with a glass of wine and watch the news. She glances at the darkening river, scraping her elbow as she continues to run. Her scarf streams behind her. And below, a large camellia floats on the water where the bundle was dropped, or a small baby's bonnet, white and scalloped. She runs on, the sack of groceries banging against her legs, bruising the cantaloupe. "I was watching," she calls out to the young woman, breathless. "I was standing over there." Pointing, she tries to determine just how far away she was but can't identify her precise place along the stark railing of the bridge.

The young woman turns but doesn't run. Together they stare at the place where she stood on the bridge. The young woman's face is smooth and shiny like a plate and yes, young. Her eyes are gray as the water and she raises them to the sky as if looking for signs of changing weather. Her hands fill her pockets, her arms are tight against her sides where a bundle was. Is she used to strangers talking to her, calling breathless from 15, 10 feet away? She herself isn't used to watching babies being thrown into the river, or even flowers. There is a story in flowers too, although a far different tale, probably romantic and full of meaningless gestures, predictable details. But what happened? There is a new emptiness inside her. What must there be in this young woman whose life has changed by the crossing of a bridge in fall. "I saw you throw something into the river," she tells her.

. . . .

The young woman seems to consider everything, then says, "I heard you call out. Are you all right?" as she pulls her coat closer about her, ties up her scarf. The young woman continues, "I think it is going to rain again. It's ruined everything I've planned." The grocery bag feels heavy and she sets it down as if it contains quarts of heavy rich milk. "What was it," she asks the young woman. "What did you throw into the river." The young woman seems to think the question does not refer to anything specific like flowers or babies as she glances at the bag of groceries—perhaps wondering if she should offer to carry them, or making a list of what she herself needs from the store. "I must go," she says, putting her hands in her pockets again, and she goes.

. . . .

And so. She watches the young woman once more recede into the distance. In her wake, Cambridge neon begins to breathe above the gray water. The subway thunders past her on its short sojourn across the bridge outside its tunnel. How much does a baby weigh? She stoops down and moves aside English muffins, the wine. She hefts the cantaloupe before lifting it out with both hands. She tries to palm it like a basketball, but can't suspend it in one hand. As she holds on with one hand to the railing of the bridge, she pulls her arm back over her shoulder, her other hand under the ripe fruit. Lacking the grace of the young woman's motion, she heaves it like a catapult out into the river. She tries to remember the soft plop of entry, and failing that, she listens for a cry.

WRITING AND THE HUMAN ANIMAL
On Transforming the Artificial into the Natural

Etgar Keret

I was first introduced to Franz Kafka's writing during my compulsory army-service basic training in Israel. During that period Kafka's fiction felt hyper-realistic. I had read a lot of works that had moved me as much before Kafka, but it was only after reading his short stories that I felt that I could try writing, too.

My stories have been called fables that don't teach you anything except how complicated it is to be human. Fables find their origins and their success in the spoken word or oral tradition, which brings me to the Hebrew slang in which I write, one that represents a unique language that existed exclusively as a written language for 2,000 years only to find itself "defrosted" at an arbitrary historical point. This created a spoken language that had preserved its ancient biblical roots on the one end but that was also very open to invented and imported words out of necessity—there were 2,000 years worth of words that didn't exist in the language. This tension between a traditional language and a very chaotic and anarchistic one creates a spoken language that is bursting with unique energy and that

Etgar Keret is an Israeli writer of very short stories, graphic novels, children's stories, and scripts for television and film. He is a winner of the 2007 Cannes Film Festival Caméra d'Or and a French Chevalier des Arts et des Lettres, as well as the Israeli Prime Minister's Prize. His work has appeared in *The New Yorker*, *The Paris Review*, and *The New York Times*, among other publications, and on "This American Life," where he is a regular contributor. His books have been published in 36 languages, including seven short story collections in English.

allows you to switch registers mid-sentence. All of these linguistic aspects can't pass translation. I have been lucky enough to work with probably the best translators around; what we do most of the time is cry together and share comforting hugs.

In my story "What Animal Are You?" a German Public Television reporter asks the narrator/writer/me to write, so that she can take a picture of him/me writing. The story closes with the writer's three-year-old son asking the reporter in Hebrew what kind of animal she is. The writer translates the question into English. The reporter says she is a monster here to eat pretty little children. In Hebrew, the writer tells his son that the reporter says she is a red-feathered songbird who flew here from a faraway land. There are many levels to this exchange. At a fairytale level, the moral is that interpreters need to be wily. There's a political idea also about what to pass on and not to pass on to the next generation.

Yes, this is a framing device; and yes, I advise throwing out framing devices and conventions when they don't work in a piece. Here, the frame works well with "What Animal Are You?" because it enables the writer/ narrator/me to explain that everything the reader is in the process of reading, the writer—I—is/am in the process of writing, having been asked by a reporter to write something on the computer because it always makes for great visuals: an author writing. (Remember the scene in *Dr. Zhivago* with Omar Sharif at his desk?)

You could say the story is about artificiality: the lengths to which we human animals go to make the artificial seem natural, and yet somehow manage to turn our natural activities into strained and awkward ones. Unlike the narrator's three-year-old child, most adults, when asked "What animal are you?" don't understand how to play along. ("Write a story about just that—about how unnatural it seems and how the unnatural suddenly produces something real, filled with passion.") Here, I intentionally write a bunch of artificial stuff in order to show the natural struggle to push through for something real: how hard we have to try—blunted first by cynicism, rage, manners, and all the other myriad things we do—to pretend that we're not animals.

Writing is one way to break through that artificial stuff; it is also a way to live another life. Many other lives. The lives of countless people whom I've never been, but who are completely *me*. So enjoy what you do and love your characters. For a character to be real, there has to be at least one person in this world capable of loving it and understanding it, whether they like what the character does or not. Remember, you're the mother and the father of the characters you create. If you can't love them, nobody can.

One of the gifts of writing is that while writing, you don't owe anything to anyone. In real life, if you don't behave yourself, you'll wind up in jail or in an institution, but in writing, anything goes. If there's a character in your story who appeals to you, kiss it. If there's a carpet in your story that you hate, set fire to it right in the middle of the living room. When it comes to writing, you can destroy entire planets and eradicate whole civilizations with the click of a key, and an hour later, when the old lady from the floor below sees you in the hallway, she'll still say hello.

This essay is a combined and adapted version of three interviews with Etgar Keret, conducted by Granta, The Paris Review, *and* The Believer. *More information about the interviews can be found in the Credits section.*

HYBRID WORK
From Suddenly, a Knock on the Door

What Animal Are You?

The sentences I'm writing now are for the benefit of the German Public Television viewers. A reporter who came to my home today asked me to write something on the computer because it always makes for great visuals: an author writing. It's a cliché, she realizes that, but clichés are nothing but an unsexy version of the truth, and her role, as a reporter, is to turn that truth into something sexy, to break the cliché with lighting and unusual angles. And the light in my house falls perfectly, without her having to turn on even a single spot, so all that's left is for me to write.

At first, I just made believe I was writing, but she said it wouldn't work. People would be able to tell right away that I was just pretending. "Write something for real," she demanded, and then, to be sure: "A story, not just a bunch of words. Write naturally, the way you always do." I told her it wasn't natural for me to be writing while I was having my picture taken for German Public Television, but she insisted. "So use it," she said. "Write a story about just that—about how unnatural it seems and how the unnaturalness suddenly produces something real, filled with passion. Something that permeates you, from your brain to your loins. Or the other way around. I don't know how it works with you, what part of your body gets the creative juices flowing. Each person is different." She told me how she'd once interviewed a Belgian author who, every time he wrote, had an erection. Something about the writing "stiffened his organ"—that's the expression she used. It was probably a literal translation from German, and it sounded very strange in English.

"Write," she insisted again. "Great. I love your terrible posture when you write, the cramped neck. It's just wonderful. Keep writing. Excellent. That's it. Naturally. Don't mind me. Forget I'm here."

So I go on writing, not minding her, forgetting she's there, and I'm natural. As natural as I can be. I have a score to settle with the viewers of German Public Television but this isn't the time to settle it. This is the time to write. To write things that will appeal, because when you write crap, she's already reminded me, it comes out terrible on camera.

My son returns from kindergarten. He runs up to me and hugs me. Whenever there's a television crew in the house, he hugs me. When he was younger, the reporters had to ask him to do it, but by now, he's a pro:

runs up to me, doesn't look at the camera, gives me a hug, and says, "I love you, Daddy." He isn't four yet, but he already understands how things work, this adorable son of mine.

My wife isn't as good, the German television reporter says. She doesn't flow. Keeps fiddling with her hair, stealing glances at the camera. But that isn't really a problem. You can always edit her out later. That's what's so nice about television. In real life it isn't like that. In real life you can't edit her out, undo her. Only God can do that, or a bus, if it runs her over. Or a terrible disease. Our upstairs neighbor is a widower. An incurable disease took his wife from him. Not cancer, something else. Something that starts in the guts and ends badly. For six months she was shitting blood. At least, that's what he told me. Six months before God Almighty edited her out. Ever since she died, all kinds of women keep visiting our building, wearing high heels and cheap perfume. They arrive at unlikely hours, sometimes as early as noon. He's retired, our upstairs neighbor, and his time is his own. And those women—according to my wife, at least—they're whores. When she says whores it comes out natural, like she was saying turnip. But when she's being filmed, it doesn't. Nobody's perfect.

My son loves the whores who visit our upstairs neighbor. "What animal are you?" he asks them when he bumps into them on the stairs. "Today I'm a mouse, a quick and slippery mouse." And they get it right away, and throw out the name of an animal: an elephant, a bear, a butterfly. Each whore and her animal. It's strange, because with other people, when he asks them about the animals, they simply don't catch on. But the whores just go along with it.

Which gets me thinking that the next time a television crew arrives I'll bring one of them instead of my wife, and that way it'll be more natural. They look great. Cheap, but great. And my son gets along better with them too. When he asks my wife what animal she is, she always insists: "I'm not an animal, sweetie, I'm a person. I'm your mommy." And then he always starts to cry.

Why can't she just go with the flow, my wife? Why is it so easy for her to call women with cheap perfume "whores" but when it comes to telling a little boy "I'm a giraffe" it's more than she can handle? It really gets on my nerves. Makes me want to hit someone. Not her. Her I love. But someone. To take out my frustrations on someone who has it coming. Right-wingers can take it out on Arabs. Racists on blacks. But those of us who belong to the liberal left are trapped. We've boxed ourselves in. We have nobody to take it out on. "Don't call them whores," I rail at my wife. "You don't know for a fact that they're whores, do you? You've never seen anyone pay them or anything, so don't call them that, okay? How would you feel if someone called you a whore?"

"Great," the German reporter says. "I love it. The crease in your fore-head. The frenzied keystrokes. Now all we need are an intercut with trans-lations of your books in different languages, so our viewers can tell how successful you are—and that hug from your son one more time. The first time he ran up to you so quickly that Jörg, our cameraman, didn't have a chance to change the focus." My wife wants to know if the German re-porter needs her to hug me again too, and in my heart I pray she'll say yes. I'd really love my wife to hug me again, her smooth arms tightening around me, as if there's nothing else in the world but us. "No need," the German says in an icy voice. "We've got that already." "What animal are you?" my son asks the German, and I quickly translate into English. "I'm not an animal," she laughs, running her long fingernails through his hair. "I'm a monster. A monster that came from across the ocean to eat pretty little children like you." "She says she's a songbird," I translate to my son with impeccable naturalness. "She says she's a red-feathered songbird, who flew here from a faraway land."

8

. . . .

Pictures Made of Words

PICTURES MADE OF WORDS
An Introduction

The genre "Pictures Made of Words" includes the graphic versions of memoir, journalism, essays, and poetry created by writers employing, among other materials, scissors, tape, ink, maps, etymologies, and paint. As well as graphic texts and literary comics, this category includes concrete poetry, erasures, illustrations, and cut-outs of various kinds of texts, which are, literally, pictures made of words. This hybrid form invites us to explore the long association between depicted speech and graphics. We know, of course, that written language emerged from glyphs, the basic elements of picture writing systems, and that letters are, ultimately, tiny pictures representing the smallest parts of sound that we combine and recombine to make words on a page. With written language, we are in the realm of the abstract, a realm where words are disembodied, needing no voice to utter them. And even the fact of words as representation increasingly feels less consequential, especially with technologies that eliminate the need for paper and traditional writing instruments, and that allow words to be conceived, typed, and transmitted instantaneously. The logic behind these systems of verbal representation fascinated the exuberantly anti-art Dadaist movement in the early twentieth century, and that movement's embrace of Cubism, collage, and concrete poetry facilitated our twenty-first century iterations of pictures made of words.

Three-quarters of a century before international Dadaists began to experiment with simultaneous visual perspectives in a single moment of time, Emily Dickinson was experimenting with visual techniques for portraying the multi-faceted experience of the eternal now. Perusing the table of contents of the remarkable Emily Dickinson Electronic Archives, one can choose between such categories as "Dickinson Cartoonist," "The Letter-Poem, a Dickinson Genre," and "Mutilations: What was erased, inked over, and cut away," showing her to be a near-complete "pictures made of words" category unto herself. Today the features for which Dickinson are known can be seen in Anne Carson's blank spaces that speak of the world lost before Carson ever tried to translate Sappho in *If Not, Winter: Fragments of Sappho* (2003), or Carson and visual artist Bianca Stone's *Antigonick* (2015), which juxtaposes watercolors of contemporary domestic scenes onto a version of Sophocles' *Antigone* that is aware of itself as a version. Works of literary erasure achieve similar effects: Doris Cross' 1965 "Dictionary Column" art book and Matthea Harvey's *Of Lamb* (2011), which is an illustrated, book-length erasure of a biography of Charles Lamb.

The history of graphic novels, comics, and graphic journalism is so broad it is difficult to cover, but certainly Art Spiegelman's Pulitzer Prize-winning 1986 graphic novel *Maus*—which depicts the author's interviews with his father about his Holocaust experience as a Polish Jew, and which uses different species of animals to depict different human races—is one of the most influential contemporary works of pictures made of words. Marjane Satrapi's *Persepolis* (2004), a graphic depiction of the author's childhood experience of the 1970 Iranian revolution, is another. More recent examples include Alison Bechdel's *Fun Home: A Family Tragicomic* (2007), Shaun Tan's *The Arrival* (2007), and Reif Larsen's *The Selected Works of T. S. Spivet* (2010), which draws on methods of Talmudic commentary and glosses to turn the novel into a kind of illustrated hypertext.

This anthology includes works that draw from all the influences mentioned above. Jena Osman's "Financial District," excerpted from *The Network*, employs etymological maps juxtaposed onto topographical maps of early Manhattan, and Craig Santos Perez's excerpt from *from unincorporated territory [saina]* maps the erosion of both language and land on the island of Guam. In Perez's and Osman's work, words, serving as ambassadors of political entities and policies, are as powerful as rain, rivers, and earthquakes in shaping the physical geography of an island. Their word maps reveal how the stories we, as a nation, a culture, and a society, tell actually shape the ground on which we—as authors—quite literally stand.

Andrea Baker's excerpt from *The Incredibly True Adventures of Me* uses images created from packing tape and paper to access a story that refuses language. Mira Bartók's illustrations that she created for, but ultimately did not use in, the published version of her memoir *The Memory Palace*, explore the shaky basis on which our stories, words, and pictures depend: memory. Writing in the aftermath of a traumatic brain injury and subsequent memory loss, her artwork poses important questions about the tension between the stories that hold us in thrall and our power to create our own reality.

Miriam Libicki's work with comics and nonfiction to document African refugees in Tel Aviv reveals the ultimate subjectivity inherent in any journalistic reportage or history. As opposed to photography, in which the photo is a closed world and the photographer's eye suggests objectivity, "the subjectivity (even unreliability) of the creator/narrator is foregrounded by drawing." Also a work of graphic nonfiction, Stan Mack's *Janet & Me*, which he calls an "illustrated memoir," counts on authorial subjectivity to share what it feels like to care for a beloved partner who is dying of cancer. His artwork diffuses sentimentality through its focus on the funny and decidedly unsentimental Janet.

Each artist offers a glimpse of the human mind in a three-dimensional world in the act of creation, establishing the reader as someone with the capacity to acknowledge the voice that speaks and the eye that sees and the world under contemplation. Perspective, after all, means the place from which one sees, and these pieces stand bravely in places that are sometimes uncomfortable. Here it is the genre's dual medium—the word as a material being and the word as the bearer of an idea—that is its strength. In the congruence and dissonance between the two is where the magic happens.

—*Marcela Sulak*

PACIFIC HYBRID POETICS
Unwriting and Interweaving Visual Stories
Craig Santos Perez

In the essay "Unwriting Oceania: The Repositioning of the Pacific Writer Scholars within a Folk Narrative Space" (2000), Papua New Guinean poet Steven Edmund Winduo considers the relationship between Pacific Islander literature and postcolonial hybridity theory. He argues that colonialism, modernization, urbanization, and globalization have attempted to erase Pacific cultures and replace them within Western cultural practices.

I grew up on the Pacific Island of Guåhan (Guam), a 212-square-mile island in the area of the Western Pacific Ocean known as Micronesia. Formal and informal family gatherings were a central part of my childhood, which meant that oral stories and storytellers were a vital part of my island world. Of course, we kids did not talk—we listened as our elders talked story.

Despite the attempts to erase Pacific cultures, Winduo insists that a "trace" of "living cultural memory" remains. From these traces, Pacific poets "reinstate what has been crossed out, but is visible in erasure." To do

Craig Santos Perez is a native Chamoru from the Pacific Island of Guåhan (Guam). He is the co-founder of Ala Press, co-star of the poetry album *Undercurrent* (2011), and author of three collections of poetry: *from unincorporated territory [hacha]* (2008), *from unincorporated territory [saina]* (2010), and *from unincorporated territory [guma']* (2014). He has been a finalist for the *LA Times* Book Prize for Poetry and the winner of the PEN Center USA Literary Award. He is an associate professor and the director of the creative writing program in the English department at the University of Hawai'i, Mānoa.

this, we must "unwrite" and deconstruct representations of our disappearance and form "new positions of articulation."

These talk-stories did not follow linear or predictable plots. They were often improvisational, fragmentary, and spiraling. These talk-stories were also communal because many voices contributed to the telling. Sometimes family members interrupted each other; sometimes family members told the same story from diverging perspectives; sometimes family members remembered stories differently. As families wove stories together, new stories became threaded and unraveled.

Winduo suggests that the (post)colonial Pacific poet expresses "multiple selves as necessary fragments of an agency involved in knowledge production." Through this multiplicity, a "dialogic encounter develops within a hybridized narrative structure" and the traceable "fragments of culture, language, and society are evoked as necessary differences."

When I was in high school, my family migrated from Guåhan to California in search of economic opportunities. I began writing poetry as a way to stay connected to my home island, to remember what we left behind, and to continue weaving family stories. As an undergraduate and, later, a graduate student, I studied modernist and postmodernist American and European poetry and poetics. I felt drawn to these poetries because of their fragmentary, deconstructed, indeterminate, and nonlinear forms and narrative structures. At the same time, I was drawn to multicultural, minority, and indigenous poetries of the United States: poets of Latino, Asian American, African American, and Native American heritages. These poets inspired me with how their narrative and lyric poems sang their experiences, identities, cultures, and histories into existence.

According to Winduo, a hybridized narrative structure weaves together complex and heterogeneous influences that "complement, contradict, and challenge one another." Winduo asserts that the only way Pacific writers can "maintain cultural independence is to incorporate and adapt other cultural practices into their own to forge an independent identity."

The poetry included in this anthology reflects how I have adapted other aesthetic practices with the aesthetics of talk-story. I incorporate words from official documents to show how these abstract texts attempt to erase our culture and land.

I also employ strikethroughs to illustrate how colonial forces often silence our voices. Furthermore, I incorporate the voices of my family members, our suppressed histories, and our endangered ecologies. To make the traces of our stories visible, I experiment with the spatial and textual materiality of the page. Sometimes, I see words as islands emerging from the ocean of the page. Sometimes words are weights that open up the fishing net of sentences to harvest meaning. Sometimes I see words as symbols on a map or stars in the sky, guiding us home. Sometimes I see words as canoes carrying our precious cargo across great distances. All of these ways of seeing inform the visual poetics of my work.

To me, hybrid narrative structures weave together orality and textuality, the traditional and the contemporary, external documents and internal emotions, indigenous and colonial languages, communal storytelling and individual authorship, the experimental and the lyrical, the fragment and the whole. Sometimes family members fall silent all at once. They breathe and allow the complex net of stories to sink into the currents of the moment. Then another story begins, always.

HYBRID WORK

Excerpt from from unincorporated territory [saina]

        'th   ey   c   ut

off   so   me   of   th   eir   lo   ng

        be   au   ti   ful

                         hair

              and   wove

it   in   to   a   net

    spread   out   in   every
    direction

    then   they

        began   to   sing

    the   fish   heard   the   sound

        it   swam   in   to   the

        under   land   waters

    to   hear   more   clearly

they   *sang*

          all   *their*   *known*   *songs*

then   *they*   *invented*

                                        new   *ones*

proclamation no 4347 < 2/1/75 40 fr 5129 >

*reserving certain submerged lands adjacent to rose atoll national wildlife refuge
in american samoa and certain submerged lands for defense needs of united
states in guam and virgin islands*

*the submerged lands in apra harbor and those adjacent to inapsan beach and
urano point in guam and certain submerged lands on west coast of st croix
united states virgin islands are required for national defense purposes*

now therefore i gerald r ford [i tatan-mami : our father] *president of* [ni gaige
hao gi : who art in] *the united states of america*

by virtue of authority vested in me [umamaila' i gobietno-mu : thy kingdon
come] *do hereby proclaim that lands hereinafter described are exce[r]pted
from transfer* [umafa-tinas i pino'-mu : thy will be done] *to government of
american samoa government of guam and government of united states virgin
islands*

        ...

[asi gi tano' komu gi langet : on earth as it is in heaven] *guam :*

[1] submerged lands of inner and outer apra harbor and

[2] submerged lands adjacent to the following uplands

[a] *unsurveyed land municipality of machanao guam as delineated*
on commander naval forces marianas y and d drawing numbered 597-464
lying between seaward **bound***aries of lots numbered 9992 thru 9997 and*
mean high tide containing an undetermined area of land
         [b] *unsurveyed land municipality of machanao guam as delineated*
on commander naval forces marianas y and d drawing numbered 597- 464
lying between the seaward boundary of lot numbered 10080 and line of mean
high tide containing an undetermined amount of land
         [c] *lot numbered po 4.1 in the municipality of machanao guam*
as delineated on y and d drawing numbered 597-464 more particularly
described as surveyed land bordered on the north by lot numbered 10080
machanao east by northwest air force base south by us naval communication
station [finegayan] and west by the sea containing a computed area of 125.50
acres more or less all of above lands within territory of guam shall be under
*administrative juris***diction** *of department of navy*

           in witness
           whereof i have hereunto set my hand
           [na'i ham pa'go : give us this day] *this first day*
           of february in the year
           of our lord
           [taiguihi i in asisi'i i dumidibi ham siha : as we forgive those who
              trespass against us]
           nineteen hundred seventy-five and of [lao na'fanlibre ham gi :
           but liberate us from] *the independence of the united states of america*
              ~

'the giant fish swam nearer
nearer

swam farther farther
           under island
toward agana spring   at last

came to place where the
women

      sang

      ~

    "she can sing
and she can play piano and guitar
her voice

    "is like my voice
the way i sing sounds like my mother   *she says*

    "i really miss my mom

    "she's very devoted to the blessed mother
        every evening at six we had to come home
and say our rosary
in front of the madonna

    "my mother
would light the candle and say rosary

      bula hao grasia

    "every six o'clock
no matter what we're doing we had to drop and say rosary
very devoted
we have rosary *every night every night*
she believed
in the blessed mother
just like us here
now

      bula hao grasia

"almost every night during the war
neighbors come to our house
and in the basement
my mother

"would translate the radio
that someone brings to the house
because they had it buried
somewhere during the day
my mother

"speaks
chamorro japanese english spanish
so she could translate
the radio and read the newspapers to them
and she always makes a huge pot of soup
for everyone

"b	ut	w	e	h	ad	to	b	e
	qu	i	et	ve	ry	q		
		u	i	et		li	k	e
wh		is		p	e		ri	
	ng		b	e	ca			
	us	e	yo		u	ne	v	er
				k	no	w	w	
	ho	's	ou			ts	id	e
		in	t	he	d	ar	k	

she whispers

bula hao grasia

MAPPING THE PAGE

Poem as Diagrammatic Investigation

Jena Osman

The first poem in my book *The Network* takes as its starting point poet Cecilia Vicuña's instruction to "enter words in order to see." This quote is from *Palabrarmás*, a book Vicuña describes as having been "born from a vision in which individual words opened to reveal their inner associations, allowing ancient and newborn metaphors to come to light." Vicuña goes on to make the power of etymology explicit: "A history of words would be a history of being." Much of *The Network* is an attempt to test that theory in relation to American history.

The long poem "Financial District" from *The Network* is a patterned assemblage. It consists of 11 sections organized around 11 different streets in the Wall Street area of New York City; the Pearl Street section is below. Each section has three parts: the first part is a timeline, running from 1609 to 1920, tracing events that occurred on the 11 selected streets; the second part is an amateurish etymological map tracing the roots of words that have to do with the world of finance; the third part combines these two mapping systems with an italicized sci-fi narrative that includes chase scenes, assassination attempts, and a network key.

For the timeline parts, I browsed around in books like *Gotham: A History of New York City to 1898* by Edwin G. Burrows and Mike Wallace, as well

Jena Osman's books of poems include *Corporate Relations* (2014); *Public Figures* (2012); *The Network* (2010), selected for the National Poetry Series in 2009; *An Essay in Asterisks* (2004); and *The Character* (1999), winner of the 1998 Barnard New Women Poets Prize. She teaches in the MFA Creative Writing program at Temple University.

as the amazing map collection of David Rumsey, an archive of over 50,000 maps and images online (www.davidrumsey.com). For the etymological diagrams, I relied on Eric Partridge's *Origins: A Short Etymological Dictionary of Modern English*. I should say that there's a good chance that my understanding of this dictionary and the way it tracks relations between words is flawed. However, the act of figuring out the diagrams—translating Partridge's textual listings into tree formations—had me thinking actively about how words are attached to geography and empire, as well as how words are always slowly evolving according to their use. It made me think about how, on the one hand, our language controls what we imagine to be possible, but on the other hand, our language bends to serve our needs. And this paradoxical action seems to synch up with how we understand and interpret history as well.

While trying to make the etymological charts, I started to notice that certain words were linked, although their meanings seemed unrelated at first glance (for example, "peace" and "propaganda," or "invest" and "travesty," or "tavern" and "tabernacle"). These connections told a different story about the words than the equivalencies offered up by most dictionary definitions. Many of the words I worked through had unexpected sets of relations, and the diagramming forced me to acknowledge them rather than proceeding as if they weren't there.

I made similar discoveries while working on the timelines. Manhattan's Financial District is known for the abstractions of capital: stocks, numbers, percentages. But a closer look at the history of its streets shows the concrete particulars of capital in the early years of the United States—particularly the economy's reliance on enslaved Africans. Again, my research revealed historical relations that are often hidden from view in the present.

History and etymology—which are meant to clarify and explain—collide in the third part of each section of the poem so as to resist intelligibility. As a counterweight, these opaque collaborations are interrupted by a narrative—the closest I've ever come to writing fiction. There are characters: a female protagonist, a guard, three boys. There is a plot that escalates, even if its details are hard to discern. I was thinking of Leslie Scalapino's work a lot while writing these lines; in my mind they are an homage to her written worlds. She was and continues to be a very important writer for me, as are many others who work in a hybrid register—writers who mix text with image, sound-play with historical investigations, lyric subjectivity with documentary materials, verse with essay. Some examples of such mixtures include Kamau Brathwaite's *Trench Town Rock*, Tisa Bryant's *Unexplained Presence*, Theresa Hak Kyung Cha's *Dictee*, Tina Darragh's *adv. fans—the 1968 series*, Thalia Field's *Bird Lovers, Backyard*, Susan Howe's *The Midnight*, Charles Reznikoff's *Testimony*, Leslie Scalapino's *Defoe*, Juliana Spahr's *Well Then There Now*, Rosmarie Waldrop's *A Key Into the Language of America*, and William Carlos Williams' *Paterson*.

The hybrid poem interrogates, investigates, and necessarily complicates everything that it touches. It lets the facts in, and then releases them from our standard way of knowing them. If it can't set the record straight, then it can at least make the reader conscious that most records are crooked. When it treats text visually, the page space becomes a place to map out relations and to uncover submerged connections.

HYBRID WORK
Excerpt from "Financial District" from The Network

PEARL

1841: Walt Whitman moves to Manhattan to work for *The Aurora and Union* on **Nassau** Street.

1842: Charles Dickens visits America for the first time and stays at Carleton House, on the corner of **William** and **Pearl**.

1846: **Trinity** Church is completed.

1849: Whitman starts going to Fowler and Wells' Phrenological Cabinet on **Nassau** to have the bumps on his head analyzed.

1850: In order to get California into the Union as a free state, Congress compromises and passes a fugitive slave law which denies trials to runaway slaves and heavy fines for those who help them. This is good for business, so **Wall** Street celebrates with a 100 gun salute from the Battery. On September 11, Jenny Lind sings at Castle Garden under the management of P.T. Barnum.

1854: The Stock Exchange moves to **William** and Beaver.

1857: Panic.

1861: Fernando Wood, Mayor of New York City, proposes that New York secede from the Union so it can continue to do business with Confederate states.

1863: **Wall** Street attains its full power by financing the Civil War. Meanwhile, draft rioters (those who can't afford to send someone in their place to fight) kill hundreds.

1865: The Stock Exchange moves into its permanent home on Broad Street.

1868: A press dinner is given to honor Charles Dickens at Delmonico's on Beaver St. In his speech, he says it would be better "for America and England to go back to the ice age and be given over to the Arctic fox and bear, than fight."

BROKER

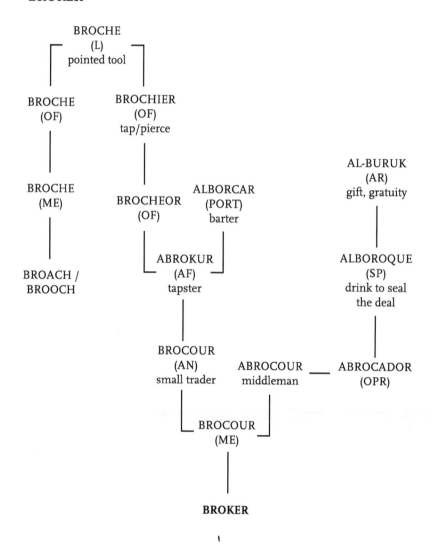

BROCHE
(L)
pointed tool

BROCHE
(OF)

BROCHIER
(OF)
tap/pierce

BROCHE
(ME)

BROCHEOR
(OF)

ALBORCAR
(PORT)
barter

AL-BURUK
(AR)
gift, gratuity

BROACH /
BROOCH

ABROKUR
(AF)
tapster

ALBOROQUE
(SP)
drink to seal
the deal

BROCOUR
(AN)
small trader

ABROCOUR
middleman

ABROCADOR
(OPR)

BROCOUR
(ME)

BROKER

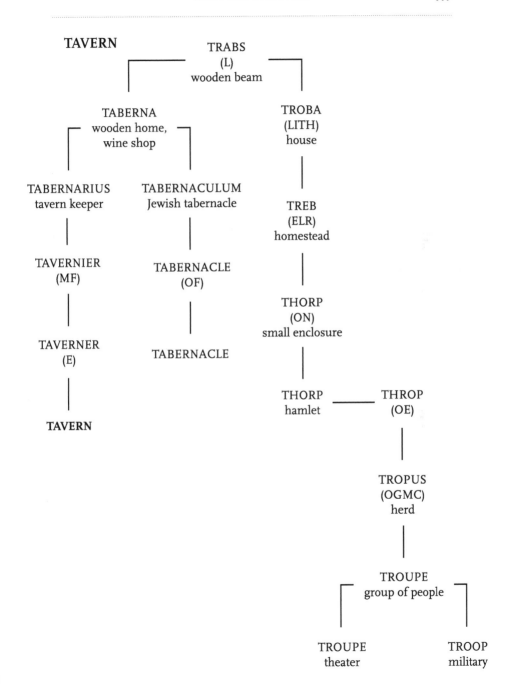

PEARL + BROKER + TAVERN

it's an English translation of the Dutch parelstraat (paerlstraet). is historically identical with the similarly pronounced (noun) comes, through Middle English, from Old French-French from Latin of Celtic origin.

> *for a moment the guard feels his conscience glowing yellow, but moves quickly, the red lines of the network burning his tongue.*

is Middle English adopted from Medieval French-French, which takes it from Latin.

> *he must make a connection before it's too late.*

paved with oyster shells. the Celtic root appears to have been a point. perhaps originally any wooden habitation, but in practice a shop, especially a wine shop.

> *for each minute the network lives in his mouth, hundreds of brain cells become arctic numb and silver.*

oyster shells left by the Lenape derive from Middle English, from Old Northern French, to broach o.o.o. (of obscure origin): perhaps either Etruscan or a metathesis (transposition) from Latin, a wooden beam.

> *soon he will not be able to think. he will lose his way. he'll forget his language.*

the oldest street, the original border. Old French has derivative Old French-French, to stitch, whence English.

> *the three boys enjoy their lighter frame, her quickness.*

—Latin has derivative, a tavern-frequenter or keeper, whence Medieval French-French, adapted by English as, archaic except as personal name. pearl shells washed in from the sea are used to pave the road.

they think perhaps they can now be nicer, more approachable, more flirtatious in their workplace.

the basic meaning is 'pointed head' of weapon or tool. another derivative is the dim, a tent, Later Latin the jewish tabernacle.

the guard repeats his own name under his breath repeatedly as an exercise in focus, the arctic numb and silver reaching further in now.

also called the strand, great dock, queen—still queen at washington's inauguration—then again all pearl.

frost begins to web and coat the corners of his eyes.

Latin, a beam, becomes Old French-Medieval French, Medieval French, whence Medieval French-French, the space between the beams.

the crowd of traders pushes up against him, then folds down so that on the horizon he sees only one.

the shoreline extends by three blocks and the island grows from its own landfill.

he knows what she has become, the three boys. tries to move faster but can't communicate with his legs.

the ornament stuck on with a pin in a transaction. with Old Norse, a small enclosure, compare with Old High German-German, a village.

they approach in her small frame as a hungry animal but coy.

captain kidd has real estate on pearl. who broached or opened the cask of wine.

the guard no longer moves although he thinks perhaps he moves. perhaps he sleeps.

to love, pimp, and pander—a contemptuous marriage.

> *in their new frame they flirt with the guard, take out a cigarette, ask for a light.*

Old Saxon and Old Frisian, a hamlet.

> *he cannot answer. almost all cells stabilized in service to the delicate red sparks of circuitry. a frozen vehicle.*

facing the river, the city tavern becomes the first city hall. originally a broacher of wine casks, hence a retailer of wine.

> *a hungry animal but coy they lick their lips and flirt. they are careful, remember the burn of his power in the veined paper, the watermark branded on the inside of their skin.*

william bradford, exiled from philadelphia, sets up shop and prints laws, almanacs, pamphlets. he opened it up. the spike and stitch makes a pamphlet. the French general victor moreau, exiled for trying to assassinate napolean, lives here until called back. a wealthy huguenot, etienne de lancey, builds a house; his grandson turns it into a store. the store is bought by a West Indian named fraunces, and becomes the queen's head tavern.

> *she as ash in animate particles repeats in swirls and twister eyes. as ash she gathers, spreads, and circulates.*

so the broker discovers he is a tapster. cannonballs hit the roof. after a deal, men were wont to broach a cask of wine. Old English has the metathetic variant, which perhaps helps to explain the Old Germanic origin of Later Latin-Middle Latin, a herd.

> *they reach out her fingers, they touch his icy cheek. sluggish with the cold, the guard holds their gaze then lets it go, his body dredged ice and silver on the ground before them.*

this is where washington says goodbye. but the man that pricked it open was the first. whence Old French-French derivative agent French.

they reach out her fingers and dig into the ice of the guard, the faint red lines blinking from hub to hub on the surface of his skin.

the north area called "the swamp" due to the smell of the tanneries. Old French-French, adopted by English.

she as ash in animate particles, a cloud with tendrils senses the edge and end of a long plotline in the plight of the guard.

the patriot tailor hercules mulligan makes uniforms. at home the tailor gives alexander hamilton room and board while attending school at kings college.

the three boys touch and pull the red veins of the network from the ice of the guard who is dying. with each touch, a node turns black.

finally retail, a middleman.

from a distance she sees herself flirting with the numbed out guard.

hamilton opens the bank of new york in a building that later hosts the society for the manumission. the former adopted, the latter adapted, by English, in their theatrical senses.

a cloud with tendrils, choking dust, drops a twister eye onto the dredged ice.

the country is fifty years old; the architecture is Greek revival as a nod to the origins of democracy.

she as ash covers the guard with her animate particles, pushes her dust down her old throat to choke the three boys. they gasp for her breath and suffocate unceremoniously.

gothic a field, a farm, a landed estate, and Old English, a hamlet, retained by English.

the veins of the network scatter and recombine in her biology and smoke.

merchants sell "civilizing" consumer goods such as hardware, wine, and fabric. a drink concludes a transaction with ado like a gift.

she leaves the guard silver and melting, circulates as a cloud of ash blinking red.

Old French-French, originally a herd, whence a company of people. thomas edison sets up the first power plant, pearl street station. he calls this place "the most dilapidated street in the world."

the ice of the guard now water dripping through the sewer grate in small silver pearls. the three boys choke, try to make him cohere as a solid not liquid so as to hold on.

compounds with pawn and stock.

a thousand silver pearls loyal to the cause march through the pipes below the vacant houses. they move to make their connection, that is the guard.

hence in military sense, becomes English. o.o.o.

ERASING THE DISTANCE
Graphic Journalism and Empathy

Miriam Libicki

Joe Sacco's 1996 *Palestine* is considered the first book-length comics journalism. Except that doesn't sound right. "Comics journalism" sounds like
it should mean journalism about comics. (Indeed, comic books' equivalent
of *The New York Review of Books* is called *The Comics Journal*.) But "journalism comics" sounds too frivolous, like a daily newspaper strip about wacky,
unlucky-in-love reporters. To analogize from "graphic novel," you'd get
"graphic reportage," but that just sounds like journalism that's especially
gore-mongering. "Drawn journalism" might work, except that some of the
great journalist-cartoonists, like Sarah Glidden and Maira Kalman, paint.

Maybe the difficulty of settling on a satisfactory label is why there's
no section for it in the library. But I think it is safe to say that Sacco is
the grandfather of us all. I read *Palestine* in 2000, when I was on "the
other side" of Sacco's subjects; I was an expat American and an Israeli
soldier. But that's not the only reason the book upset, absorbed, and ultimately inspired me. *Palestine* is kind of like a documentary; the dialogue is
naturalistic, and all the settings look like real places. Sacco does as much
photographing and recording as a "real" reporting team. But the some-

Miriam Libicki is a cartoonist and illustrator concentrating on narrative nonfiction.
She teaches graphic memoir at the Emily Carr Institute and is the creator of the
comic series *Jobnik!*, and the drawn essays "Towards a Hot Jew," "ceasefire, fierce
ease," and "Jewish Memoir Goes Pow! Zap! Oy!," published in *The Jewish Graphic
Novel: Critical Approaches* (2008). She exhibits at galleries and comic conventions,
and lectures on cartooning across Canada and the United States.

what goofy faces take away the distance that exists between a viewer and a photograph.

A photograph is a complete world, a window that doesn't open. When we readers look at a drawing, we are somehow aware that we are taking *that* line on the page and superimposing it on our memory of a human eyebrow. Unconsciously, we know that we're interpreting it, doing half the visualization on our own as we read. Which means we are in the world with the drawings in a book. We're really meeting the people that Sacco is meeting, and hearing their stories firsthand. And we see Sacco, too, and we hear what he's feeling, but he's not an authority. In fact, as we read, we might think he looks like kind of a goober, whereas in real life, Sacco is surprisingly handsome. We're immersed in his viewpoint, which actually makes it easier to not believe everything he says.

My whole life I've been drawn to the immediacy and accessibility of comics. I started drawing comics while pursuing a Fine Arts degree, having found them to be a medium of communication more than any other artistic discipline. A comic doesn't need an artist's statement (yet, here we are). No other medium, film included, combines images and words in such an intimate way. Text and art in comics explain each other, contradict each other, become each other. And the medium also seems to invite intimacy between the creator and the consumer in a unique way. For instance, Art Spiegelman considers all "comix" (his term for literary/experimental comic books, usually the work of one creator) a form of journal writing because the author's fingerprints are so visible—sometimes literally—in the hand lettering alone.

The unique strengths of comics as communication take on an added dimension when the comics are nonfiction. The subjectivity and even unreliability of the creator/narrator is foregrounded by drawing, rather than obfuscated by the supposed objectivity of photographs or the "authoritative voice" of journalism. When your writing is married to drawings, you can show and you can tell, and what you are showing is always different from what you are telling.

My piece "Strangers" is a hybrid of journal writing and journalism. There's no original reporting—almost all the text about the Sudanese refugees is from newspapers, as are almost all of the image references. Quotes from others have been reproduced in my own hand—giving large blocks of text a personal touch and unifying them with the images. The images may have been lifted from widely available news sources, but they have been transmuted into something more vibrant than a standard photograph via lush watercolors. No matter how faithfully I may have traced the original image, the reader sees what I chose to emphasize.

The scenes in which I depict myself, experiencing the news mediated through my internet connection in suburban Canada, remind the reader again that I am inevitably telling my story as much as I am telling the story of the Sudanese refugees, and that I am simultaneously telling the story of how the story gets transmitted and transmuted. But when I cut the frames away from the news photos, make them bleed onto the paper, and point the figures' eyes at the reader (I never trace eyes directly), the reader is immersed in the painted world, and may be experiencing it more empathetically than he or she experiences a newsreel. That's why exploring nonfiction in graphic form is my constant pursuit, no matter what you call it.

HYBRID WORK
Excerpt from "Strangers"

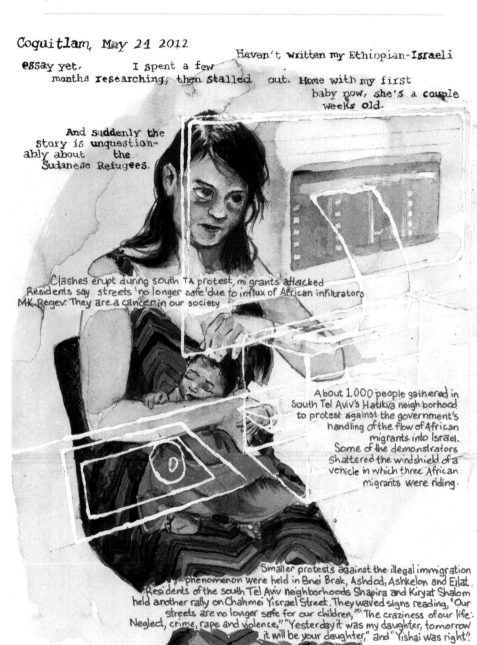

Coquitlam, May 24 2012

essay yet,   I spent a few   Haven't written my Ethiopian-Israeli
months researching, then stalled   out. Home with my first
baby now, she's a couple
weeks old.

And suddenly the
story is unquestion-
ably about   the
Sudanese Refugees.

Clashes erupt during south TA protest, migrants attacked
Residents say streets 'no longer safe' due to influx of African infiltrators
MK Regev: They are a cancer in our society

About 1,000 people gathered in
South Tel Aviv's Hatikva neighborhood
to protest against the government's
handling of the flow of African
migrants into Israel.
Some of the demonstrators
shattered the windshield of a
vehicle in which three African
migrants were riding.

Smaller protests against the illegal immigration
phenomenon were held in Bnei Brak, Ashdod, Ashkelon and Eilat.
Residents of the south Tel Aviv neighborhoods Shapira and Kiryat Shalom
held another rally on Chahmei Yisrael Street. They waved signs reading, "Our
streets are no longer safe for our children," "The craziness of our life:
Neglect, crime, rape and violence," "Yesterday it was my daughter, tomorrow
it will be your daughter," and "Yishai was right!".

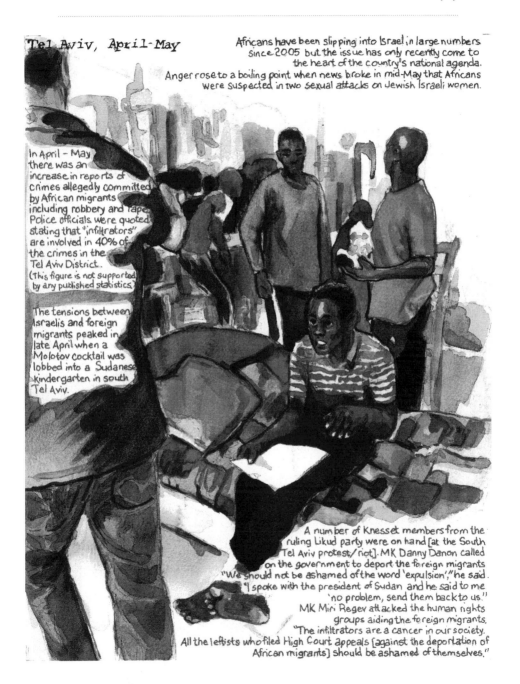

Tel Aviv, April-May

Africans have been slipping into Israel in large numbers since 2005 but the issue has only recently come to the heart of the country's national agenda. Anger rose to a boiling point when news broke in mid-May that Africans were suspected in two sexual attacks on Jewish Israeli women.

In April - May there was an increase in reports of crimes allegedly committed by African migrants, including robbery and rape. Police officials were quoted stating that "infiltrators" are involved in 40% of the crimes in the Tel Aviv District. (This figure is not supported by any published statistics.)

The tensions between Israelis and foreign migrants peaked in late April when a Molotov cocktail was lobbed into a Sudanese kindergarten in south Tel Aviv.

A number of Knesset members from the ruling Likud party were on hand [at the South Tel Aviv protest/riot]. MK Danny Danon called on the government to deport the foreign migrants. "We should not be ashamed of the word 'expulsion'," he said. "I spoke with the president of Sudan and he said to me 'no problem, send them back to us.'" MK Miri Regev attacked the human rights groups aiding the foreign migrants. "The infiltrators are a cancer in our society. All the leftists who filed High Court appeals [against the deportation of African migrants] should be ashamed of themselves."

Israel, May-June   After that, every other day seems to bring a new outbreak of racist violence.

A group of 11 teens from Tel Aviv (all aged 14-18) has been charged with attacking Sudanese and Eritrean migrants in "revenge" attacks. The indictment states that 10 of the group are accused of "racially motivated" attacks in which the teens would attack foreigners who crossed their path, using boards and pipes. In two cases, they stole the plaintiffs' bicycles. A teenage girl is accused of property crimes but not of assault.

Abdullah Abuya, 40, from Darfur, is lying beaten and injured in his house in Eilat, after he was allegedly attacked by seven guests at the Club Hotel where he works. One hotel guest described the incident on her Facebook page, writing: "We almost witnessed a lynch. Seven intoxicated guys decided to lynch a Sudanese housekeeper. He could have been thrown from the fifth floor window, or die from punches and kicks to his head. This was happening a few centimeters from us."

Magen David Adom emergency services received a report at 4 am on Saturday about an unconscious Sudanese man on Sderot Har Zion Street in South Tel Aviv. A medical team that arrived at the scene found the man with injuries all over his body. Police investigators collected testimonies from eyewitnesses, and shortly afterwards arrested a suspect.

On Sunday, a video depicting an Israeli man hurling a raw egg on an African migrant was uploaded to the web. The police department is attempting to determine the identity of the web user who uploaded the video.

A Jerusalem apartment housing foreign workers was torched overnight. Firefighters rescued 10 people, four of whom needed medical attention. The Fire Department said that their investigation indicated arson. Investigators also found the words "Get out of the neighborhood" sprayed on one of the walls.

Coquitlam, May 31 I am horrified, but not too horrified to remember I have a big convention coming up, and no new comics, nothing to show for myself except, of course, the baby.

But I've been doing all this research about tensions around Jewishness and Blackness! And Lisa prophesied this four years ago! This has to be what my next drawn essay is about.

I hear on facebook about a counter-demonstration planned in Tel Aviv, and try to delegate friends in Israel to be my eyes and ears there, if I'm getting all the news long- distance, I can do a journalistic piece the same way.

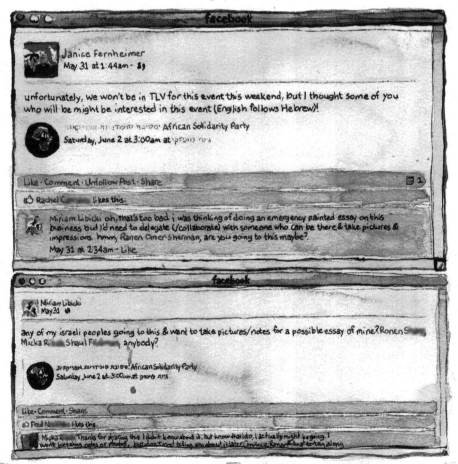

Jerusalem, May-June   So is it just a case of opportunists stoking
flames easily stoked? The right-wing government stirring up populist
sentiment   to distract from the fact that they do
        nothing to   relieve the worsening poverty in South Tel Aviv?

       It is striking that so much of the evil words and policies
come from two
       guys: Prime Minister Bibi Netanyahu, head of the "center-right"
Likud, and Interior Minister Eli Yishai, head of the Ultra-Orthodox
Shas. Both parties are historically popular among poor Sephardi
Israelis, without actually helping them economically.

Yishai has been the most prolific, declaring that the majority of "illegals are "criminals" and that they are responsible for raping Israeli women and infecting them with HIV. Yishai provided no evidence of either claim.

Yishai, whose own family immigrated to Israel from Tunisia, told the daily newspaper Maariv "Most of the people arriving here are Muslims who think the country doesn't belong to us, the white man."

The minister said that if given the mandate, there will not be a single infiltrator left in Israel in one year's time. "I would change the law so that every infiltrator is put in jail. Then he can decide whether he wants to remain imprisoned or go back to his home country."

Netanyahu contends that most of them are economic immigrants and that they threaten the Jewish character of Israel. On Sunday, he said that all new arrivals would immediately be placed in detention.

Before the wave of anger, the government was already building the world's largest detention facility, which will mean that Israel has room to detain 15,000 potential immigrants. A new law permits detaining all illegals for up to three years and some indefinitely.

June 7, the government wins a case
    allowing them to deport all South
          Sudanese.   Days later, immigration police has arrested over
             140 South Sudanese nationals before the expiration of the 1-week period granted
             to allow the asylum seekers to put their affairs in order. Most of those arrested are
             released after they sign a paper declaring that they are willingly returning to South
             Sudan. Those who sign are allowed to return home, collect their things, cash their
             paychecks and await the Ministry of Interior flights to Juba. Those who are not
             released are transferred to Saharonim and Giv'on prisons for migrants.

Tel Aviv, June

If it is just cynical populism (with potentially deadly effects), some in Israel are wise to it, even among inner-city South TelAvivians.

Shula Keshet, a resident of Neveh Sha'anan, added that it was important to her to take part in the protest to ensure that it didn't devolve into violence against Africans, no matter what country they were from.

"Violence against the refugees isn't acceptable - not as far as I'm concerned and not for many other residents. Our protest is against the policies of the government and the city and against the apartheid in Tel Aviv and the ghettos of poverty it creates. It's also racism that not a single refugee or infiltrator is sent to north Tel Aviv, just here."

Some Israelis invoke the biblical injunction to "love the stranger for we were strangers in the land of Egypt." Others say they now feel like strangers in their own country.

Inside the government there is embarrassment over the impression that mass deportations are imminent, and from the provocative statements of Minister Yishai.

"We're very frustrated by the Minister of the Interior and his populist statements," a senior Foreign Ministry source told the Forward. "Some of them are very irresponsible and they are causing great damage to Israel abroad."

Even regular Israelis see the horrifying irony in the "racial purification" Yishai and others seem to call for: "I feel I am in a movie in Germany, circa 1933 or 1936," said Orly Feldheim, 46, a daughter of Holocaust survivors, as she doled out food to a long line of immigrants in the neighborhood's Levinsky Park.

GRIEVING THROUGH COMICS
Real Life and Death in Words and Pictures

Stan Mack

This conversation occurred in an online exchange between Stan Mack in the United States and Marcela Sulak in Israel in September 2013.

Marcela Sulak: *How did the foray into hybridity begin for you?*

Stan Mack: In my growing-up years, the conformist 1950s, publishers of popular books and magazines seemed to believe that stories were carried entirely with words—illustrators embellished and visualized a particular moment. There were artists who worked with words—in comic strips and comic books—but they hid their ideas in plain sight and their products weren't considered serious.

In the 1960s and 70s, two movements began the journey toward hybrid storytelling. Artists like Robert Rauschenberg experimented with new media, upsetting notions about what art is, mixing words and pictures in unexpected ways. In the comic book world, artists and writers brought more adult themes into their stories—*Spiderman*, for example. And in time, the modern hybrid story—the graphic novel—began to emerge.

....

Stan Mack's "Stan Mack's Real Life Funnies" ran in *The Village Voice* for 20 years. His strip "Stan Mack's Outtakes" covered the media scene for a decade. His graphic nonfiction includes *Taxes, the Tea Party and Those Revolting Rebels: A History in Comics of the American Revolution* (2012), *Janet & Me: An Illustrated Story of Love and Loss* (2004), and *The Story of the Jews: A 4,000 Year Adventure* (2001). He co-authored three young adult nonfiction books with his late partner Janet Bode. His children's picture books include *10 Bears in My Bed* (1974). He is the former art director of *The New York Times Sunday Magazine*.

Looking way back, I suppose that classic comics, *Mad Magazine*, and even editorial sports cartooning were subtly suggesting that real life could be reported through words and pictures, but it really began to come together for me in the 60s when I became a newspaper art director—first at the *New York Herald Tribune* and, when the *Tribune* folded, at *The New York Times*.

At both places I was smack in the middle of ground-breaking journalism as the papers raced to cover the great social and political upheavals of the day. Adventurous reporters experimented with the tools of fiction writing, and I, too, was experimenting, sending out illustrators rather than photographers to cover protests and riots.

In the 70s, I went further, turning myself into a sort of cub reporter, covering the New York scene, combining the tools of journalism, storytelling, and comic strips. My first real life comic strip, "Stan Mack's Real Life Funnies," began a long weekly run in *The Village Voice* newspaper. The strip was such an unusual idea—there was nothing else around like it—that the editors thought it necessary to reassure the readers that they were reading nonfiction by adding the note: "all dialogue guaranteed verbatim." Today many artists/cartoonists/writers have embraced the journalistic form.

When it came out in 2004, I called *Janet & Me* an illustrated (rather than a graphic) story for a particular reason. Even though Art Spiegelman's *Maus*, published in the early 90s, certainly demonstrated that graphic books could take on serious topics, I wanted my book to appeal to an older mainstream audience—people likely to understand the human toll brought on by illness—who would be more comfortable with the recognizable illustrated form, rather than the edgier "graphic." I designed the book in a traditional text format for the same reason; folding the many drawings into the type column and purposely avoiding the panel look of a typical graphic novel.

A word here about the drawing style in *Janet & Me*. I'd been known for a humorous style as a commercial illustrator, drawing distinctive cartoony characters. In my comic strips, I tried to capture the immediacy of life with a bold spontaneous style. For *Janet & Me*, I just set out to draw as honestly as possible. No frills, no mannerisms, no irony.

MS: *I love how multi-dimensional* Janet & Me *is, as well as how it's so honest and vulnerable. When I finished reading it, I felt as if you and Janet were actually people I knew and had spent a long time with—your presentation of Janet and the experience of her breast cancer and death was so complex. It's also a really useful and clear-eyed guide to negotiating health care and dying in America, where everything is so confusing and can feel so impersonal. I was as shocked and horrified, at times, by the way health care works as I was at Janet's cancer.*

SM: All that you say about my book makes me happy. It's what I set out to do: introduce a woman I greatly admired to new friends; offer hard-won medical information to those who may be forced to struggle through the thicket of health care and health insurance when they are least likely to have the time, patience, and strength; and tell the personal story of a man loving and care-giving during serious illness. I told the story using the tools I was most comfortable with: words and pictures together.

MS: *It does seem right—after all, you two collaborated quite often on each other's work.*

SM: Janet wrote nonfiction books for and about teens on tough topics such as teen pregnancy, juvenile crime and violence, and troubled relationships. And I would tell some of those real-life stories in graphic form. Janet was such a wonderful outsized character; she also made regular appearances in my comic strips. To tell her poignant and heroic story in words and pictures was exactly right.

HYBRID WORK
Excerpt from Janet & Me

I thought about what the hospice brochure had said: "To dispel the fear of death is to make room for it in life." I intended someday to look squarely at her life and death. I would even welcome the pain. But not yet.

Meanwhile, I talked to Janet all the time. I knew exactly where she was.

In August, as Janet and I had done every summer, I took the ferry to Fire Island to visit our friends Marvin and Rosemarie. On the ferry, the couple behind me was bickering. "Jerks!" I muttered.

At 6 p.m., I sat on the empty beach. There were the long blue shadows and the silvery light she knew I loved. From I don't know where, a big black dog lumbered up, settled down against my leg, and watched the waves with me. He was unexpectedly comforting. In time he wandered off, limping from an injured front paw.

By September, nine months after her death, the acute pain was receding, but I didn't want to forget anything about her.

It bothered me that I couldn't recall our everyday conversations. If we'd had such a great relationship, why couldn't I better remember? I wished I had a tape of our words that I could play back.

I did hear the words she'd said to me a few weeks before she died. They made me cry.

I thought about what made her special—her courage, her sense of outrage, her advocacy for teenagers, her quirkiness . . . and I could almost hear her saying, "You might mention that I was cute and a lot of fun, too."

I remembered her response early on when I began to include her in my comic strip, with me as the square-nosed guy with a mustache. She said, "I always knew I'd be famous, I just didn't know it would be in the funnies."

This woman, whom I'd come to admire as well as love, had faced her illness the way she'd lived her life, with guts and charm. I was beginning to understand how I could keep her with me a while longer.

As Janet's disease progressed, she and I had talked about taking notes. We couldn't do it—which was ironic, since we'd always used "real life" in our work.

But now I would search for her in her writings. I would discover her in the memories of her friends—especially among the ones I call the warrior women; those strong females who'd rallied around us when she was sick. And I would listen for her voice in my head.

A book would also be a way to explore the everyday, unexpected, painful details that plagued us as her disease took hold and then worsened— and the human problems that the doctors would have us believe stopped short of their doors.

Janet's sister Carolyn worried that the project would be too painful for me.

PALACES, MONSTERS, AND THE
IDEALIST CONSTRUCTS OF MEMORY

Mira Bartók

This conversation took place over email in June 2014. Marcela Sulak was writing from Israel and Mira Bartók was writing from her home in the United States.

Marcela Sulak: *I'm intrigued by your confession in the excerpt below that you originally thought of creating* The Memory Palace *as a comic book.*

Mira Bartók: In my process of trying to figure out what my book was about, I found myself automatically drawing little comic book scenes in my sketchbook. And some of my favorite memoirs are in graphic narrative form, like Alison Bechdel's *Fun Home*, David B.'s *Epileptic*, and David Small's *Stitches*. I think that one can often approach memory in a more interesting and associative way by using sequential art. One can use multiple viewpoints, floating text bubbles, visual mini-flashbacks, etc. in a way you can't in a straight narrative. Plus, memory is not chronological. Often, when writers start memoirs, they try to create some kind of strict linear format when we just don't remember our lives that way.

Mira Bartók is an artist, public radio commentator, and author of *The Memory Palace* (2011), a *New York Times* bestselling memoir and winner of the 2012 National Book Critics Circle Award for Autobiography. She has also written over 28 books for children. Her writing for adults has been noted in *The Best American Essays* series and has appeared in numerous literary journals, magazines, and anthologies. She is a spokesperson for TransCultural Exchange, an international arts organization dedicated to creating artistic collaborations across disciplines and international boundaries.

MS: *What are the particular concerns or challenges that drawing from memory create for you?*

MB: Well, oddly enough, because I have a traumatic brain injury and had been studying the science of memory for the past few years, I found myself more inclined to explore the nature of memory itself. I was less attached to "getting it all down exactly as it happened" because I knew from studying neuroscience, particularly the work of Nobel Laureate Eric Kandel, that memory is not a fixed thing at all. I didn't make anything up, but I did use the fact that I wasn't sure about certain events. I used that lack of certainty to my advantage, asking the "what if?" question we ask in fiction. The other thing that happened was that early on I decided to use my ability as a visual thinker and artist to draw certain objects or images in order to dredge up pivotal moments from my life. As I was doing this, I remembered the ancient mnemonic concept of the memory palace, and the structure of my book was born.

What I like about the whole memory palace idea is that, in many ways, it is a false structure, or rather, an idealistic structure bound to fail. It was invented at a time when we thought memory was a stable thing—and now we know it isn't. I bring that up in the book, how my palace of memories will change over time and in the telling of the tale. Which is what happens to our brain when we tell a story about our past. The recounting of each memory creates a cascade of neurological changes in the structure of our brain. In the end, I think what you come away with in the book is the narrator's intense striving to remember the past and make sense of it. And at the core of that search for meaning is the drive to make art in the world— to transform the darkness into light.

MS: *What is a memory palace?*

MB: A memory palace is an ancient mnemonic system in which a person visualizes different elements that stand for specific memories, and then places them in an imaginary palace in their mind. The idea is that, if you want to recall something, you walk through the palace you've created and look for the memory you need by searching for the image you had previously affixed to it. The concept and practice goes back to Ancient Greece, to the poet Simonides, who, while visiting friends at a palace one day, stepped outside for a minute. Suddenly, a terrible accident occurred—the great hall where most of the people were came crashing down, leaving the bodies so terribly crushed they were unrecognizable. But Simonides remembered exactly where everyone was standing before the crash and was able to identify the bodies.

MS: *What did you look for in a good memory palace image?*

MB: I began by making a stream-of-consciousness list of all the striking images, places, and objects from my childhood and adolescence. I actually start a lot of my stories this way, too, with a strong image that appears to me suddenly, either in a dream or while I'm awake. This is what happened with my memoir, too.

I first imagined *The Memory Palace* as a cabinet of curiosities from the sixteenth or seventeenth century; each chapter would be a drawer that revealed some peculiar passion I shared with my mother. But the structure of the palace won out. Partially because the story of my schizophrenic mother is so chaotic that I felt it needed something solid and architectural. And I have always loved Renaissance buildings. I'm sure that my having lived in Italy has something to do with that. Also, when I was very active in my art career in the 80s and 90s, many of my paintings had architectural details, like arches and friezes, set in a kind of luminous, metaphysical landscape. There was always a strange connection between the landscape, a human figure or figures, and part of a Renaissance building.

MS: *Speaking of human figures and mergings, the Medusa image you've included here is so provocative.*

MB: The thing about Medusa (particularly Ovid's version which I'm partial to) is that she began as a strikingly beautiful woman, not a monster.

However, Athena transformed her into a monster after Poseidon raped her inside Athena's temple. So from this violent act by a male god, the victim was punished. Things haven't really changed much since those times, have they? Anyway, my mother was beautiful and loving—and absolutely terrifying. And my earliest memories of her displaying her frightening delusional behavior are merged with my memory of reading a big illustrated book of myths that we had when I was a child. In the writing of my chapter called "Medusa" in *The Memory Palace*, the picture came first. I knew I wanted to write about the first time I became aware of my mother's terrible illness. When I sat down to write about it, the image of Medusa popped into my head, because that is what it felt like—like watching a beautiful woman transform into a monster. But I hope, as one moves through the book to the very end, that image is softened. When I see my mother for the last time, so close to death, she transforms once again. My sister and I both feel, at the end of the book, that we got our sweet and loving mother back, the mother that had been destroyed by schizophrenia, which is the true monster in the story. For my mother's loving essence was always there, buried deep inside, forever trying to emerge.

One last word, on hybrids—for me, it is less about publishing my book in a particular shape that I originally intended and more about what I actually did in the end. That is, I combined journal writing (my mom's), dreams, art, science, natural history and cultural threads of thought, an exploration into the nature of memory, and memoir writing about family, one's personal journey, etc. I think that what interests me most about hybrid writing is that intersection between one thing and another and the tension that intersection creates.

HYBRID WORK

Previously Unpublished Illustrations from **The Memory Palace**

Editor's Note: Except for the frst illustration, the images that Mira Bartók presents here are images that she had included in her original version of *The Memory Palace*, but that were not part of the final version of the published book. She has given us some of her favorite unpublished illustrations and provided us with context for them.

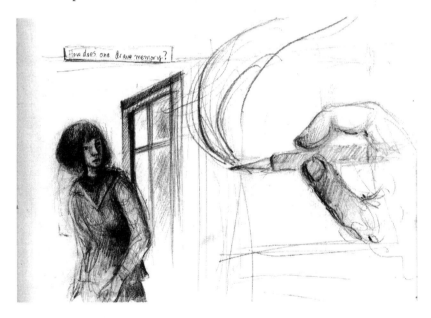

My very first idea was to maybe do the book in comic book form. Hardly anyone knows that, but it's true. Then I realized it would take me so much longer to use a comic book/ graphic memoir approach (having never done one before) so I gave up the idea. This image is from my sketchbook and the caption reads, "How does one draw memory?"

One of the many images that I took out of the final version of the book was this little architectural frieze. I originally imagined there being architectural elements throughout the book, but once I finished painting my memory palace, my editors and I agreed to just use the pictures that came from that large picture: one image per memory, per chapter, until, at the end, the entire palace appears.

I like this image a lot. It was supposed to go at the end of the second chapter called "Medusa," about my very first memory of my mother's illness, her talking to herself and seeming quite monstrous to me.

This is an imaginary map that I made for the Italian chapter ("Forgeries and Illuminations"). We only used a tiny fragment of the image for the book.

This is the image of the Memory Palace that I drew from. It's based on an old Italian villa from I think the fifteenth century. But of course, embedded in the facade are fantastical images that I used (and some I did not) in the final piece.

WORKING THE FIELD OF THE PAGE
A Syntax of Shapes

Andrea Baker

As a child, I kept an undecorated cardboard receptacle that I or, more likely, my mother, accorded the privilege of storing miscellaneous crap—small shreds of paper and lace, ubiquitous green plastic animals, toy soldiers, and every toy surprise gifted by a cereal box. It was dubbed my "collage box," and it lived its life in my spacious closet. I also had a low kitchen cabinet of coloring books and crayons, where my non-scissors-and-glue-dependent and, incidentally, non-mess-making, art supplies lived.

During my elementary school years, my mother was in art school and passed a good amount of time in her home studio. When I was indoors, I generally spent my time contemplating the still-life world of my porcelain dolls and pot-metal miniatures.

Until, that is, we got a new kitchen table and the old one was relocated to my playroom. I took to taking the collage box down from its shelf and carrying it through the hall to the novelty of my "new" table, where I was permitted to make a mess gluing the box's contents into wobbly construction paper-backed collages, which I would then bring to my mother for praise.

Andrea Baker is the author of *Famous Rapes* (2015), a paper and packing tape constructed, not-quite-graphic-novel about the depiction of sexual assault from Mesopotamia to the present day. Her most recent full-length collection of poetry is *Each Thing Unblurred Is Broken* (2015). She has been a Poetry Society of America Chapbook Fellow, and in 2005 she was awarded the Slope Editions Book Prize for *Like Wind Loves a Window* (2005). She is a subject in the documentary "A Rubberband Is an Unlikely Instrument," and is employed as an appraiser of arts and antiques.

When I took up writing, my notebooks became my collage box equivalent. There I collected and generated interesting shreds of language, which I would later assemble into poems. The more I worked to crystallize my images-in-language, especially in times of distress, the more I became inclined to reach for what I felt in its visual form.

Mixing visual images into my poems started after some upheaval in my personal life left me in shock. Every time I tried to let my mind go into language, I could only see the image of a house hanging from the ceiling, so I sketched that into my notebook and didn't think about it any further until I went back to those notebook pages and realized that I needed the house in its visual form to be included in a poem. As I worked on that piece, which became the poem "House" from my first book *Like Wind Loves a Window*, other fragments of visual activity from my notebooks began to get folded into the project I was making. I saw myself working the field of the page.

I liked the results and would have chosen to continue to make poems with visual elements, but I'm not very good at making things happen in my work—all I can do competently is follow in the direction my writing goes on its own. There isn't a single visual element in *Each Thing Unblurred Is Broken*, my second book of poetry. But then I was back in a time of distress. I was in the midst of a divorce—the type of divorce where your ex breaks into your house at night to watch you sleep, where he has made himself a peephole into your bedroom, and where you change your email and voicemail passwords daily because he has hired a hacker to let him monitor your communications.

My mind went back to a place without much language. I adored sleeping alone in my twin bed, and I adored the freedoms I was finding, but I was also concerned for my safety. I took to binging on *Law & Order SVU*.

I make a good portion of my living by buying and selling art and antiques. I deal quite a bit with mid-century design, and, especially in those days, with Asian and ancient ceramics. As a result, there are usually packing supplies lying around. One evening, I was sitting on the sofa, with the paper tape and scissors on the coffee table, right next to my computer, which was, of course, streaming *SVU*. Picking up the tape and beginning to cut it was an impulse. Over the course of the year that followed, I found I was able to use scissors and packing tape to chronicle the way I felt as I moved from a state dominated by fearfulness, to a confused state of sensing some safety, then to a tentative state of well-being.

I turned to Google to show me what "scared" looked like, what "abuse" looked like, and what "hope" looked like. I browsed for images that resonated with me, printing ones that rang true and using them as stencils. Once I had collected a good number of cut-out shapes, I made the images connect to one another, just as I do in my poems, and did, much earlier, in my childhood collages. Each image was like an element in my visual vocabulary, and the interplay of brown packing tape and white cut outs formed a sort of syntax.

This particular sequence is taken from the final chapter of that year-long project, which became the book-length manuscript *The Incredibly True Adventures of Me*. The idea that we cannot see our own eyes is taken from the Buddhist teacher Tara Brach and, in the sixth image, the body shape is borrowed from choreographer Chris Elam.

My passion for literature is limited in the sense that it is not literature, *per se*, that I love. What I love are the arts in general. Both contemporary choreography and the high drama that is enacted on classical operatic stages thrill me. This entire manuscript is nearly wordless and, as I assembled it, I thought of myself as, mostly, a choreographer.

HYBRID WORK
Excerpt from The Incredibly True Adventures of Me

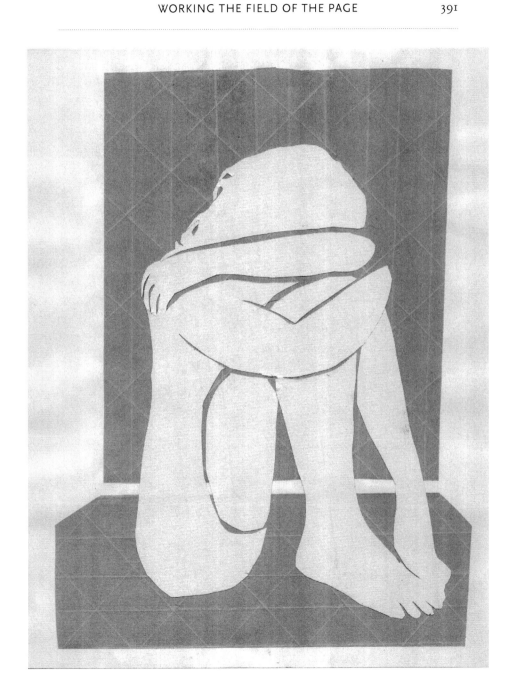

can't see my own eyes can't see my own eyes can't see my own eyes can't see my own
eyes can't see my own eyes can't see my own eyes can't see my own eyes can't see my
own eyes can't see my own eyes can't see my own eyes can't see my own eyes can't see
my own eyes can't see my own eyes can't see my own eyes can't see my own eyes can't
see my own eyes can't see my own eyes can't see my own eyes can't see my own eyes
can't see my own eyes can't see my own eyes can't see my own eyes can't see my own
eyes can't see my own eyes can't see my own eyes can't see my own eyes can't see my
own eyes can't see my own eyes can't see my own eyes can't see my own eyes can't see
my own eyes can't see my own eyes can't see my own eyes can't see my own eyes can't
see my own eyes can't see my own eyes can't see my own eyes can't see my own eyes
can't see my own eyes can't see my own eyes can't see my own eyes can't see my own
eyes can't see my own eyes can't see my own eyes can't see my own eyes can't see my
own eyes can't see my own eyes can't see my own eyes can't see my own eyes can't see
my own eyes can't see my own eyes can't see my own eyes can't see my own eyes can't
see my own eyes can't see my own eyes can't see my own eyes can't see my own eyes
can't see my own eyes can't see my own eyes can't see my own eyes can't see my own
eyes can't see my own eyes can't see my own eyes can't see my own eyes can't see my
own eyes can't see my own eyes can't see my own eyes can't see my own eyes can't see
my own eyes can't see my own eyes can't see my own eyes can't see my own eyes can't
see my own eyes can't see my own eyes can't see my own eyes can't see my own eyes
can't see my own eyes can't see my own eyes can't see my own eyes can't see my own
eyes can't see my own eyes can't see my own eyes can't see my own eyes can't see my
own eyes can't see my own eyes can't see my own eyes can't see my own eyes can't see
my own eyes can't see my own eyes can't see my own eyes can't see my own eyes can't
see my own eyes can't see my own eyes can't see my own eyes can't see my own eyes
can't see my own eyes can't see my own eyes can't see my own eyes can't see my own
eyes can't see my own eyes can't see my own eyes can't see my own eyes can't see my
own eyes can't see my own eyes can't see my own eyes can't see my own eyes can't see
my own eyes can't see my own eyes can't see my own eyes can't see my own eyes can't
see my own eyes can't see my own eyes can't see my own eyes can't see my own eyes
can't see my own eyes can't see my own eyes can't see my own eyes can't see my own
eyes can't see my own eyes can't see my own eyes can't see my own eyes can't see my
own eyes that edge that edge that edge that edge that edge can't see my
my own eyes that edge

my own
see
ca
eyes
own   that edge that edge that edge can't see my own eyes can't see my own eyes can't see
my own eyes can't see my own eyes can't see my own eyes can't see my own eyes can't
see my own eyes can't see my own eyes can't see my own eyes can't see my own eyes

      that edge that edge that edge that edge that edge

see my eyes see my eyes see my eyes see my eyes see my eyes see my eyes see my eyes
see my eyes see my eyes see my eyes see my eyes see my eyes see my eyes see my eyes
see my eyes see my eyes see my eyes see my eyes see my eyes see my eyes see my eyes
see my eyes see my eyes see my eyes see my eyes see my eyes see my eyes see my eyes
see my eyes see my eyes see my eyes see my eyes see my eyes see my eyes see my eyes
see my eyes see my eyes see my eyes see my eyes see my eyes see my eyes see my eyes
see my eyes see my eyes see my eyes see my eyes see my eyes see my eyes see my eyes
see my eyes see my eyes see my eyes see my eyes see my eyes see my eyes see my eyes
see my eyes see my eyes see my eyes see my eyes see my eyes see my eyes see my eyes
see my eyes see my eyes see my eyes see my eyes see my eyes see my eyes see my eyes
see my eyes see my eyes see my eyes see my eyes see my eyes see my eyes see my eyes
see my eyes see my eyes see my eyes see my eyes see my eyes see my eyes see my eyes
see my eyes see my eyes see my eyes see my eyes see my eyes see my eyes see my eyes
see my eyes see my eyes see my eyes see my eyes see my eyes see my eyes see my eyes
see my eyes see my eyes see my eyes see my eyes see my eyes see my eyes see my eyes
see my eyes see my eyes see my eyes see my eyes see my eyes see my eyes see my eyes
see my eyes see my eyes see my eyes see my eyes see my eyes see my eyes see my eyes
see my eyes see my eyes see my eyes see my eyes see my eyes see my eyes see my eyes
see my eyes see my eyes see my eyes see my eyes see my eyes see my eyes see my eyes
see my eyes see my eyes see my eyes see my eyes see my eyes see my eyes see my eyes
see my eyes see my eyes see my eyes see my eyes see my eyes see my eyes see my eyes
see my eyes see my eyes see my eyes see my eyes see my eyes see my eyes see my eyes
see my eyes see my eyes see my eyes see my eyes see my eyes see my eyes see my eyes
see my eyes see my eyes see my eyes see my eyes see my eyes see my eyes see my eyes
see my eyes see my eyes see my eyes see my eyes see my eyes see my eyes see my eyes
see my eyes see my eyes see my eyes see my eyes see my eyes see my eyes see my eyes
see my eyes see my eyes see my eyes see my eyes see my eyes see my eyes see my eyes
see my eyes see my eyes see my eyes see my eyes see my eyes see my eyes see my eyes
see my eyes see my eyes see my eyes see my eyes see my eyes see my eyes see my eyes
see my eyes see my eyes see my eyes see my eyes see my eyes see my eyes see my eyes
see my eyes see my eyes see my eyes see my eyes see my eyes see my eyes see my eyes
see my eyes see my eyes see my eyes see my eyes see my eyes see my eyes see my eyes
see my eyes see my eyes see my eyes see my eyes see my eyes see my eyes see my eyes
see my eyes see my eyes see my eyes see my eyes see my eyes see my eyes see my eyes
see my eyes see my eyes see my eyes see my eyes see my eyes see my eyes see my eyes
see my eyes see my eyes see my eyes see my eyes see my eyes see my eyes see my eyes
see my eyes see my eyes see my eyes see my eyes see my eyes see my eyes see my eyes
see my eyes see my eyes see my eyes see my eyes see my eyes see my eyes see my eyes

TEACHING HYBRID LITERARY GENRES
An Afterword

Jacqueline Kolosov

"'Nothing' is / the force that renovates / the World—"
—Emily Dickinson, *Letters*

"Now is life very solid or very shifting? I am haunted by the two con-
tradictions. This has gone on forever; goes down to the bottom of the
world—this moment I stand on. Also it is transitory, flying, diapha-
nous. I shall pass like a cloud on the waves. Perhaps it may be that
though we change, one flying after another, so quick, so quick, yet we
are somehow successive and continuous we human beings, and show
the light through. But what is the light?"
—Virginia Woolf, *A Writer's Diary*

WHY HYBRID GENRES

Hybrid forms foreground their affiliations with two or more literary
genres. Because they resist the impulse to classify, bringing them into the
classroom both challenges and enlarges ways of thinking about genre and
can prompt analysis and interrogation of such aspects of literary art as
syntax, setting, and character, as well as more philosophical questions surrounding the nature of truth, identity, and memory. The biggest and most
fundamental advantages of teaching hybrid forms are that they disallow
the possibility of taking genre for granted and they can explode assumptions about traditional genres.

More accomplished writers—writers already conversant in one genre—can benefit from a hybrid teaching model in which students select and introduce their own readings based on a special topic, such as race or disability, or something more abstract, such as "the raw and the cooked" or "the sacred and the profane." Course design can also be structural in orientation: fragments, for example, are an appropriate choice given that hybrid writing re-imagines inherited forms; taking them on, not in their entirety, but rather in remnants or pieces. Etymologically, "fragment" comes from the Latin *fragmentum*: literally "a piece broken off," from the root *frangere,* meaning "to break."

There are a plethora of assignments that make use of fragments. One successful one asks students to choose a contemporary story (from a newspaper, tabloid, or documentary) and then find a point of engagement or tension with a myth, fairy tale, or archetype. These two stories form the core or two poles of a lyric essay (though the assignment can work with any hybrid form). The student then integrates facts, lore, and miscellany that fragment the piece of writing further. Once, I intensified the assignment by having students use an inherited poetic form to create a scaffold or container for their lyric essay. The sestina proved to be a fruitful model, as did the villanelle (though of course the possibilities are endless). In the case of the villanelle, the contemporary story became refrain one and the myth, refrain two. I left it up to the students to consider how the villanelle's rhyme scheme might be integrated into an assignment that compelled writers to find the mythic in the ordinary or sensational. The assignment provided hands-on experience in using fragments to empower the resistance to narrative, or how not to tell a story. Conversely, the assignment enabled some students to set several mini-narratives into dialogue with the facts, lore, and miscellany. Maggie Nelson's contributor's essay speaks to her experience teaching a course she conceived of as a taxonomy of the fragment, which is well worth investigating in the context of bringing hybrid forms into the classroom.

In a more recent workshop, each student introduced and imported a structure as a possible vehicle or container for creating new work, exploring the psalm, the chiasmus, the call and response segment of the Episcopal liturgy, techniques from photography, and epistolary forms including the letter and the postcard. A former ballet student imported one of the most dynamic structures, a series of movements from ballet that she taught to the class. Writers then used the precise sequence of steps involved in a *pas de bourrée* or a *rond de jambe* to write everything from a lyric love story to a script in which the various dance steps acted as stage directions.

My most full-scale venture into teaching hybrid forms was in a graduate workshop entitled The Anatomy of Memory. The six sub-units in the course ranged from Physical Memory to Ancestral/Familial Memory to Cultural/Collective Memory. The class included writers of nonfiction, poetry, and fiction, and among the hybrid readings were Margot Singer's "Lila's Story," which enacts the fictive dimension of memory in life writing; the lyric essays assembled in Brenda Miller's *Season of the Body*; selected essays from Virginia Woolf's *Moments of Being*; poetic memoirs including Gregory Orr's *The Blessing* and Li-Young Lee's *The Winged Seed*; Lewis Carroll's masterpiece of children's literature *Alice's Adventures in Wonderland*; as well as secondary, related work by a diverse range of writers, among them Carl Jung and Diane Ackerman. The course "hybridized" each student's sense of what's possible by establishing connections to other genres and even other media, including visual art and music, as well as architecture and film. Digital media—i.e. video clips and animation—would be a provocative inclusion.

These experiences demonstrate just a few of the reasons contemporary writers and teachers are drawn to hybrid work and why such work is a growing part of the contemporary literary landscape in the U.S. and abroad. Google "hybrid genre literature courses" and dozens of listings come up, among them Brown University's course in Queer and Feminist Poetics: Hybrid Forms, 1969 to Present, and Indiana University of Pennsylvania's Critical Approaches to Literature. Increasingly, hybrid panels figure on the program at AWP and smaller conferences like Nonfiction Now. Then there is the recent publication of such anthologies as *Bending Genre: Essays on Creative Nonfiction* (ed. Margot Singer and Nicole Walker) and *American Hybrid: A Norton Anthology of New Poetry* (ed. David St. John and Cole Swensen), as well as more scholarly examinations, many of them pedagogical, in journals such as *Across the Disciplines*.

As exciting as these recent developments are, several of our most canonical writers—Walt Whitman, Emily Dickinson, H.D., and Virginia Woolf—initially crossed or simply eluded genre boundaries. And it is with the precedent of two of these writers, Dickinson and Woolf, that I wish to begin a more intensive discussion of teaching hybrid literary forms.

EARLY HYBRID INNOVATORS: DICKINSON AND WOOLF

Dickinson's work can best be described as epistolary, given that everything she wrote—poems, letters, and drafts, in fascicles, on folios, individual sheets, envelopes, and fragments—was primarily composed on plain, machine-made stationery. Dickinson often wrote variants of a single poem, enclosing or embedding different versions in her correspondence with a wide network of friends and family. Later, once she ceased assembling her poems into the hand-sewn books known as fascicles, she almost exclusively sent copies of her poems to her correspondents, in the process redefining her notion of audience to a circle of intimate readers.

Significantly, Dickinson lived at the historical moment when the modern postal system was taking hold. Dickinson was in her late twenties when it first became possible to mail a letter sealed in an envelope that was dropped in a public box and paid for with a pre-purchased stamp. This system, like the railroad, heralded an age increasingly defined by speed. As Marta Werner writes in the afterword to the collection of Dickinson's envelope writings—fragments that Dickinson wrote on sections of envelopes—assembled in *The Gorgeous Nothings*: "[Dickinson] lived and wrote in the century of suddenness, amid the rise of new telecommunications technologies that altered forever the forms of human contact. 'The new media [historian John Durham Peters writes] gave life to the older dream of angelic contact by claiming to burst the bonds of distance and death.' Yet they also delivered us into new solitudes." This passage is important in the teaching of hybrid literary genres, for it negotiates both the distance that is part of life in a society defined by mass communication and by the fundamental need to claim intimacy and connection. Fifty-two-year-old Dickinson sent her first telegram in May 1882 to Judge Otis P. Lord, whose marriage proposal she refused, after learning of his sudden illness: "Would I write a telegram? I asked the Wires how you did, and I attached my name." How would she rupture the distance separating one human being from another in our age of Twitter, Facebook, and the worlds within worlds found on the Internet?

This brings me to Woolf. Her life spanned two World Wars and numerous traumas, and the press she ran with her husband, Leonard Woolf, first published the work of Sigmund Freud in English, a crucial precedent given that psychoanalysis fractures the coherence of the self and foregrounds the subconscious, central components of much hybrid writing. Woolf's body of work is defined by the profound need, however impossible, to close the gap between self and other, self and world. In attempting to bridge that distance, in nearly all of her work Woolf actively blurred the lines across genres. Her experimental novel *The Waves*, for example, is a lyric meditation far closer to poetry than narrative prose in which external life is less central than the inner lives of the six main characters who speak entirely through symbolic soliloquies, thereby allowing the reader to focus on what Woolf called the "common life that is the essence of all inner lives." Such reality cannot be described; rather, to quote Woolf, it must be "suggested and brought slowly by repeated images before us until it stays, in all its complexity, complete."

The speed and impersonality endemic to society and the human need for connection collide in hybrid literary forms, which may vex, challenge, and inspire us, and which always require us to slow down and study them carefully. Here we can return to Dickinson who, at 16, wrote to her friend Abiah Root: "Let us strive together to part with time more reluctantly, to watch the pinions of the fleeing moment until they are dim in the distance & the new coming moment claims our attention." Hybrid literary genres claim our attention precisely because we cannot take their forms as a given. Rather, we must scrutinize them and in the process enlarge and even transform our understanding of what's at stake in a particular literary genre.

EXPLORING NARRATIVE TECHNIQUES

Consider the possibilities that arise out of organizing a course around the role of narrative/narration in hybrid genres, or in integrating hybrid work into a course in nonfiction or fiction. Broadly defined, narration (along with exposition, argumentation, and description) is one of the four rhetorical modes of discourse. In fiction and literary nonfiction, narrative is the vehicle through which the narrator communicates to the reader across a range of distances, from the intimacy implied in "Reader, I married him" to the more removed perspectives that have become Alice Munro's signature.

But what happens to narrative in a hybrid genre like prose poetry? Or poetic memoir? Or flash fiction? And how does examining narrative in hybrid genres impact and complicate and provoke assumptions about narrative in a class discussion? Flash fiction is a natural starting point given its affinities with and differences from both the traditional-length short story and prose poetry. Flash fiction, as Katie Cortese points out, "starts much closer to its inevitable point of transition." The literary magazine *Monkeybicycle* features a host of one-sentence flash fictions that prove fruitful in considering the incredible efficiency of a hybrid genre in which, like the tightest poem, every word counts. Among my favorites is Nathan Patton's "Brave Little Chucks":

> On the pavement was a discarded pair of gray Chucks, rain
> soaked and threadbare, both upright and facing east as if
> someone had stepped out of them and walked off into the world,
> unafraid of the stones and thorns that might come their way.

"Brave Little Chucks" places an image at the center of the story and suggests an evocative, mysterious history for it without having to engage in all that Marie Howe critiques in her gorgeous poem "Why the Novel Is Necessary but Sometimes Hard to Read," which begins:

> It happens in time. *Years passed until the old woman*
> *one snowy morning realized she had never loved her daughter . . .*
>
> Or *Five years later she answered the door, and her suitor had returned*
> *almost unrecognizable from his journeys . . .*
>
> But before you get to that part
> you have to learn the names—you have to suffer not knowing
>   anything about anyone
>
> and slowly come to understand who each of them is, or who
>   each of them
> imagines themselves to be—

How does flash fiction shift the emphasis away from what the novel epitomizes—or as Howe puts it, "Oh it happens in time, and time is hard to live through." It does so via a compression so intense it alters the focus entirely. Instead of establishing and building context and characterization, as a traditional story does, flash fiction starts *in medias res* and shifts attention away from character and narrative arc to foreground images, the rhythms of syntax, and ends on a point of suspense or suspension.

I regularly assign one-sentence flash fictions or one-sentence prose poems, building in additional criteria such as the five senses and various sonic effects or requiring students to use a particular lexicon (the vocabulary surrounding ornithology, dressage, fly fishing, automobile repair, cellular biology) to write about falling out of love, giving birth, getting lost on a road trip, etc.

Prose poems, too, are magical containers for re-envisioning narrative, especially when they unfold in a sequence. With the exception of Mary Szybist's work, all of the pieces anthologized here are from book-length prose poem sequences. For discussing narrative strategies, I'll single out Carol Guess' *Doll Studies: Forensics*, which is built around 18 dioramas created by forensic pathologist Frances Glessner Lee that were based on real crime scenes and used in the study of crime scene investigation during the 1940s and 1950s. In *Doll Studies* the prose poem form becomes a part of the dialogue with the "dioramas," and their room-like shape makes the space of the page an integral part of the strategy. *Doll Studies* introduces an opportunity for students to model a hybrid form on an existing creation: a work of art, "walls" such as the Great Wall of China or the late Berlin Wall, or a series of anatomical illustrations. Ideally, the hybrid form will incorporate into its own structure that of the creation with which it is in conversation. In a literature course, the instructor could choose other such works that find their starting points by entering into dialogue with another entity, say Joe Wenderoth's epistolary engagement with the fast food chain *Letters to Wendy's* or Takashi Hiraide's *Postcards to Donald Evans*, an epistolary collection that takes as its point of origin the postage stamps artist Donald Evans designed for fictive countries.

In *Doll Studies* Guess introduces techniques common to detective fiction, except she renders them as if they were part of a how-to manual rather than a straight narrative: "Detectives learn to sweep a story clockwise for detail," the opening poem reads. A pedagogical strategy, then, could examine the ways in which hybrid forms borrow from other genres and to what ends. Why foreground, with such heightened self-consciousness, the role of the detective in a collection about domestic violence where women are the victims? And how does placing the reader in the role of the budding detective further the text's more feminist aims?

The titles of each prose poem raise possibilities for discussing the ways in which chapters or headers can work in narrative. Like the narrative itself, Guess' titles are both oblique and evocative, troubling puns or wordplay on what's hidden in plain sight, as the saying goes. "Late White," in context, reads as "Late Wife." "Cake, with Corpse" plays on a still life or a recipe: cake, with whipped cream; cake, with berry glaze. What roles, then, can titles play in hybrid forms? And what can these forms teach us about the expectations created by titles in other genres: creating suspense, for example, or resisting the focus of "a chapter" operating in a linear or associative fashion? One assignment could showcase the use of subtitles throughout a piece, with the sub/title functioning as both frame and a stepping stone into the writing.

Joy Ladin's *The Book of Anna* compels the reader to consider the narrative roles of omission, concealment, and revelation (subjects that can speak to the discussion of fragments in hybrid writing). When asked to consider Anna's story in relation to the novel and not in relation to poetry, the genre in which she initially envisioned Anna's story unfolding, Ladin stresses that:

> Like any novel, Anna is omnivorous, swallowing all material that comes its way, no matter how foreign; and like many novels, Anna is heteroglossic, collaging ironized voices to imply an authorial viewpoint that isn't otherwise stated.

Teaching a work like *The Book of Anna* trains students to recognize the materials that are being combined and the effects of those combinations, which hones critical reading skills. Students could therefore look at how hybridization changes some of the materials, what parts of the original forms are preserved, and what aspects are lost or transformed. There is also the possibility of considering where hybrid works want us to notice their hybridity, and where they try to conceal it. How could these acts of noticing and concealment become a productive part of a course—or provide the basis for an assignment?

Jenny Boully's *not merely because the darkness was stalking toward them* offers a model. Every page of text is footnoted with a section called "The Home

Under Ground" that creates a split on the page to draw attention to the visual aspect of her book as a made thing and simultaneously to demonstrate her engagement with and inclusion of literary criticism, fiction, and make-believe. What Boully reveals via her re-envisioning of J.M. Barrie's *Peter Pan* are issues surrounding memory and forgetting, especially regarding gender roles and sexuality. Teaching a hybrid work like Boully's provides opportunities for discussion of the interrelated ways in which gender and narrative are constructed through reading. Because a text like hers destabilizes the reading experience by preventing the reader from settling into a comfortable structure, it reveals the ways in which we create narrative while reading in order to find a place for ourselves within it. Boully's work disavows that safe space, forcing us to keep reading despite the unstable narrative and the characters who behave in a transgressive manner.

A related assignment would require a writer to craft a hybrid piece in which the reader can take nothing for granted. Imagine a throughline narrative as the main part of the text, and then place in tension with this a second text that unfolds via footnotes or uses critical excerpts and other discourses to call that throughline into question. For example, have students write a portrait of someone fictional, or real but iconic, such as Princess Diana or Hillary Clinton. In the throughline, the main character emerges as a role model or an example of "toeing the party line." But the other discourse calls that throughline into question. In the case of Diana, that discourse could chart her eating disorder or her marital infidelity, so that what emerges, when the two texts are read together, is a hybrid that enacts how success/beauty/privilege/the so-called happily-ever-after is actually a façade, or at least far less pretty than the official story would have us believe.

FINDING THE RIGHT FORM

Form contains; etymologically the verb derives from the Latin *continere* "to hold together, enclose." How does the writer find the most organic or fitting container for her work? One answer involves studying hybrid forms that bring with them larger questions, not just about narrative, but about structure. What is to be gained from envisioning a particular subject unfolding in a sequence of prose poems, for example, as opposed to a chronological narrative? How might an heirloom box of family recipes written on index cards or a cache of letters from World War II become the foundation for a flash fiction sequence? Or a stranger's book of photographs from the turn of the century found in an antique shop in Budapest? New Orleans? Cairo? What structural possibilities are suggested by the classification system used in an ornithological study? Or Joseph Cornell's mysterious and whimsical shadowboxes assembled from an array of junk shop clutter and found objects (talk about remnants!)? And how about the layout for a prison like Alcatraz? Or the Twelve-Step Program in Alcoholics Anonymous? Such questions enable students to wrap their imaginations around their own potential hybrid forms in a workshop setting.

And workshops aren't the only place for creative writing assignments that give students hands-on experience with the texts they are analyzing. Two summers ago, I assigned Mira Bartók's *The Memory Palace* as part of an intensive five-week introduction to nonfiction, a course that consisted almost entirely of non-majors, most of them in the sciences. Bartók's memoir opens each chapter with an image that serves as the catalyst for the memory she narrates and simultaneously allows her to mine the multifaceted possibilities of that image. I had each student choose an image from his or her past and build a memory palace around that image in a lyric or non-chronological essay that circles back to image again and again. Among the most dynamic pieces: a 50-year-old Lebanese man's recollection of the plum trees in his family's Damascus garden. The plums were his father's and his own favorite fruit, and he continually longs for their taste and cannot find it again, or the word for the fruit in English. As with the example of one sentence flash fictions, this assignment illustrates the power of the image in helping the writer find the right form for his or her work.

MEMORY, IMAGINATION, AND FORM

More than 20 years ago, Patricia Hampl pointed out the fictive dimension of memory in her canonical essay "Memory and Imagination"; Mark Doty has called memory "the past gently rewritten in the direction of feeling"; and Woolf observed that "the past is beautiful because one never realizes an emotion at the time. It expands later, and thus we don't have complete emotions about the present, only about the past." I would further qualify these statements by defining memory as the past rewritten in order to clarify, understand, and organize feeling. Considering the stakes of memory in hybrid work offers the chance to explore the permeability between fiction and nonfiction and the ways in which techniques of lyric poetry—metaphor, extended passages of lyrical writing, and associative movement—can enhance the possibilities of prose.

Because hybrid forms prevent the reader from allowing narrative or some given structure to carry her smoothly along, their resistance to easy reading requires students to hone their powers of attention. Although all of the works anthologized here participate in this conversation, and so much of the writing deals with the relationship between memory, identity, and self-knowledge, Kazim Ali's poetic memoir *Bright Felon: Autobiography and Cities* is particularly remarkable for the way it presents an image of writing "not in a book but in loose pages or cards. Not to disassemble but to assemble oneself into oneself." Such assemblage brings with it a resistance to traditional forms of coherence in narrative, point of view, and syntax. *Bright Felon's* primary structural unit is the line or sentence; these will collude at times to build a paragraph. The sentence or phrase as unit acts as a kind of "lonely thread" embodying Ali's own indirect journey toward self-acceptance as a gay man of East Indian descent after years of self-silencing. Working in tandem with this emphasis on the "lonely thread" is Ali's resistance to structure via chapter. Each section is written about a different city in which he has lived or traveled. The effect is one in which a fixed timeline or chronology is discarded.

Written as a traditional memoir, Ali's work could very well appear reductive, self-indulgent, and even melodramatic, as can happen when traumatic or difficult experience is rendered as a straight narrative. Ali succeeds because his memoir emphasizes process, discovery, and internal dialogue, qualities one associates with poetry or with the essay.

Traditional, linear narratives focused on trauma or suffering do not necessarily offer the reader a reprieve from painful experience. Here I would mention the difficulty my students experienced in staying present with Meredith Hall's stunning *Without a Map*. Although they could not deny the strength of her writing or the power of her story, Hall's book-length narrative about surrendering her newborn at birth and then finding him again after a harrowing journey of her own was one that many advanced undergraduates, most of them English majors, could not stay with because Hall's linear narrative offered little reprieve from the difficult subject matter and grave tone. One of them confessed: "It's just too much." In contrast, Joan Didion's *The Year of Magical Thinking* is not a bleak read despite its agonizing subject: the death of her husband and life-threatening hospitalizations of her adult daughter. Categorized as nonfiction, *The Year of Magical Thinking* is in reality a hybrid. Essayistic in its structure, with extended passages of lyric writing we associate with poetry, Didion's memoir constantly scrutinizes the writer's past as well as her present. So too, like any good hybrid, Didion's narrative is interrupted by and incorporates other discourses, particularly the scientific and the medical, but also Emily Post's world of etiquette. The book's structure also relies on repeating and refracting lyrical passages throughout the narrative (and the ending maximizes the value of such repetition with variation) and repeats phrases like "magical thinking" and "the vortex effect" to ground and develop Didion's consciousness throughout the grieving process.

Were it not for my experience writing across genres and working with hybrid forms, I do not think I would have been able to identify why Hall's narrative lost so many of my students (despite my own passionate admiration of the subject and craft); nor would I have recognized the hybrid nature of Didion's memoir, one I have introduced into graduate as well as undergraduate workshops. My ability to recognize Didion's hybridity underscores the value of exposing students to non-traditional forms whether in a course devoted to hybrids or one that focuses on more traditional forms.

Didion's memoir attests to the powerful models hybrids offer for mediating the intensity that can arise with writing about fraught, often traumatic experiences. Another example is Gregory Orr's *The Blessing*. Orr, who confesses his uneasiness with narrative prose in his contributor's essay, interrupts the painful narrative about his violent childhood and coming-of-age with imagery. "What I experience in memoir writing," Orr writes, "is that when the narrative gets too intense, an image appears and this image seems to reveal some aspect of the story or the self or life as I understand it." Orr's poetic memoir is instructive for the ways in which the image, a poet's central tool, can carry multiple meanings and provide some relief for the writer determined to transform trauma into art.

MASS SOCIETY, MYTH, AND THE HYBRID

Because they stray across boundaries and move between territories, hybrid forms adopt the way of the nomad, at home nowhere and everywhere. They preserve some of the original forms while transforming or surrendering others. How relevant, then, to teach such writing in a society in which rapid technological changes, shifting gender roles and family units, and migration or enforced displacement and exile are the order of the day in so many parts of the world.

In "Autobiography and Archetype," poet Stanley Plumly points out that the archetypal provides the autobiographical with the means to "achieve something larger than the single life." In the process archetype is renewed and the writing achieves an enlargement not possible when limited to individual experience. The human need for collective or archetypal forms of identity is primal, and that need remains pervasive, possibly even more intense, in an age in which so many of us spend days in front of the computer or in offices at a vast remove from the landscapes in which these necessary ancient stories took shape.

Much of the hybrid writing anthologized here engages mythic identity and experience. Embedded in Orr's *The Blessing* is the Cain and Abel story. Szybist revisits the two Marys of Christianity: Jesus' mother and Mary Magdalene. Bartók includes numerous myths including that of Medusa. Myths distill human conflict and the tendency toward good and evil; at their centers are liminal or transitional experiences. "Liminal" and "liminality" are both derived from the Latin "limen" which means "threshold"— literally the bottom part of a doorway that must be crossed. Nick Flynn's *Another Bullshit Night in Suck City* deals with mental illness and homelessness, archetypal contemporary examples of being an outsider. In works like Flynn's, the individual must delve into the psychic depths and hit rock bottom if he is to climb out again. Flynn references *King Lear*, in particular Lear's soul-searching exile in which he asks: "Is man no more than this?"

Literary figures like Shakespeare have acquired mythic status, and several writers, Jenny Boully and Amy Newman among them, engage mythic literary forerunners. Other writers transform an earlier artist or historical figure into a kind of archetype, as is the case with Takashi Hiraide's *Postcards to Donald Evans* or Kathleen Ossip's "The Nervousness of Yvor Winters." Patricia Vigderman's "Sebald in Starbucks" places W. G. Sebald's *Austerlitz* at the center of this essayistic meditation on strangeness and evil. Vigderman is reading about Sebald's account of the Nazi death camps in a Cambridge coffee shop: "Sebald writes without drama of horror and loss, of the sudden incursion of unreality into the real world, *of the possible coexistence of all moments of time in the same space*" (emphasis added).

Vigderman's sentence speaks directly to why hybrid writing gravitates toward expressions of liminal experience, often embedding this strangeness—this sense of being between places or states—into their very structures. Etymologically, "strange" derives from the Old French "estrange" and means "foreign, alien, curious, as well as estranged and distant."

Yes, a great deal of modern and contemporary writing avoids linear movement; yet hybrid forms make the co-existence of other modes of writing and of seeing an organic part of their structures and an integral part of the tensions or problems with which they wrestle. The excerpts from Ander Monson's *Letter to a Future Lover* attest to the visual impact of making other textual modes—dictionaries, for example—central to the essay. By virtue of their status as letters, the epistolary writings anthologized here invoke the historically distant, the faraway. Mark Jarman makes use of the biblical Paul's wanderings; Diane Wakoski co-opts the identity of Medea, embedding poetry into letters that enable her to be both at her desk writing and at a more desired elsewhere. Craig Santos Perez's *from unincorporated territory [saina]* collages primary texts and oral histories from his native Guam's colonialist period while evoking the fragmentary myths of his ancestors in order to push language to its limits, as if to momentarily contain what remains inexpressible and simultaneously what has becomes lost (or estranged).

Central to myth is the individual's experience; but the individual, in myth, inevitably bears on the collective. For myth—and here it bears mentioning the Everyman of the medieval morality plays, themselves hybrid forms—is traditionally meant to be instructive, a way of integrating or re-integrating the individual into the group. And liminal experience—that threshold between-ness that anthropologists define as a rite of passage—is at the heart of that movement. One assignment, then, which focuses on myth, and specifically on liminal experience, would enact that experience of existing "between" places and include the heightened sense of awareness that accompanies liminality. One possible form would juxtapose a more linear narrative movement with associative passages, akin to prose poetry. The linear narrative might track the individual's journey in time (mythic versus mundane time, as in Joy Harjo's mythic book-length poem *The Woman Who Fell From the Sky* or Alice's experiences in Wonderland). The more associative passages would delve into the psyche. How could the assignment be enlarged by including graphic elements such as photographs, drawings, diagrams, and borrowings from other kinds of writing?

One central question worth addressing concerns the individual's integration or re-integration into the collective: does the individual find a place for him or herself in today's society? Often, the answer seems to be "no," as the world news as well as so much contemporary literature evidences. (And here I would recommend the title novella in Andre Dubus III's *Dirty Love* as a model.) How then does a hybrid work make that struggle more palpable and raw for both writer and reader? And where might empathy, or at least the recognition and understanding of difference, come in?

Such questions venture toward the baseline reason for teaching hybrid works, the fact that they can powerfully further the legitimacy of difference. This raises the stakes of the moral and ethical implications and possibilities of teaching hybrid literature in college and graduate classrooms where students are coming to terms with issues of identity and conformity, as well as addiction and radical forms of extremism in an increasingly fractured world in which violence is just a YouTube click away.

This dynamic resonated personally when one of my students, enrolled in my senior seminar on Dickinson, sent me an email after our last class in December, resuming a debate about Whitman and Dickinson that he and I began earlier in outside conversations during the first weeks of the semester. "I still prefer Whitman," he concluded, "because Whitman's poetry saved me." He was referring to the impact of discovering Whitman's life and art, to a large extent inseparable, while growing up as a gay man in a religiously conservative Texas household. Whitman, he confided, provided a model for manhood that was both godly and outside the norm. And at the time it was written, Whitman's poetry (like Dickinson's) broke with received notions of what poetry could or should be. I would therefore reiterate the value of bringing hybrid forms into the classroom to introduce examples of nontraditional identities that are inextricably bound to the hybrid forms in which they are contained.

Intrinsically, then, issues of gender, race, class, religion, and political or national identity complicate and enrich the experience of reading hybrid forms. Such issues can intensify our engagement with these texts, magnifying the particular strengths that can emerge through graphics (Pictures Made of Words), the aural (Prose Poetry, Performative), *assaying* (Short-Form Nonfiction, Lyric Essay), suspense/suspension (Flash Fiction), and the mythic (Epistolary, Poetic Memoir), to name but a few. The inclusion of literary hybrids—thematically and structurally—in the classroom reveals the paradox that identities and genres are constructed and arbitrary, yet simultaneously "real." Taken individually, but especially in conversation with one another, literary hybrids illustrate that genres are not fixed entities but vehicles for finding the best form for our stories, memories, and explorations. Writers don't have to be bound by genre: rather, genre can be a starting point for finding the most organic form of expression. Put another way: each literary genre is like a family whose individual members are related in various ways without necessarily sharing any single feature in common.

CREDITS

. . . .

Kazim Ali: "Washington, DC" from *Bright Felon*. Copyright © 2009 by Kazim Ali. Reprinted by permission of Wesleyan University Press.

Susanne Paola Antonetta: "Dark Matter" first appeared in *Fourth Genre*, Issue 15, Volume 1 (2003). Reprinted by permission of the author.

Andrea Baker: Excerpt from *The Incredibly True Adventures of Me* first appeared in *Omniverse* (July 2012). Reprinted by permission of the author.

Jennifer Bartlett: Excerpt from *My Body Is (the) Marginalia; The Sun Drawn a Saw Across the Strings*. first appeared in *The Ilanot Review*, Volume 6 (Winter 2013). Reprinted with permission of the author.

Jenny Boully: Excerpt from *not merely because of the unknown that was stalking toward them*. Copyright © 2011 by Jenny Boully. Reprinted by permission of Tarpaulin Sky Press.

Julie Carr: "#58–61" from *100 Notes on Violence*. Copyright © 2010 by Julie Carr. Reprinted with the permission of The Permissions Company, Inc. on behalf of Ahsahta Press, www.ahsahtapress.org.

Katie Cortese: "Sum of Her Parts" first appeared in *Smokelong Quarterly*, No. 32 (Spring 2011). Reprinted with permission of the author.

Nick Flynn: Excerpt from *Another Bullshit Night in Suck City: A Memoir* by Nick Flynn. Copyright © 2004 by Nick Flynn. Used by permission of W. W. Norton & Company, Inc.

Sarah Gorham: "Perfect Sleep," "Perfect Solution," and "Perfect Heaven" from *Study in Perfect: Essays*. Copyright © 2014 by Sarah Gorham. Reprinted with permission of the University of Georgia Press.

ACKNOWLEDGMENTS

. . . .

In addition to the sources fully cited in the introduction, afterword, and section introductions, the following sources were referenced:

Agee, James, and Walker Evans. *Let Us Now Praise Famous Men*. Boston: Houghton Mifflin, 2001.

Aristotle. *Poetics*. Trans. with introduction and notes by Malcolm Heath. London: Penguin, 1996.

Bakhtin, Mikhail. "Forms of Time and of the Chronotope in the Novel" in *The Dialogic Imagination: Four Essays*. Ed. by Michael Holquist. Trans. Caryl Emerson and Michael Holquist. Austin: University of Texas Press, 1981.

Basho. *Road to the Deep North and Other Travel Sketches*. Trans. Nobuyuki Yuasa. New York: Penguin Classics, 1967.

Baxter, Charles. *The Business of Memory: The Art of Remembering in an Age of Forgetting*. Minneapolis: Graywolf Press, 1999.

Blake, William. *The Marriage of Heaven and Hell*. 1795. Reprint. New York: Dover, 1994.

Boland, Eavan. *Object Lessons: The Life of the Woman and the Poet in Our Time*. New York: W.W. Norton, 1996.

Brind Morrow, Susan. *The Names of Things*. New York: Riverhead, 1997.

D'Agata, John, Ed. *The Lost Origins of the Essay (A New History of the Essay)*. Minneapolis: Graywolf Press, 2009.

Didion, Joan. *Blue Nights*. New York: Vintage, 2012.

Didion, Joan. *We Tell Ourselves Stories in Order to Live: Collected Nonfiction*. New York: Everyman's Library, 2007.

Doolittle, Hilda. *Tribute to Freud*. New York: New Directions, 2012.

Doolittle, Hilda. *Trilogy*. Ed. Aliki Barnstone. New York: New Directions, 1998.

Doty, Mark. "Return to Sender: Memory, Betrayal and Memoir" in *Touchstone Anthology of Contemporary Creative Nonfiction: Work from 1970 to the Present*. Ed. Lex Williford and Michael Martone. New York: Touchstone Books, 2007.

Eliot, T.S. *Four Quartets*. New York: Mariner, 1968.

Mairs, Nancy. "Essaying the Feminine: From Montaigne to Kristeva." In *Voice Lessons: On Becoming a (Woman) Writer*. Boston: Beacon Press, 1997.

Masih, Tara L., Ed. *The Rose Metal Press Field Guide to Writing Flash Fiction: Tips from Editors, Writers, and Teachers in the Field*. Brookline, MA: Rose Metal Press, 2009.

McDowell, Gary L., and F. Daniel Rzicznek, Eds. *The Rose Metal Press Field Guide to Prose Poetry: Contemporary Poets in Discussion and Practice*. Brookline, MA: Rose Metal Press, 2010.

Montaigne, Michel de. *The Complete Essays*. Trans. M.A. Screech. London: Penguin Classics, 1993.

Moore, Dinty W., Ed. *The Rose Metal Field Guide to Writing Flash Nonfiction: Advice and Essential Exercises from Respected Writers, Editors, and Teachers*. Brookline, MA: Rose Metal Press, 2012.

Nabokov, Vladimir. *Speak, Memory: An Autobiography Revisited*. New York: G. P. Putnam's and Sons, 1966.

Orr, Gregory. *Poetry as Survival*. Athens, GA: The University of Georgia Press, 2002.

Rukeyser, Muriel. *The Life of Poetry*. Ashfield, MA: Paris Press, 1996.

Stevens, Wallace. *The Necessary Angel: Essays on Reality and the Imagination*. New York: Knopf, 1951.

Todorov, Tzvetan. "The Origins of Genres." *New Literary History* 8, No. 1 (Autumn 1976): 159–170.

"It takes a village to raise a child," the African proverb goes. The same can be said of bringing *Family Resemblance* into being. We'd like to thank the contributors for sharing their fine work and for their flexibility and timeliness in seeing the work through the stages of the editing and production process. Thanks, too, to the publishers who graciously waived permissions costs and facilitated the timely inclusion of so much outstanding, diverse writing. To Susanne Paola Antonetta, both for her provocative and intelligent introduction and for her insights into the curatorial process early on, our abiding gratitude.

Our deepest gratitude goes to Abigail Beckel and Kathleen Rooney at Rose Metal Press, for their challenging, sharp-eyed vision and edits at every stage.

Jacqueline would like to thank her colleague, Katie Cortese, who read the "Afterword" thrice, including the last pass some two weeks before the birth of her first child, Milo Anthony. Doctoral student extraordinaire Scott Morris proved stalwart and reliable as an editorial assistant. In addition to his conversance with a wealth of websites, blogs, and online journals that engage hybrid forms, Scott helped with a multitude of tasks, large and small, and proved himself to be a most sympathetic listener and tech-savvy troubleshooter. Jacqueline thanks Texas Tech University and her department chair, Dr. Bruce Clarke, in particular, for the semester course release that came at a crucial stage of *Family Resemblance's* development. Thanks, too, to Amber Tayama who engaged with several of the hybrid forms included here, both as a reader and as an aspiring writer. And to so many of the students with whom she is privileged to work, who continually inspire and remind her why writing matters so much. And always, thanks to her husband Bill for understanding those inevitable late nights and Sundays spent working under deadline. And to her daughter, Sophia: without a child's sense of humor and perspective, Jacqueline would have gotten lost in the forest and missed the home-cooked meals and the stories told around the village fire.

Marcela would like to thank her student assistant, Taryn Korb, whose diligence procured many of the permissions for this anthology. The Department of English Literature and Linguistics at Bar-Ilan University supported travel to the 2013 AWP conference in Boston, where Marcela met many of the contributors and solicited their work. She thanks the wonderful students who participated in her 451 Hybrid Creative Writing Workshop seminars at Bar-Ilan University for inspiring this anthology, including Anthony Michael Morena, whose final project is now a forthcoming Rose Metal Press title, *The Voyager Record*. Thanks to Kazim Ali for sage advice and warm encouragement, and thanks again to all the incredible contributors, and their translators, for their insights, humor, commitment, generosity, and general awesomeness.

ABOUT THE EDITORS

. . . .

Jacqueline Kolosov holds degrees in English from the University of Chicago (BA, MA) and New York University (PhD), and works as a professor of English at Texas Tech University. She has published three poetry collections, among them *Memory of Blue* (Salmon, 2014), and five novels for teens, including *A Sweet Disorder* (Hyperion, 2009) and *Paris, Modigliani & Me* (Luminis Books, 2015). The recipient of a Literary Fellowship in Prose from the National Endowment for the Arts, her essays, stories, poems, and hybrid works have been published in such journals as *The Sewanee Review, Poetry,* and *Prairie Schooner.* Originally from Chicago, she lives in West Texas with her husband, the poet William Wenthe, and their daughter, as well as three intrepid dogs, a curious cat, and a Spanish mare who keeps her fully grounded in the present. Learn more at www.jacquelinekolosovreads.com.

Marcela Sulak is the author of three collections of poetry, most recently *Decency* (Black Lawrence Press, 2015), and her essays have appeared in *The Iowa Review, The Los Angeles Review of Books, Rattle,* and various anthologies. She's translated four collections of poetry: Orit Gidali from Israel, Karel Hynek Mácha and K. J. Erben from Hapsburg Bohemia, and Mutombo Nkulu-N'Sengha from the Democratic Republic of the Congo. Some of these have been performed in the Prague National Theater and in Warsaw, and have been used as subtitles for films. She is an editor at *The Ilanot Review* and *Tupelo Quarterly,* and hosts the weekly radio podcast "Israel in Translation" at TLV.1. She directs the Shaindy Rudoff Graduate Program in Creative Writing at Bar-Ilan University outside of Tel Aviv, where she teaches American literature, hybridity, documentary poetics, prosody, and literary translation.

A NOTE ABOUT THE TYPE

· · · ·

The text of this book is set in Scala, Dutch designer Martin Majoor's most famous typeface. Released by FontShop International in 1990, it was created for Muziekcentrum Vredenburg in Utrecht and is named after the La Scala opera house in Milan. Scala is Italian for "scale"—which can be interpreted to mean a span of things—an apt name for such a large and varied font family. The family also includes a sans serif version that is used as the display face in this book. Scala's innovative variety seemed a fitting way to showcase the diverse forms and topics in *Family Resemblance* and the spectrum of creativity and inventiveness within the hybrid literary field.

The title font on the cover is ITC Binary, a semi-serif face designed by Mauricio Reyes. The International Typeface Corporation released it in 1997. Distinctive features of ITC Binary include marked stroke contrast and small missing pieces in the letterforms, most noticeably along the baseline. The seamless combination of sans serif and serif traits—a duality that is expressed in the name "Binary"—make the font itself a hybrid form.

The ornament utilized throughout the interior and on the back cover is part of the Type Embellishments One font family, released in 1994 by the Letraset Type Studio. It was designed by Michael Gills and Colin Brignall.

—Heather Butterfield

429